CATWAD

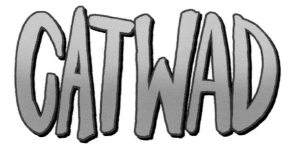

IT'S ME, TWO.

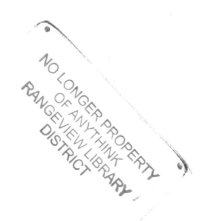

© 2019 Jim Benton

ISBN 978-1-338-32603-1

10 9 8 7 6 5 4 3 2 1   19 20 21 22 23

Printed in China   62

First edition, September 2019

Edited by Michael Petranek
Book design by Katie Fitch

IT'S ME, TWO.

JIM BENTON

graphix
AN IMPRINT OF
SCHOLASTIC

CLEAN

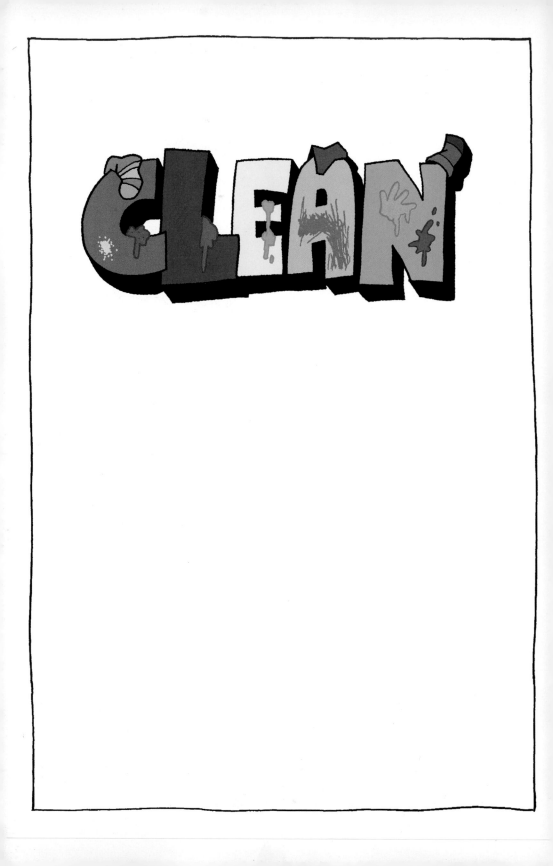

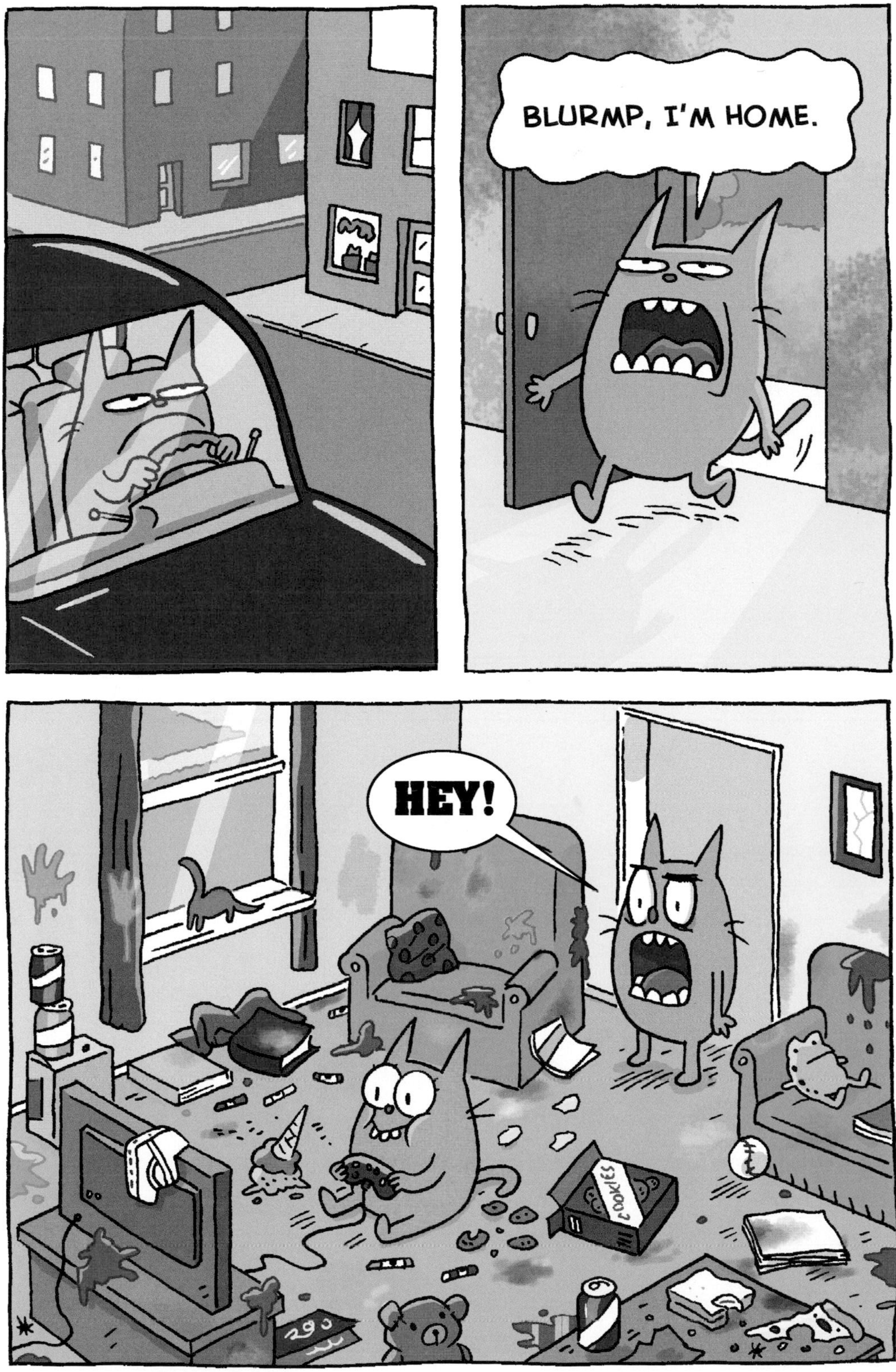
BLURMP, I'M HOME.
HEY!
COOKIES

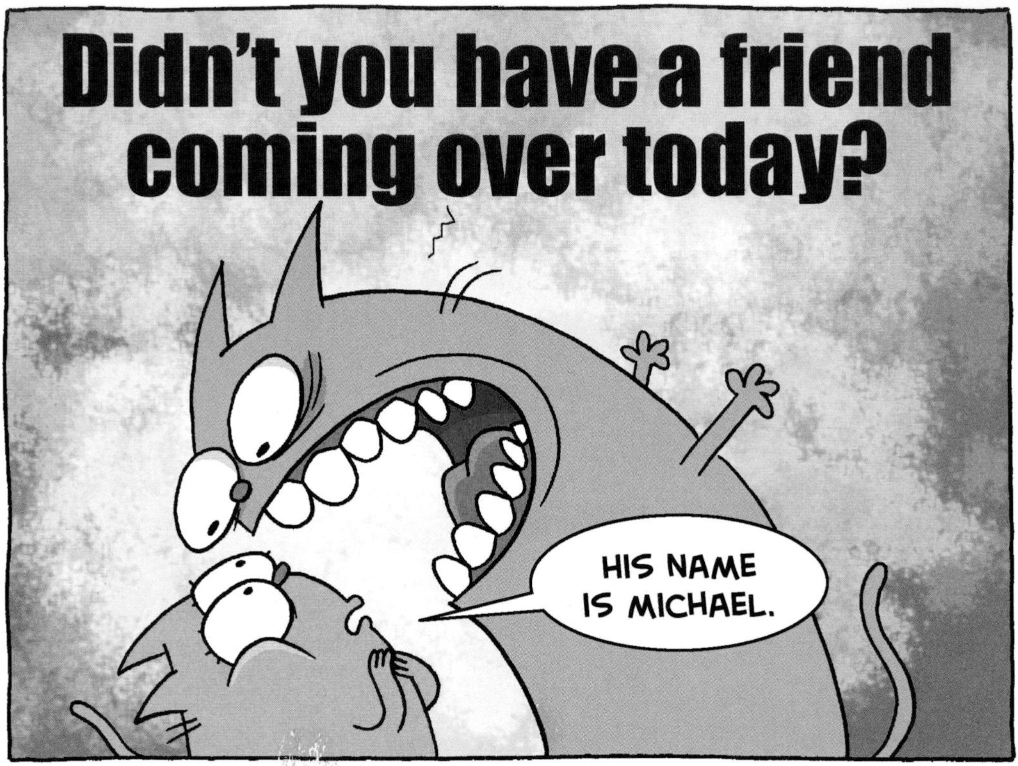
Didn't you have a friend coming over today?
HIS NAME IS MICHAEL.

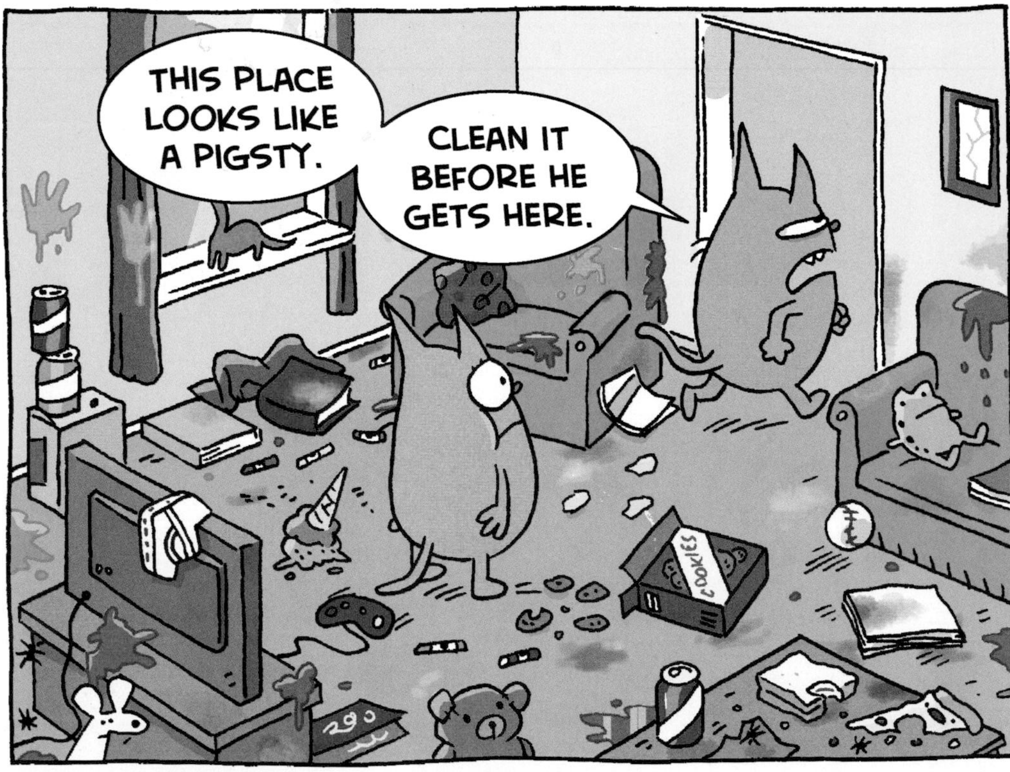
THIS PLACE LOOKS LIKE A PIGSTY.
CLEAN IT BEFORE HE GETS HERE.
COOKIES

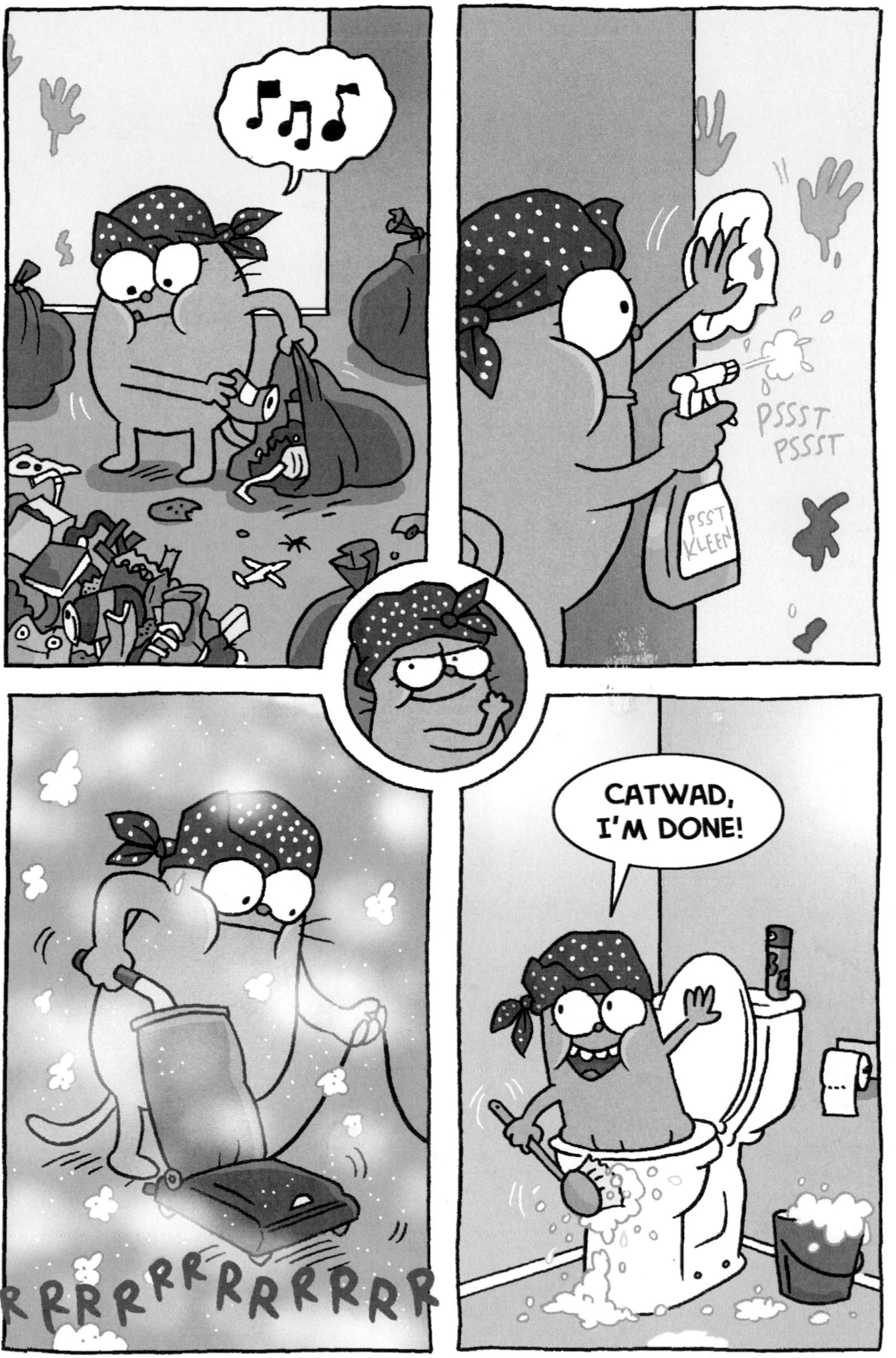
PSSST
PSSST
PSST KLEEN
CATWAD, I'M DONE!
RRRRRRRRRRRRR

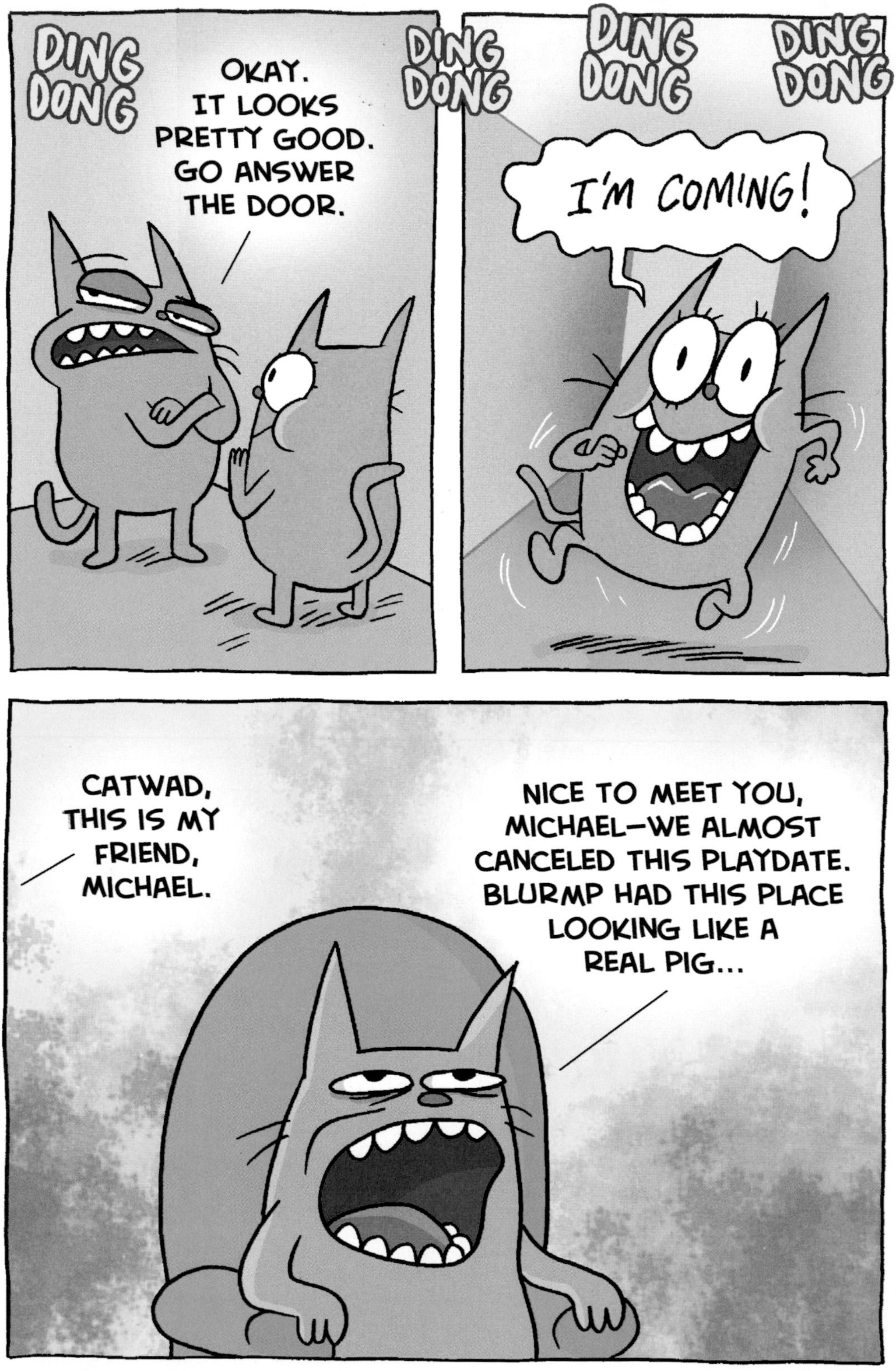
DING DONG
OKAY. IT LOOKS PRETTY GOOD. GO ANSWER THE DOOR.
DING DONG
DING DONG
DING DONG
I'M COMING!
CATWAD, THIS IS MY FRIEND, MICHAEL.
NICE TO MEET YOU, MICHAEL—WE ALMOST CANCELED THIS PLAYDATE. BLURMP HAD THIS PLACE LOOKING LIKE A REAL PIG...

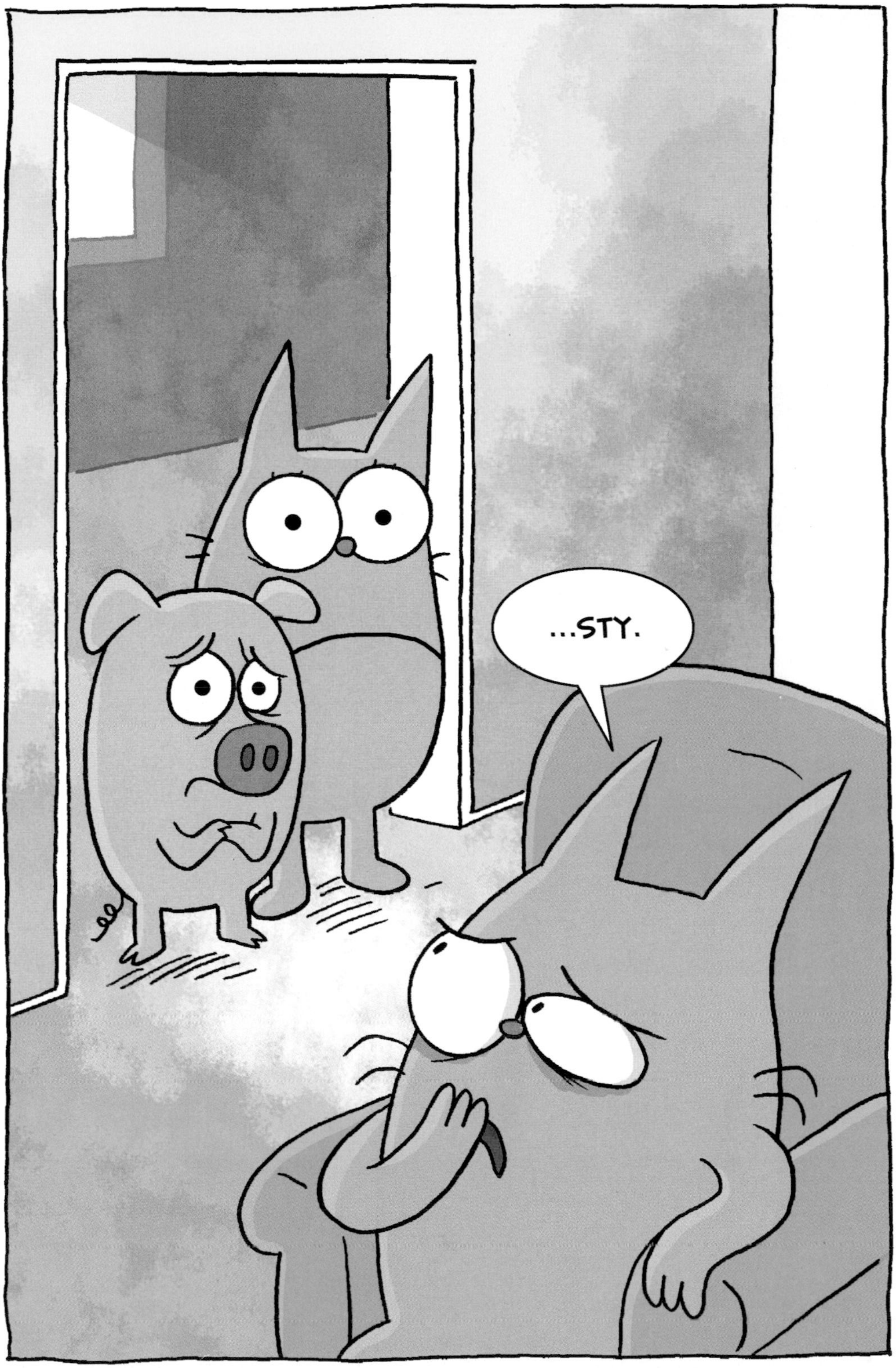
...STY.

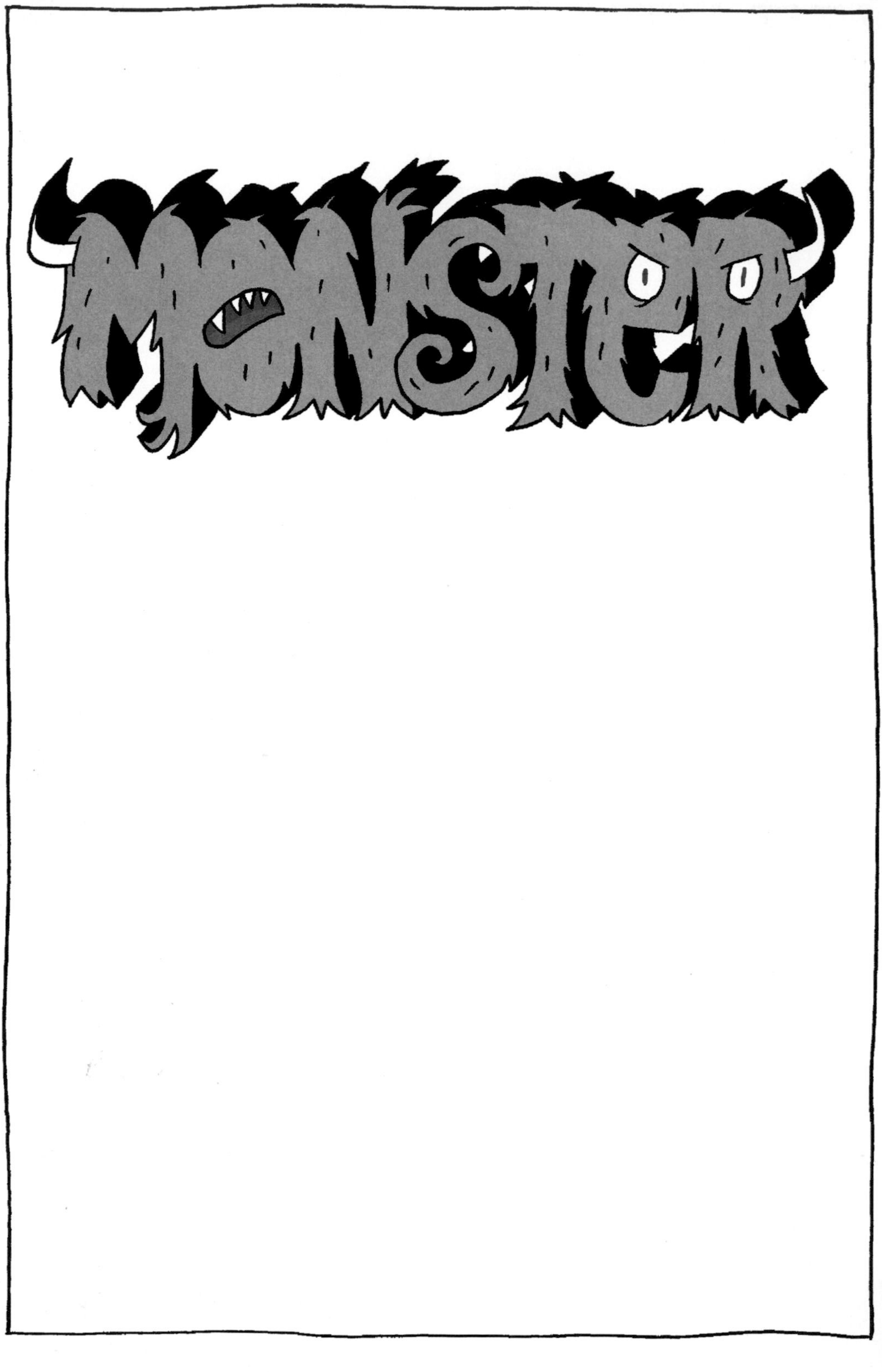
MONSTER

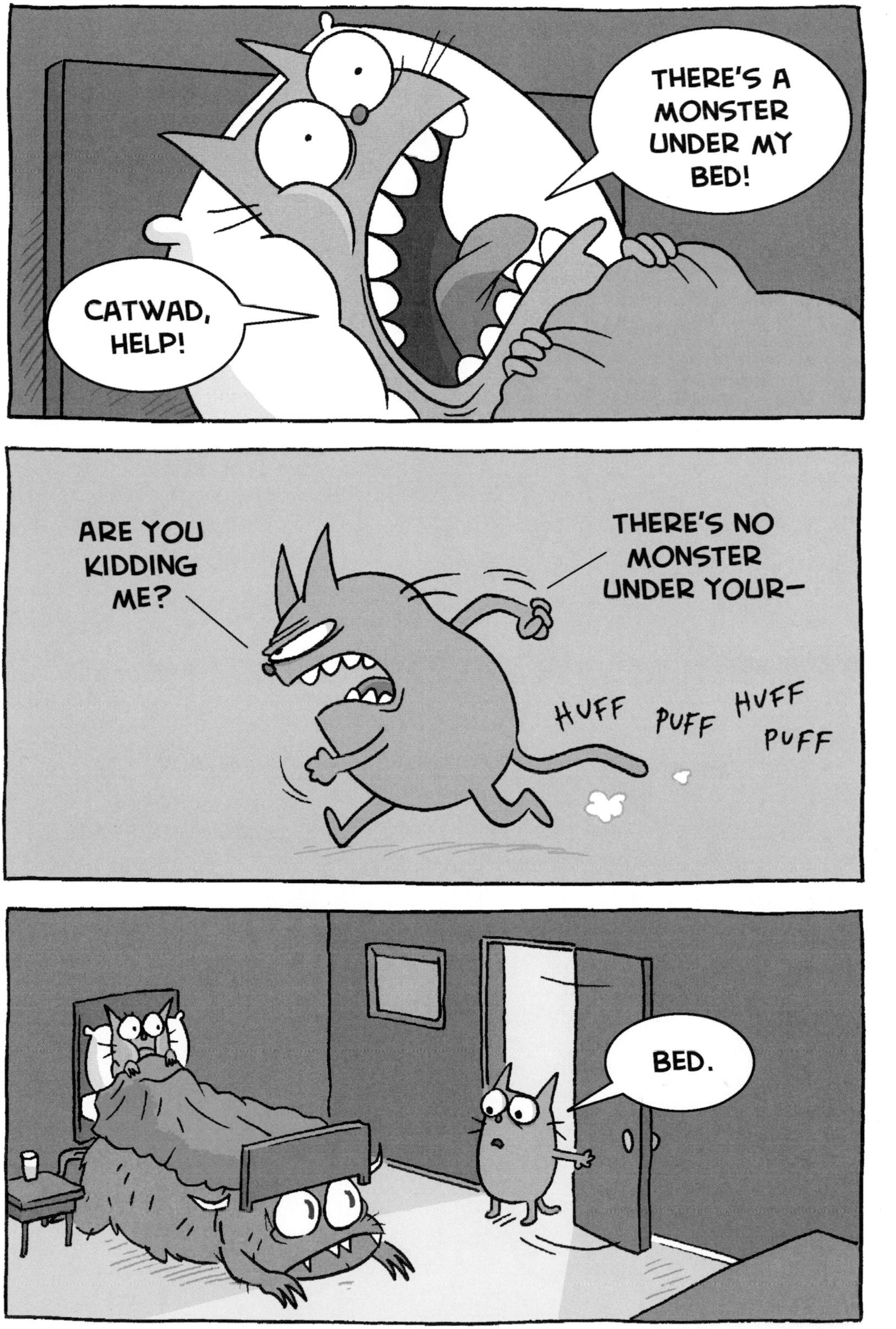
THERE'S A MONSTER UNDER MY BED!
CATWAD, HELP!
ARE YOU KIDDING ME?
THERE'S NO MONSTER UNDER YOUR—
HUFF PUFF HUFF PUFF
BED.

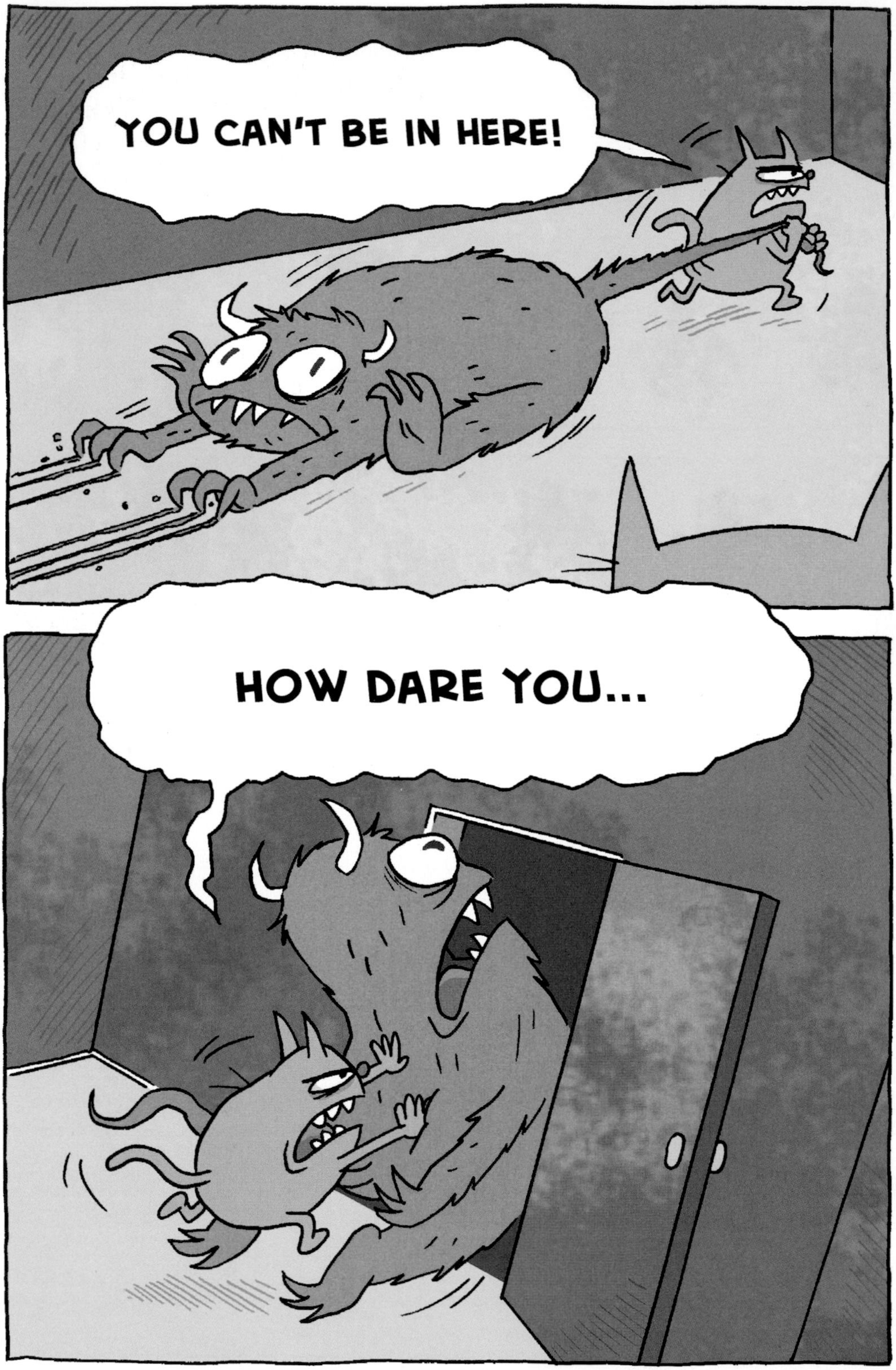
YOU CAN'T BE IN HERE!
HOW DARE YOU...

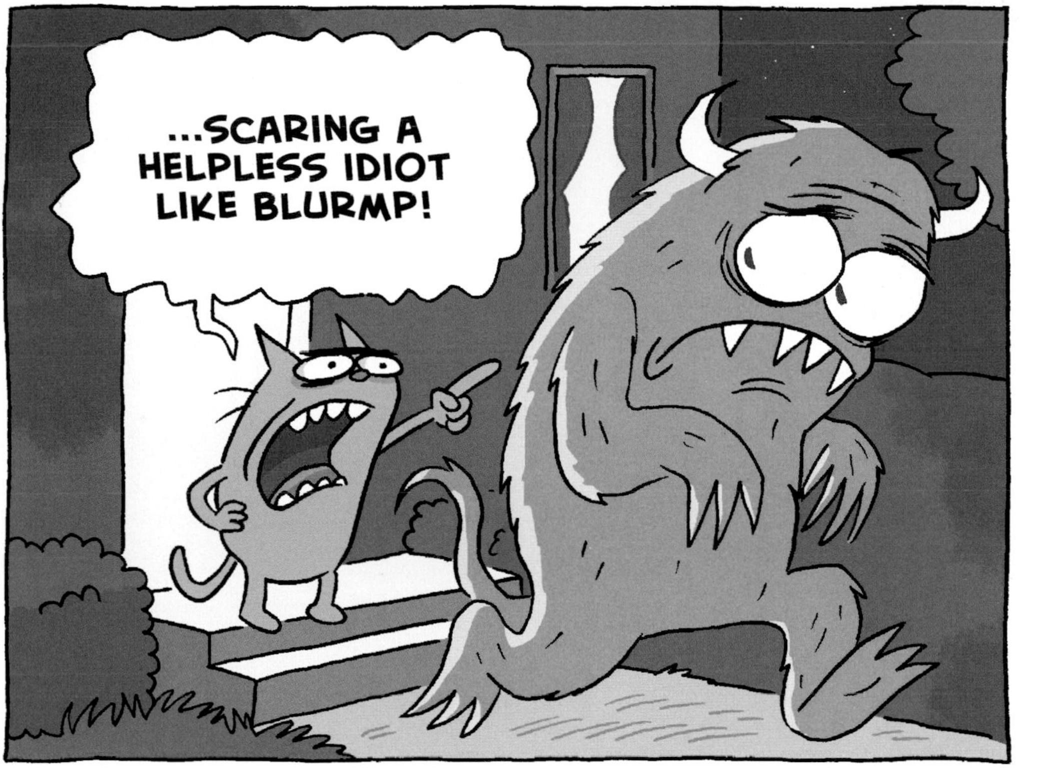
...SCARING A
HELPLESS IDIOT
LIKE BLURMP!

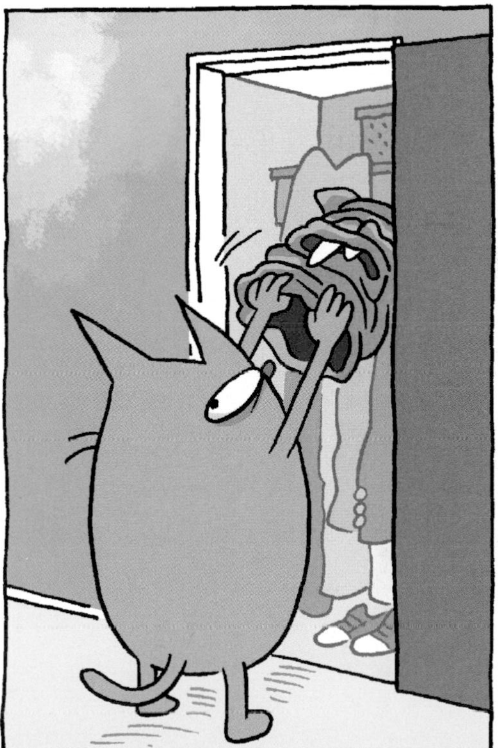

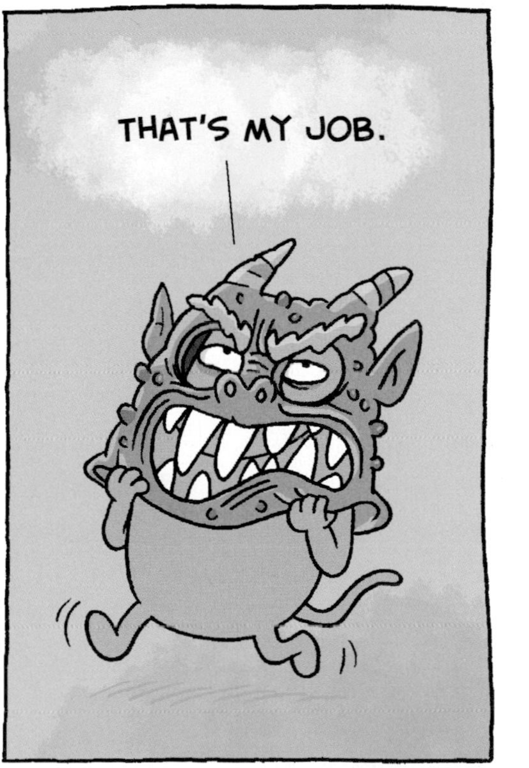
THAT'S MY JOB.

GAMING

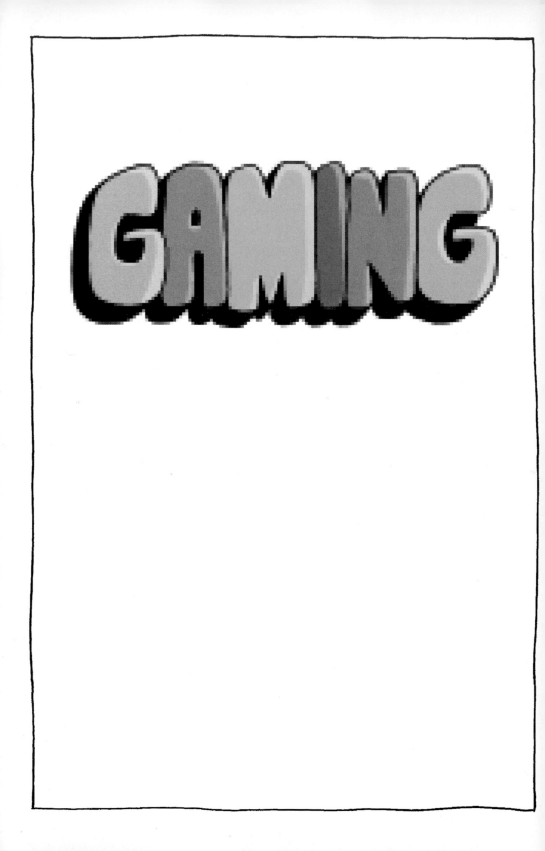

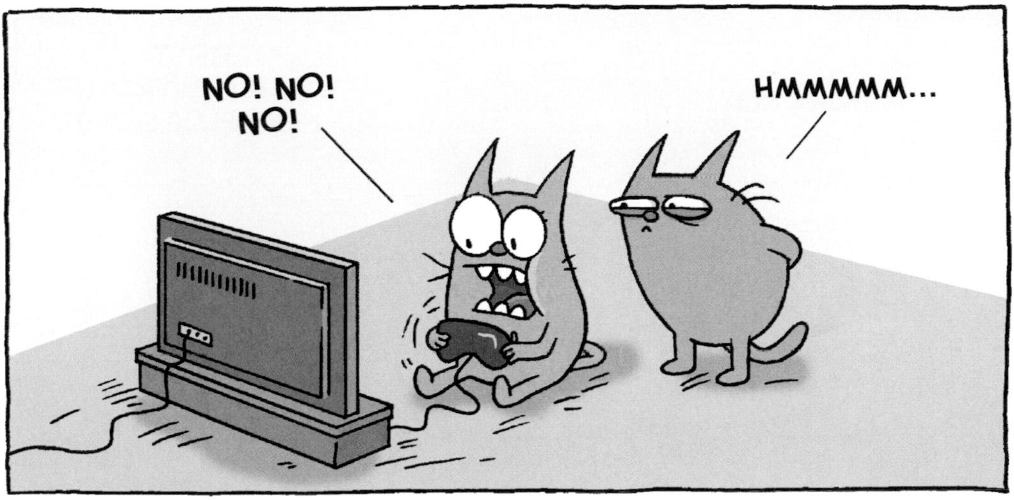
NO! NO!
NO!
HMMMMM...

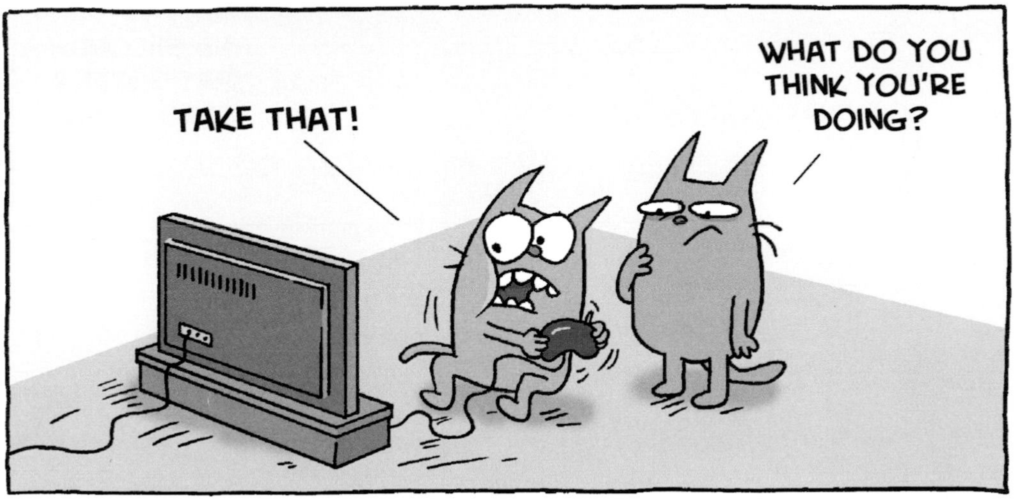
TAKE THAT!
WHAT DO YOU
THINK YOU'RE
DOING?

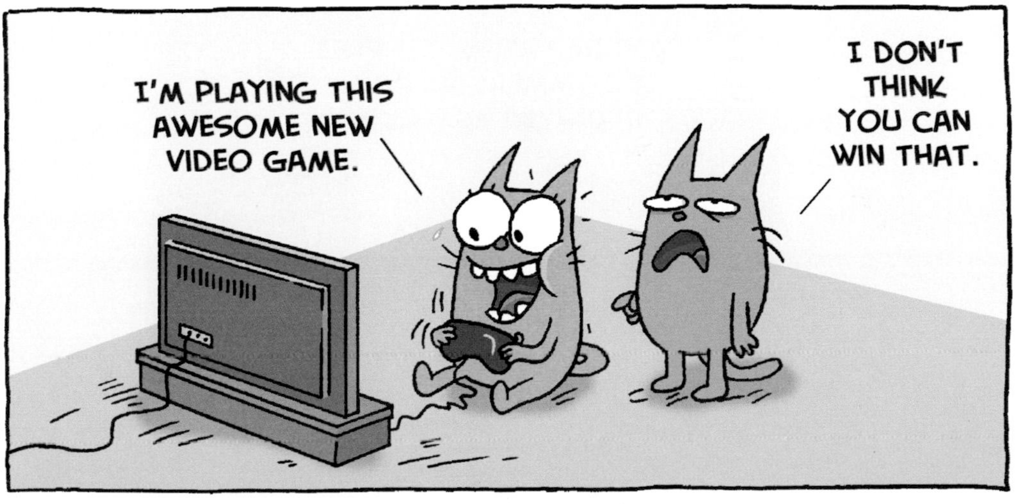
I'M PLAYING THIS
AWESOME NEW
VIDEO GAME.
I DON'T
THINK
YOU CAN
WIN THAT.

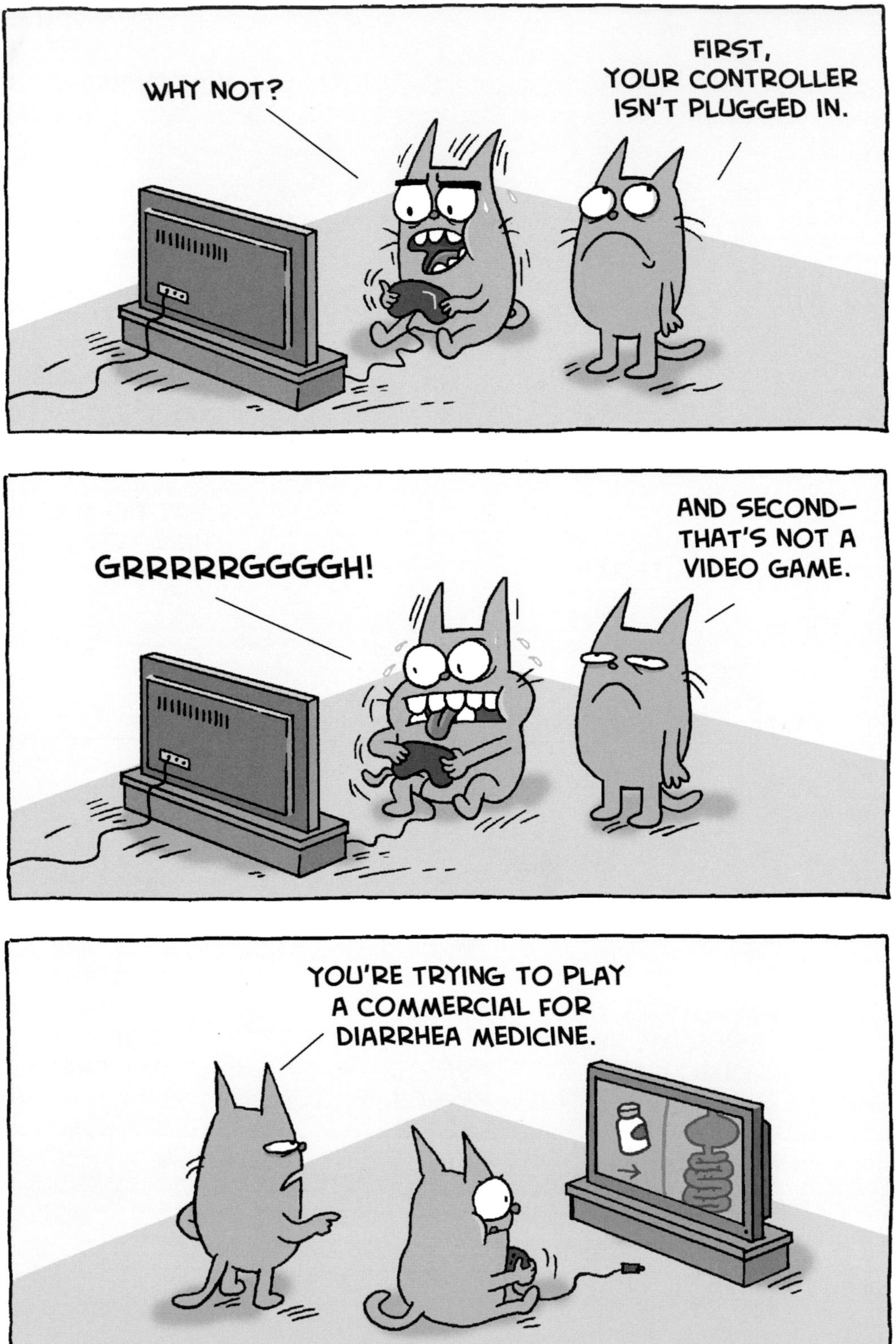
WHY NOT?
FIRST, YOUR CONTROLLER ISN'T PLUGGED IN.
GRRRRRGGGGH!
AND SECOND– THAT'S NOT A VIDEO GAME.
YOU'RE TRYING TO PLAY A COMMERCIAL FOR DIARRHEA MEDICINE.

THOSE ARE GOOD POINTS.
I'M STILL GOING
TO KEEP PLAYING.

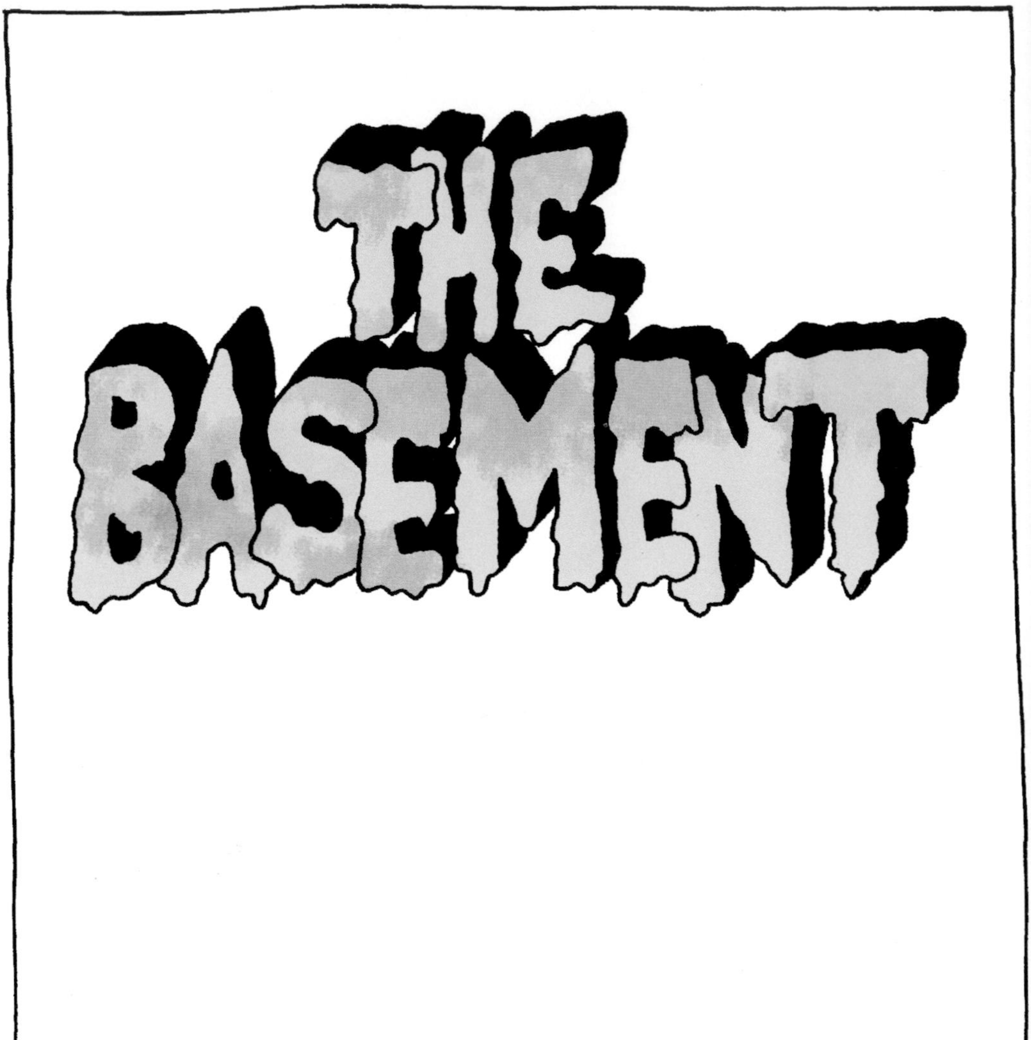
THE BASEMENT

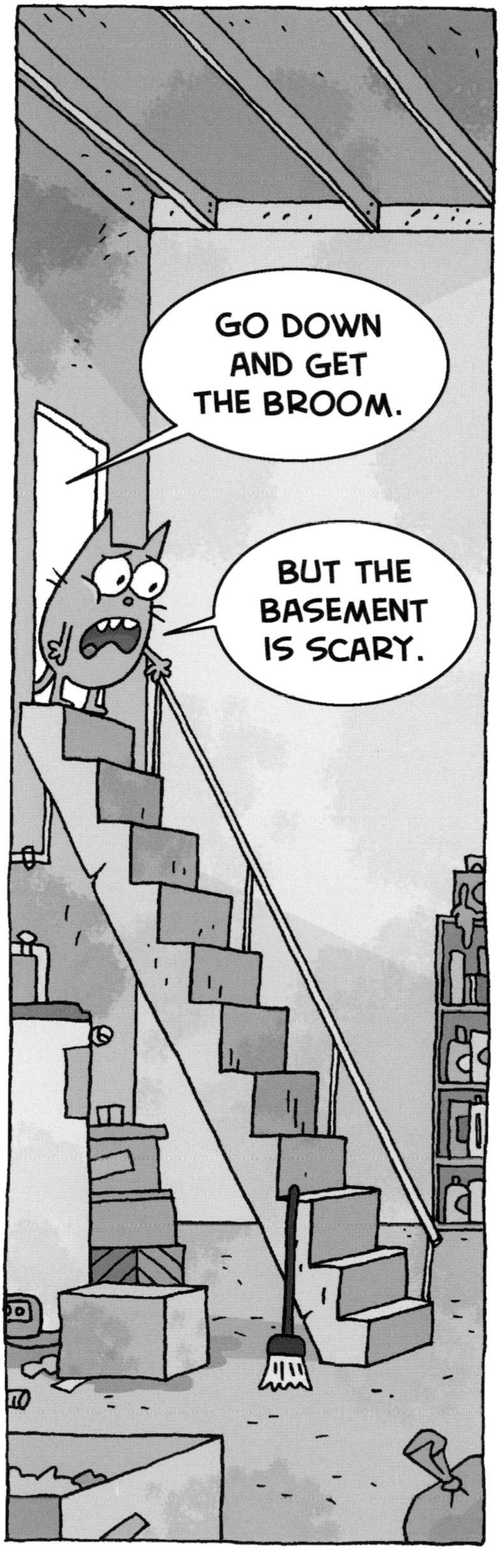
GO DOWN AND GET THE BROOM.
BUT THE BASEMENT IS SCARY.

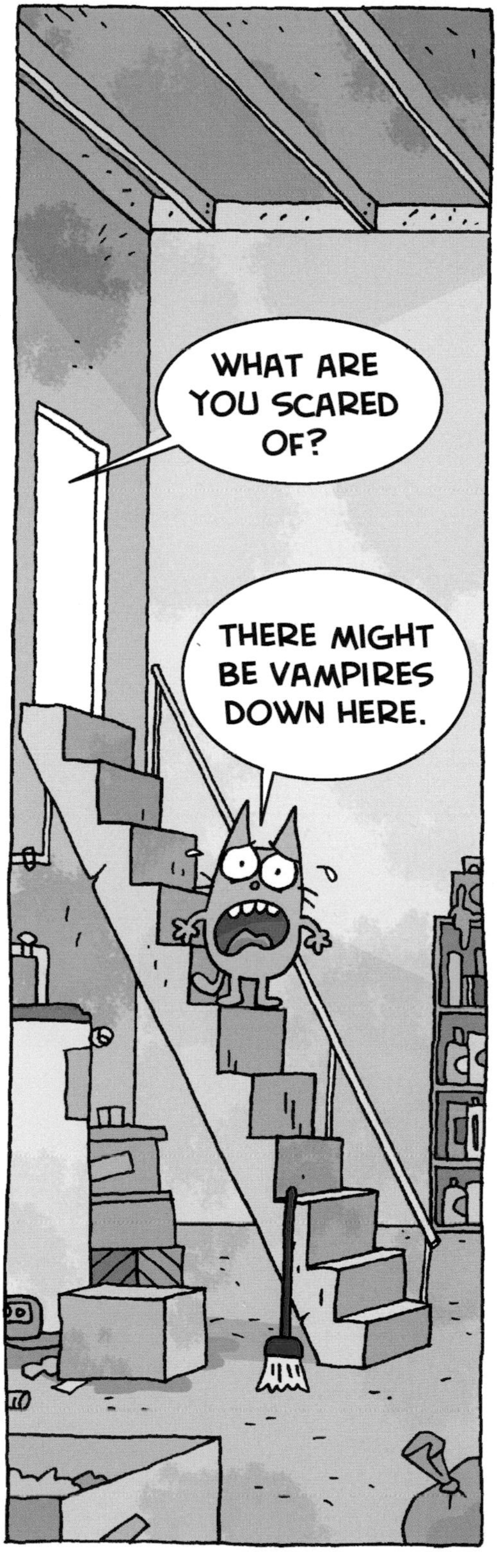
WHAT ARE YOU SCARED OF?
THERE MIGHT BE VAMPIRES DOWN HERE.

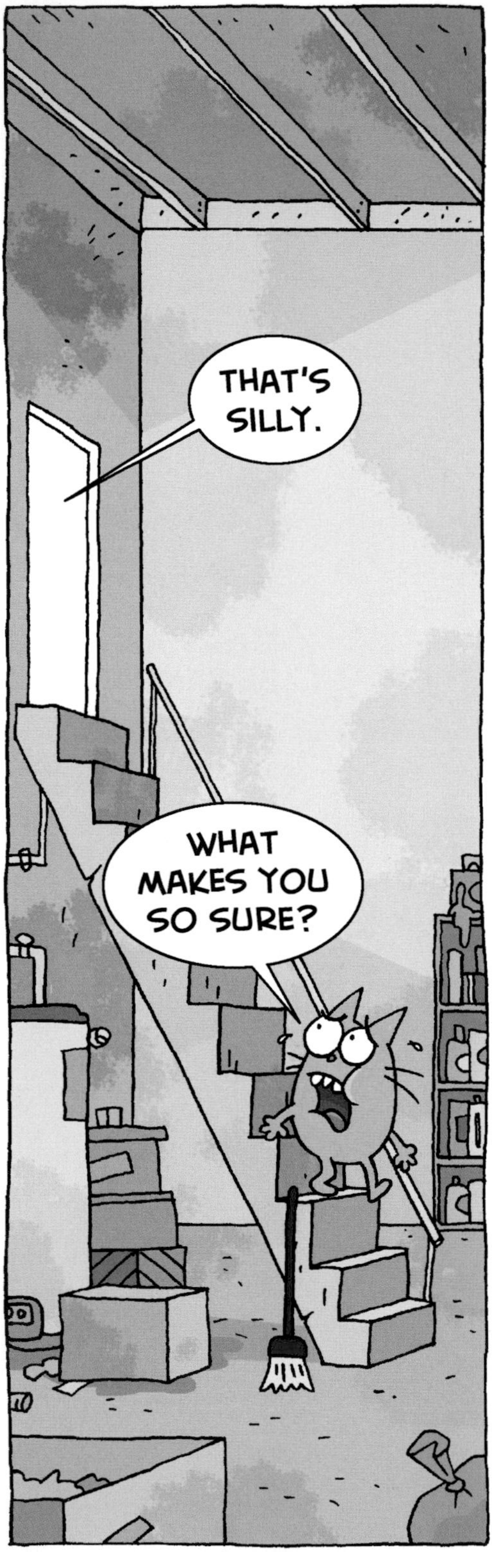
THAT'S SILLY.
WHAT MAKES YOU SO SURE?

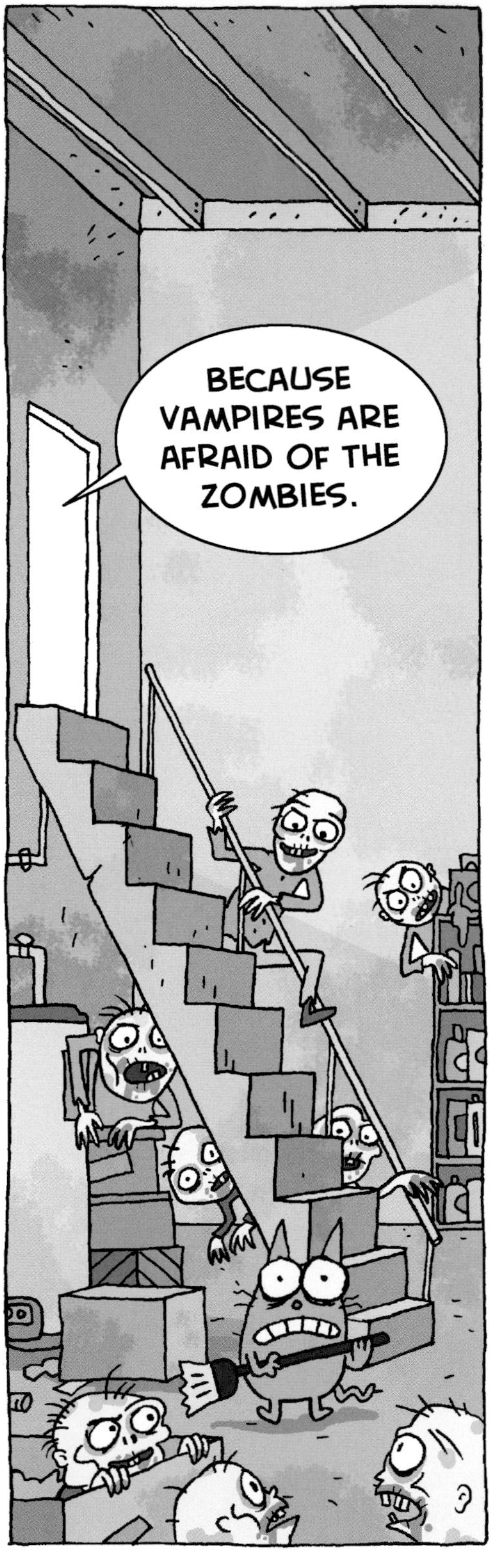
BECAUSE VAMPIRES ARE AFRAID OF THE ZOMBIES.

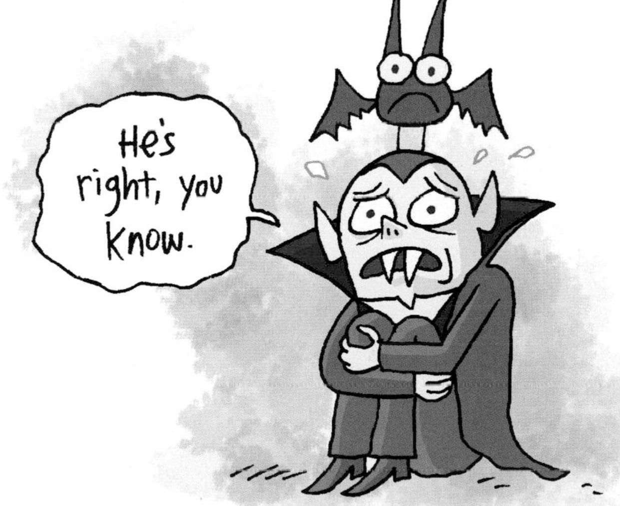
He's right, you know.

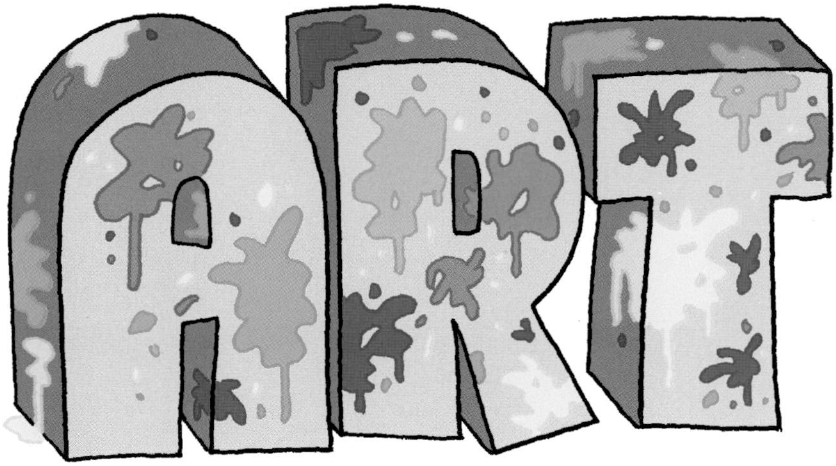
ART

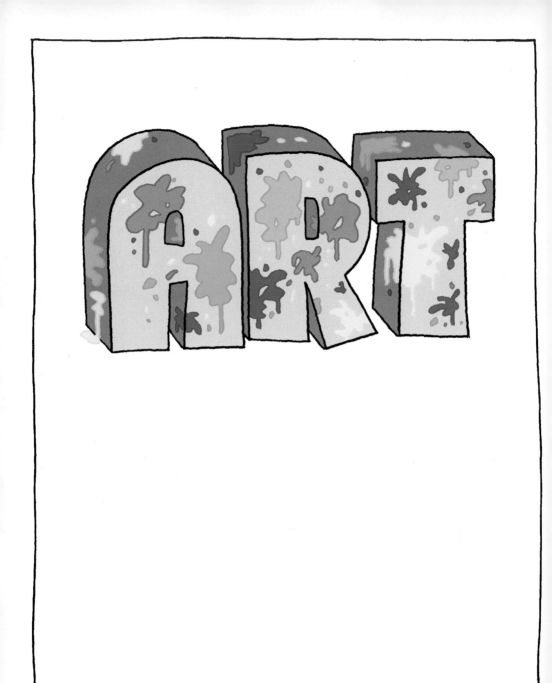

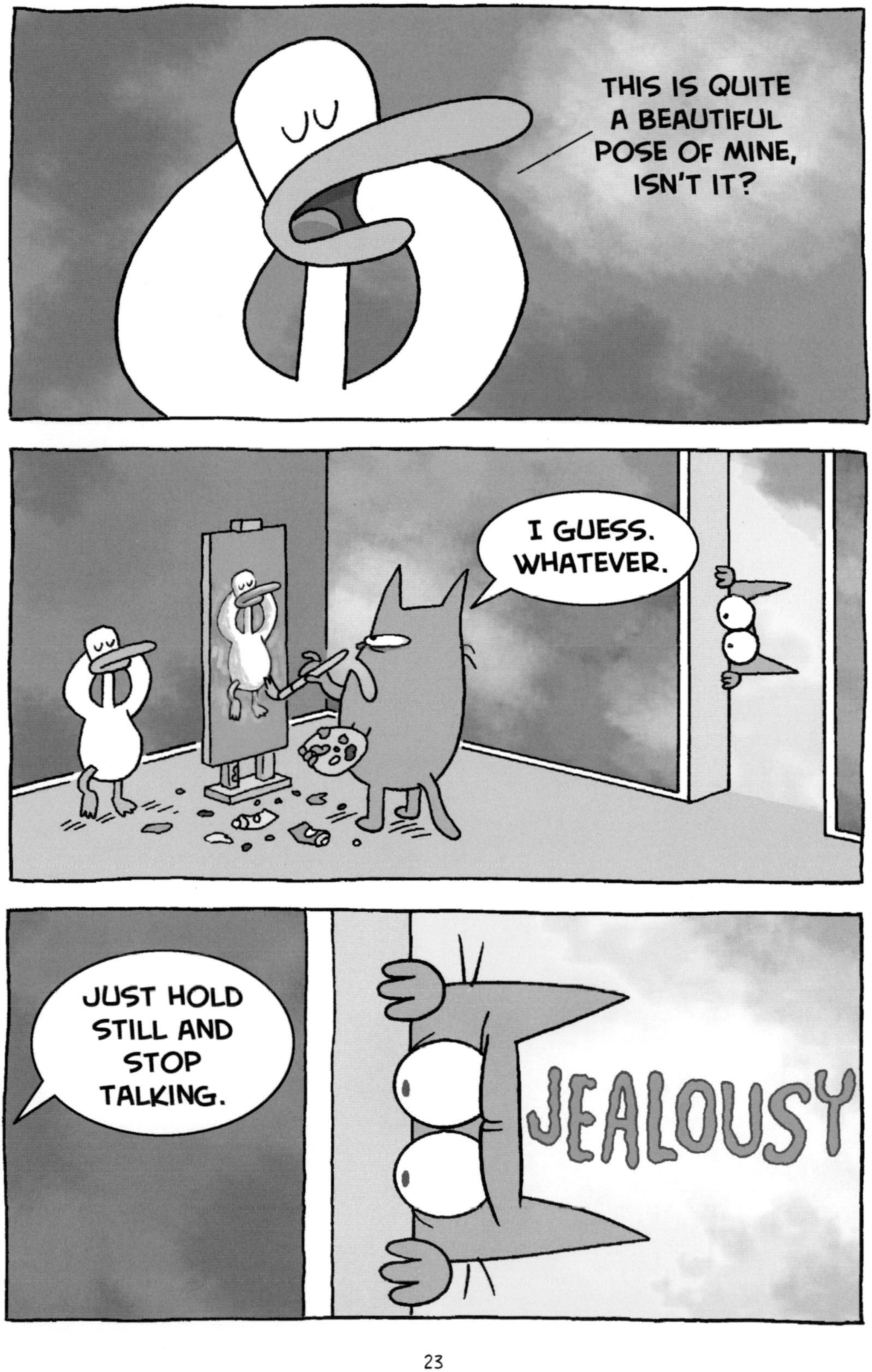
THIS IS QUITE A BEAUTIFUL POSE OF MINE, ISN'T IT?
I GUESS. WHATEVER.
JUST HOLD STILL AND STOP TALKING.
JEALOUSY

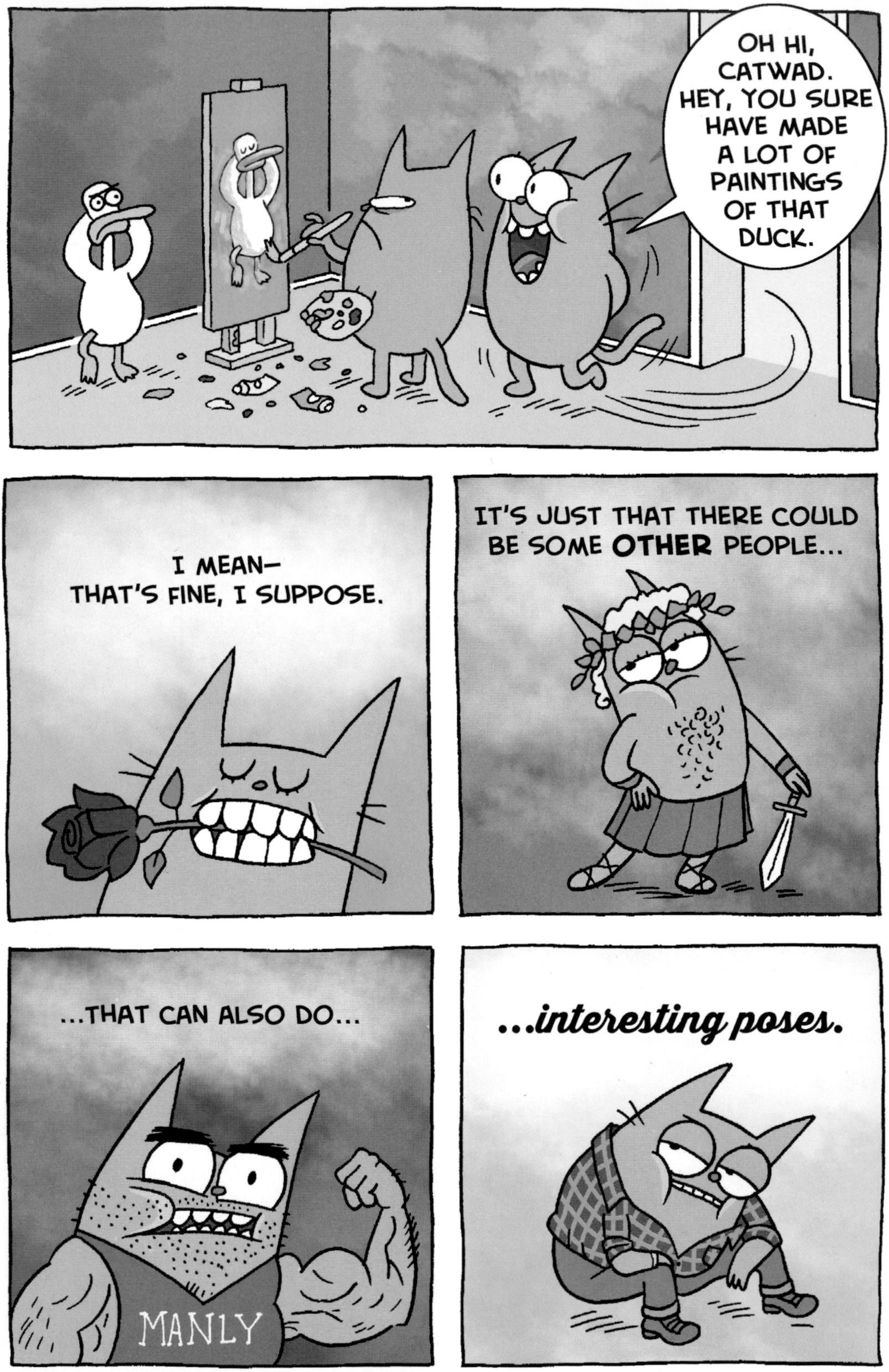
OH HI, CATWAD. HEY, YOU SURE HAVE MADE A LOT OF PAINTINGS OF THAT DUCK.
I MEAN— THAT'S FINE, I SUPPOSE.
IT'S JUST THAT THERE COULD BE SOME **OTHER** PEOPLE...
...THAT CAN ALSO DO...
MANLY
...interesting poses.

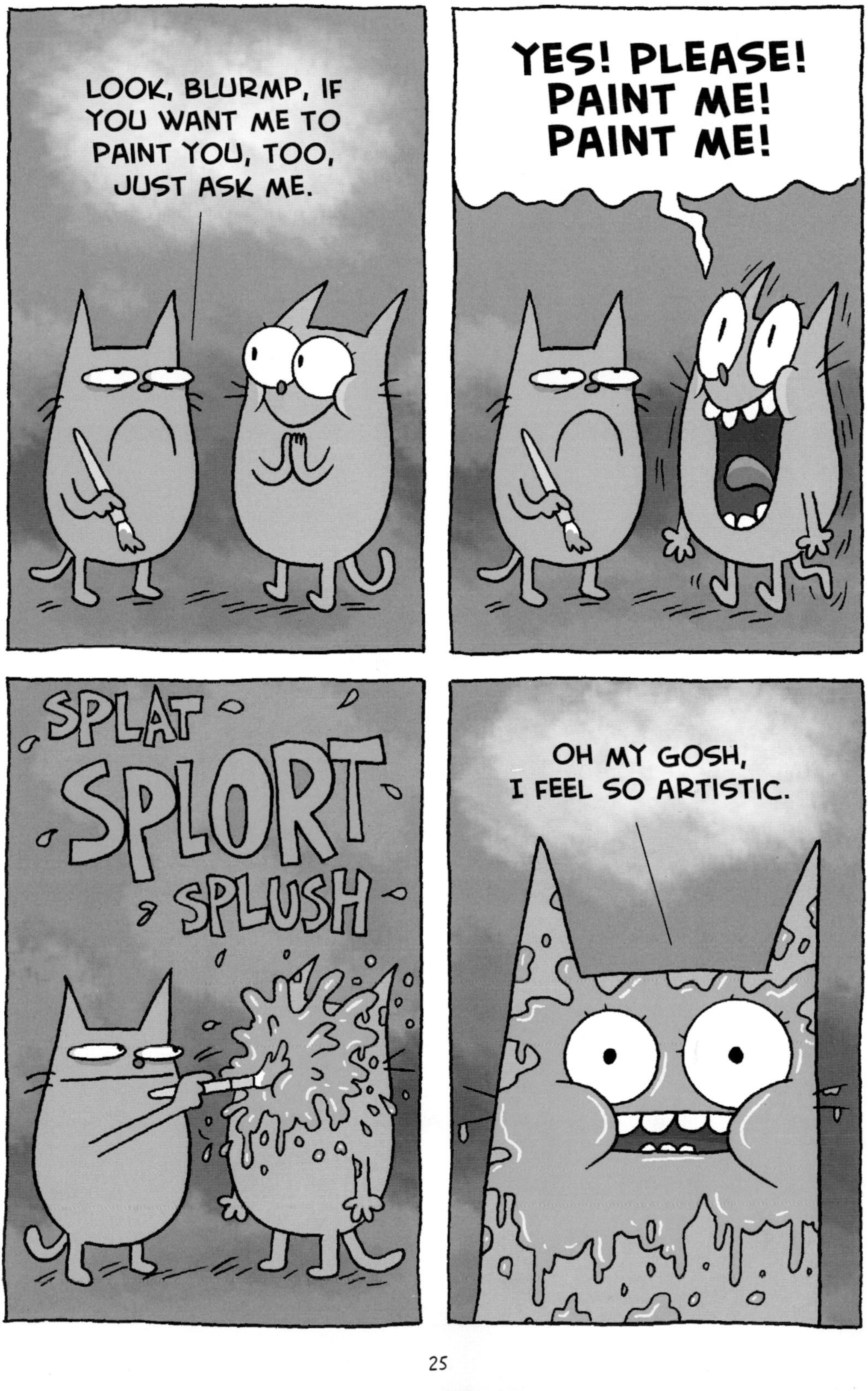
LOOK, BLURMP, IF YOU WANT ME TO PAINT YOU, TOO, JUST ASK ME.
YES! PLEASE! PAINT ME! PAINT ME!
SPLAT
SPLORT
SPLUSH
OH MY GOSH, I FEEL SO ARTISTIC.

CRAFTY

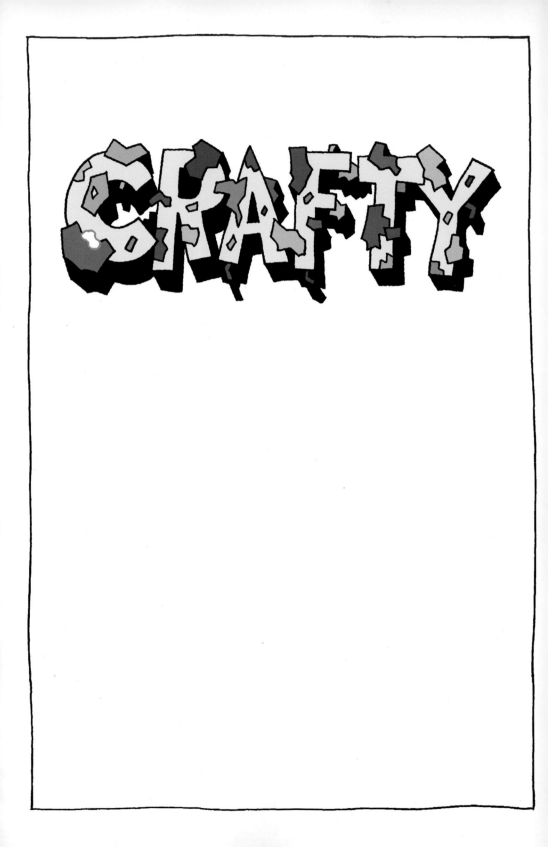

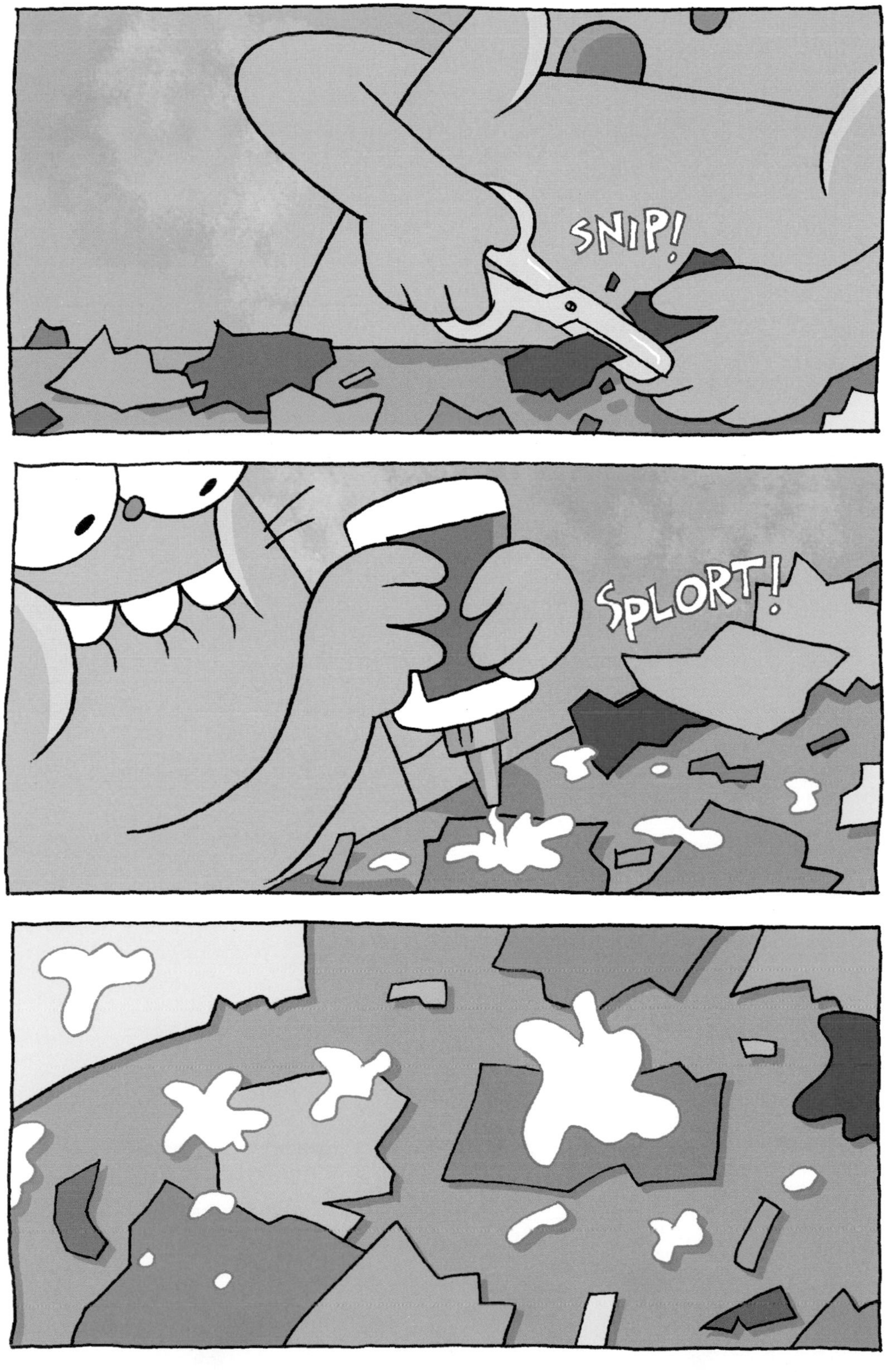
SNIP!
SPLORT!

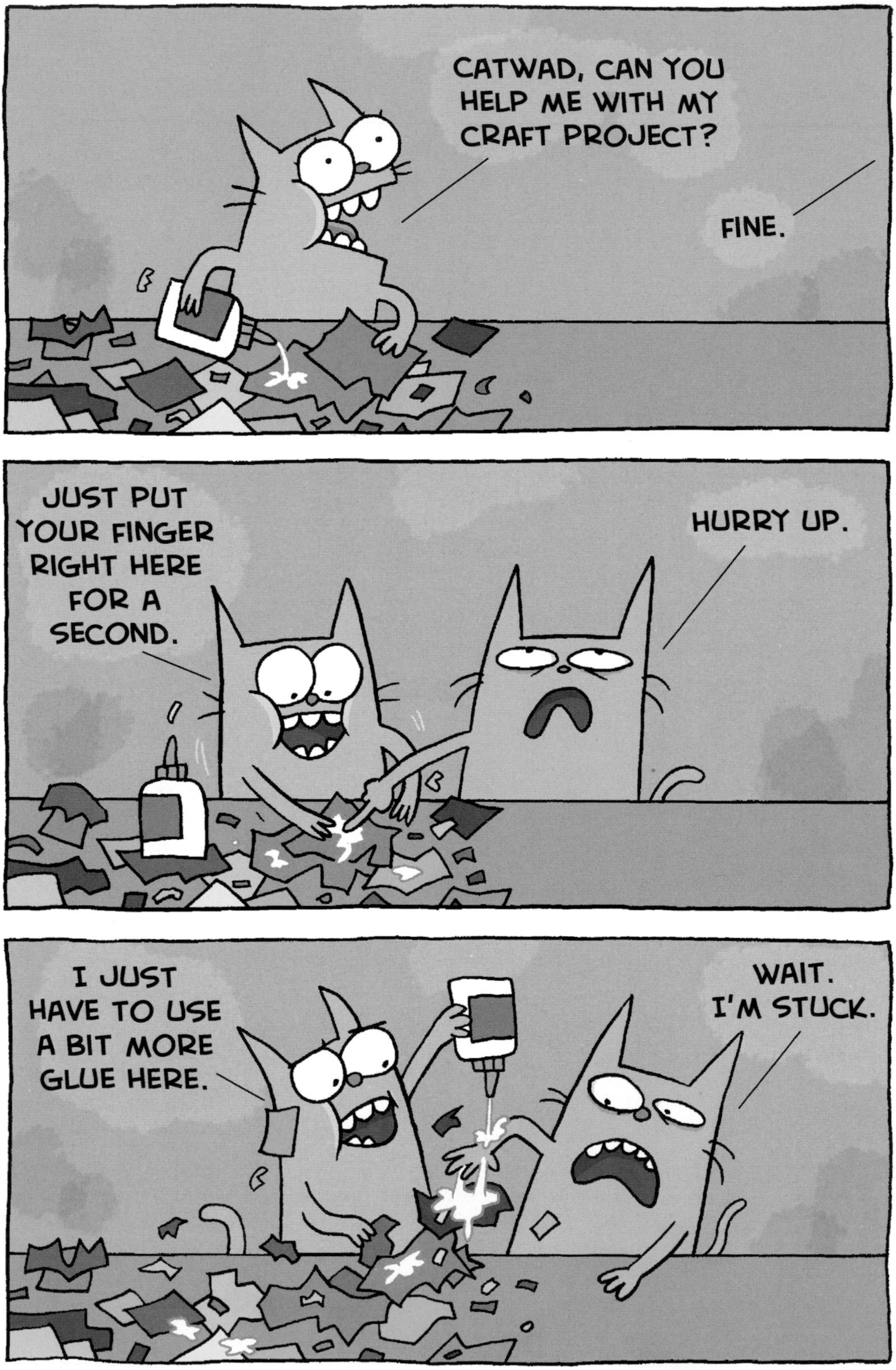
CATWAD, CAN YOU HELP ME WITH MY CRAFT PROJECT?
FINE.
JUST PUT YOUR FINGER RIGHT HERE FOR A SECOND.
HURRY UP.
I JUST HAVE TO USE A BIT MORE GLUE HERE.
WAIT. I'M STUCK.

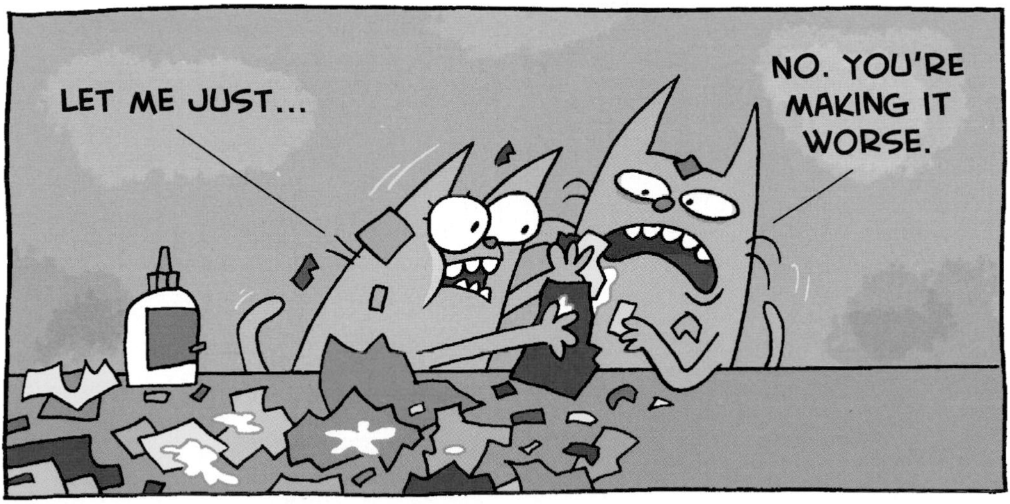
LET ME JUST...
NO. YOU'RE MAKING IT WORSE.

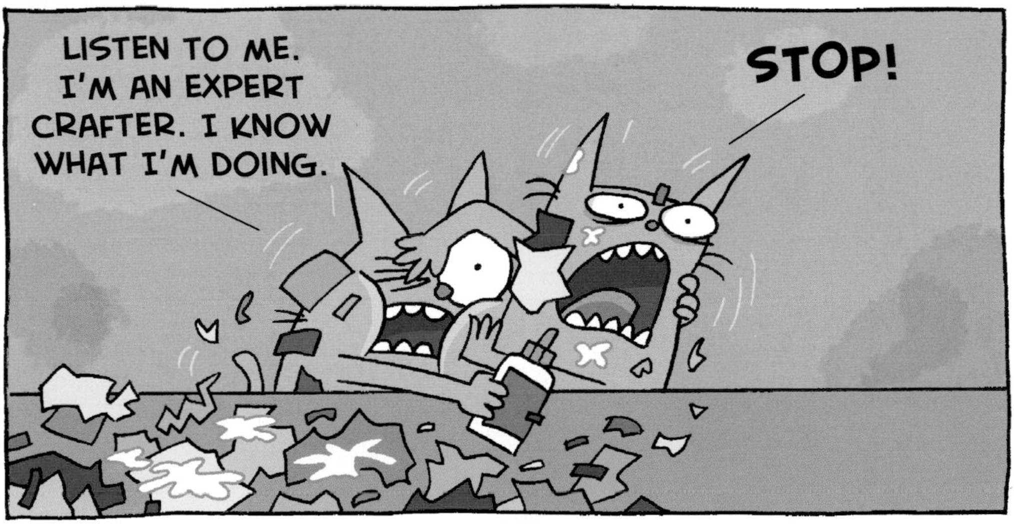
LISTEN TO ME. I'M AN EXPERT CRAFTER. I KNOW WHAT I'M DOING.
STOP!

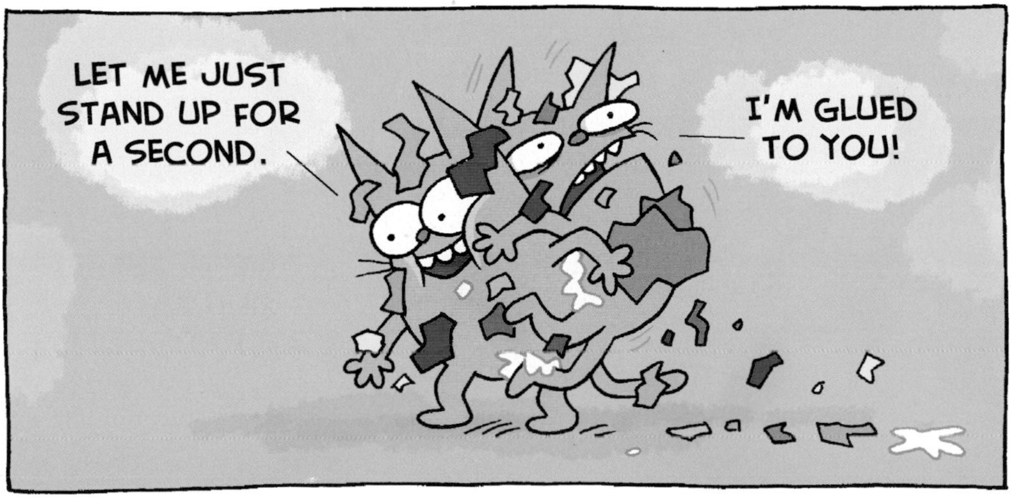
LET ME JUST STAND UP FOR A SECOND.
I'M GLUED TO YOU!

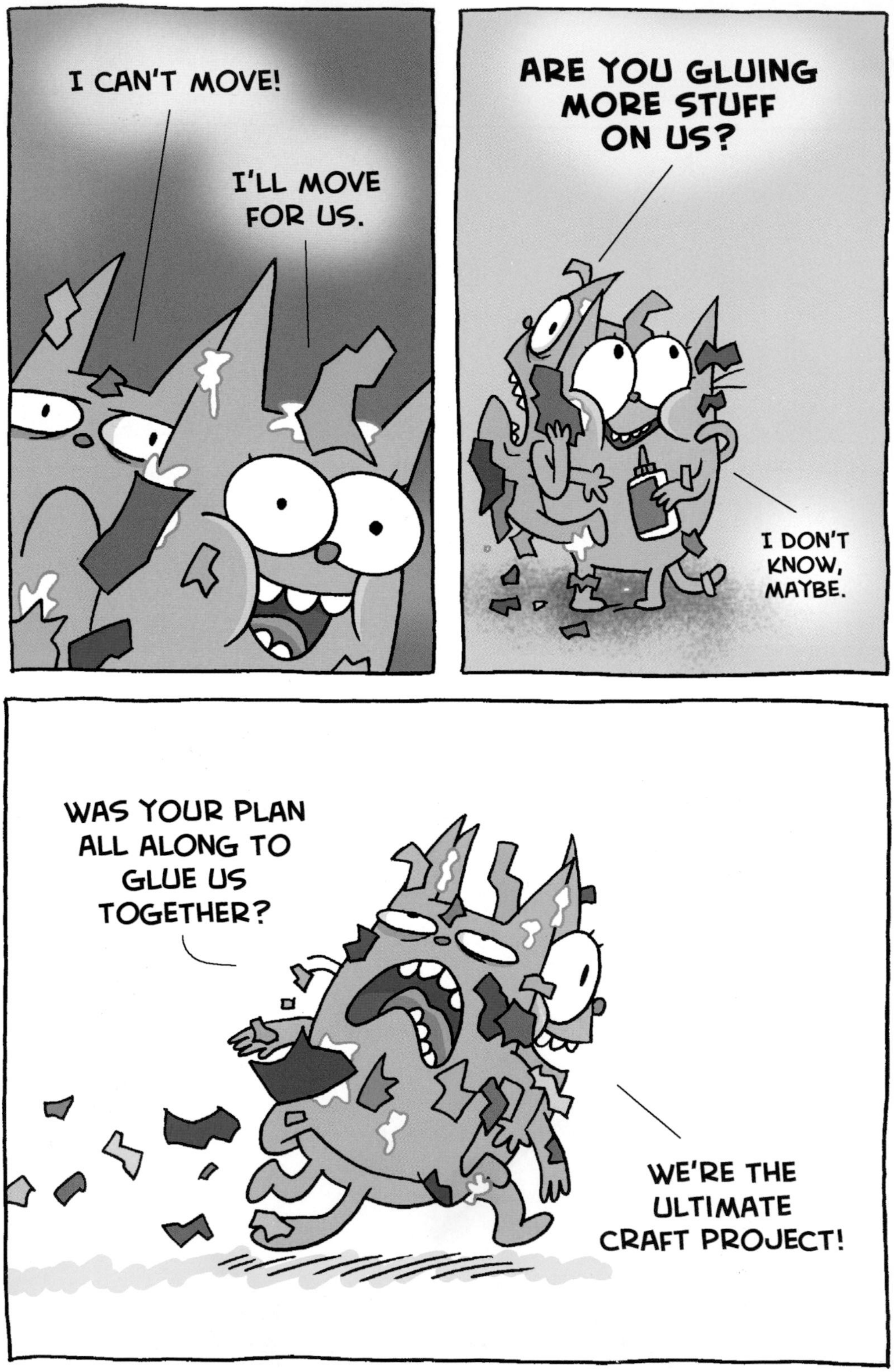
I CAN'T MOVE!
I'LL MOVE FOR US.
ARE YOU GLUING MORE STUFF ON US?
I DON'T KNOW, MAYBE.
WAS YOUR PLAN ALL ALONG TO GLUE US TOGETHER?
WE'RE THE ULTIMATE CRAFT PROJECT!

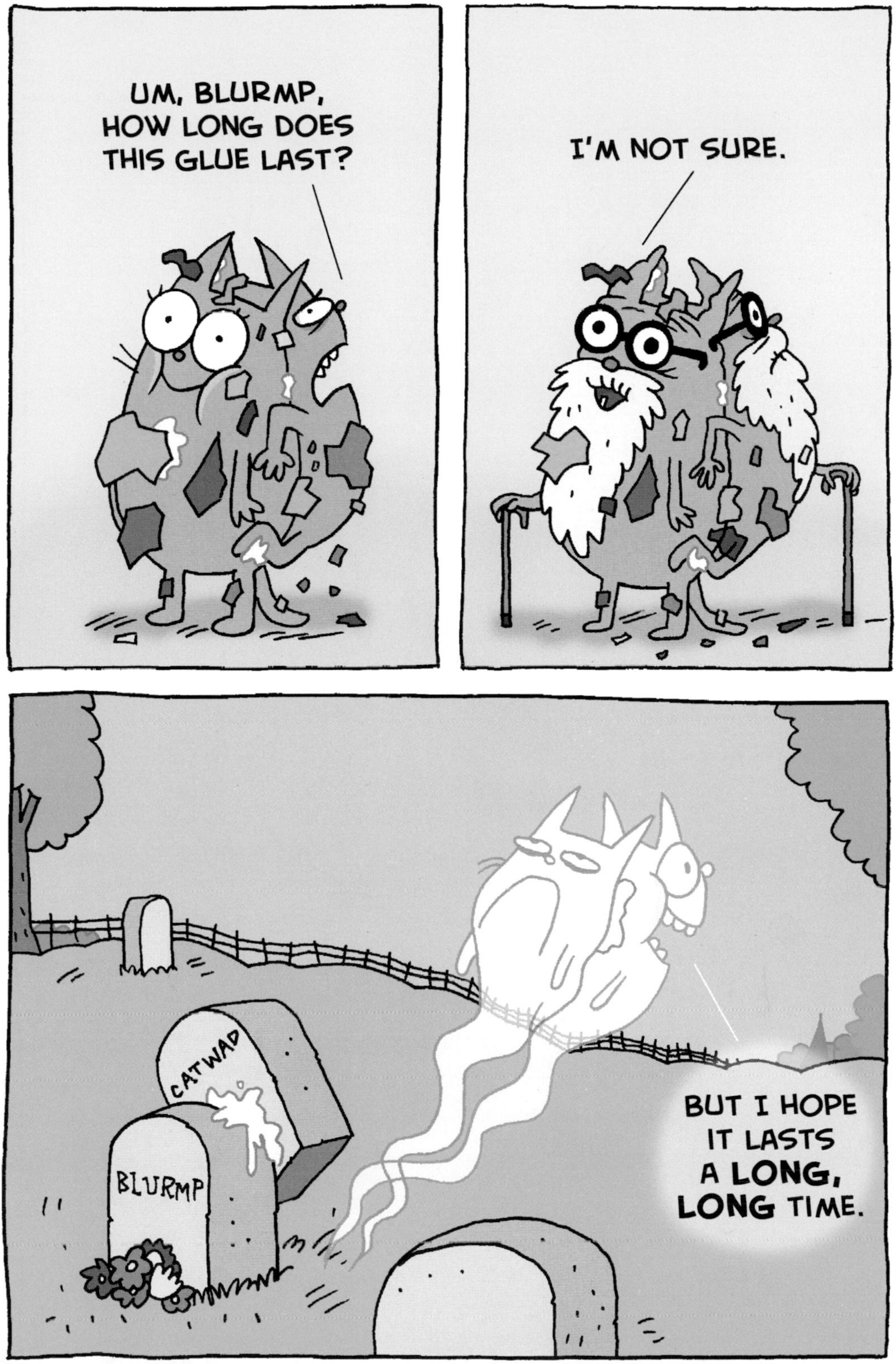
UM, BLURMP, HOW LONG DOES THIS GLUE LAST?
I'M NOT SURE.
CATWAD
BLURMP
BUT I HOPE IT LASTS A LONG, LONG TIME.

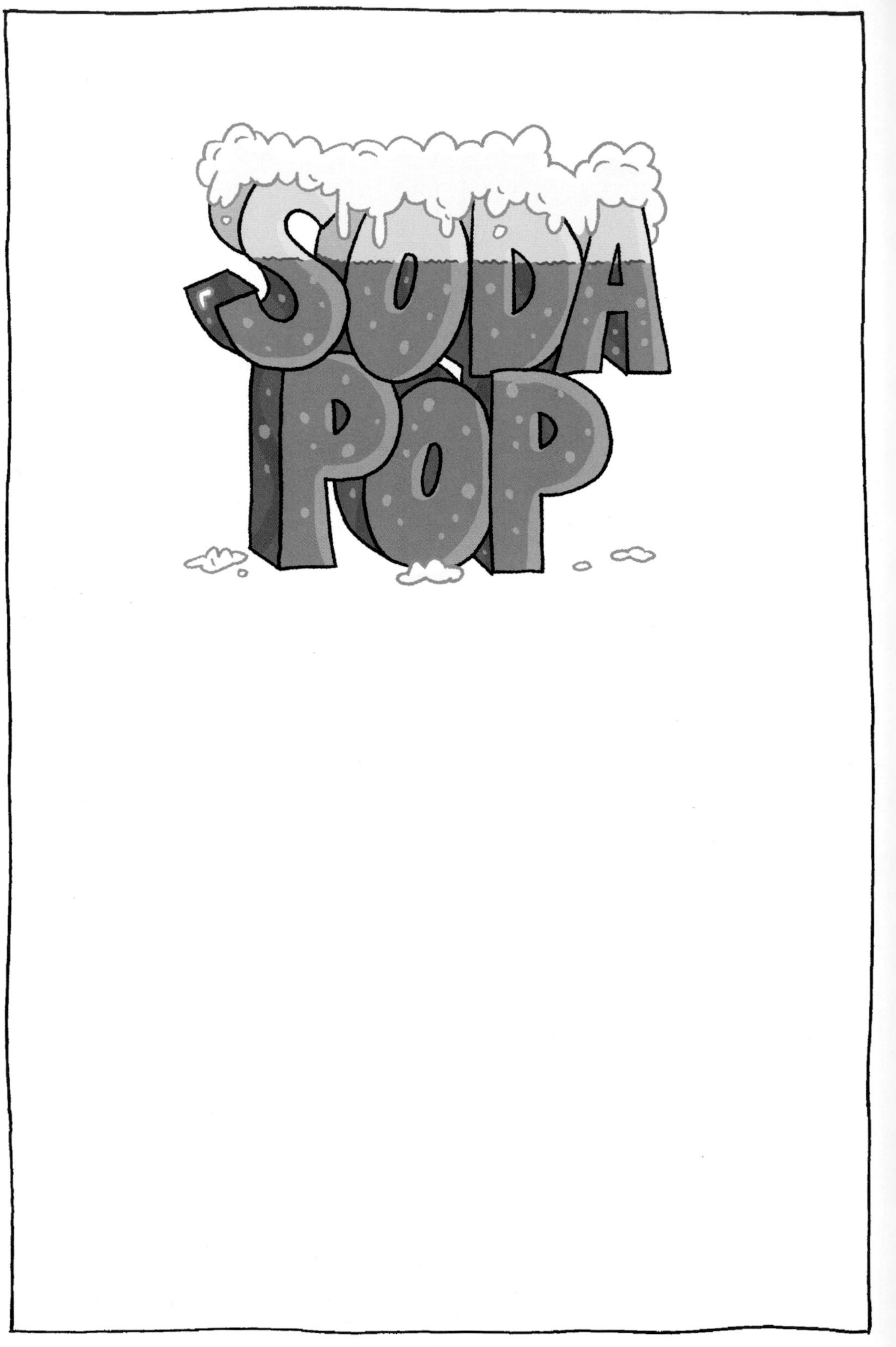
SODA
POP

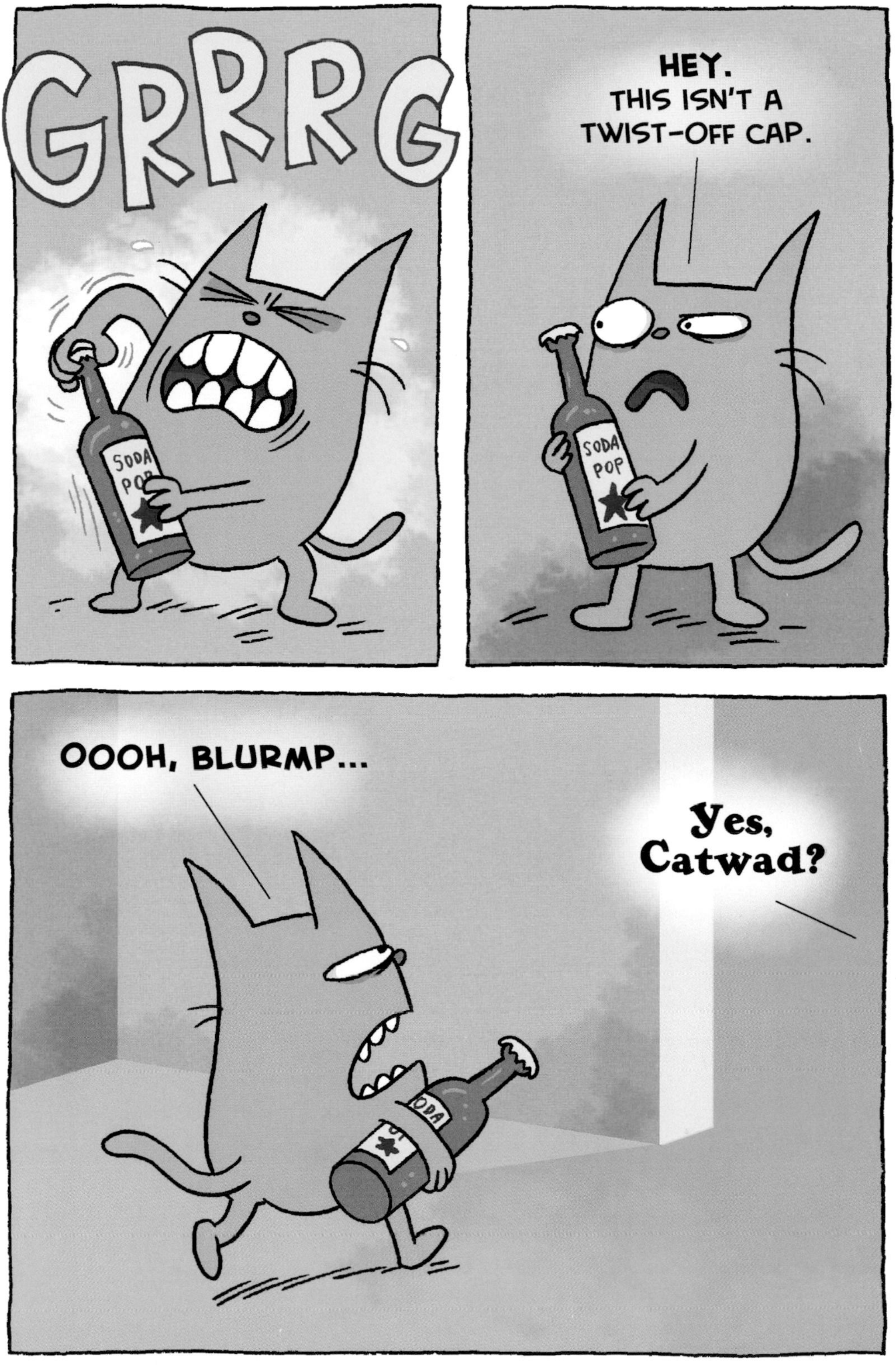
GRRRG
HEY.
THIS ISN'T A
TWIST-OFF CAP.
SODA POP
OOOH, BLURMP...
Yes,
Catwad?

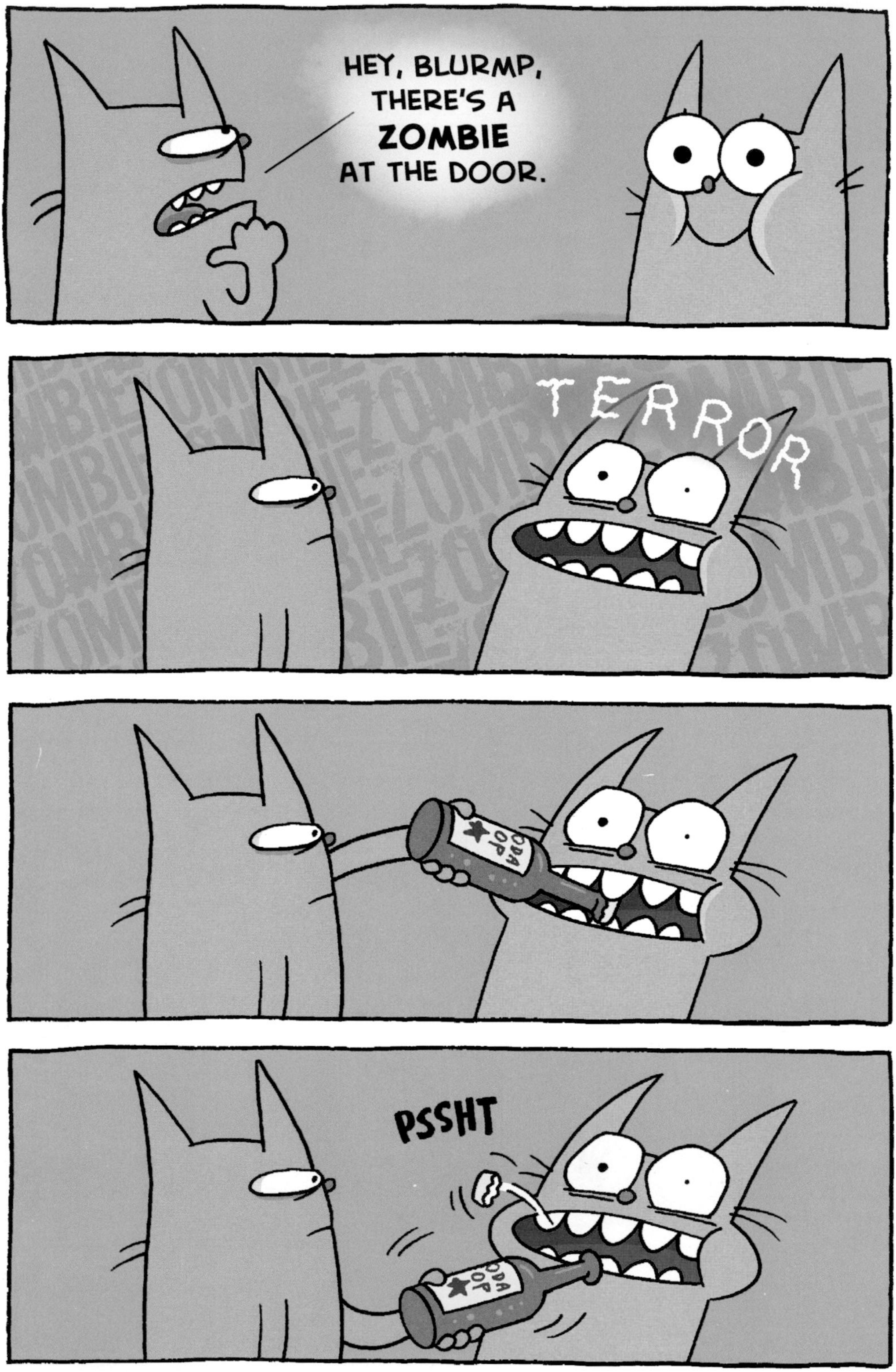
HEY, BLURMP, THERE'S A **ZOMBIE** AT THE DOOR.
TERROR
PSSHT

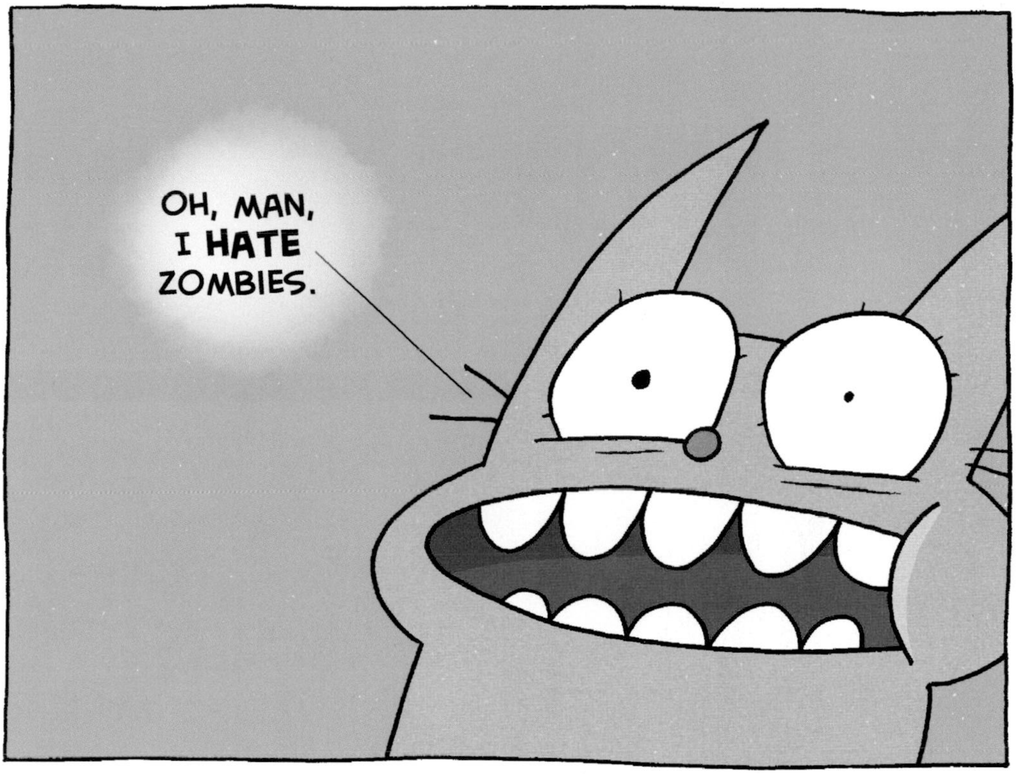
OH, MAN, I **HATE** ZOMBIES.

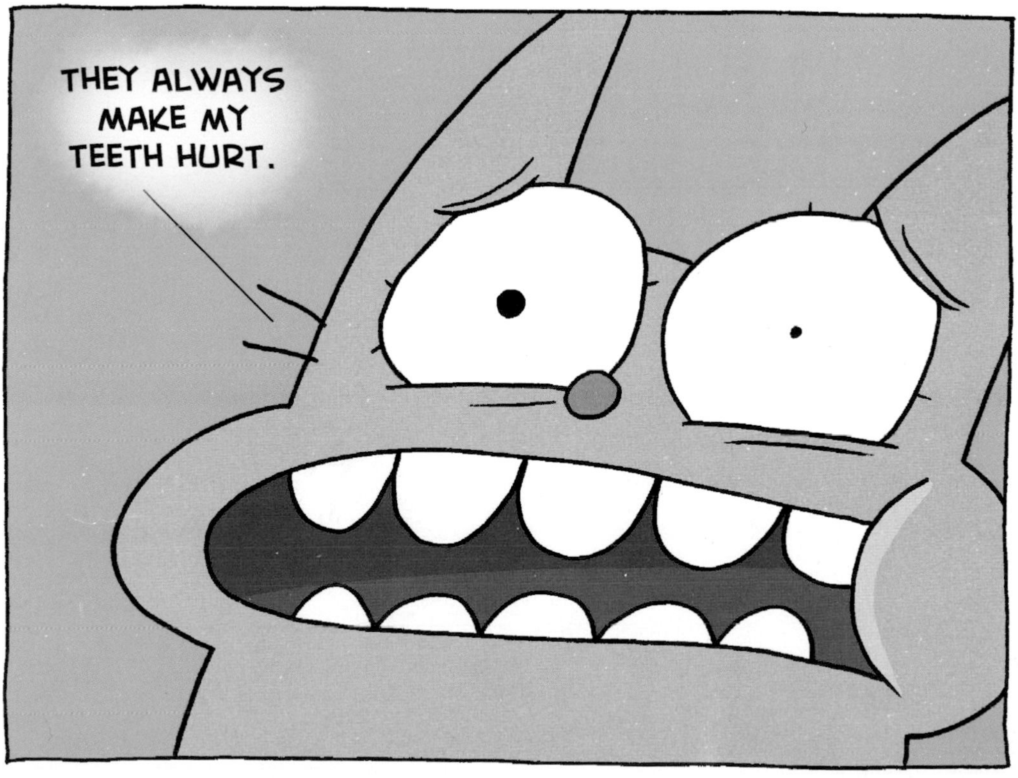
THEY ALWAYS MAKE MY TEETH HURT.

FISH

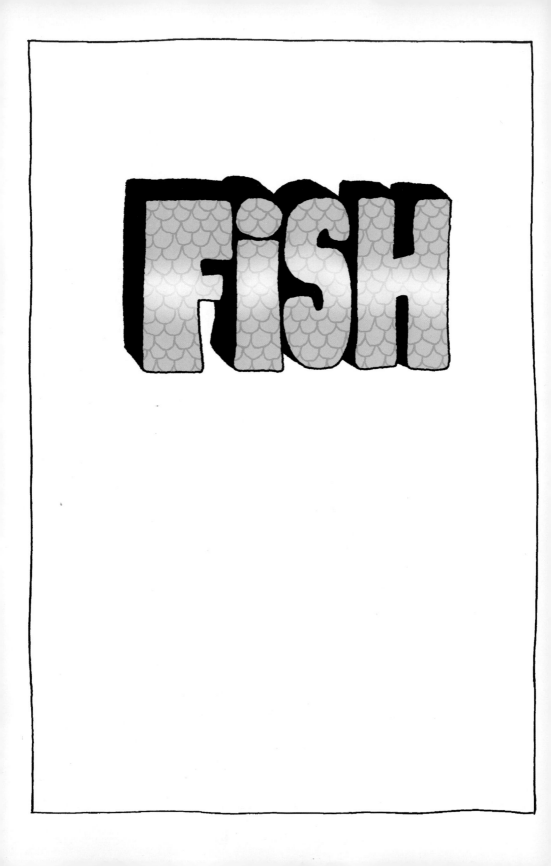

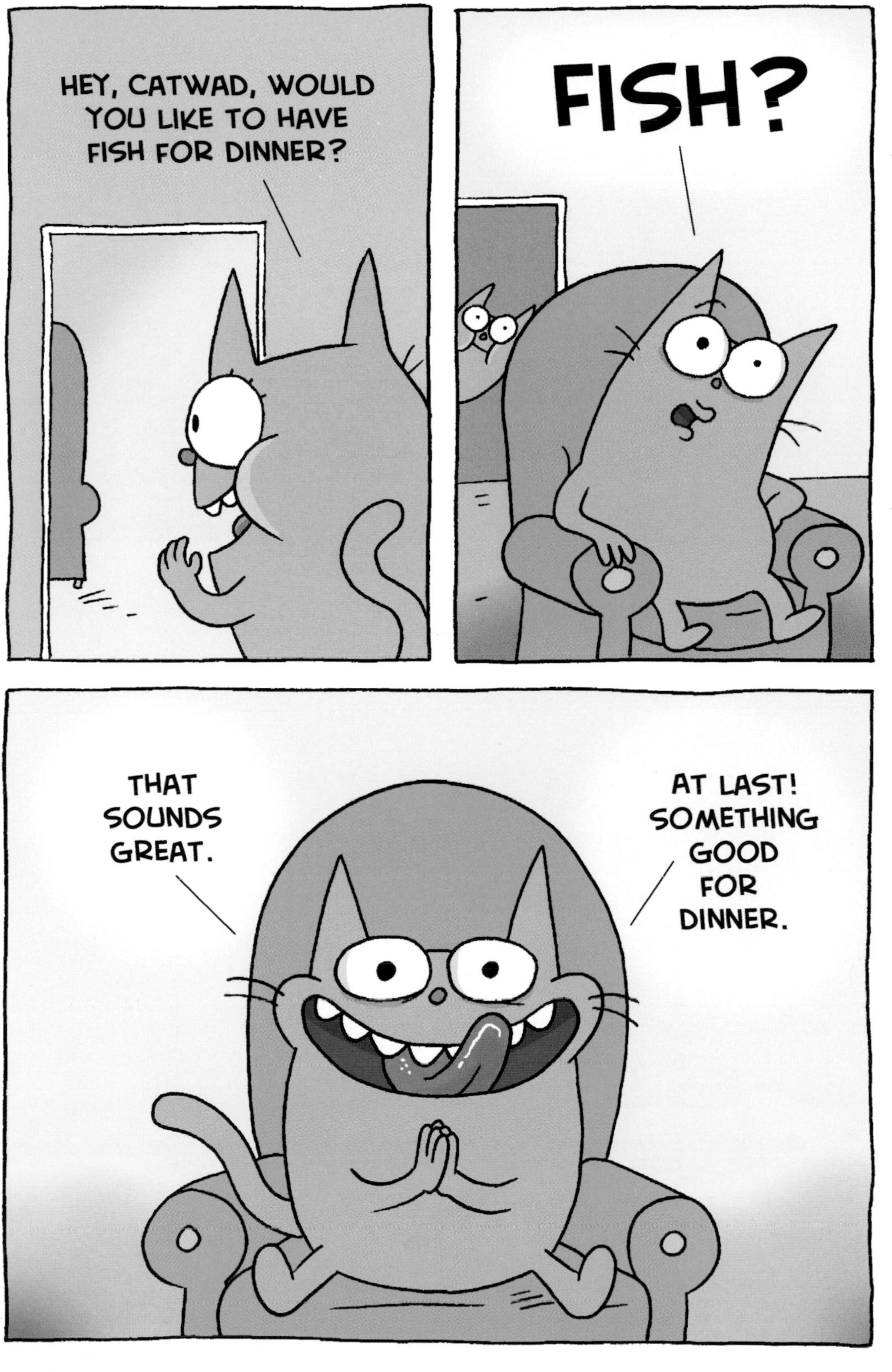
HEY, CATWAD, WOULD YOU LIKE TO HAVE FISH FOR DINNER?
FISH?
THAT SOUNDS GREAT.
AT LAST! SOMETHING GOOD FOR DINNER.

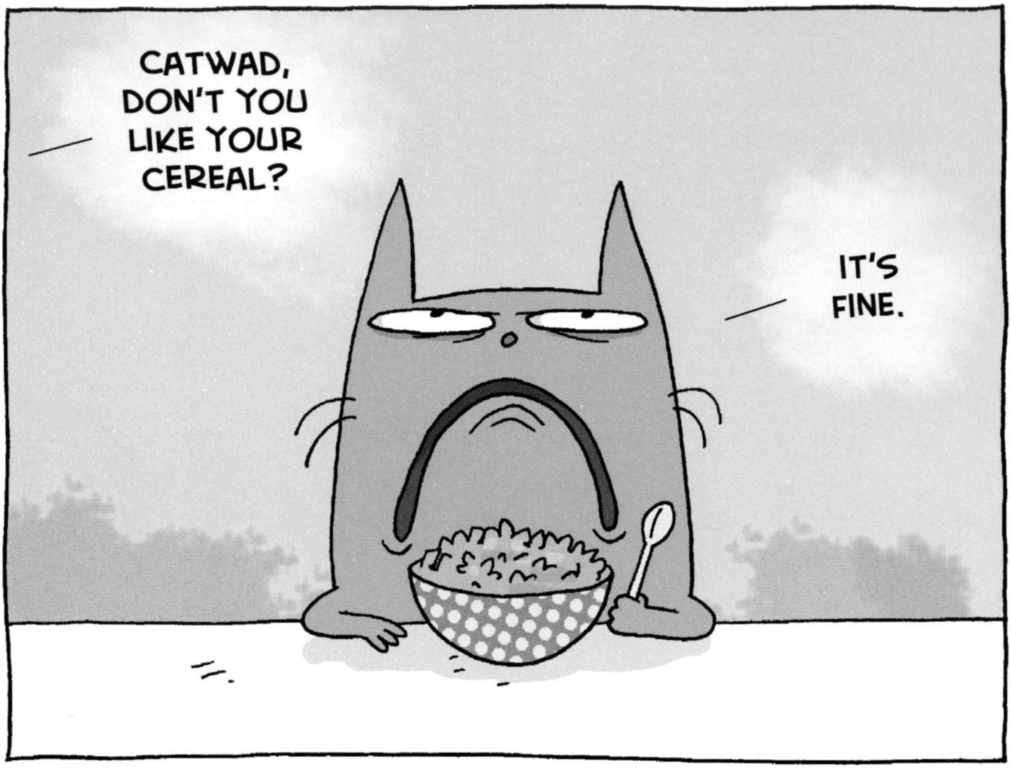
CATWAD, DON'T YOU LIKE YOUR CEREAL?
IT'S FINE.

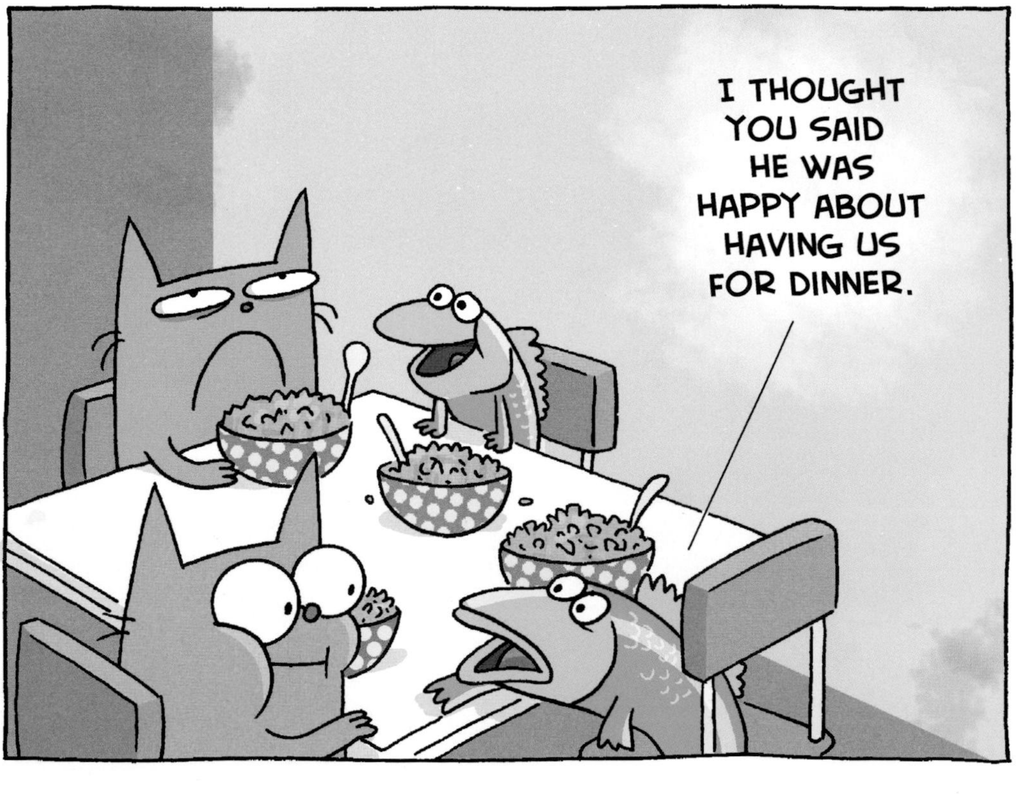
I THOUGHT YOU SAID HE WAS HAPPY ABOUT HAVING US FOR DINNER.

ISN'T
THIS FUN,
MR. CATWAD?

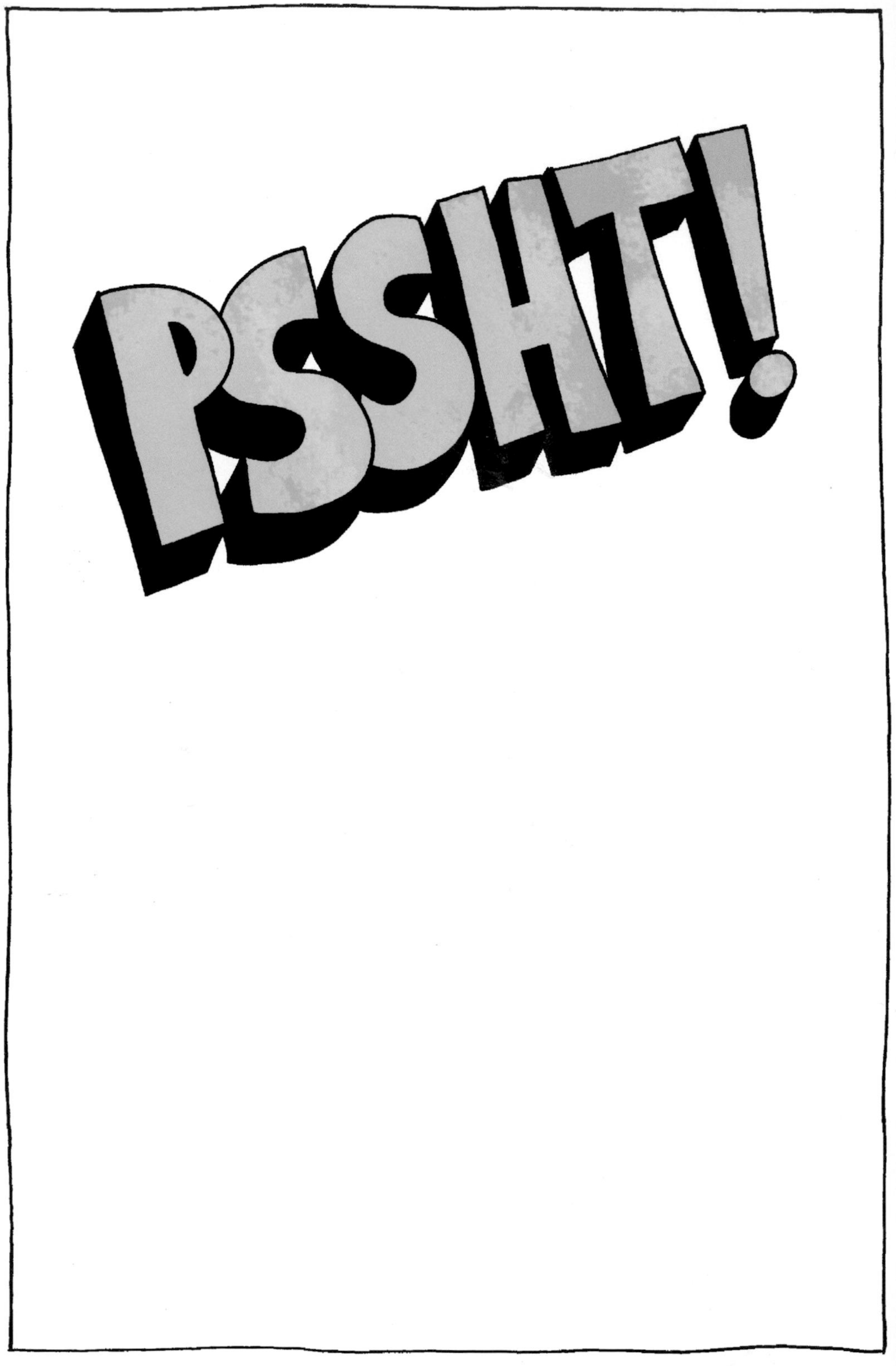
PSSHT!

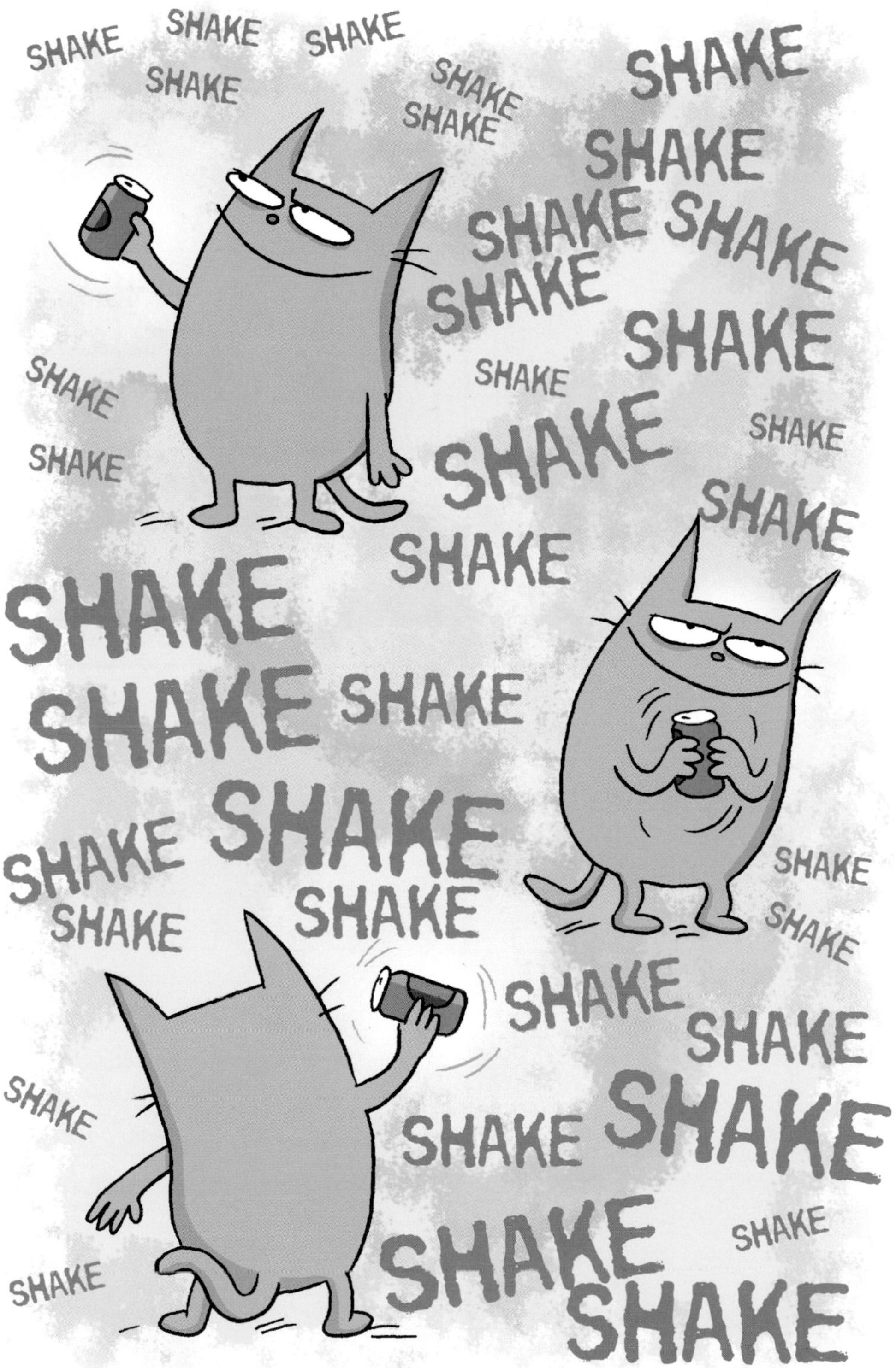
SHAKE
SHAKE
SHAKE
SHAKE
SHAKE
SHAKE
SHAKE
SHAKE
SHAKE
SHAKE
SHAKE
SHAKE
SHAKE
SHAKE
SHAKE
SHAKE
SHAKE
SHAKE
SHAKE
SHAKE
SHAKE
SHAKE
SHAKE
SHAKE
SHAKE
SHAKE
SHAKE
SHAKE
SHAKE
SHAKE
SHAKE
SHAKE
SHAKE
SHAKE
SHAKE

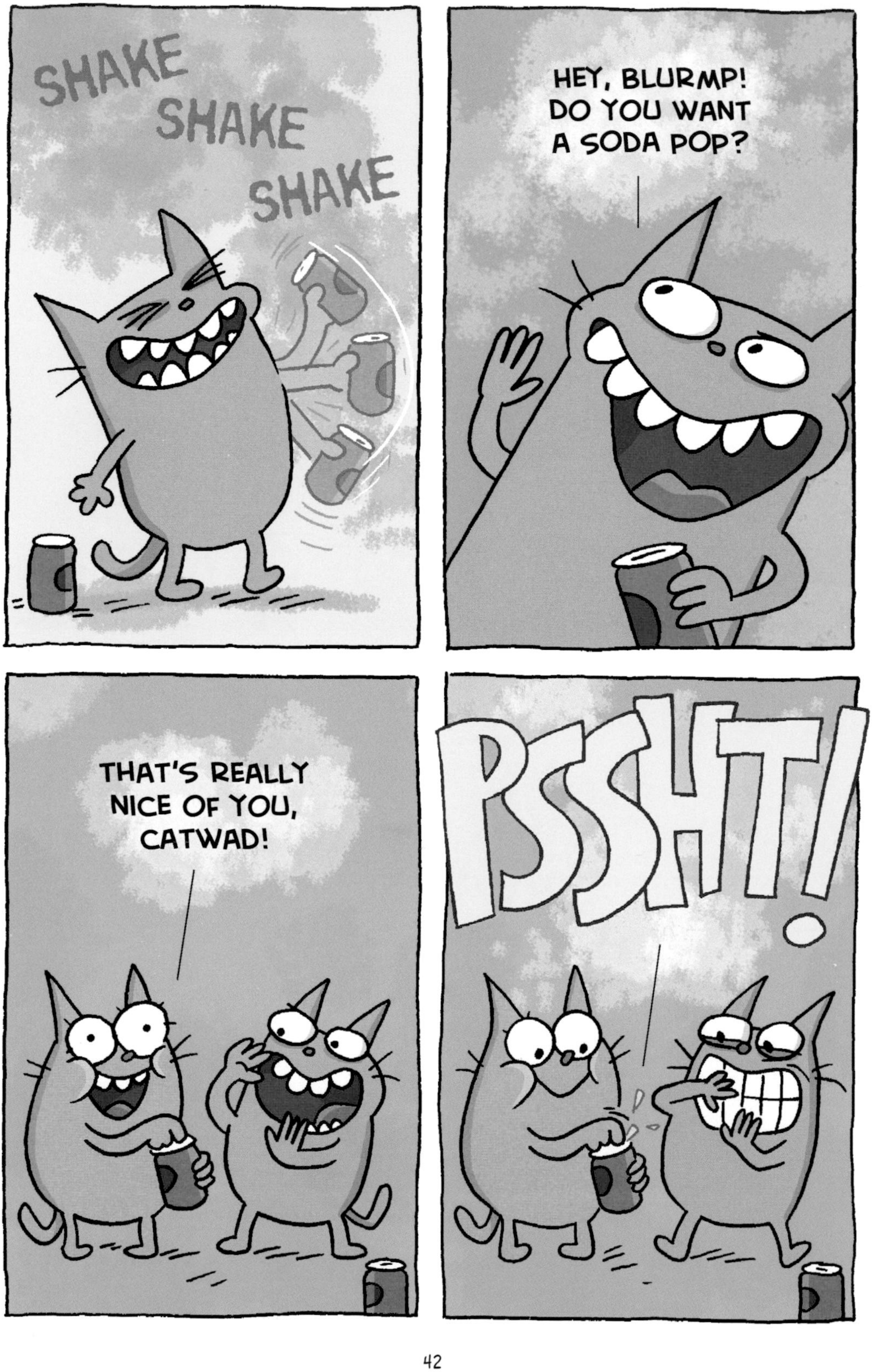
SHAKE
SHAKE
SHAKE
HEY, BLURMP! DO YOU WANT A SODA POP?
THAT'S REALLY NICE OF YOU, CATWAD!
PSSHT!

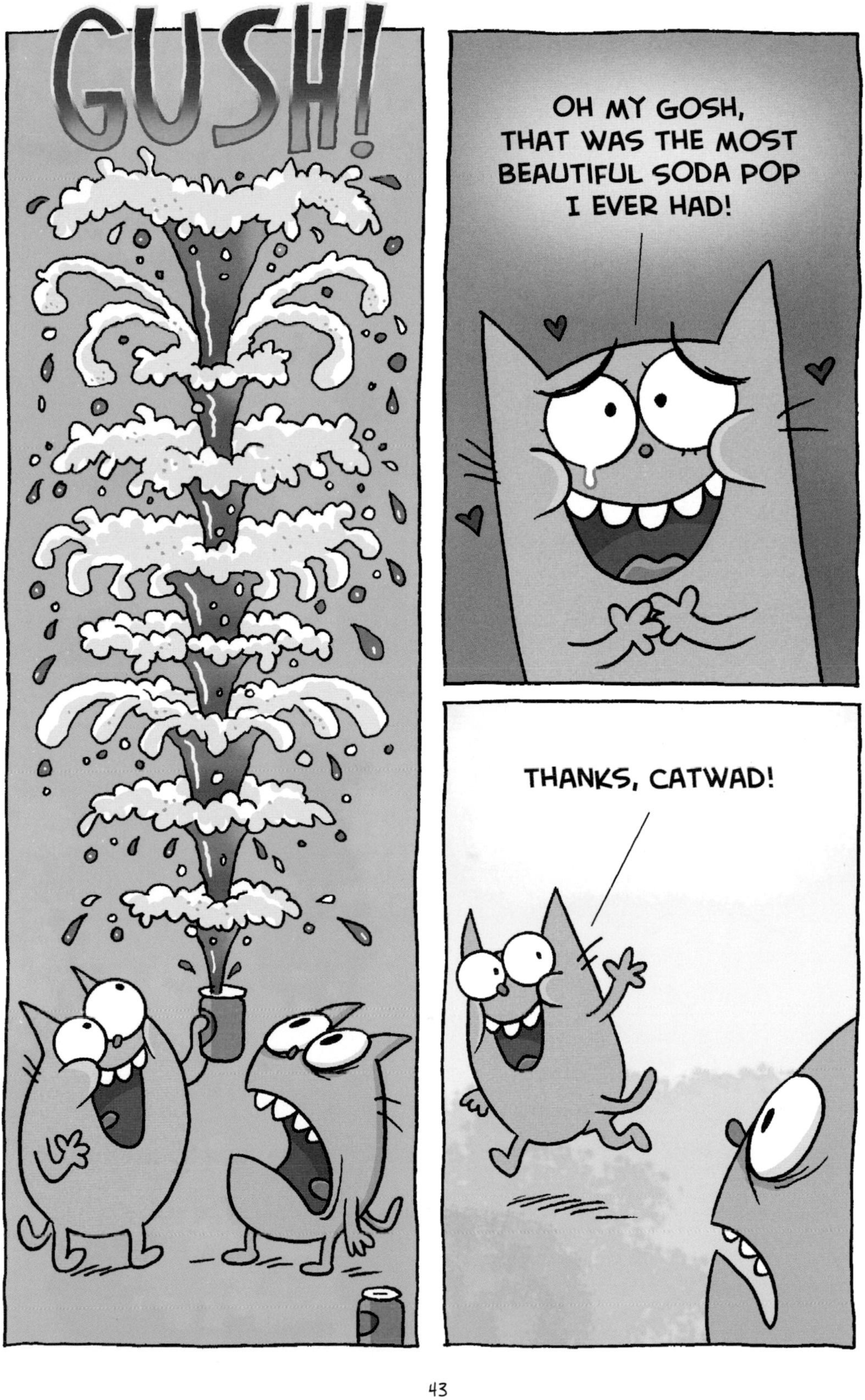
GUSH!
OH MY GOSH, THAT WAS THE MOST BEAUTIFUL SODA POP I EVER HAD!
THANKS, CATWAD!

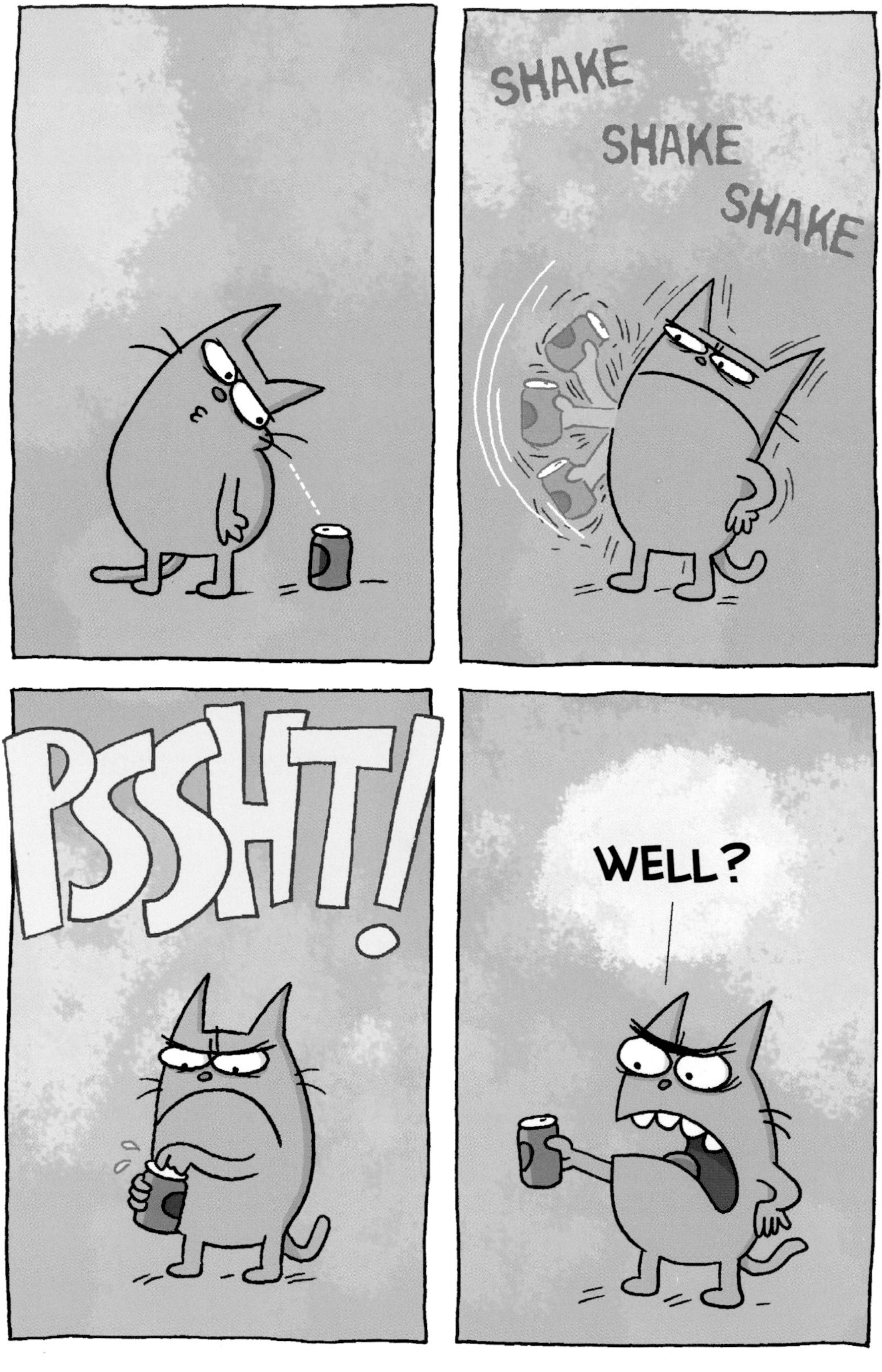
SHAKE
SHAKE
SHAKE
PSSHT!
WELL?

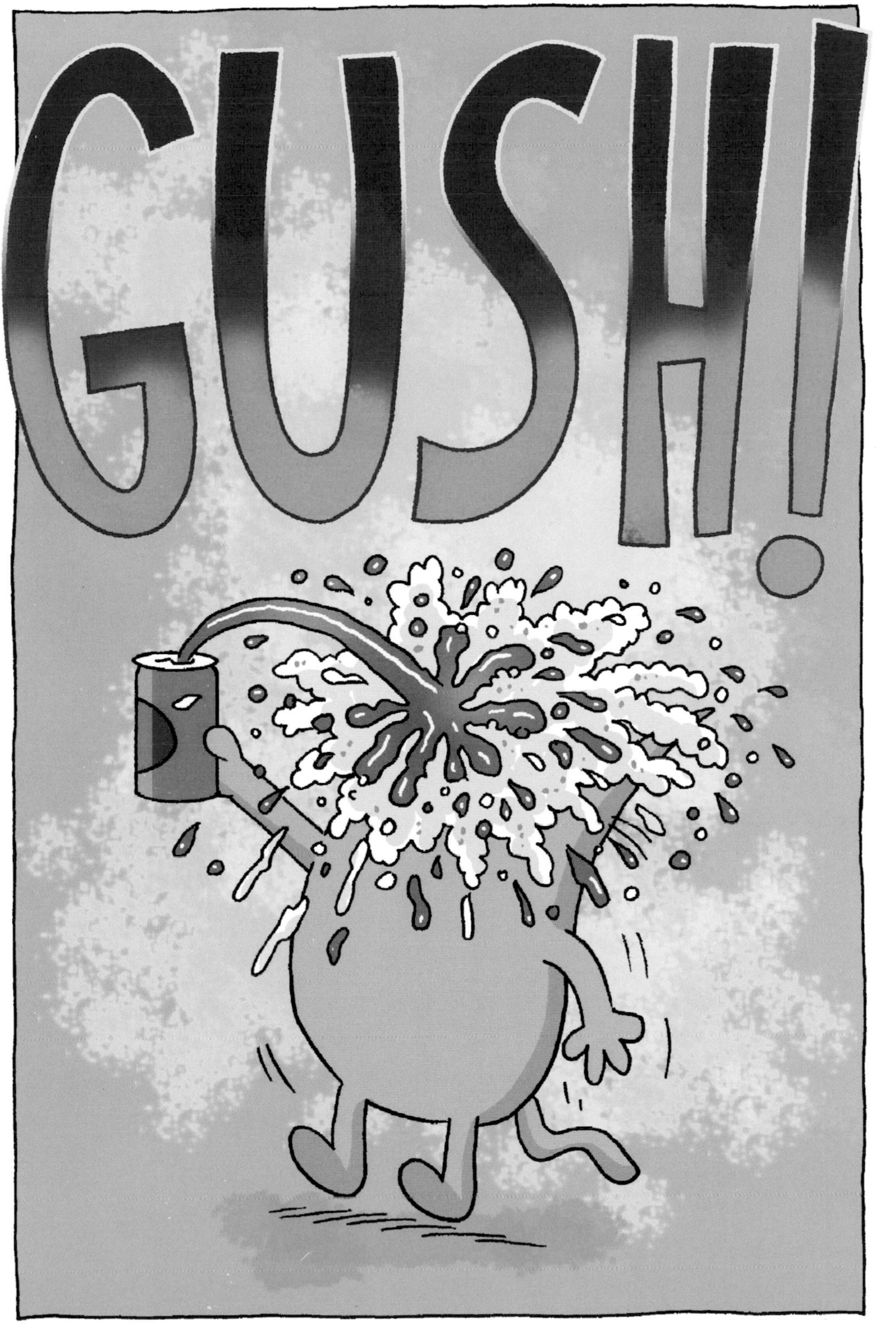
GUSH!

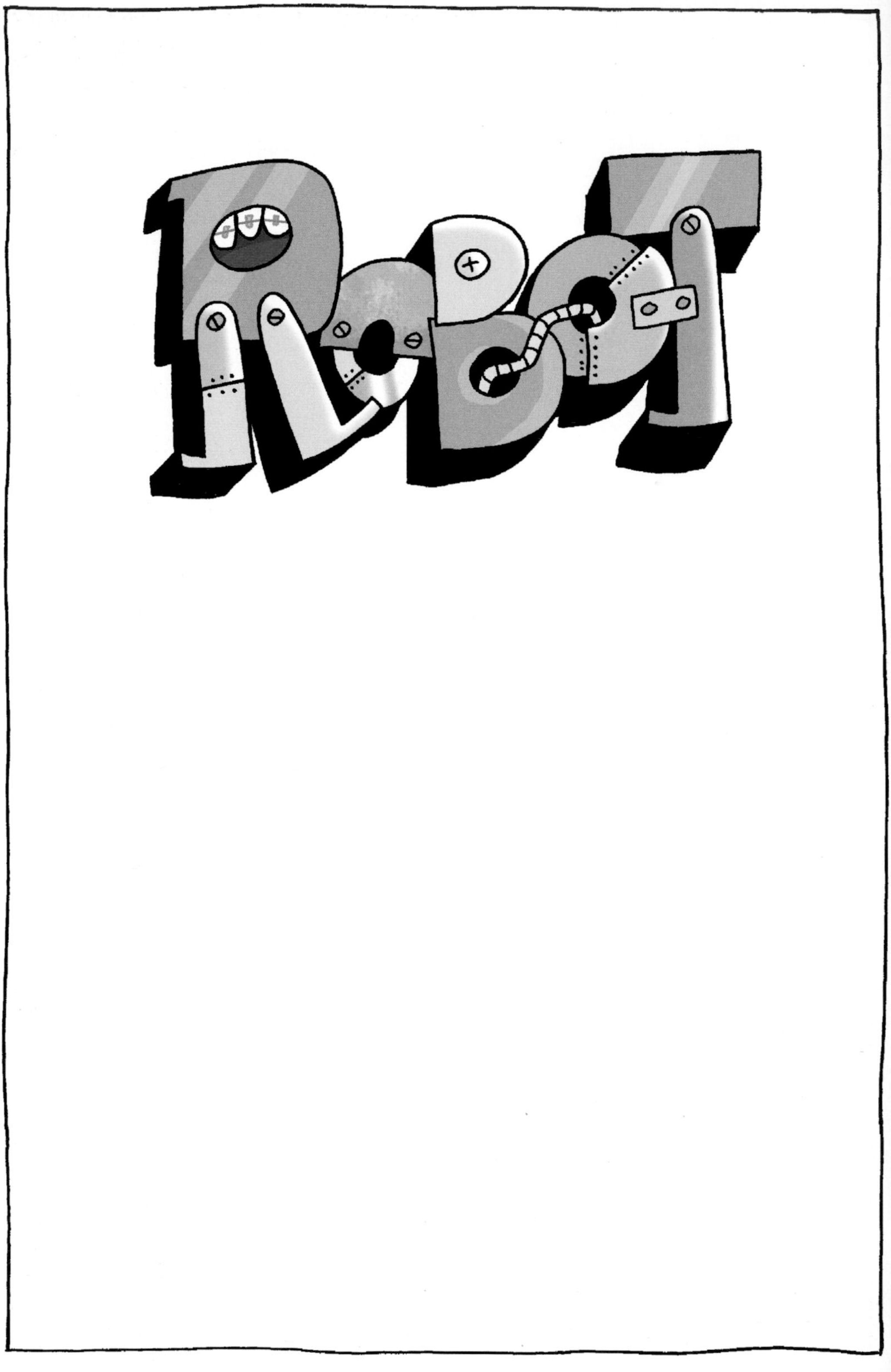
ROBOT

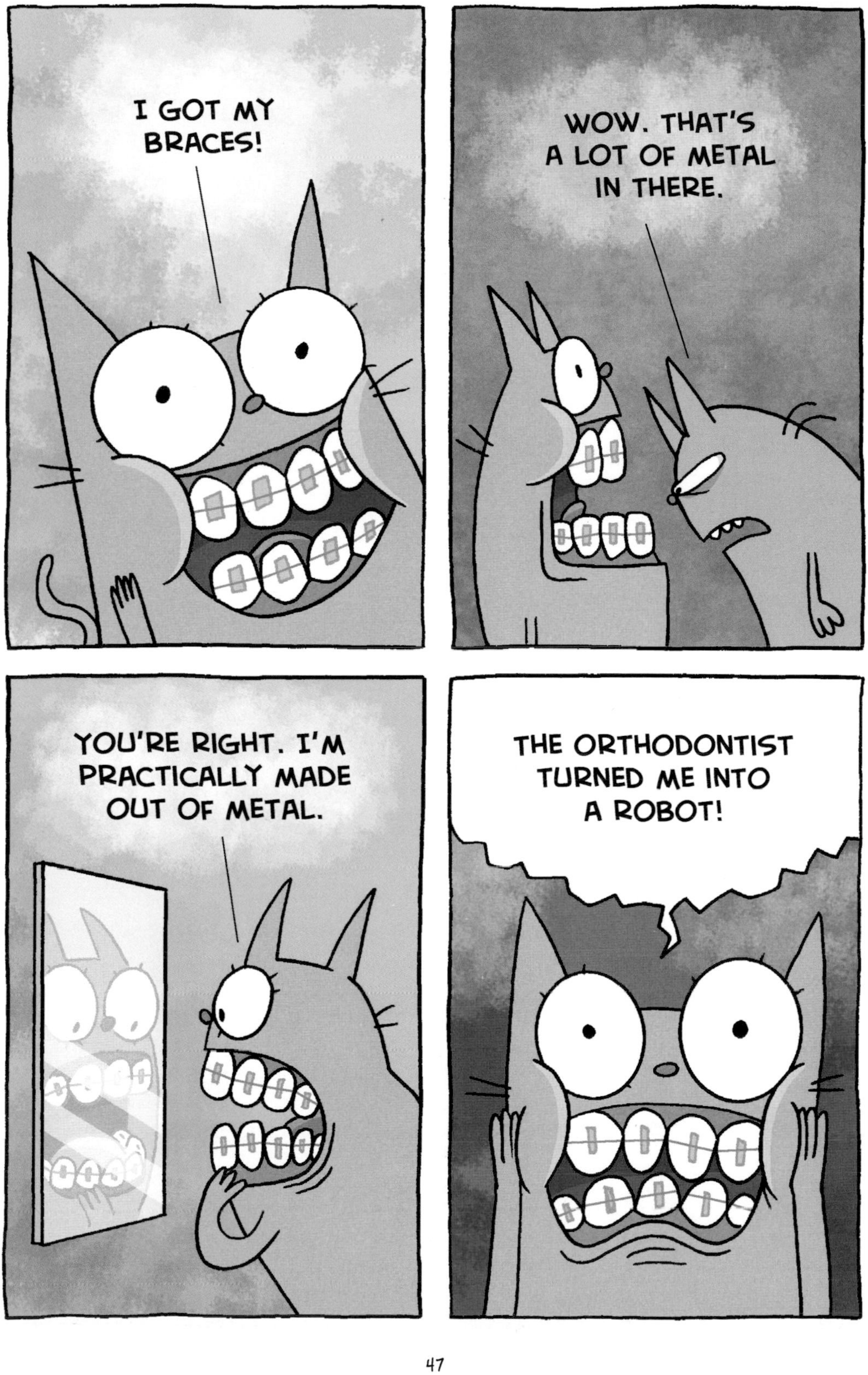
I GOT MY BRACES!
WOW. THAT'S A LOT OF METAL IN THERE.
YOU'RE RIGHT. I'M PRACTICALLY MADE OUT OF METAL.
THE ORTHODONTIST TURNED ME INTO A ROBOT!

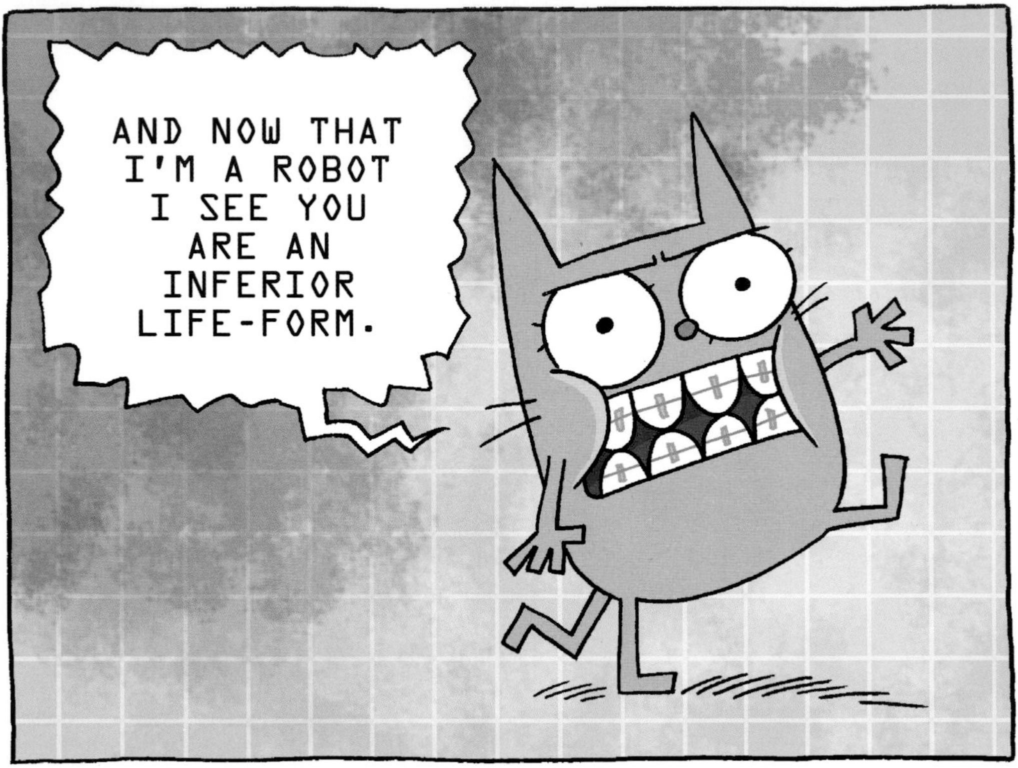
AND NOW THAT I'M A ROBOT I SEE YOU ARE AN INFERIOR LIFE-FORM.

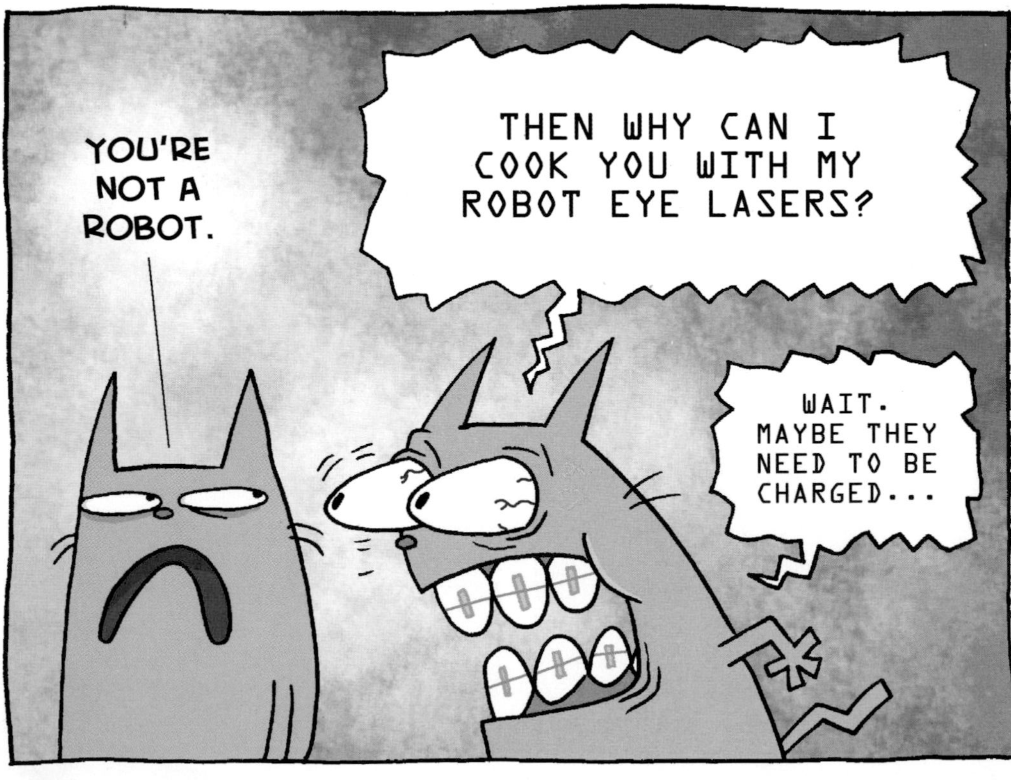
YOU'RE NOT A ROBOT.
THEN WHY CAN I COOK YOU WITH MY ROBOT EYE LASERS?
WAIT. MAYBE THEY NEED TO BE CHARGED...

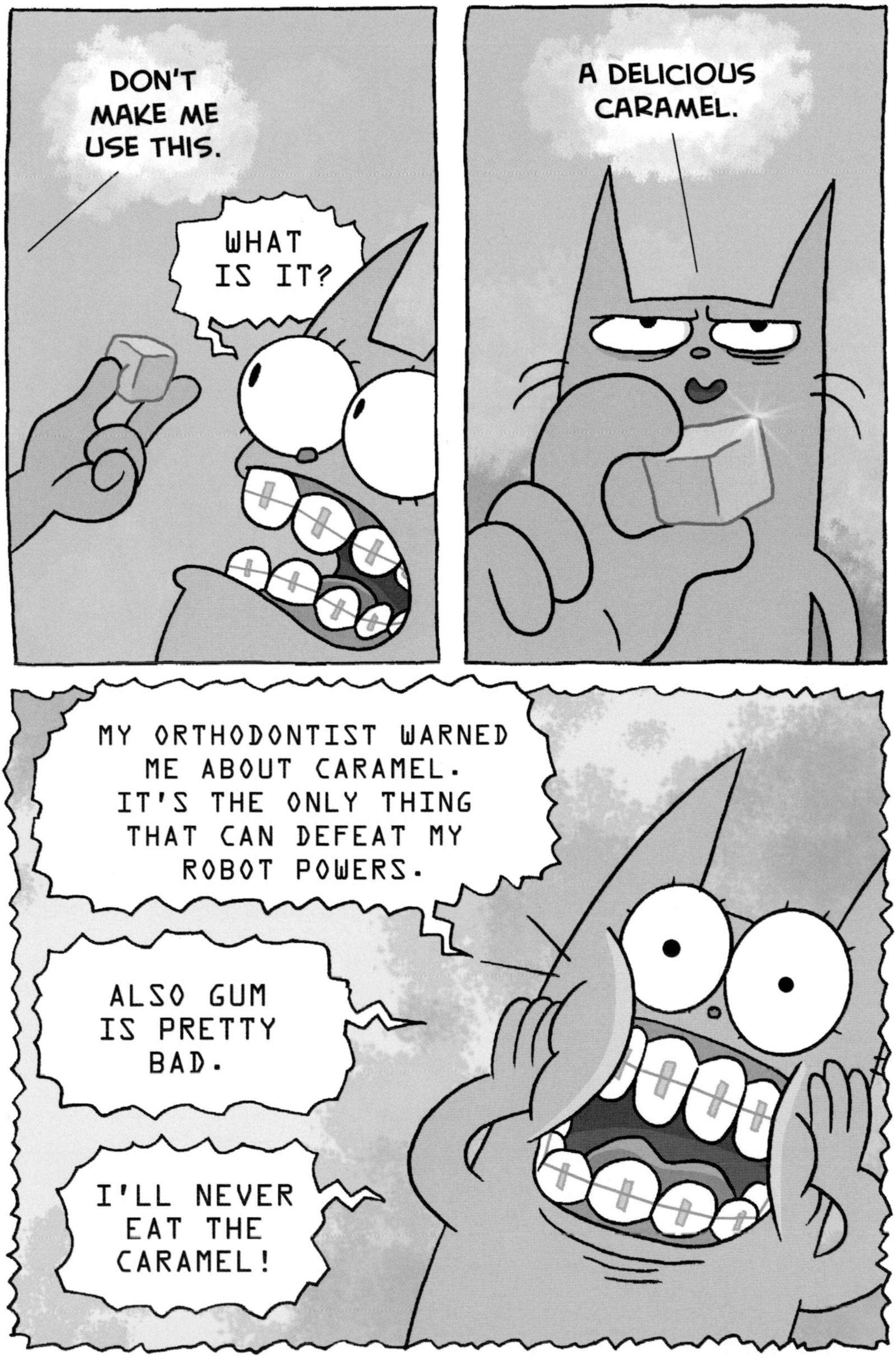
DON'T MAKE ME USE THIS.
WHAT IS IT?
A DELICIOUS CARAMEL.
MY ORTHODONTIST WARNED ME ABOUT CARAMEL. IT'S THE ONLY THING THAT CAN DEFEAT MY ROBOT POWERS.
ALSO GUM IS PRETTY BAD.
I'LL NEVER EAT THE CARAMEL!

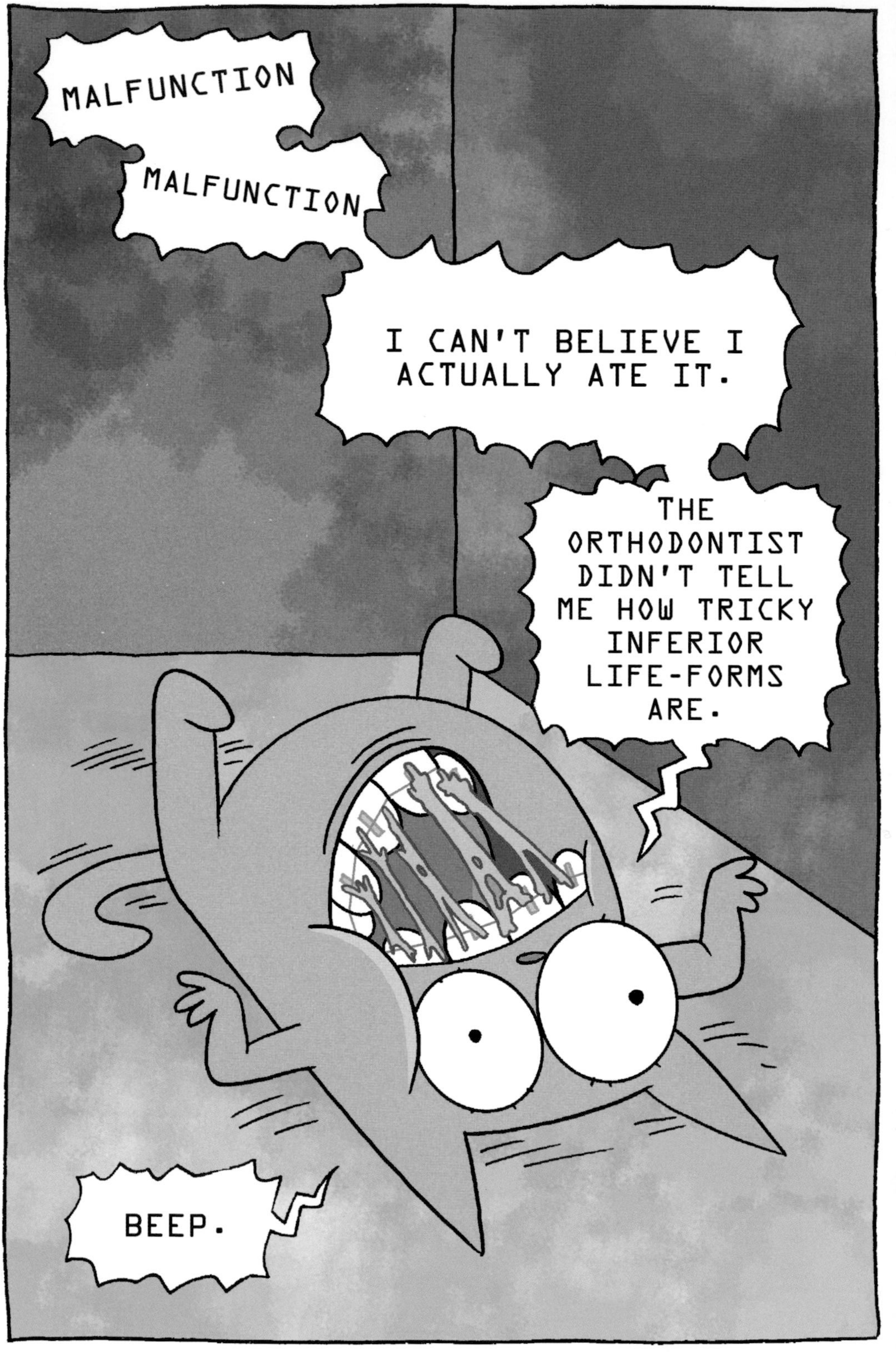
MALFUNCTION
MALFUNCTION
I CAN'T BELIEVE I ACTUALLY ATE IT.
THE ORTHODONTIST DIDN'T TELL ME HOW TRICKY INFERIOR LIFE-FORMS ARE.
BEEP.

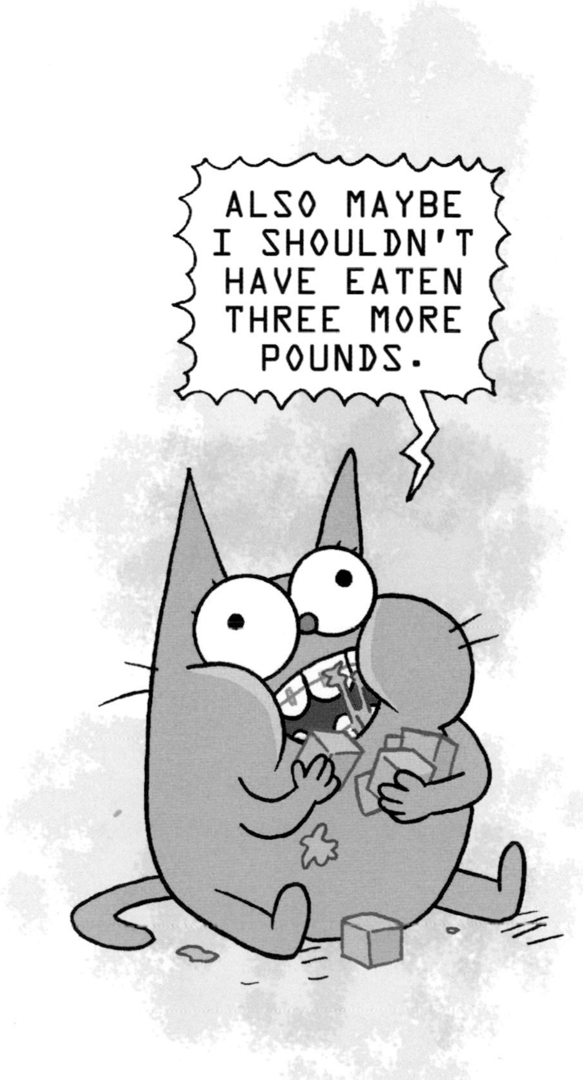
ALSO MAYBE I SHOULDN'T HAVE EATEN THREE MORE POUNDS.

SALAD

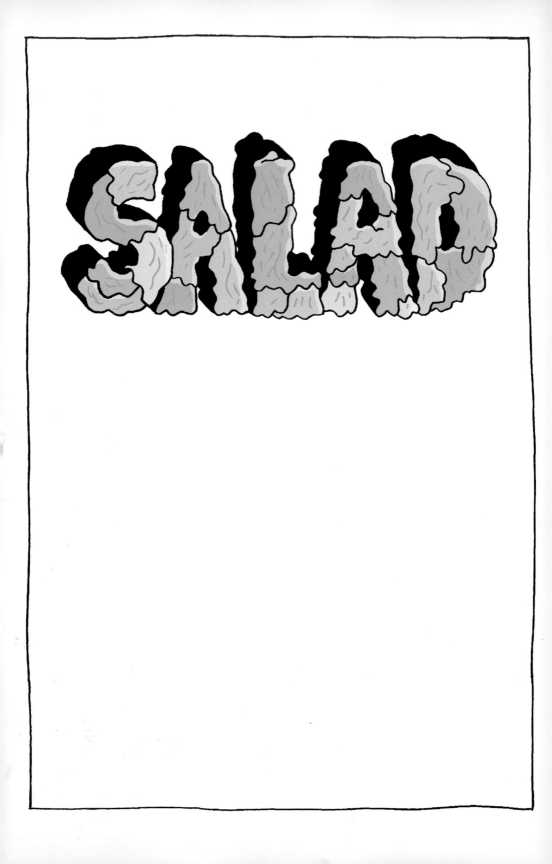

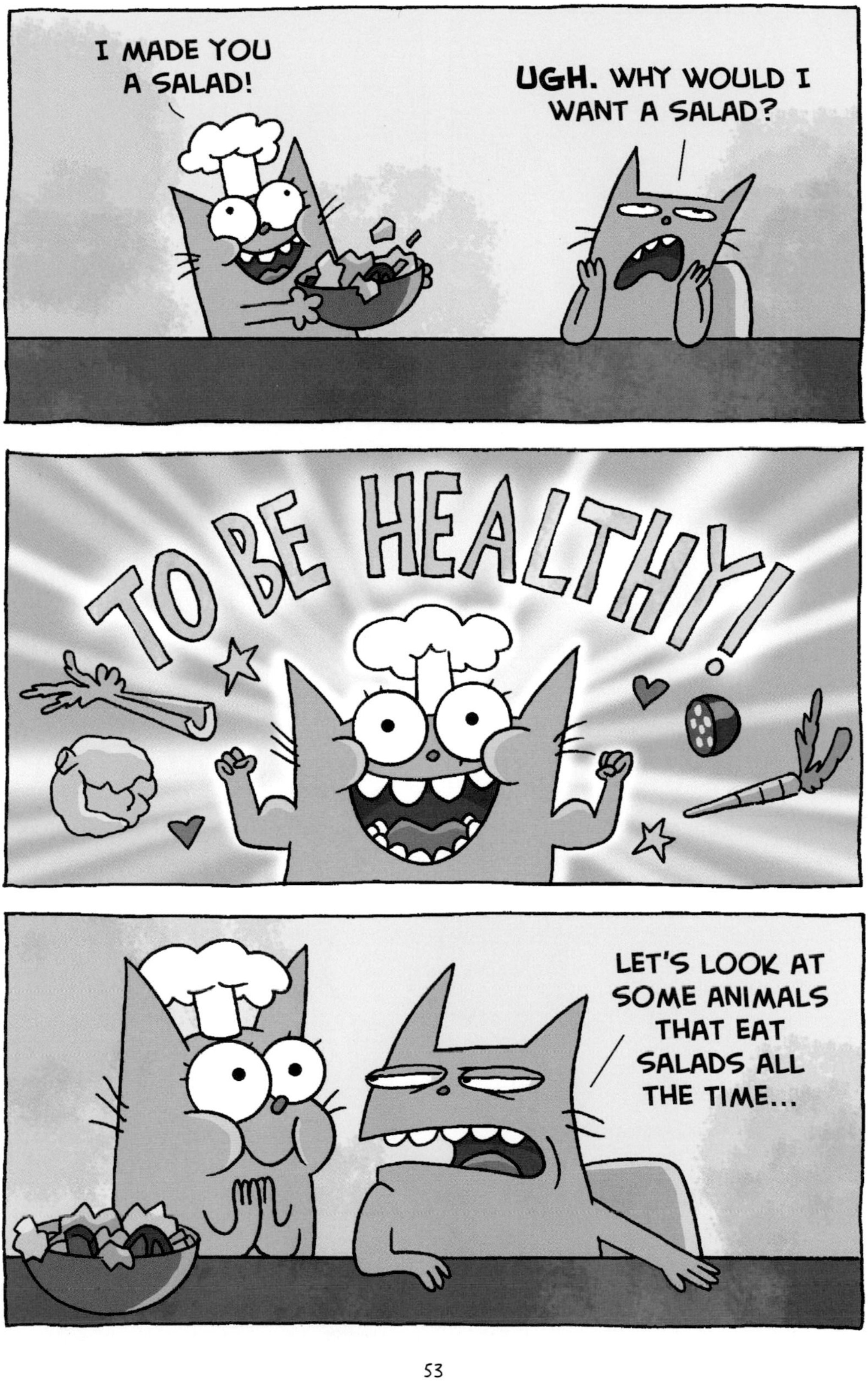
I MADE YOU A SALAD!
UGH. WHY WOULD I WANT A SALAD?
TO BE HEALTHY!
LET'S LOOK AT SOME ANIMALS THAT EAT SALADS ALL THE TIME...

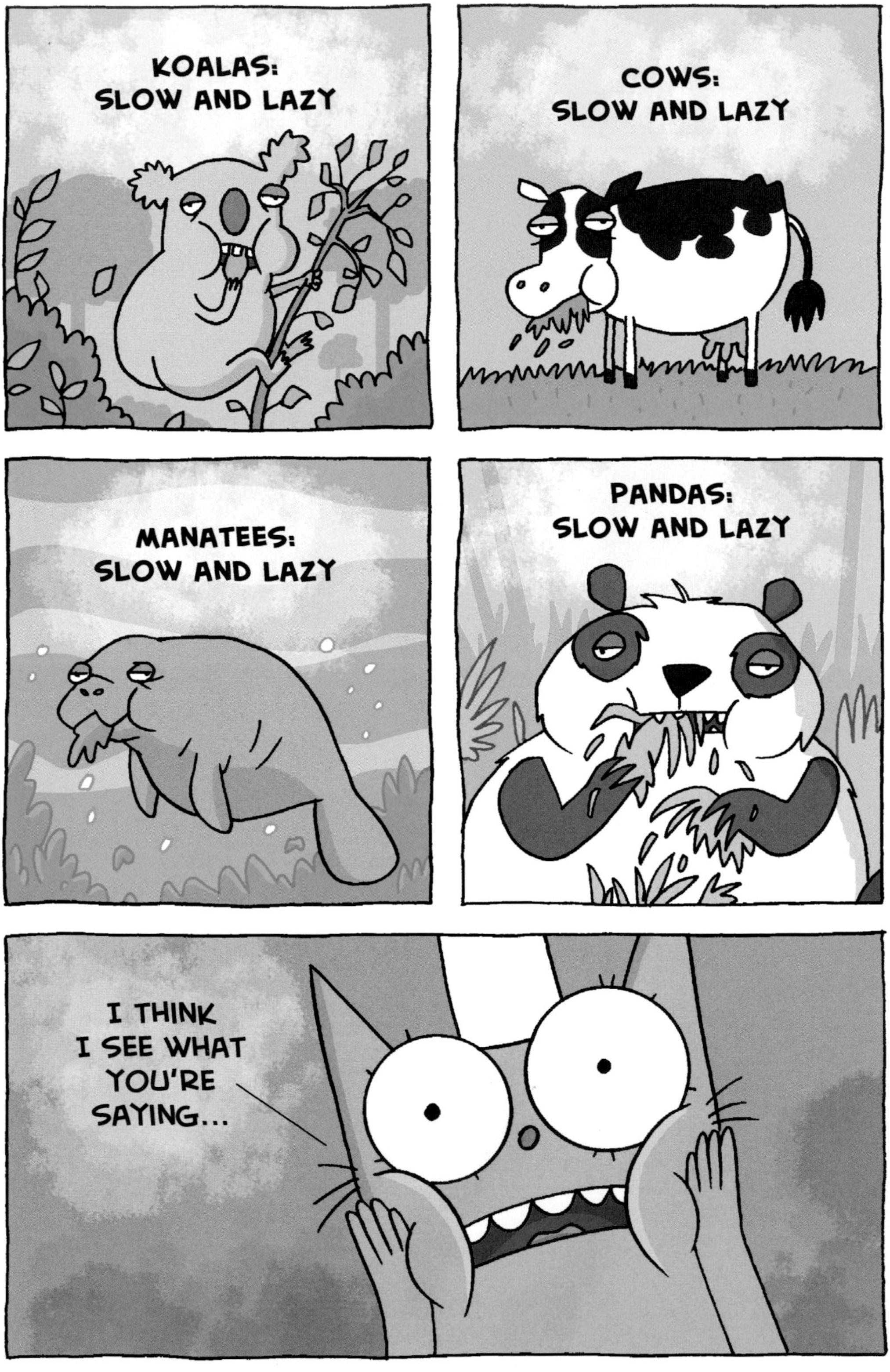
KOALAS:
SLOW AND LAZY
COWS:
SLOW AND LAZY
MANATEES:
SLOW AND LAZY
PANDAS:
SLOW AND LAZY
I THINK I SEE WHAT YOU'RE SAYING...

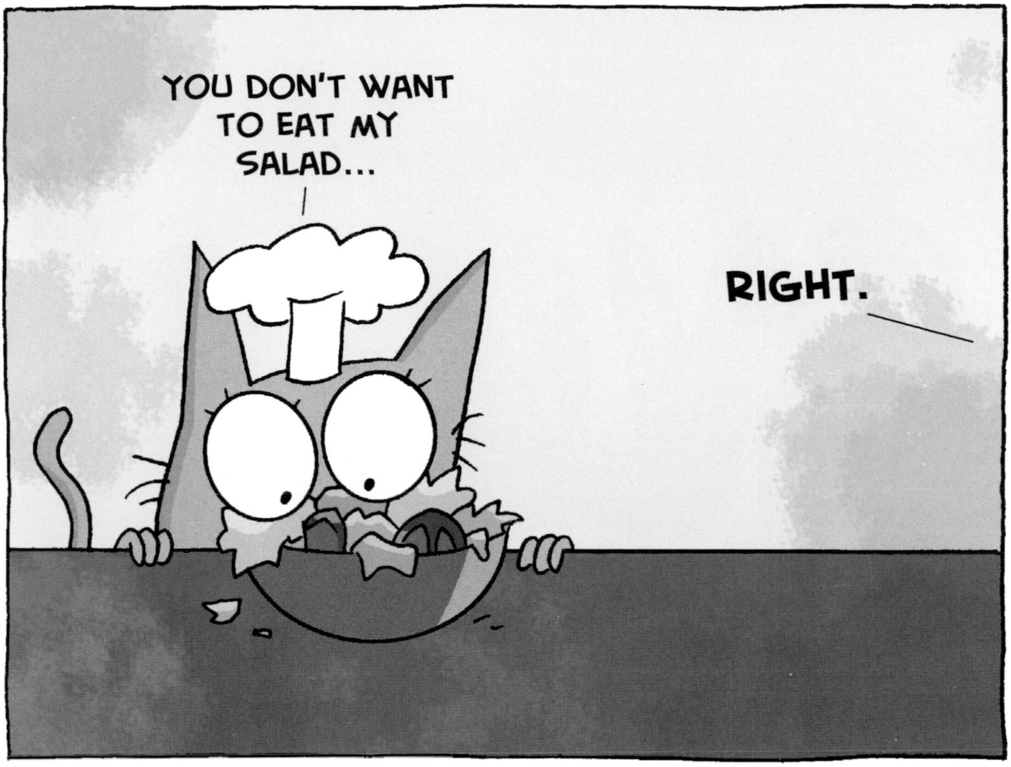
YOU DON'T WANT TO EAT MY SALAD...
RIGHT.

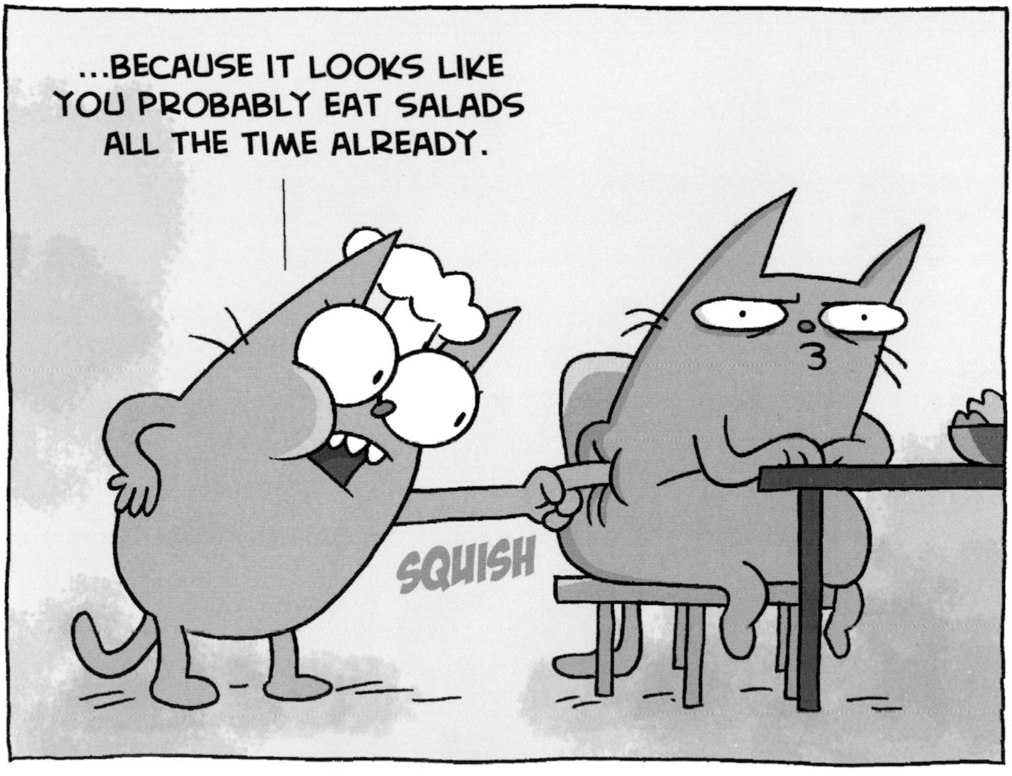
...BECAUSE IT LOOKS LIKE YOU PROBABLY EAT SALADS ALL THE TIME ALREADY.
SQUISH

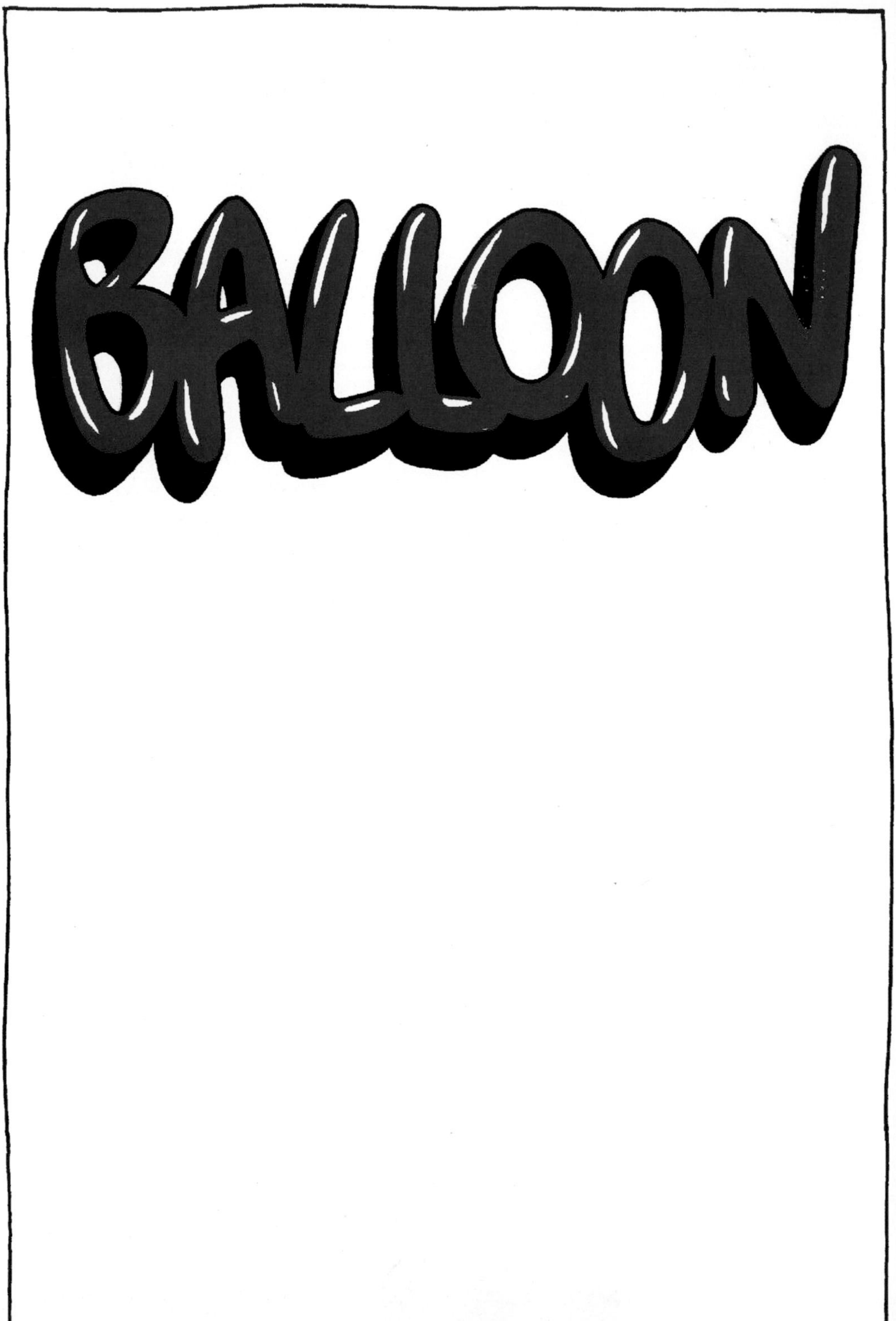
BALLOON

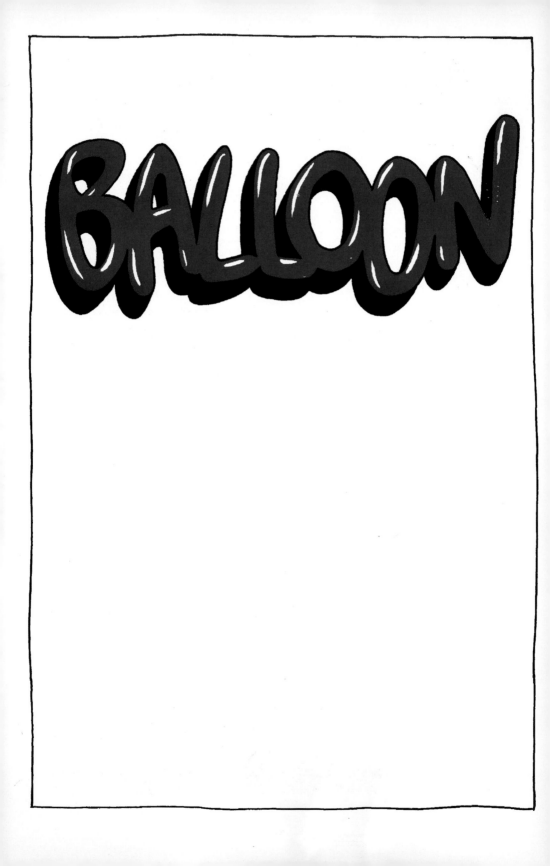

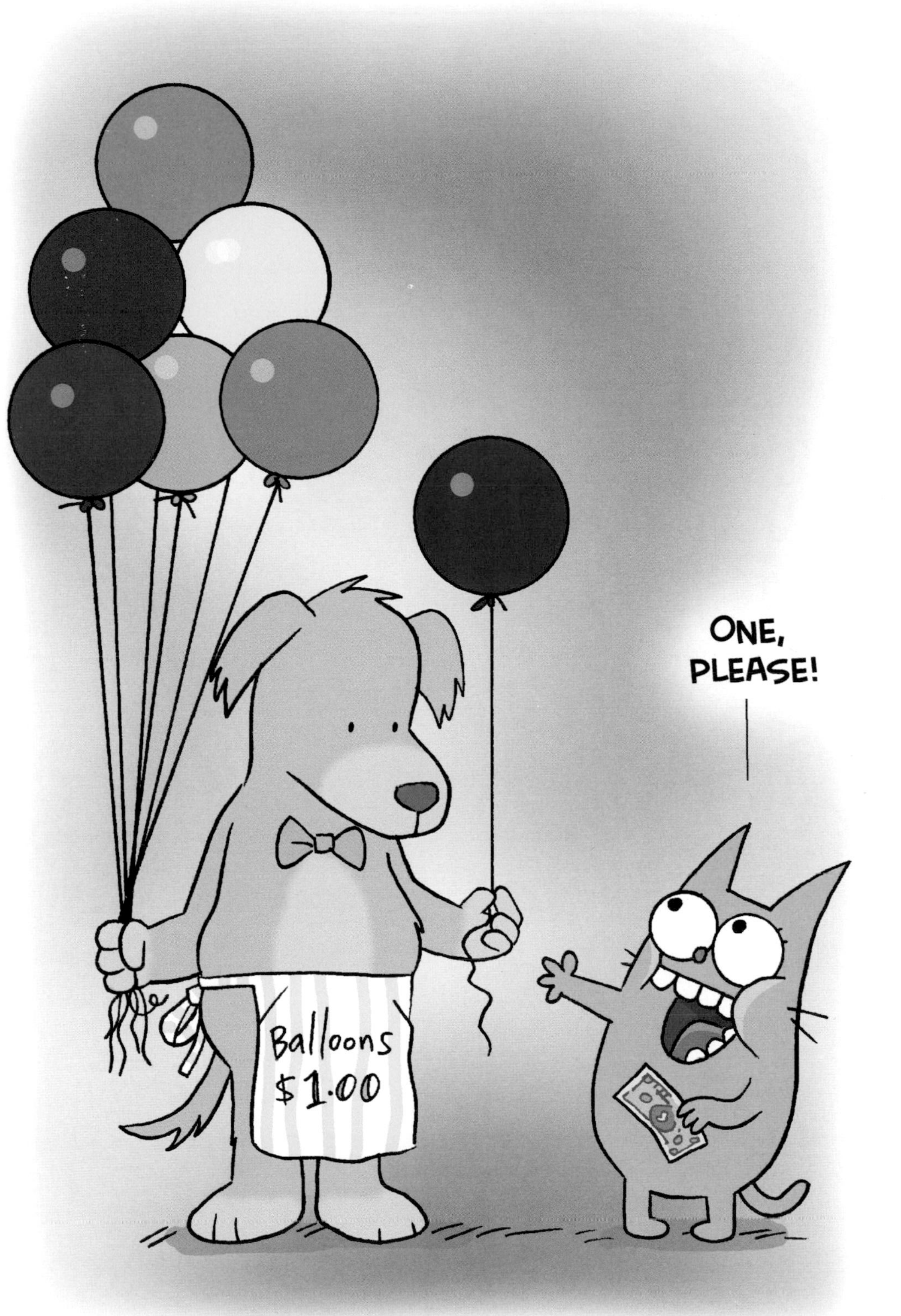
ONE, PLEASE!
Balloons $1.00

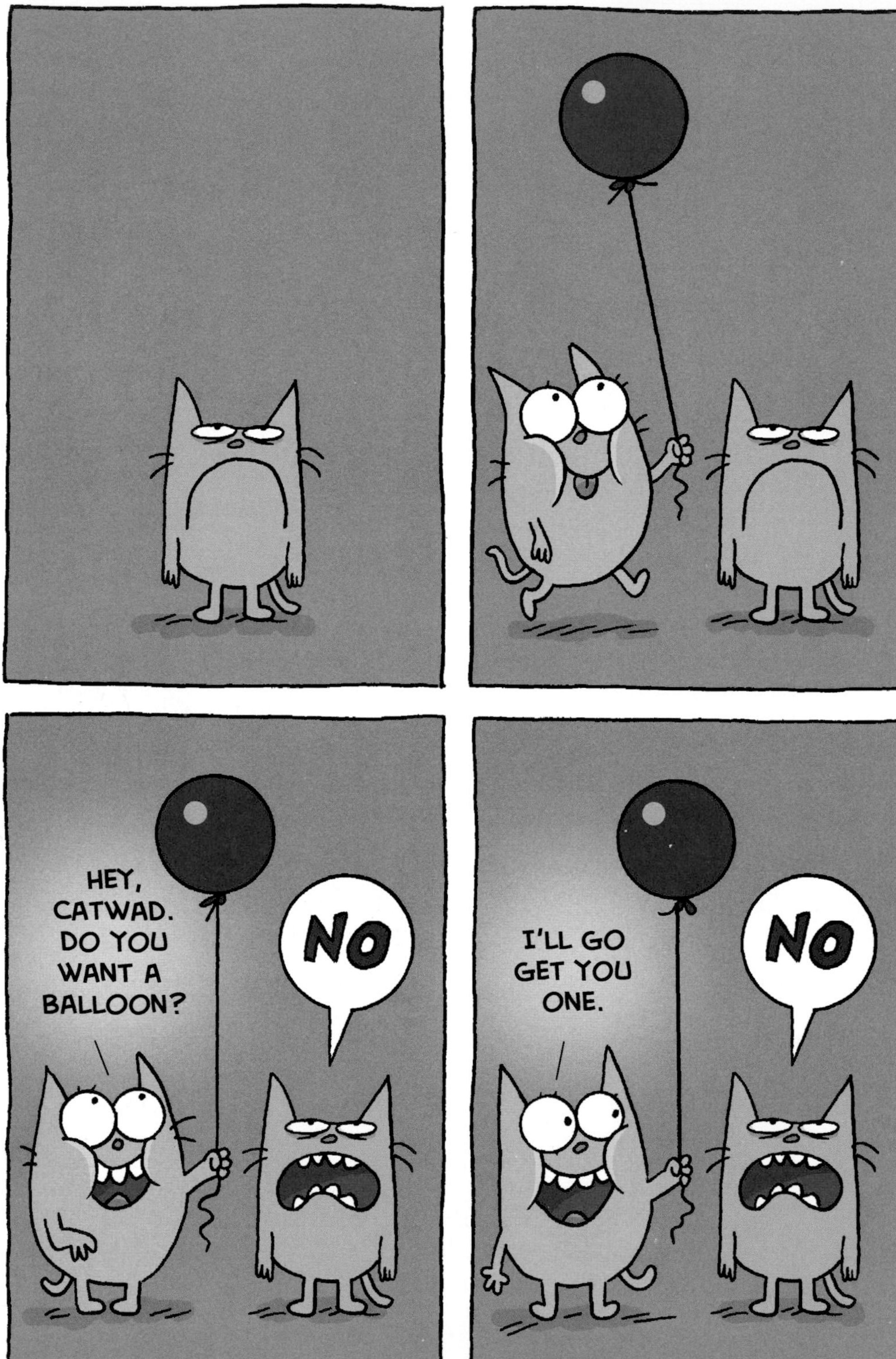
HEY, CATWAD. DO YOU WANT A BALLOON?
NO
I'LL GO GET YOU ONE.
NO

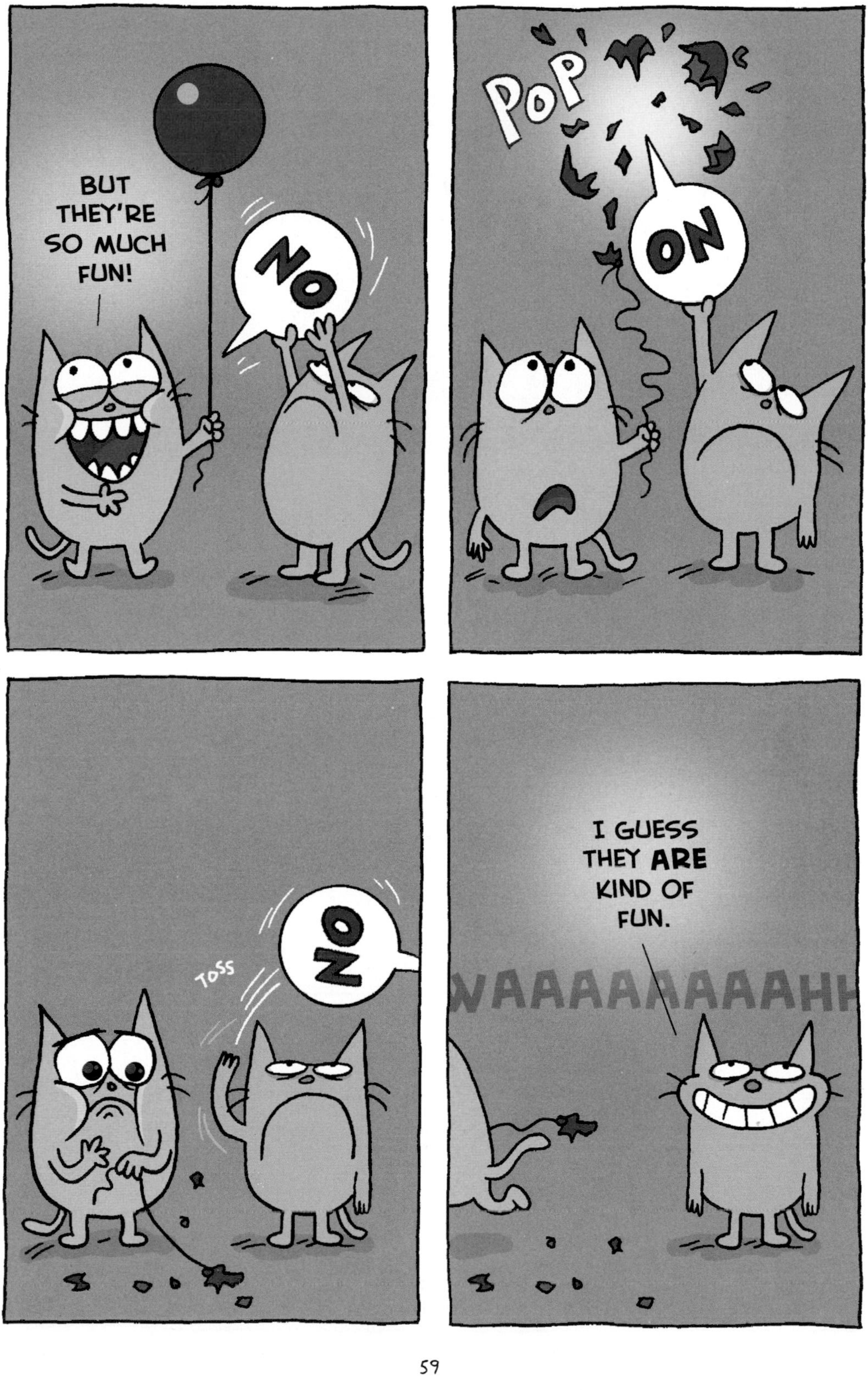
BUT THEY'RE SO MUCH FUN!
NO
POP
ON
TOSS
ON
I GUESS THEY **ARE** KIND OF FUN.
WAAAAAAAAAHH

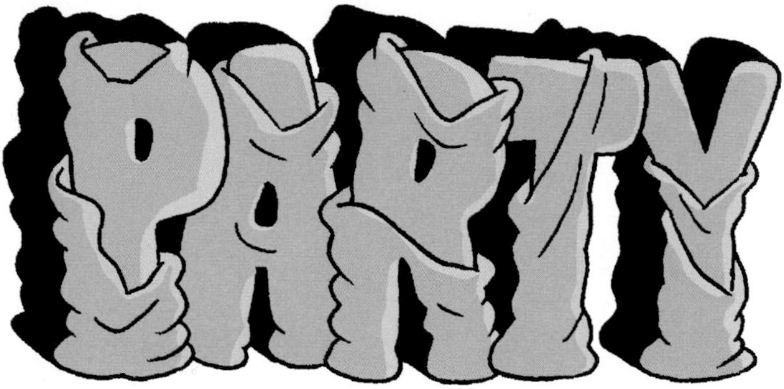
PARTY

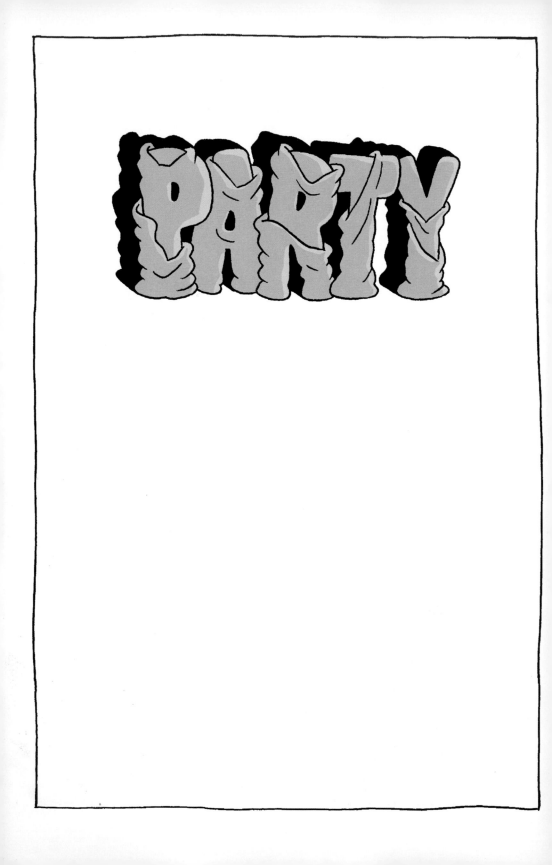

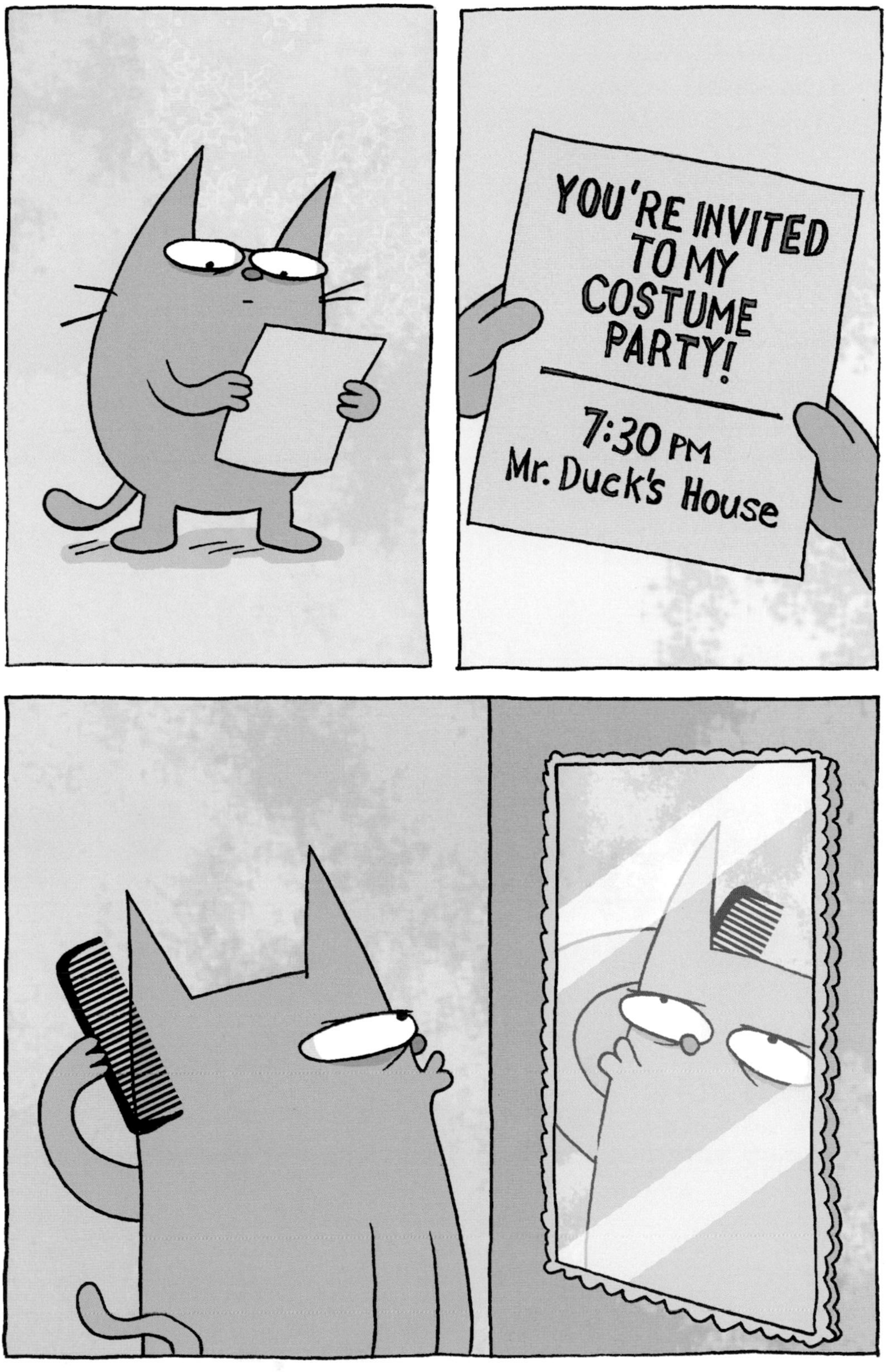
YOU'RE INVITED TO MY COSTUME PARTY!
7:30 PM
Mr. Duck's House

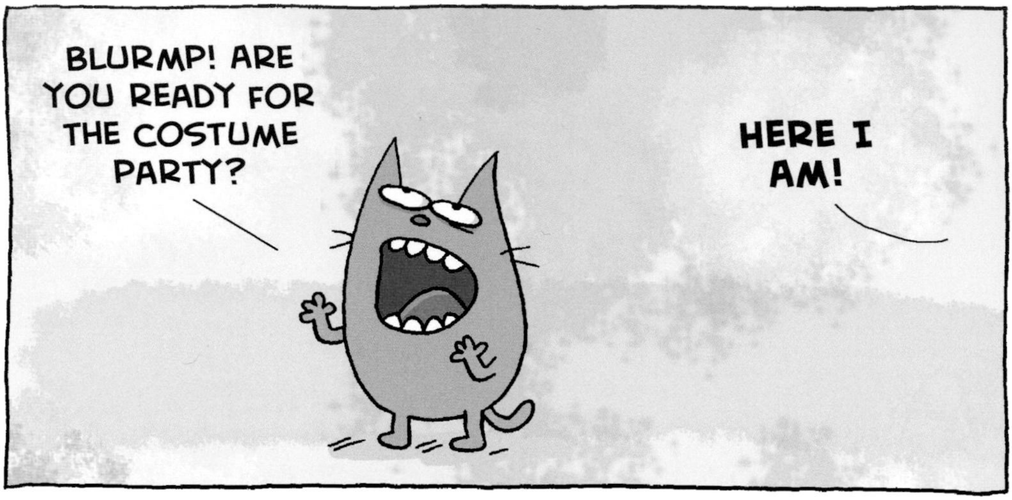
BLURMP! ARE YOU READY FOR THE COSTUME PARTY?
HERE I AM!

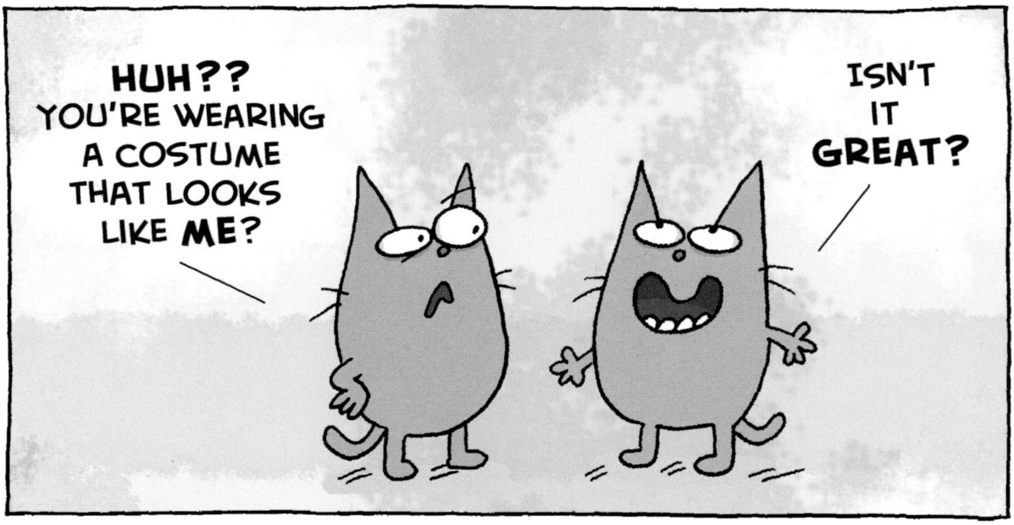
HUH?? YOU'RE WEARING A COSTUME THAT LOOKS LIKE ME?
ISN'T IT GREAT?

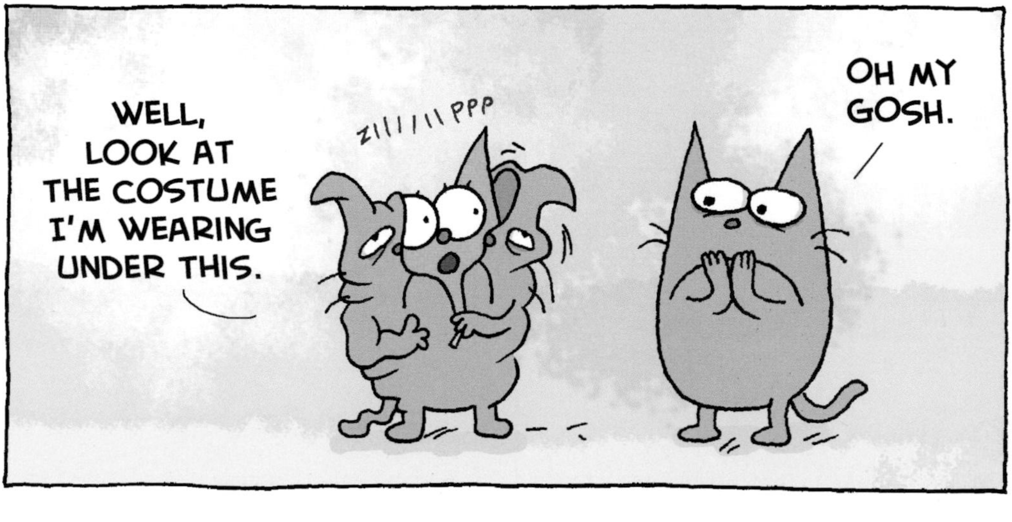
WELL, LOOK AT THE COSTUME I'M WEARING UNDER THIS.
ZIIIIIIPPP
OH MY GOSH.

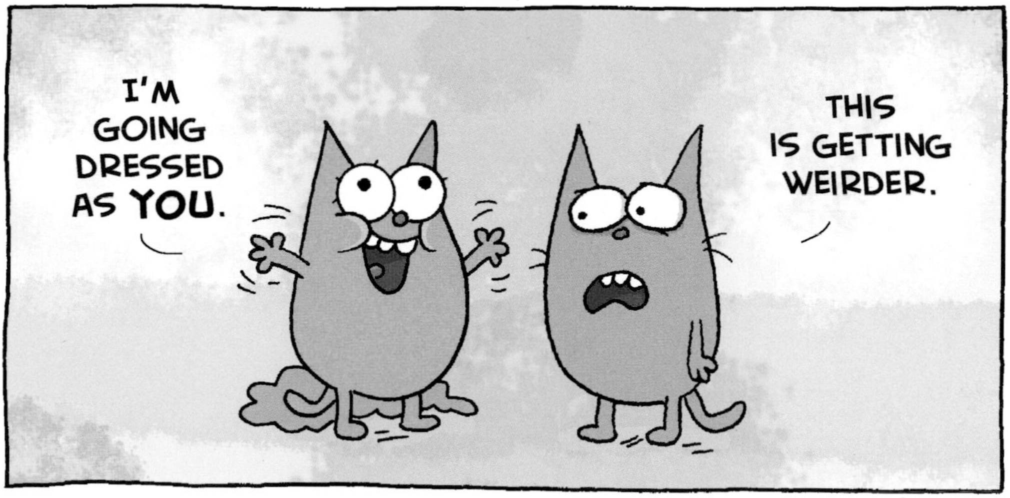
I'M GOING DRESSED AS YOU.
THIS IS GETTING WEIRDER.

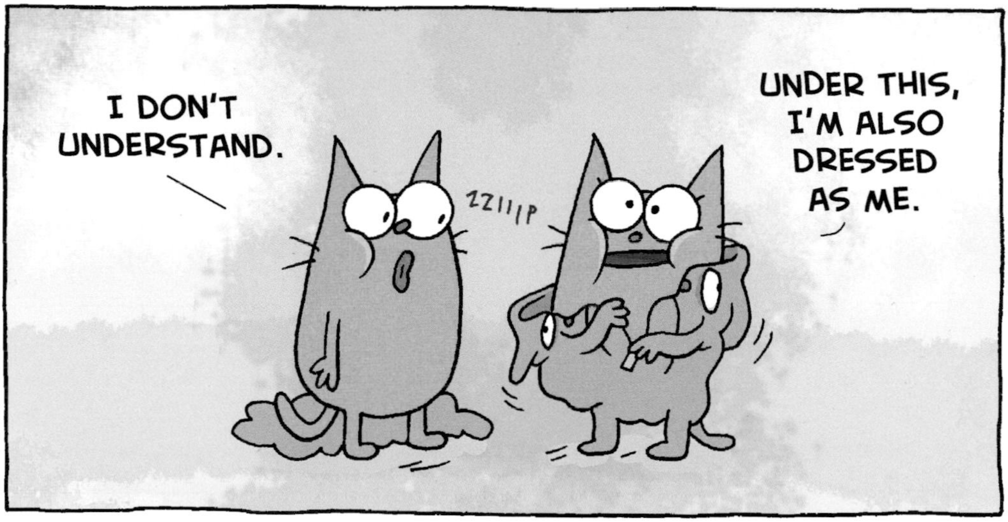
I DON'T UNDERSTAND.
ZZIIIP
UNDER THIS, I'M ALSO DRESSED AS ME.

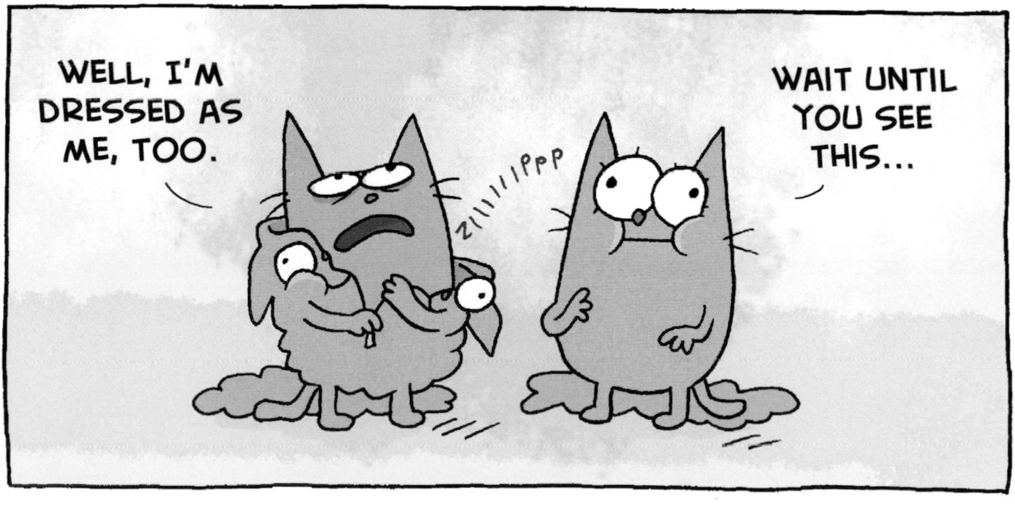
WELL, I'M DRESSED AS ME, TOO.
ZIIIIIPPP
WAIT UNTIL YOU SEE THIS...

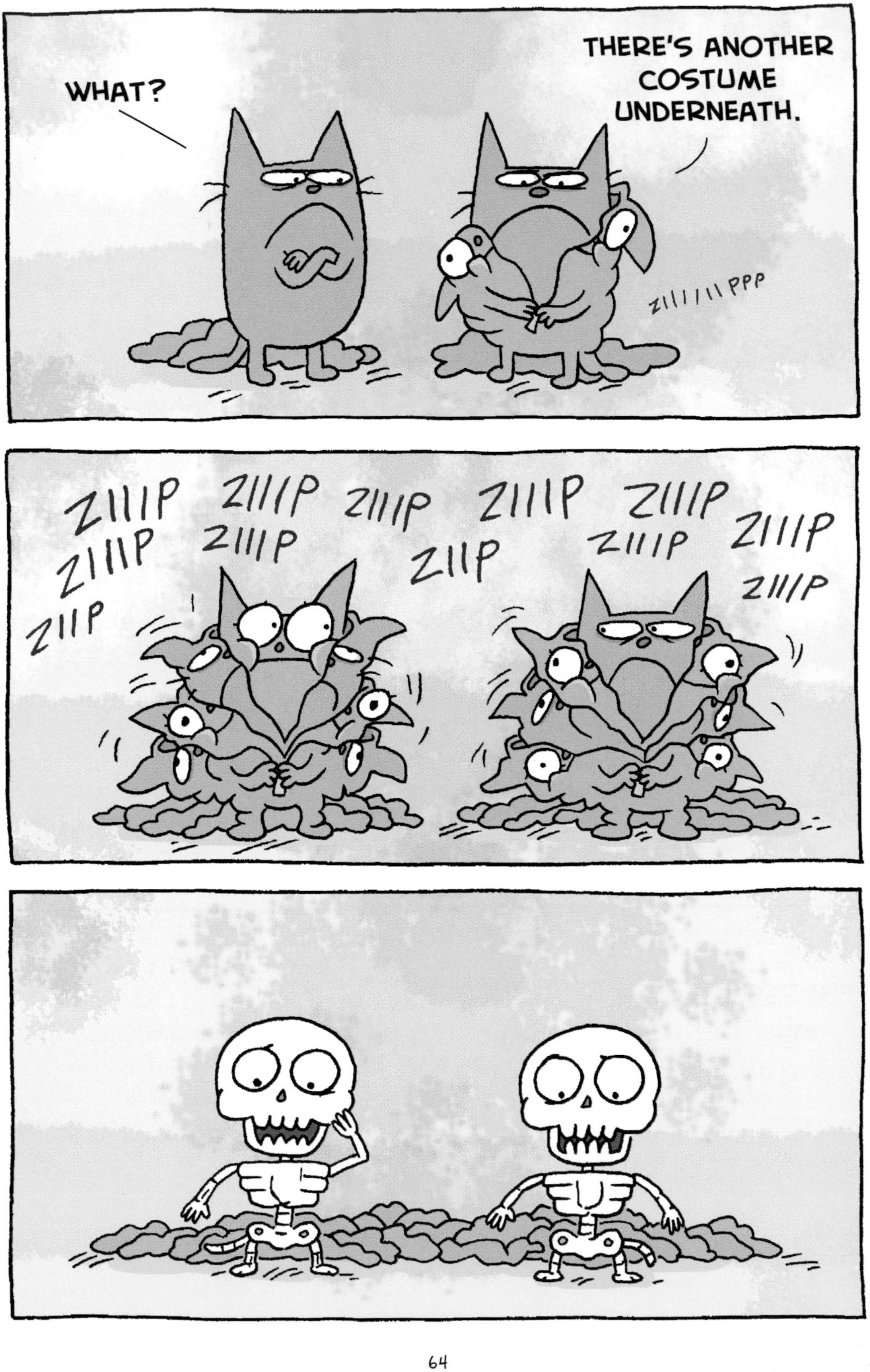
WHAT?
THERE'S ANOTHER COSTUME UNDERNEATH.
ZIIIIIIPPP
ZIIIP
ZIIIP
ZIIIP
ZIIIP
ZIIIP
ZIIIP
ZIIIP
ZIIP
ZIIIP
ZIIIP
ZIIIP
ZIIP

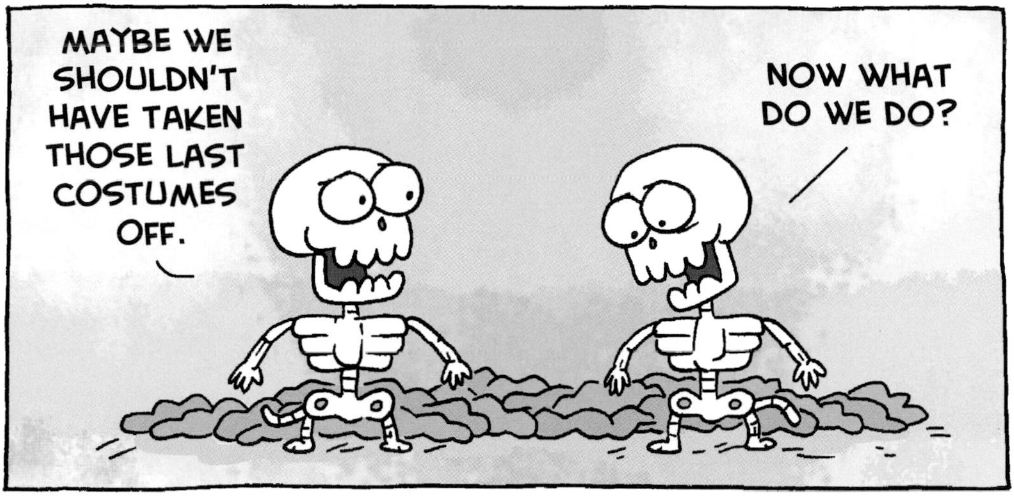
MAYBE WE SHOULDN'T HAVE TAKEN THOSE LAST COSTUMES OFF.
NOW WHAT DO WE DO?

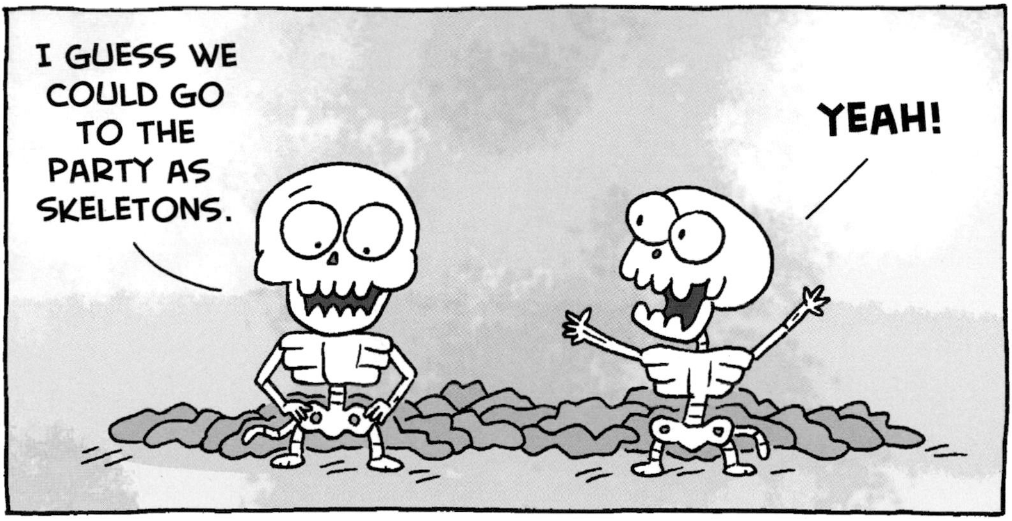
I GUESS WE COULD GO TO THE PARTY AS SKELETONS.
YEAH!

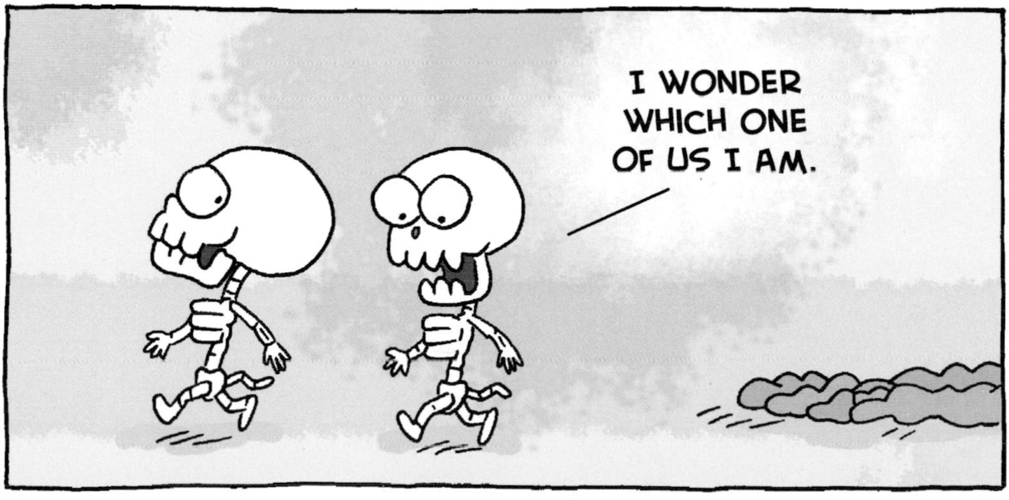
I WONDER WHICH ONE OF US I AM.

DUMB

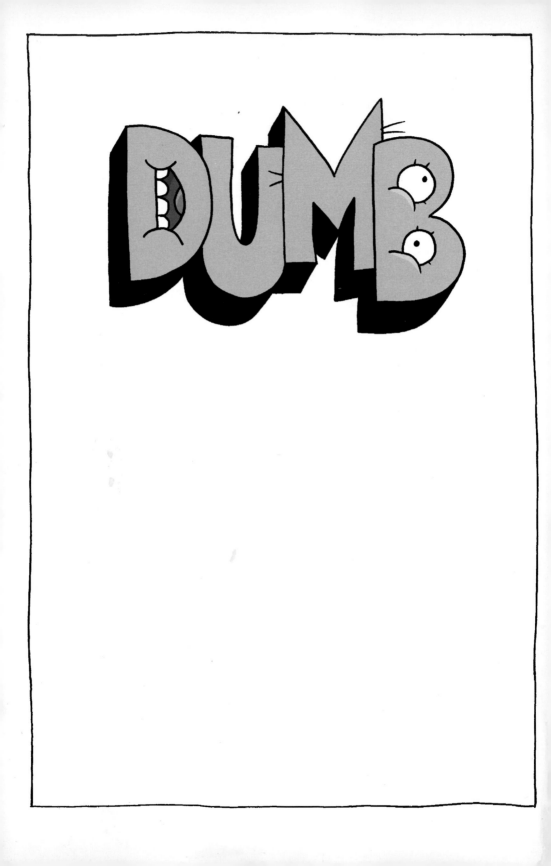

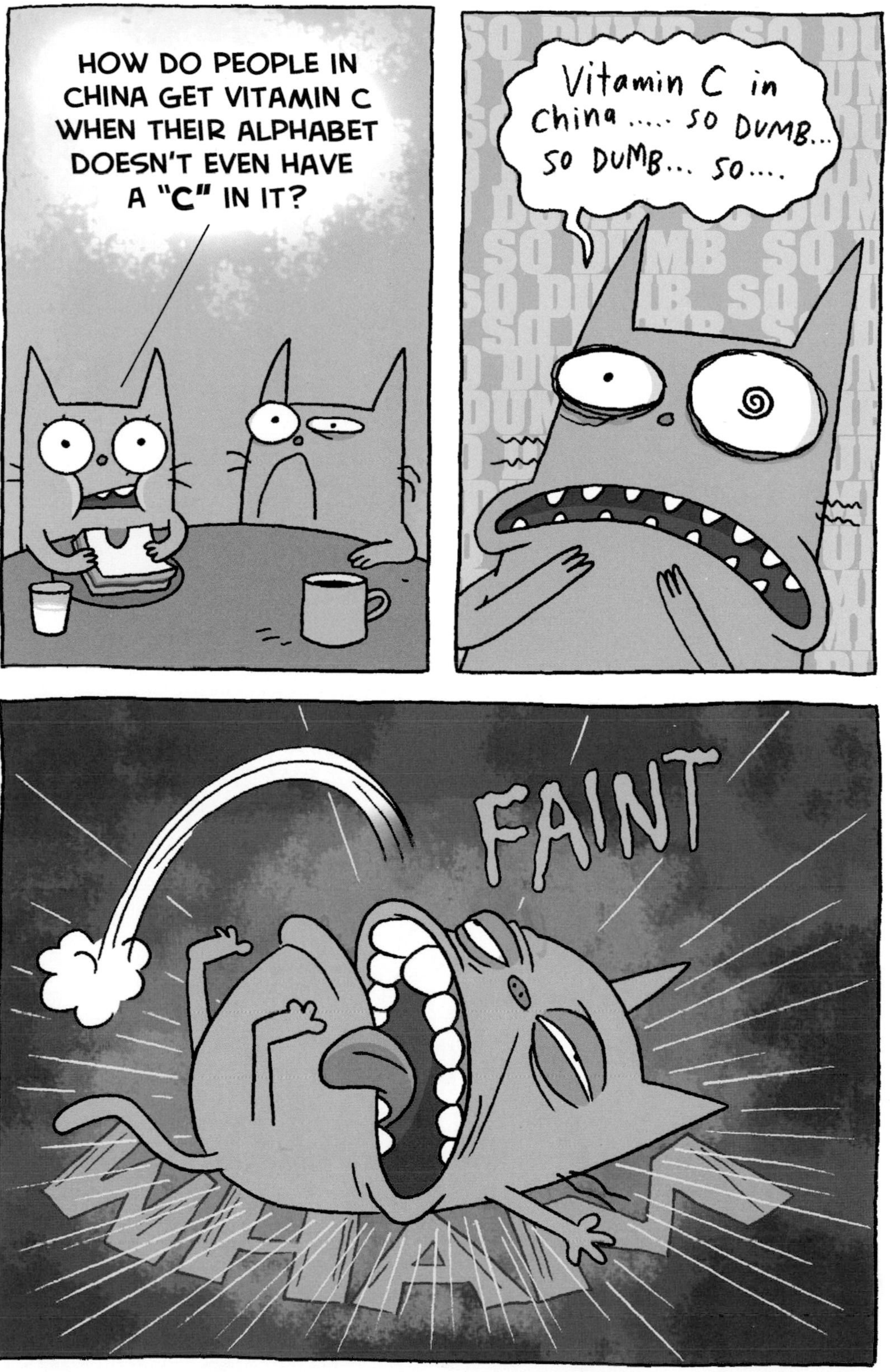
HOW DO PEOPLE IN CHINA GET VITAMIN C WHEN THEIR ALPHABET DOESN'T EVEN HAVE A "C" IN IT?
Vitamin C in China ..... so DUMB... so DUMB... so....
FAINT

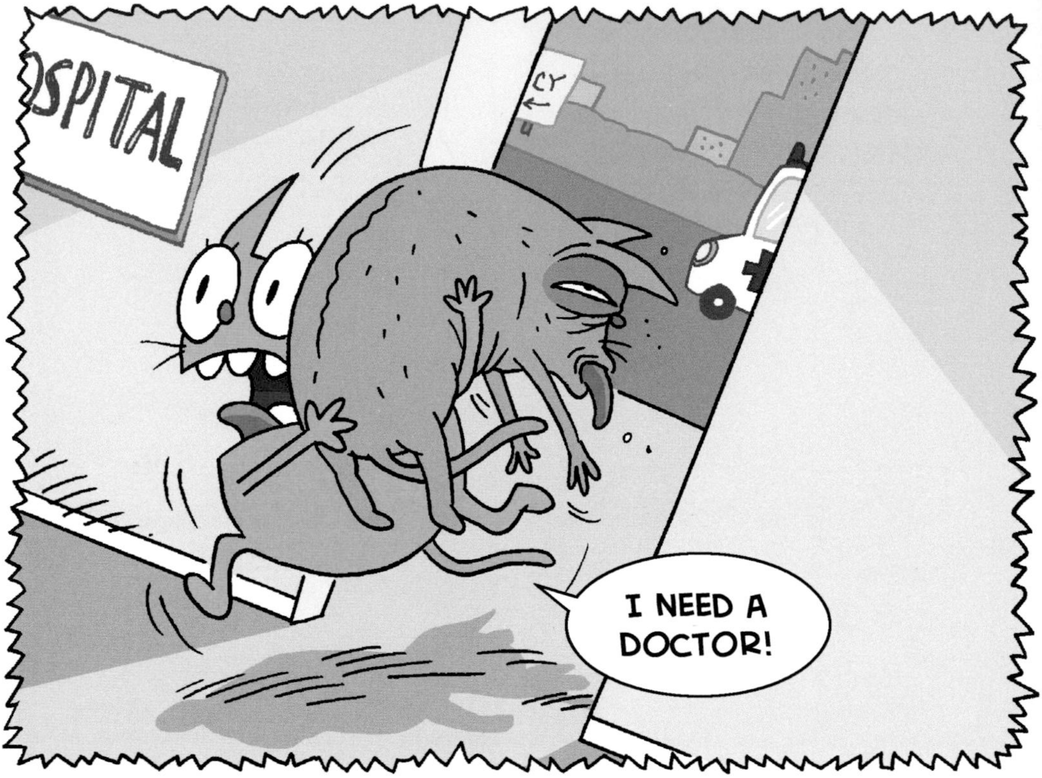
SPITAL
CY
I NEED A DOCTOR!

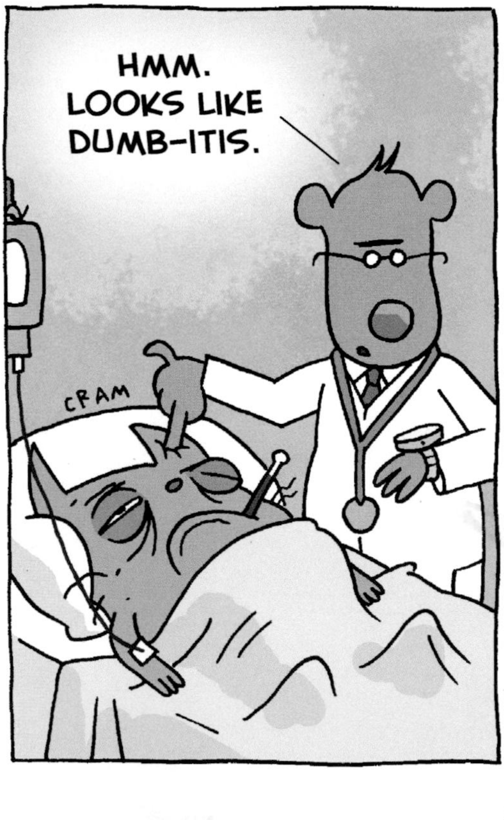
HMM. LOOKS LIKE DUMB-ITIS.
CRAM

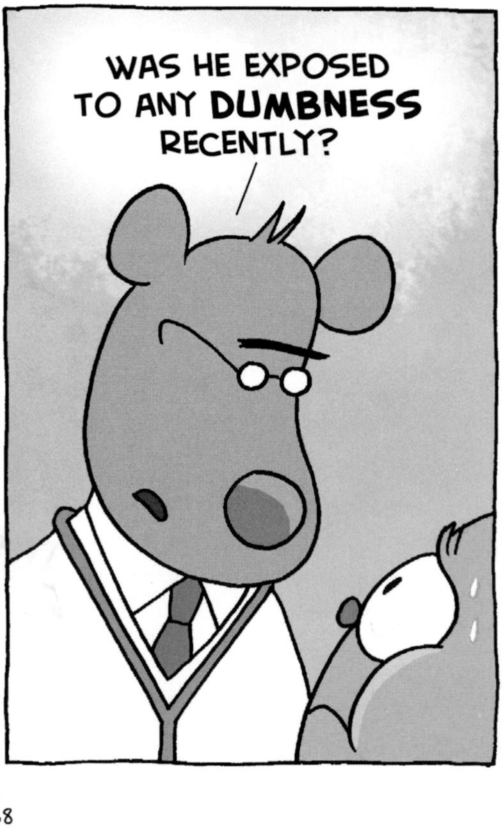
WAS HE EXPOSED TO ANY **DUMBNESS** RECENTLY?

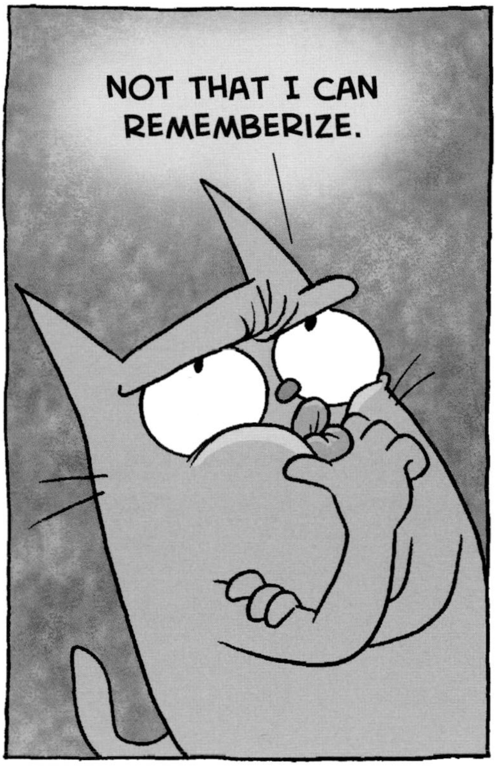
NOT THAT I CAN REMEMBERIZE.

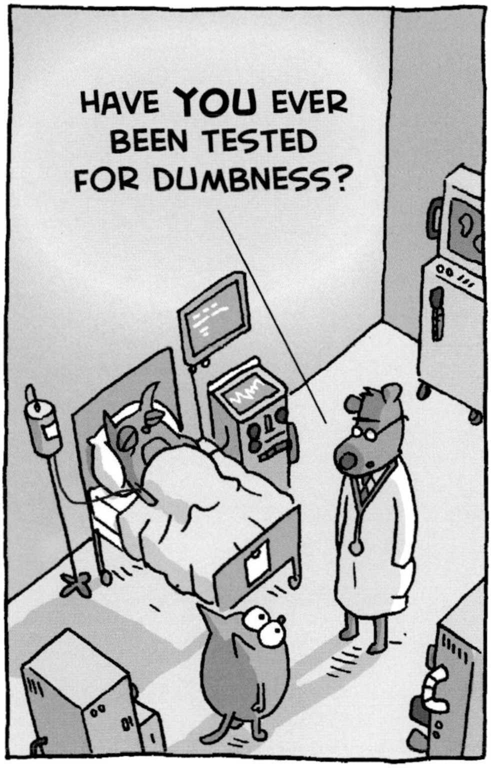
HAVE YOU EVER BEEN TESTED FOR DUMBNESS?

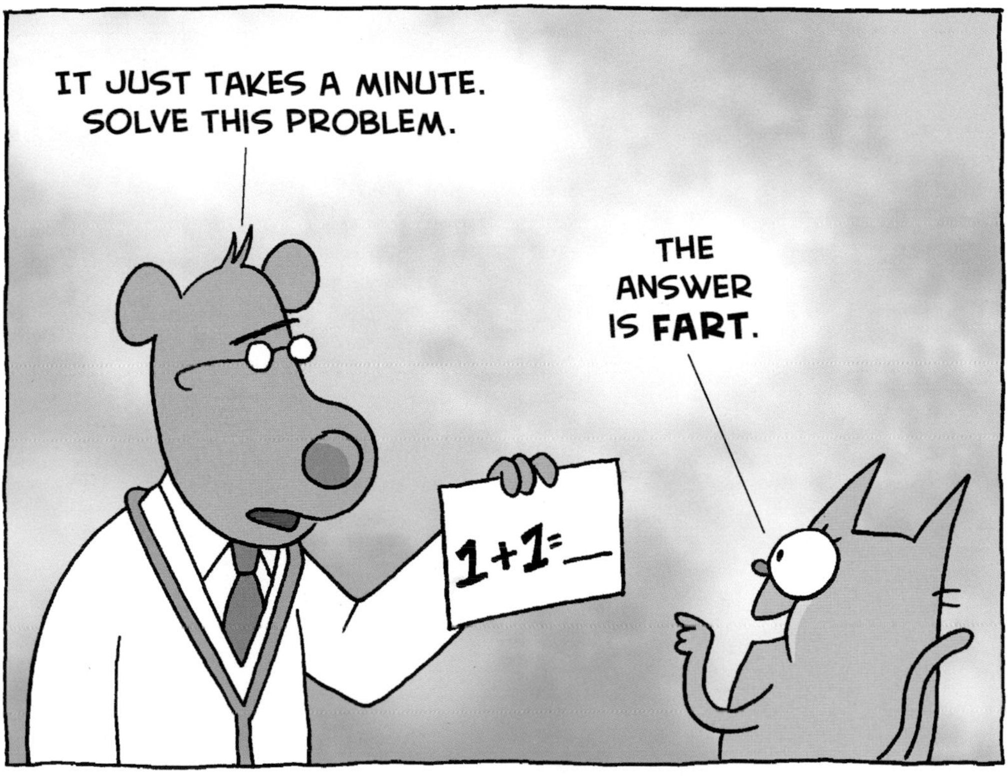
IT JUST TAKES A MINUTE. SOLVE THIS PROBLEM.
1+1=__
THE ANSWER IS FART.

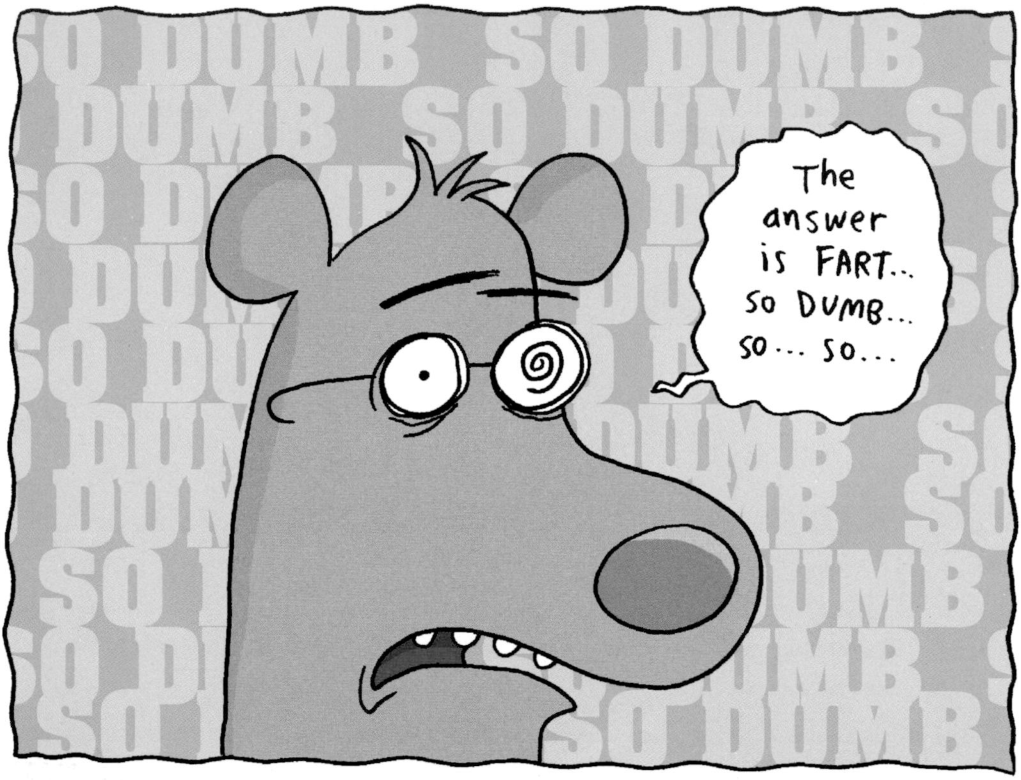
SO DUMB SO DUMB
The answer is FART... so DUMB... so... so...

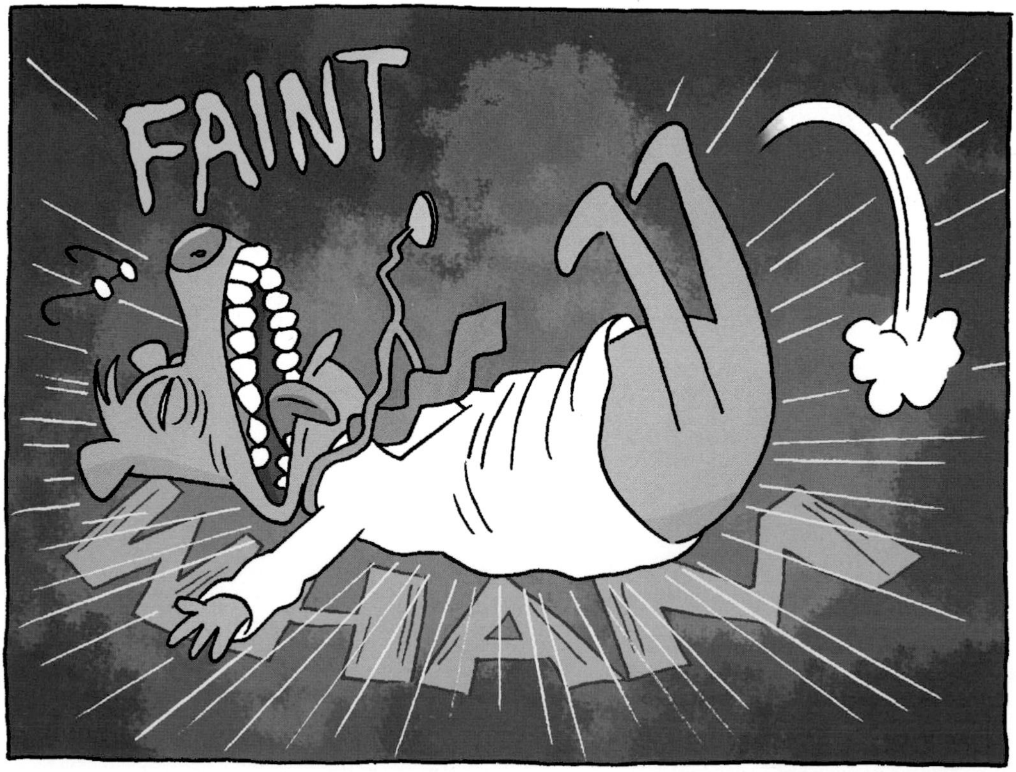
FAINT

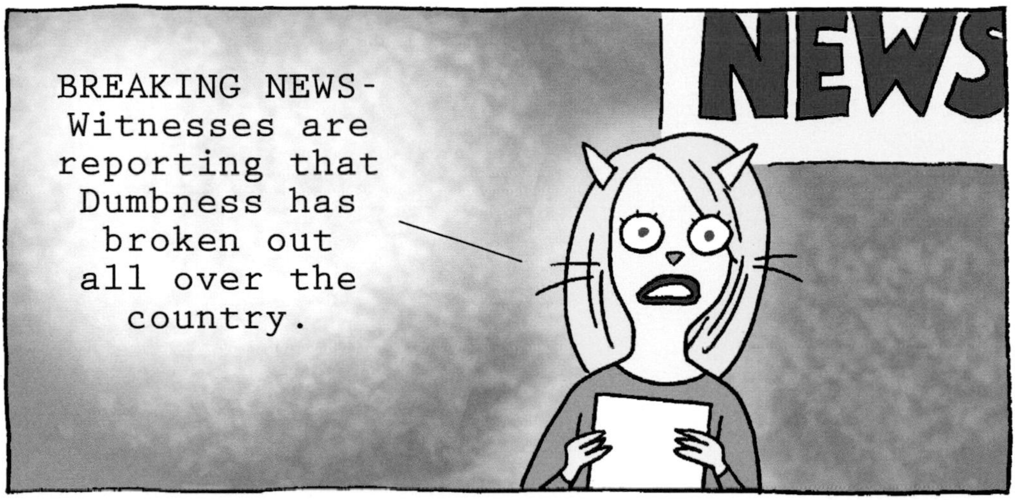
NEWS
BREAKING NEWS- Witnesses are reporting that Dumbness has broken out all over the country.

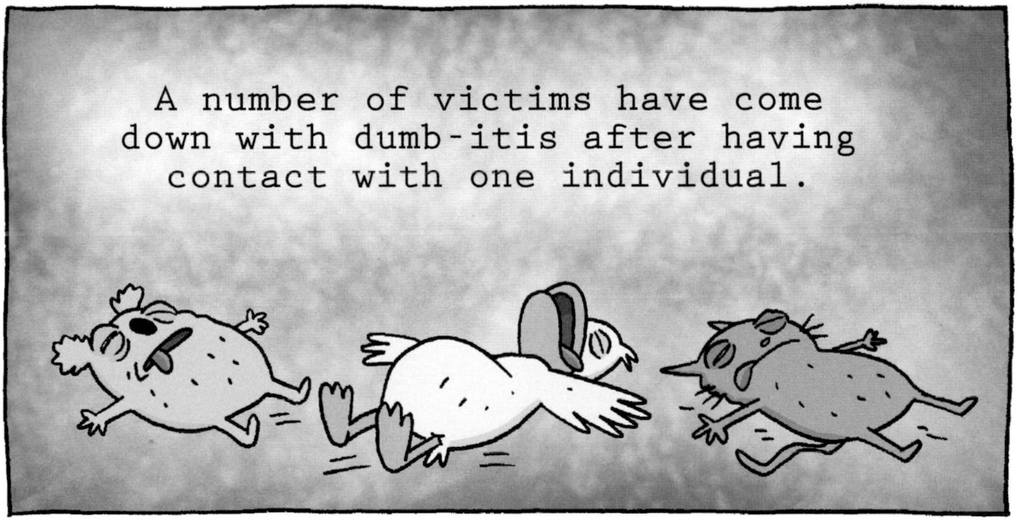
A number of victims have come down with dumb-itis after having contact with one individual.

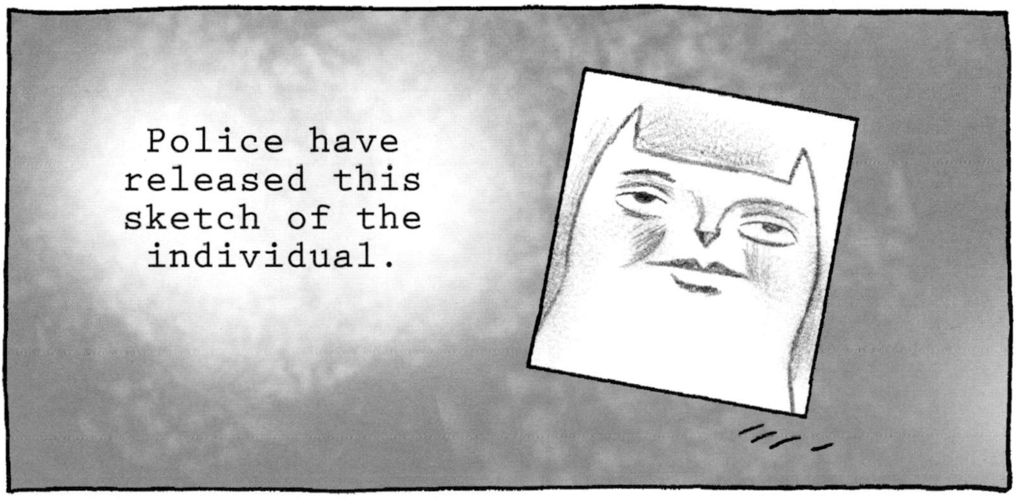
Police have released this sketch of the individual.

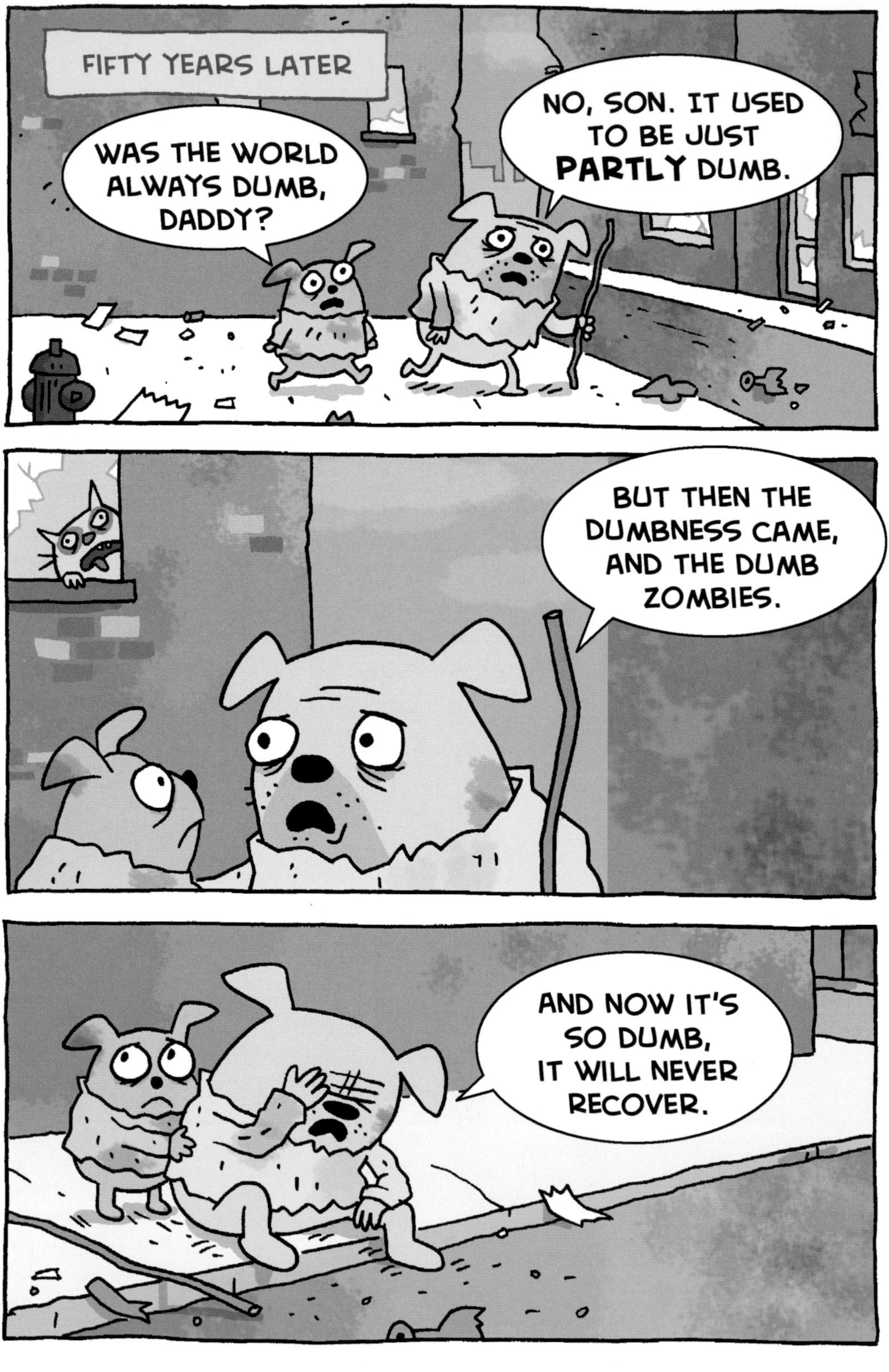
FIFTY YEARS LATER
WAS THE WORLD ALWAYS DUMB, DADDY?
NO, SON. IT USED TO BE JUST **PARTLY** DUMB.
BUT THEN THE DUMBNESS CAME, AND THE DUMB ZOMBIES.
AND NOW IT'S SO DUMB, IT WILL NEVER RECOVER.

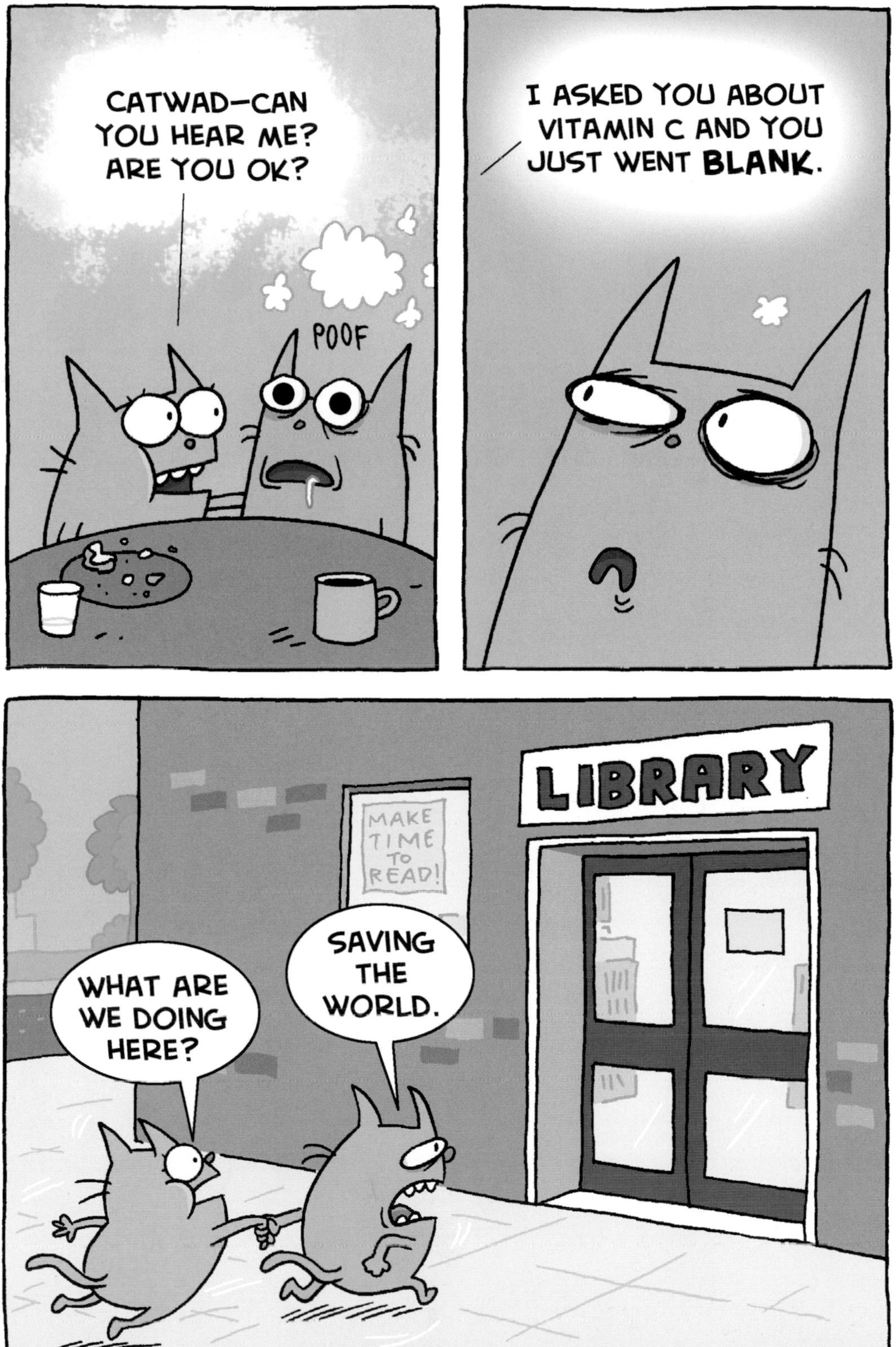
CATWAD—CAN YOU HEAR ME? ARE YOU OK?
POOF
I ASKED YOU ABOUT VITAMIN C AND YOU JUST WENT BLANK.
LIBRARY
MAKE TIME TO READ!
WHAT ARE WE DOING HERE?
SAVING THE WORLD.

A NEW FRIEND

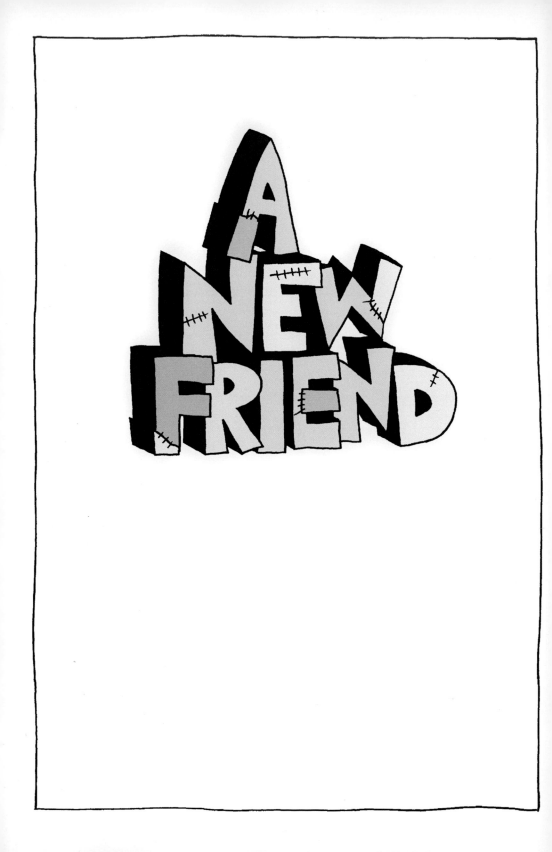

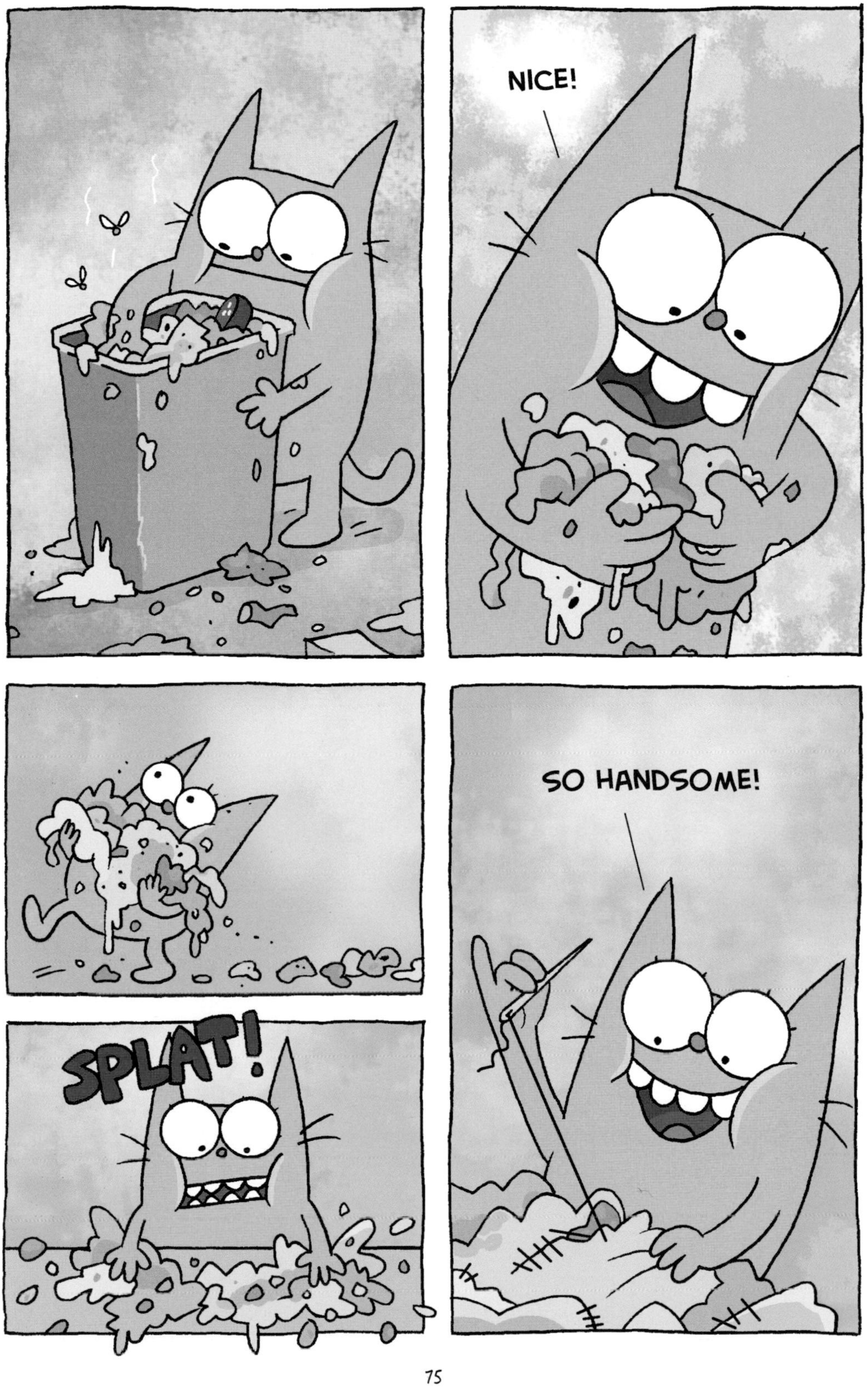
NICE!
SPLAT!
SO HANDSOME!

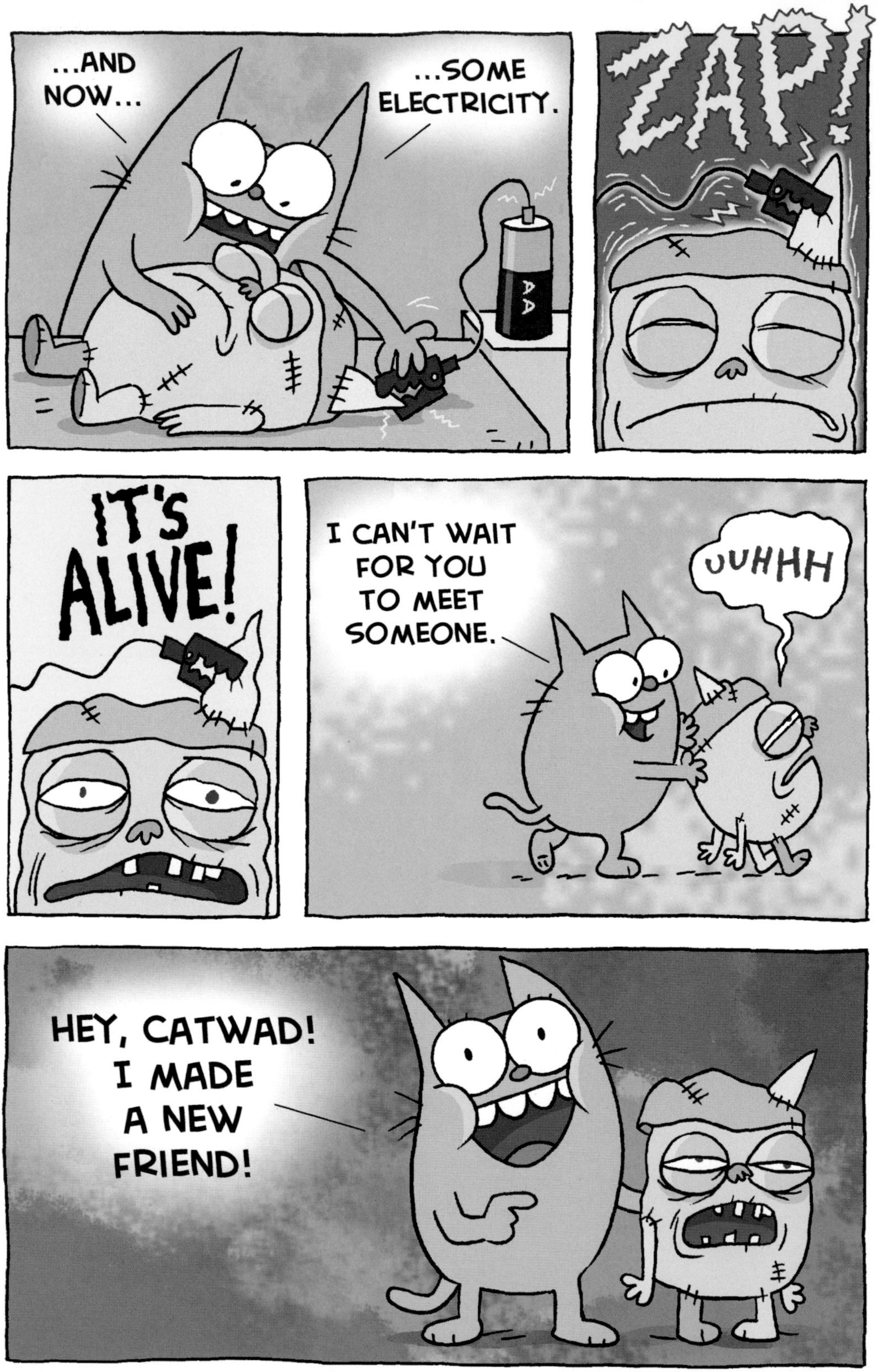

...AND NOW...
...SOME ELECTRICITY.
ZAP!
IT'S ALIVE!
I CAN'T WAIT FOR YOU TO MEET SOMEONE.
UUHHH
HEY, CATWAD! I MADE A NEW FRIEND!

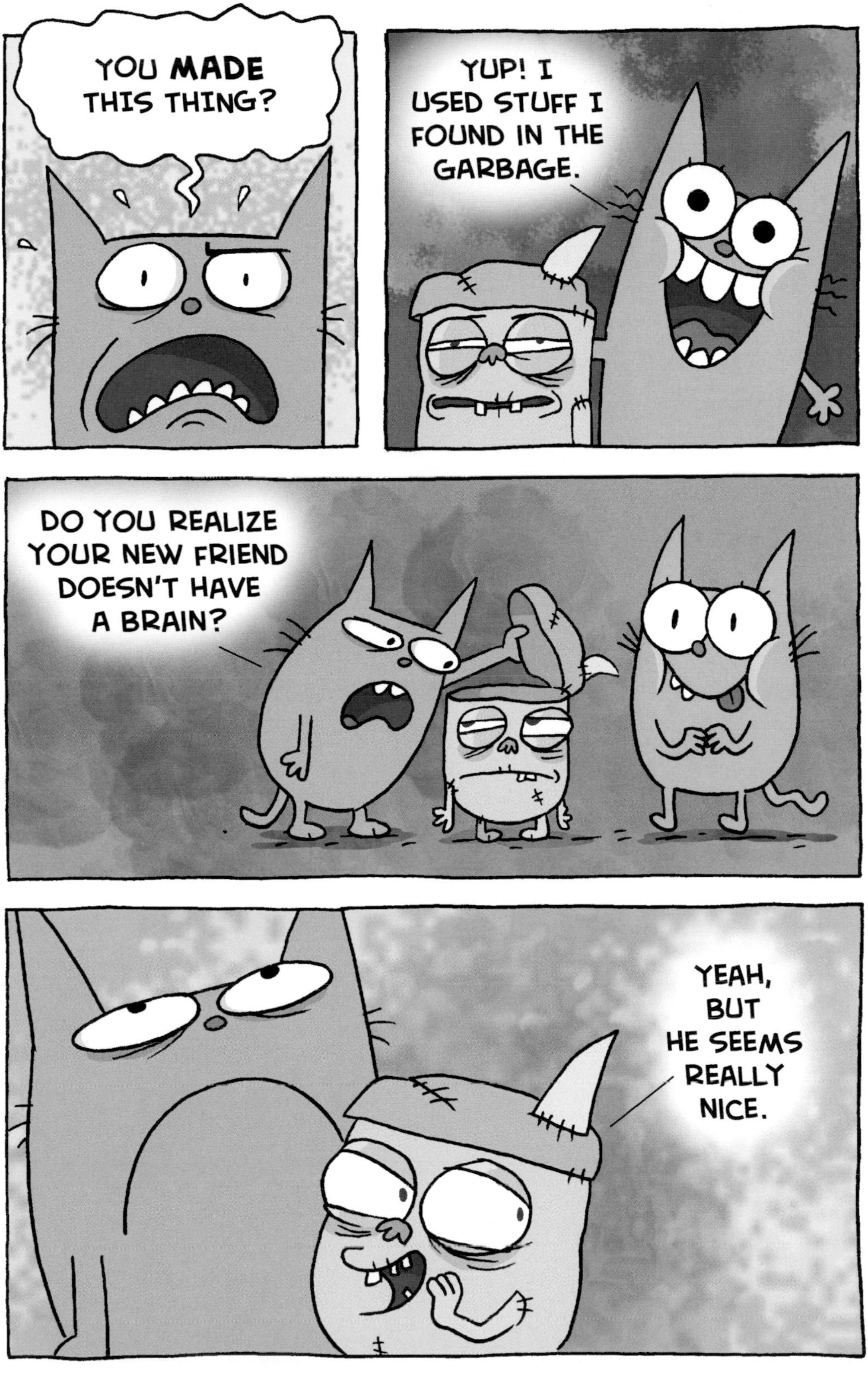
YOU **MADE** THIS THING?
YUP! I USED STUFF I FOUND IN THE GARBAGE.
DO YOU REALIZE YOUR NEW FRIEND DOESN'T HAVE A BRAIN?
YEAH, BUT HE SEEMS REALLY NICE.

MUSIC

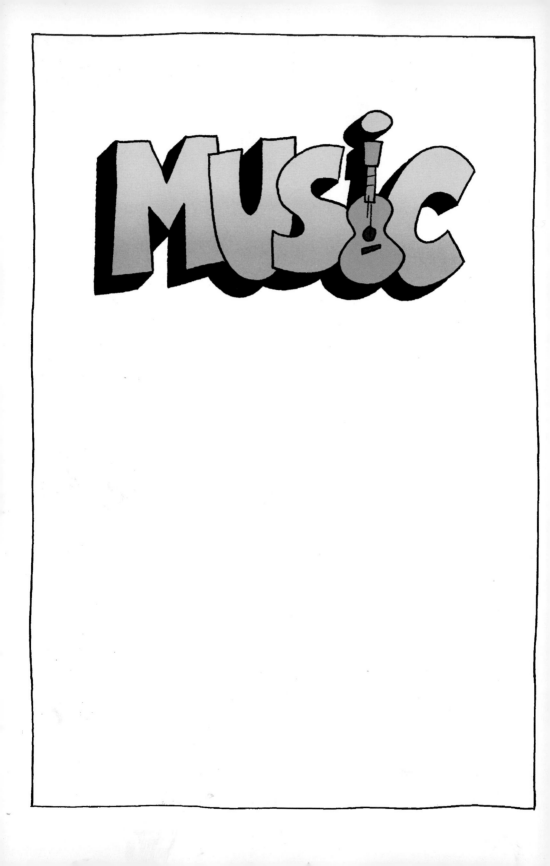

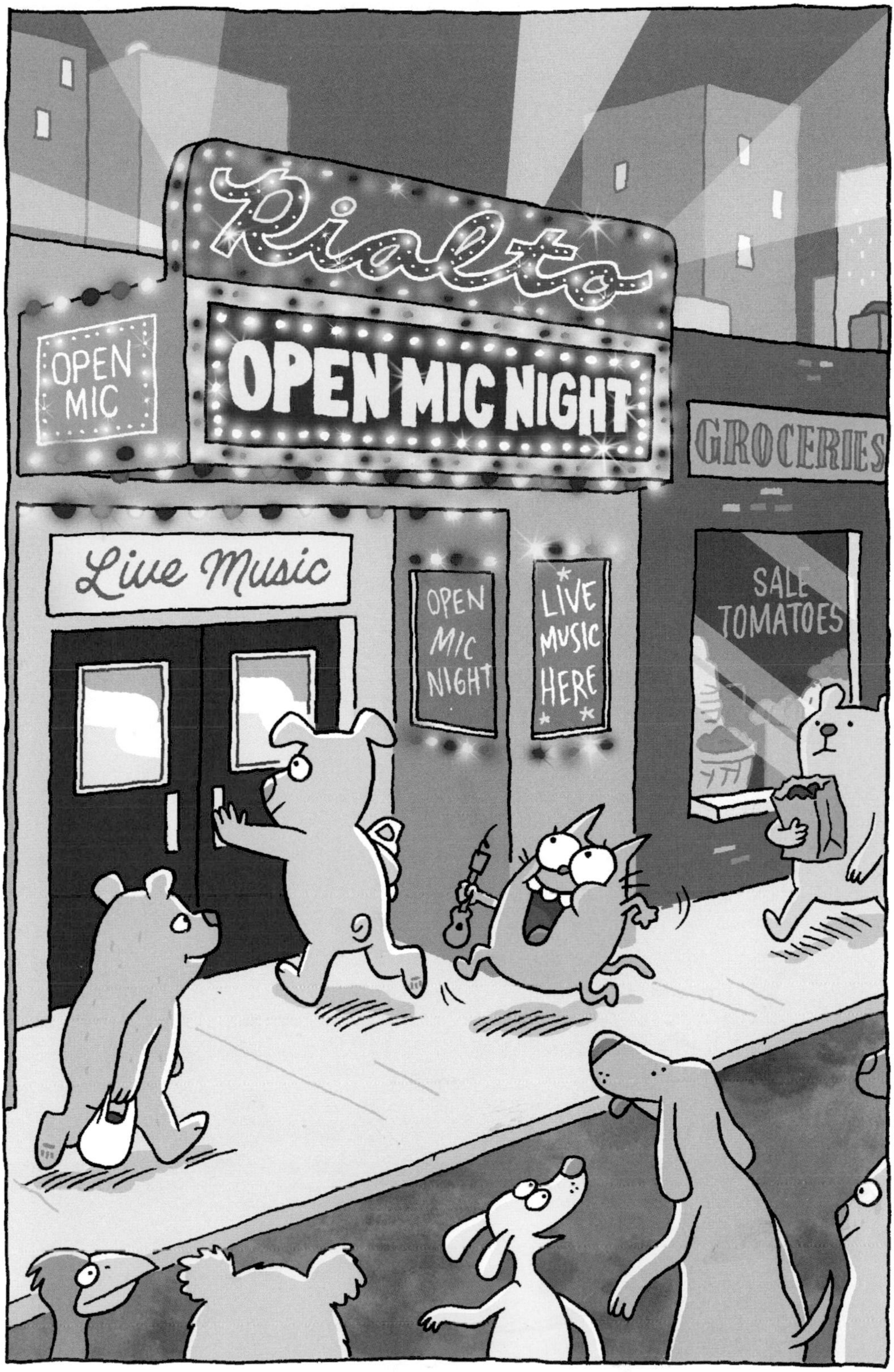
Rialto
OPEN MIC
OPEN MIC NIGHT
GROCERIES
Live Music
OPEN MIC NIGHT
LIVE MUSIC HERE
SALE TOMATOES

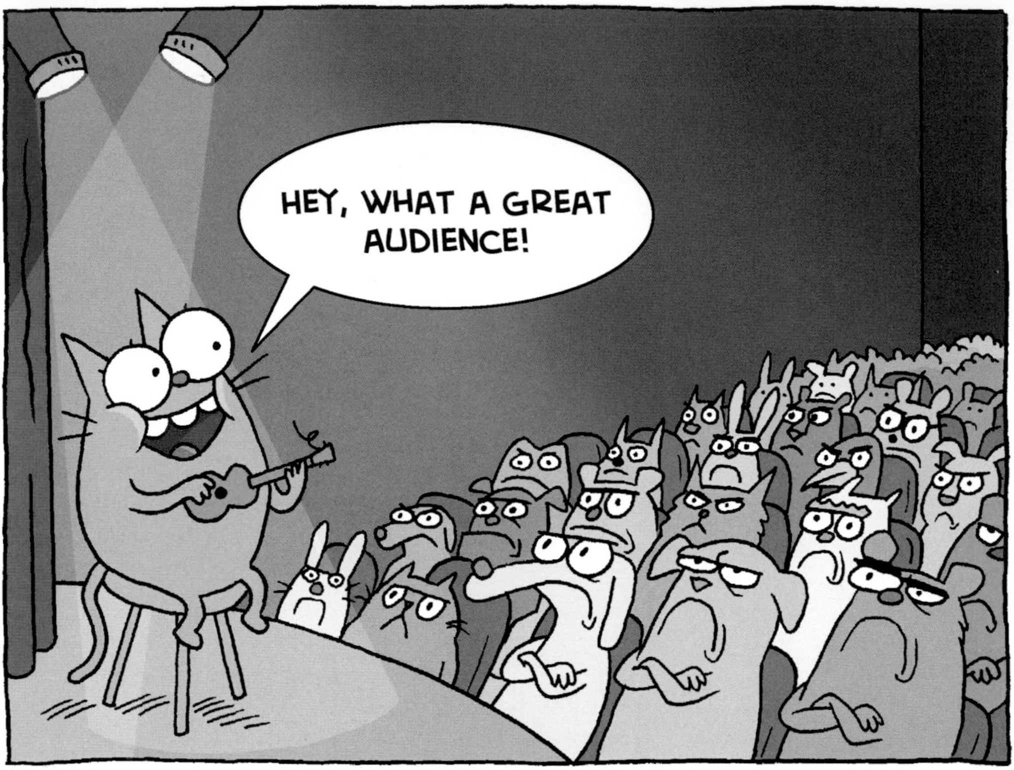
HEY, WHAT A GREAT AUDIENCE!

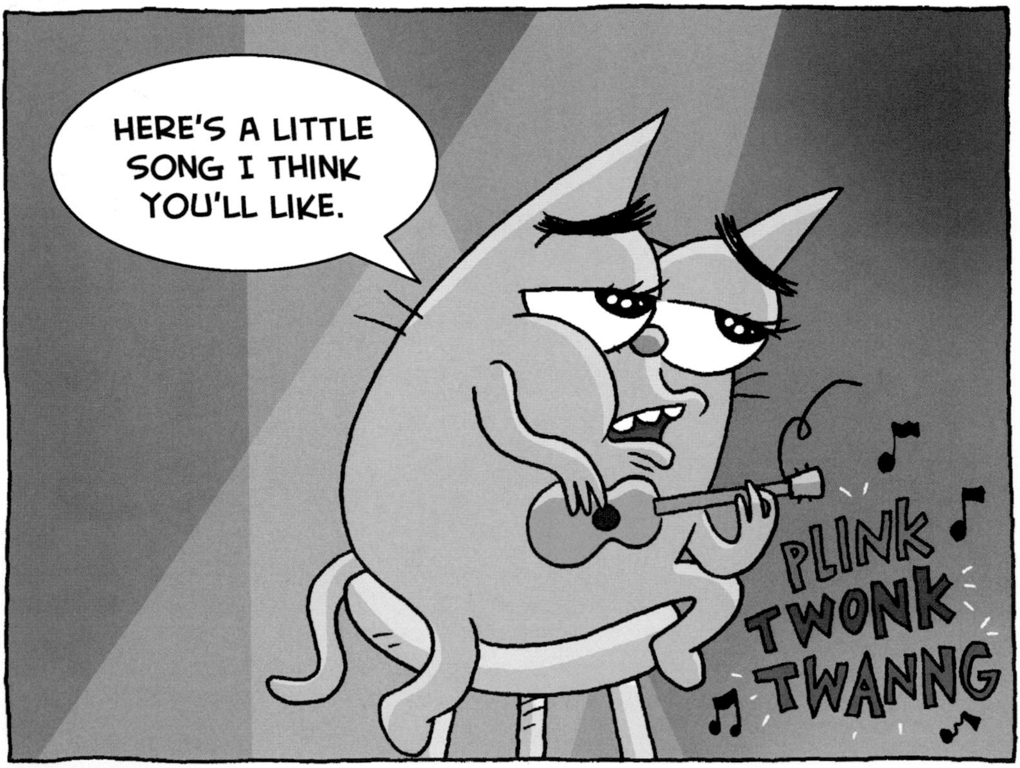
HERE'S A LITTLE SONG I THINK YOU'LL LIKE.
PLINK
TWONK
TWANNG

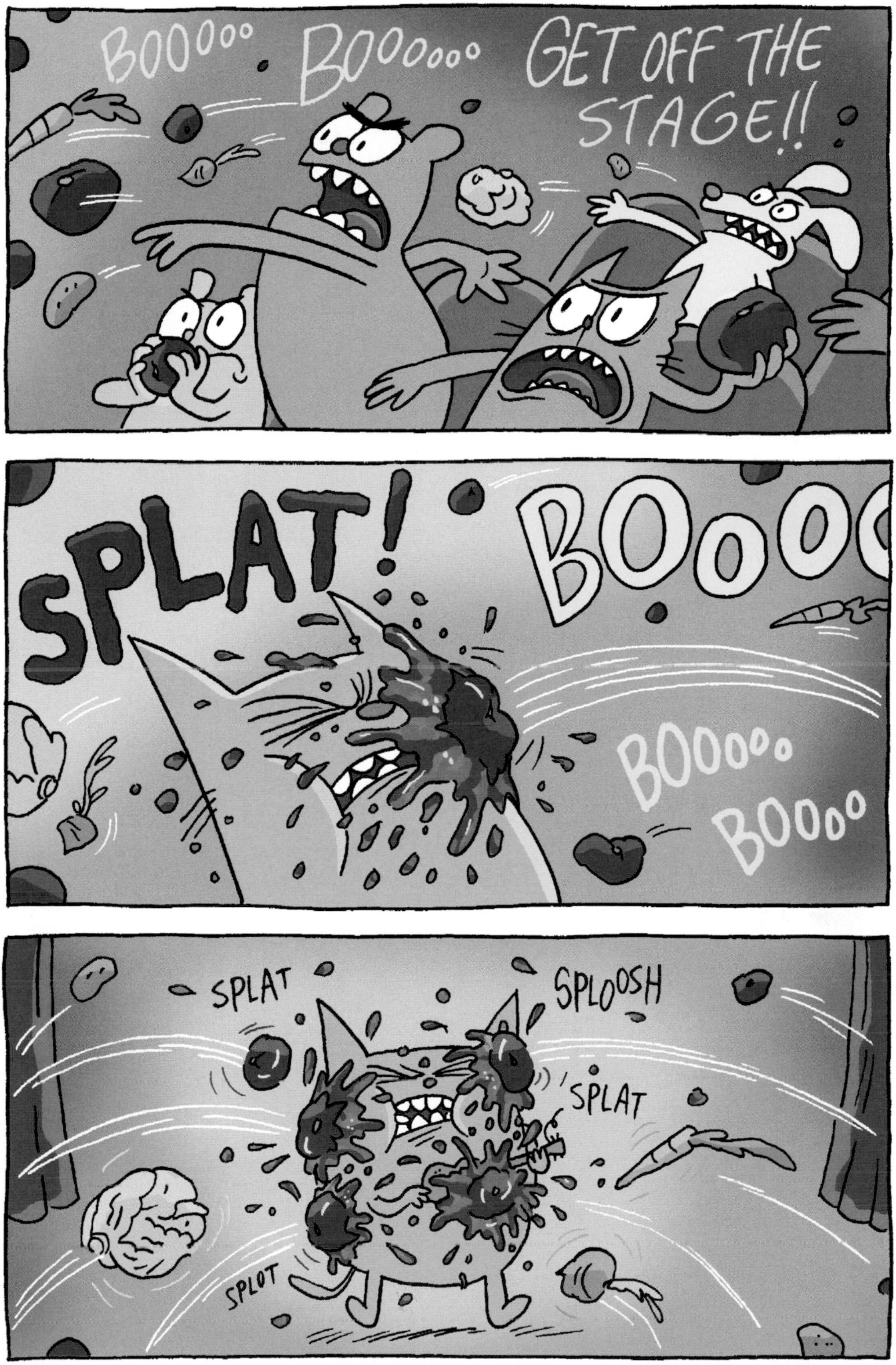

BOOooo
BOOoooo
GET OFF THE STAGE!!
SPLAT!
BOOOO
BOOooo
BOOooo
SPLAT
SPLOOSH
SPLAT
SPLOT

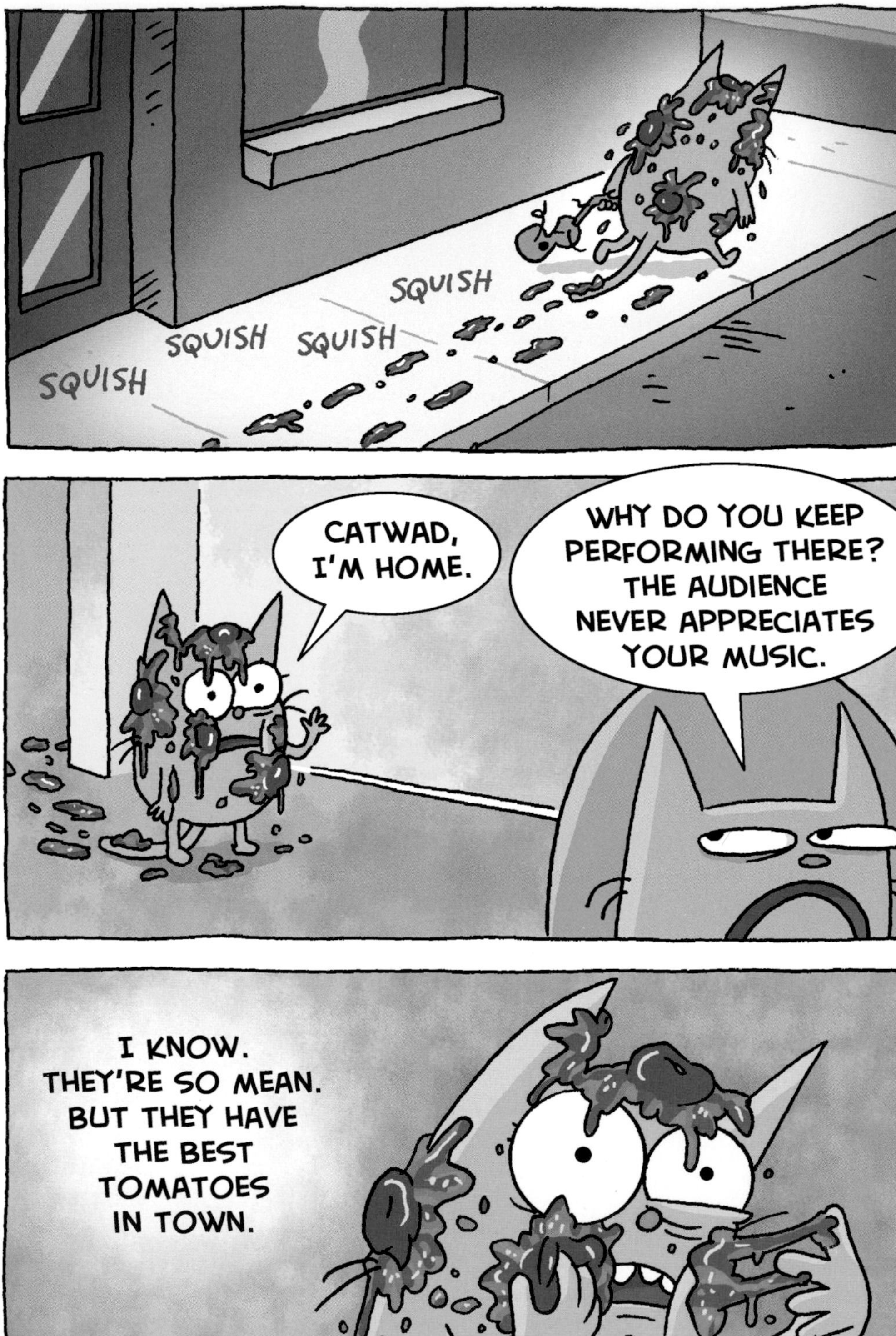
SQUISH
SQUISH
SQUISH
SQUISH
CATWAD, I'M HOME.
WHY DO YOU KEEP PERFORMING THERE? THE AUDIENCE NEVER APPRECIATES YOUR MUSIC.
I KNOW. THEY'RE SO MEAN. BUT THEY HAVE THE BEST TOMATOES IN TOWN.

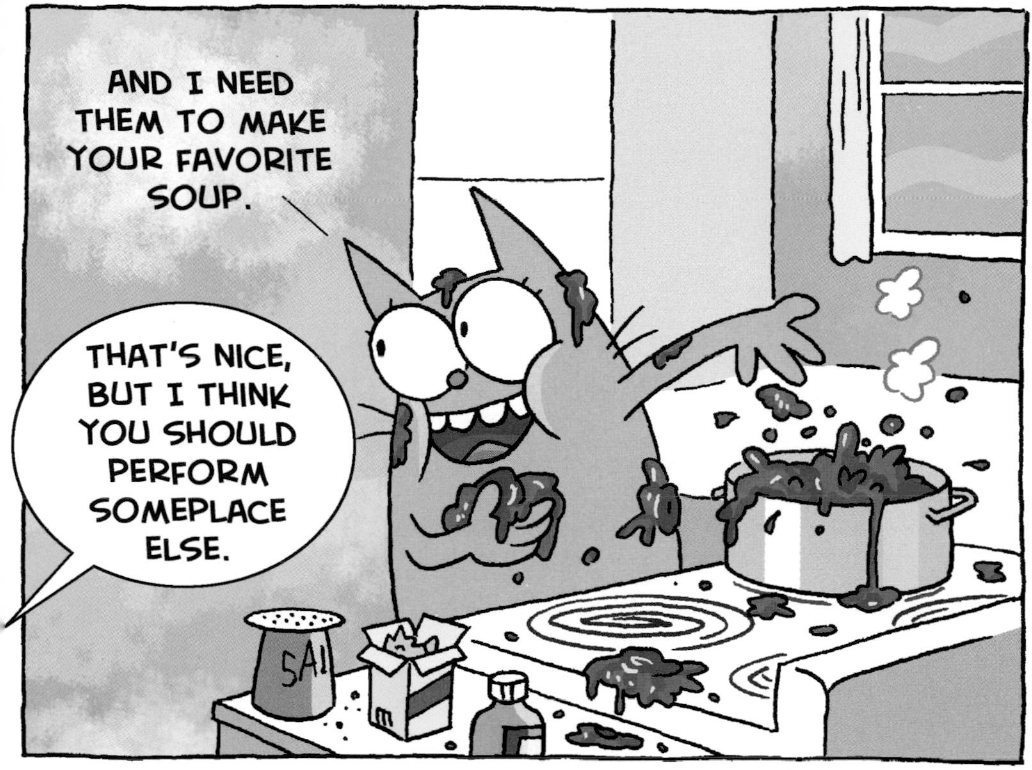
AND I NEED THEM TO MAKE YOUR FAVORITE SOUP.
THAT'S NICE, BUT I THINK YOU SHOULD PERFORM SOMEPLACE ELSE.

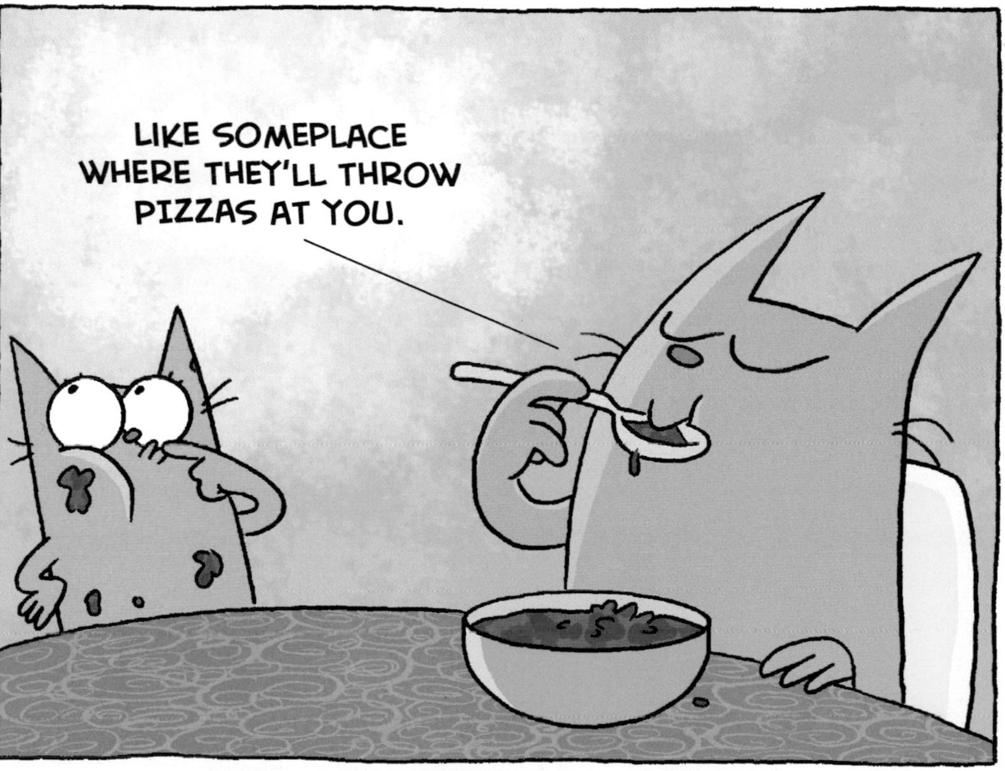
LIKE SOMEPLACE WHERE THEY'LL THROW PIZZAS AT YOU.

SWIM

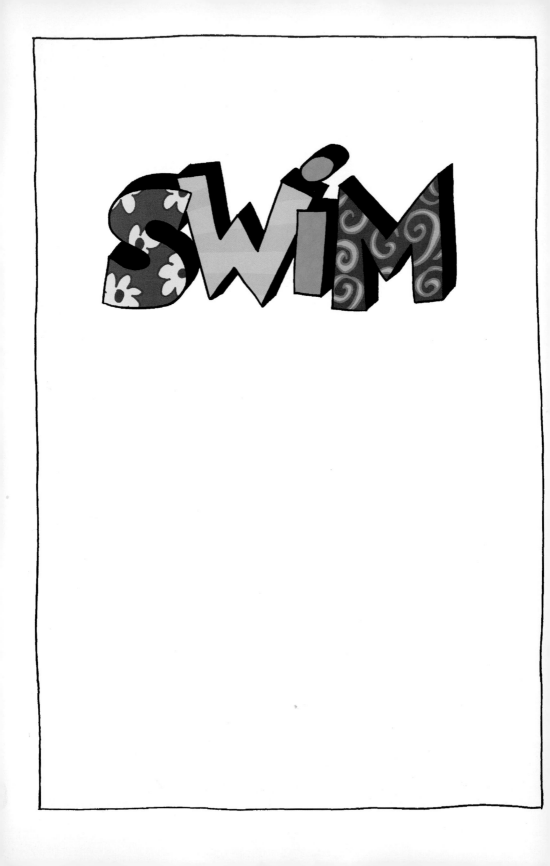

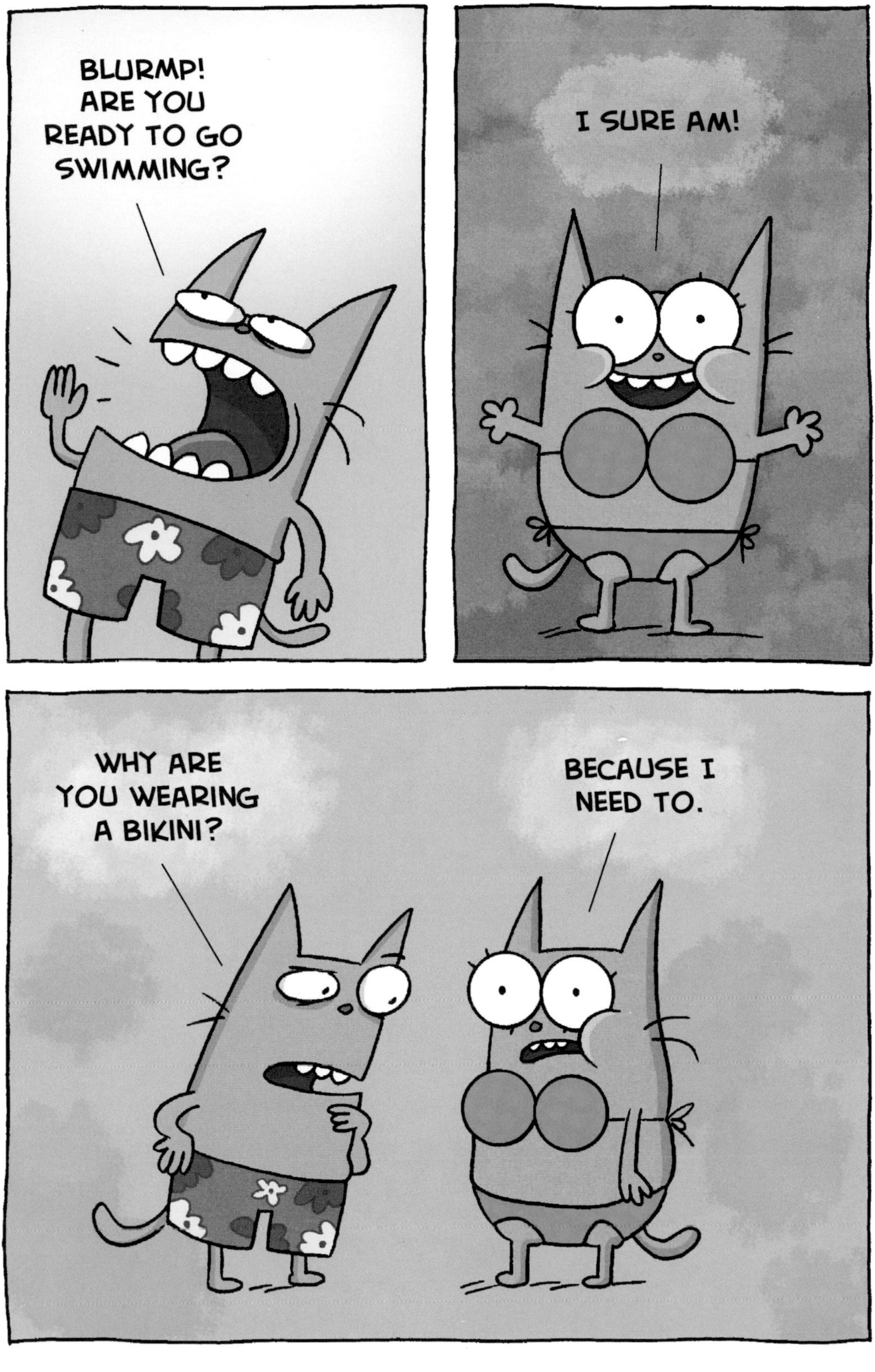
BLURMP! ARE YOU READY TO GO SWIMMING?
I SURE AM!
WHY ARE YOU WEARING A BIKINI?
BECAUSE I NEED TO.

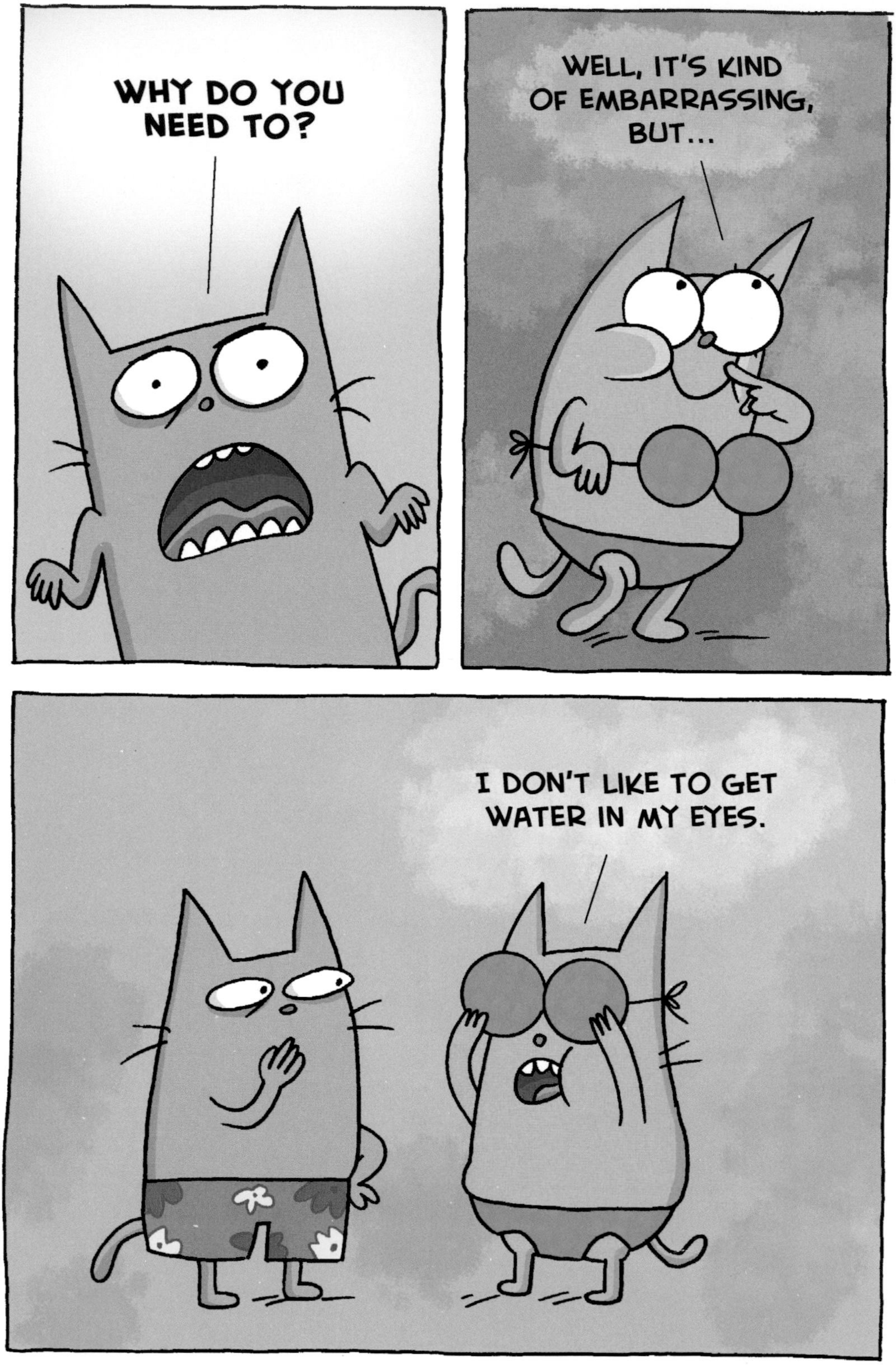
WHY DO YOU NEED TO?
WELL, IT'S KIND OF EMBARRASSING, BUT...
I DON'T LIKE TO GET WATER IN MY EYES.

CATWAD?
YOU'RE STILL
THERE, RIGHT?

SMART

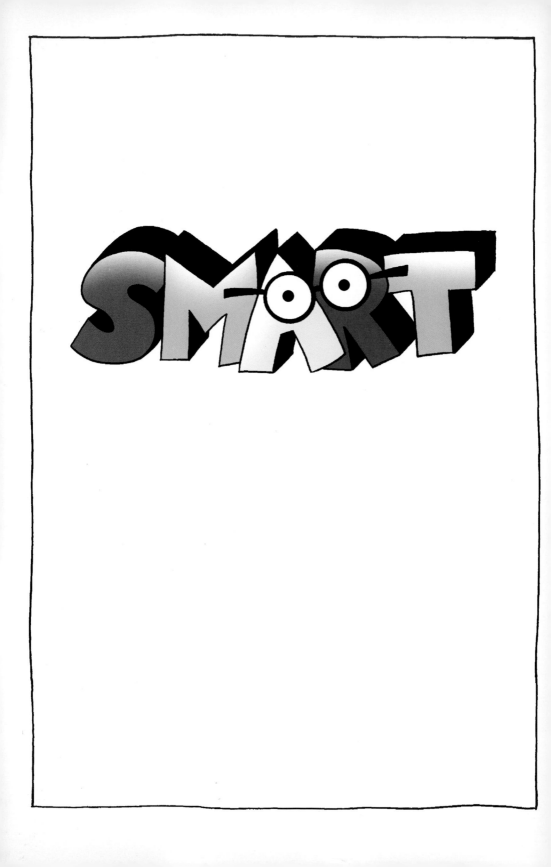

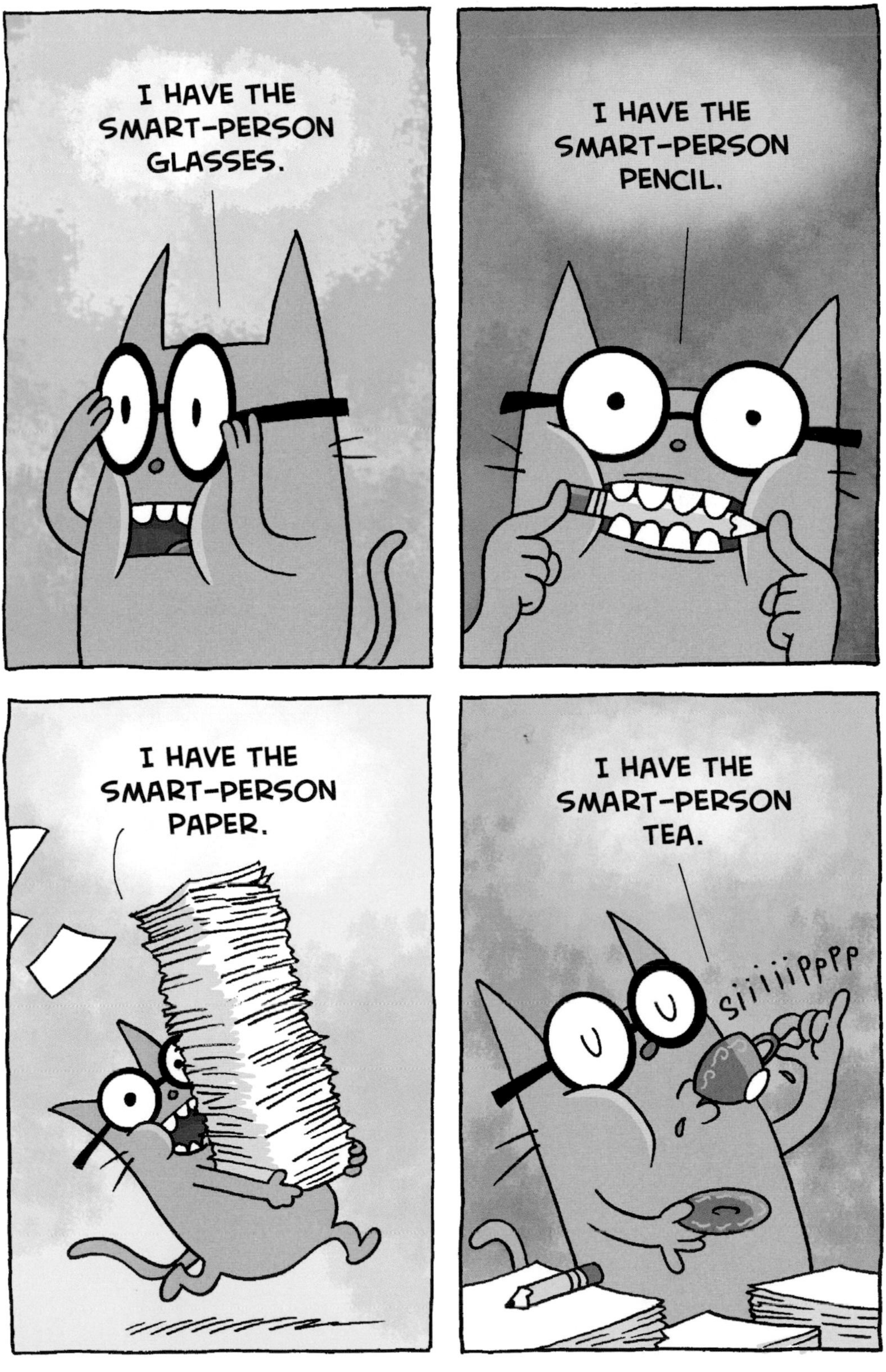
I HAVE THE SMART-PERSON GLASSES.
I HAVE THE SMART-PERSON PENCIL.
I HAVE THE SMART-PERSON PAPER.
I HAVE THE SMART-PERSON TEA.
SIIIIIPPPP

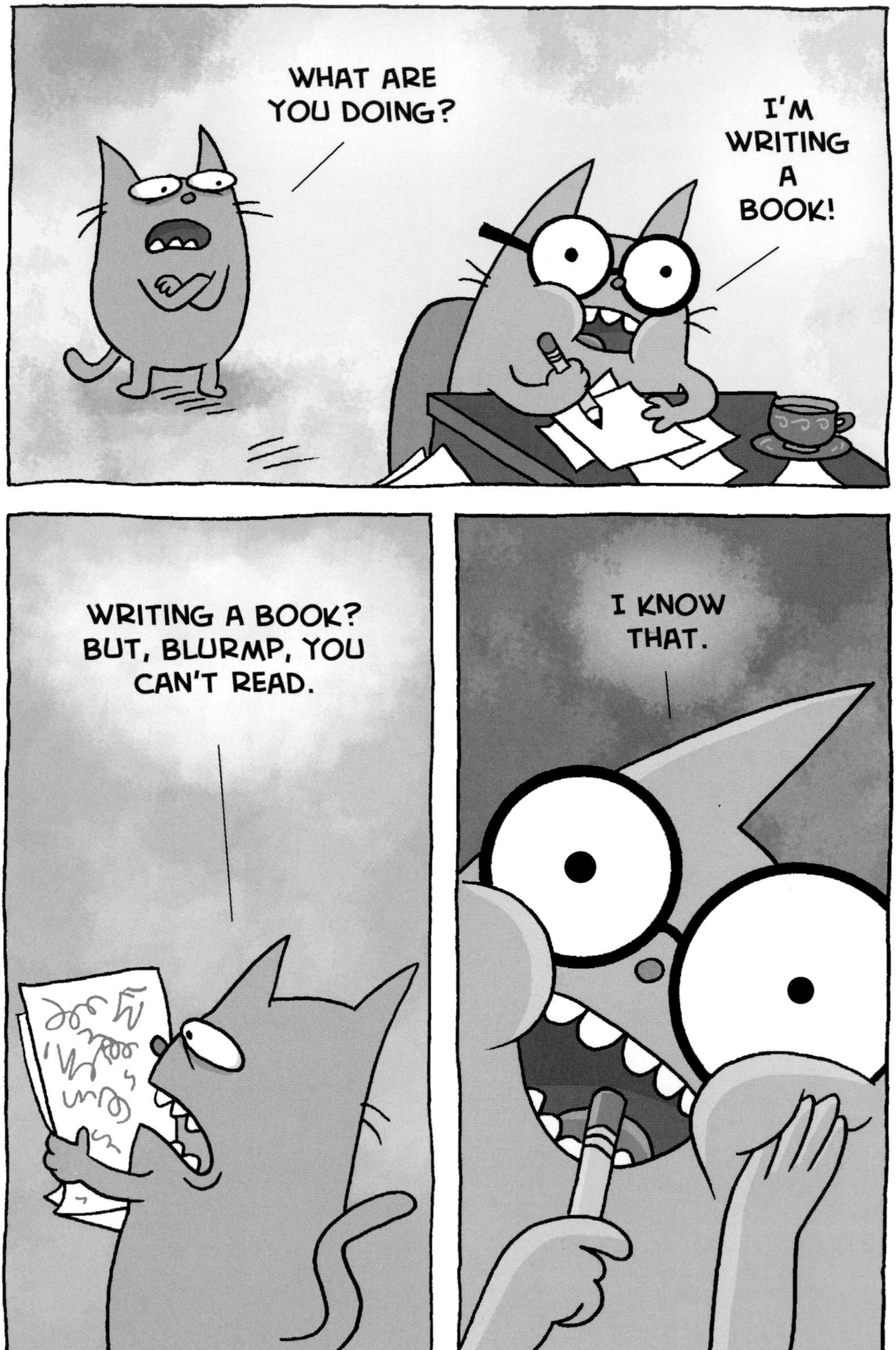
WHAT ARE YOU DOING?
I'M WRITING A BOOK!
WRITING A BOOK? BUT, BLURMP, YOU CAN'T READ.
I KNOW THAT.

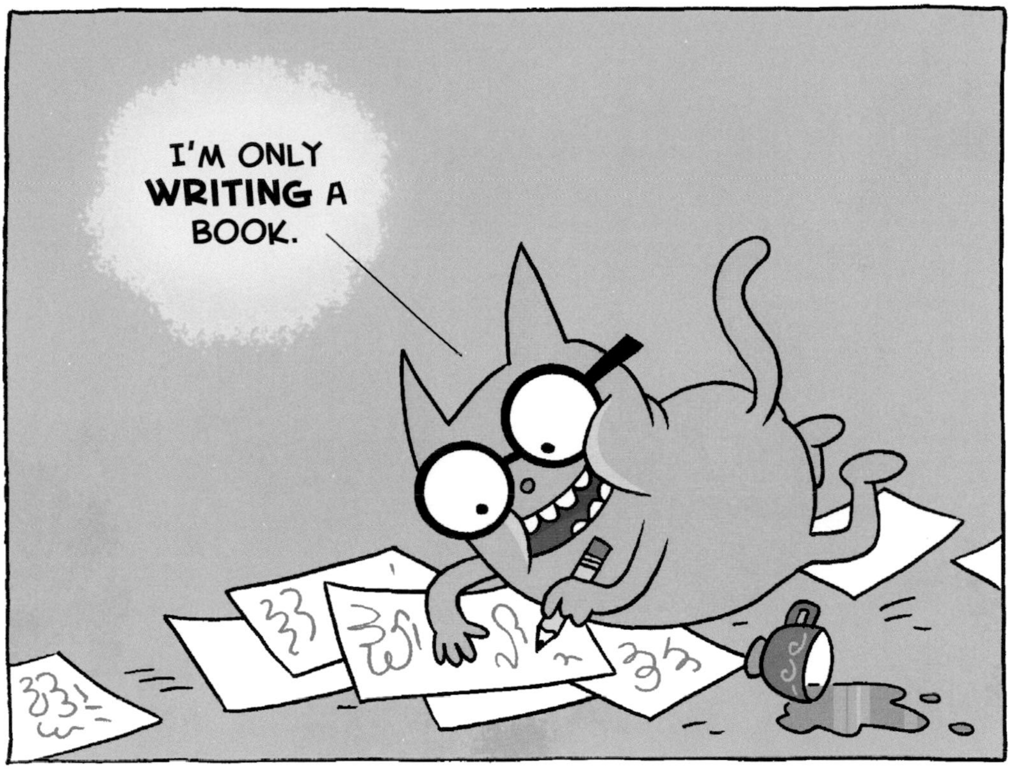
I'M ONLY WRITING A BOOK.

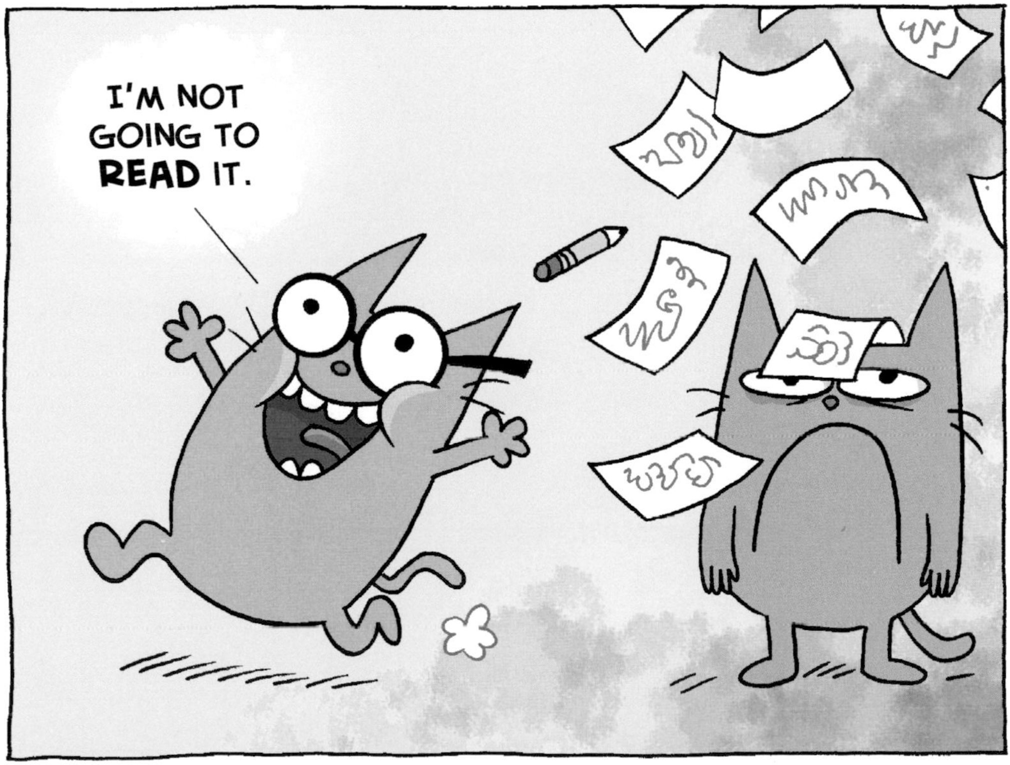
I'M NOT GOING TO READ IT.

WEIGHTS

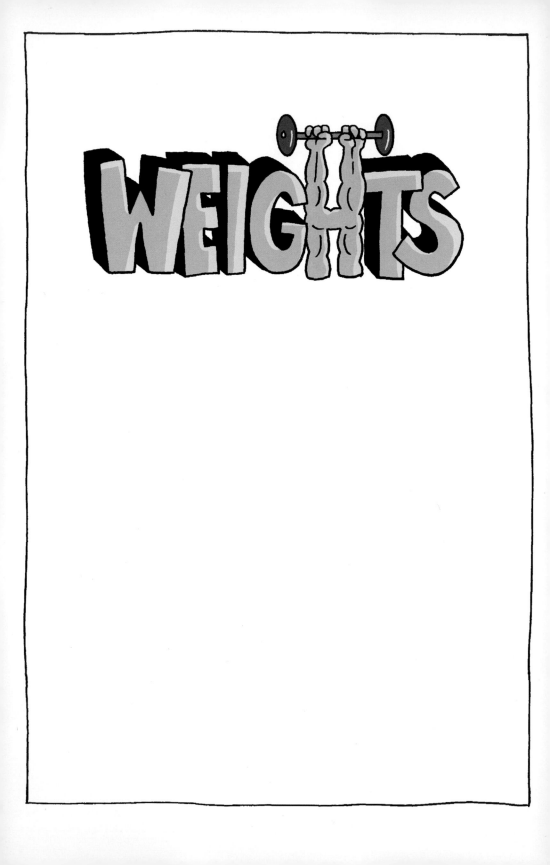

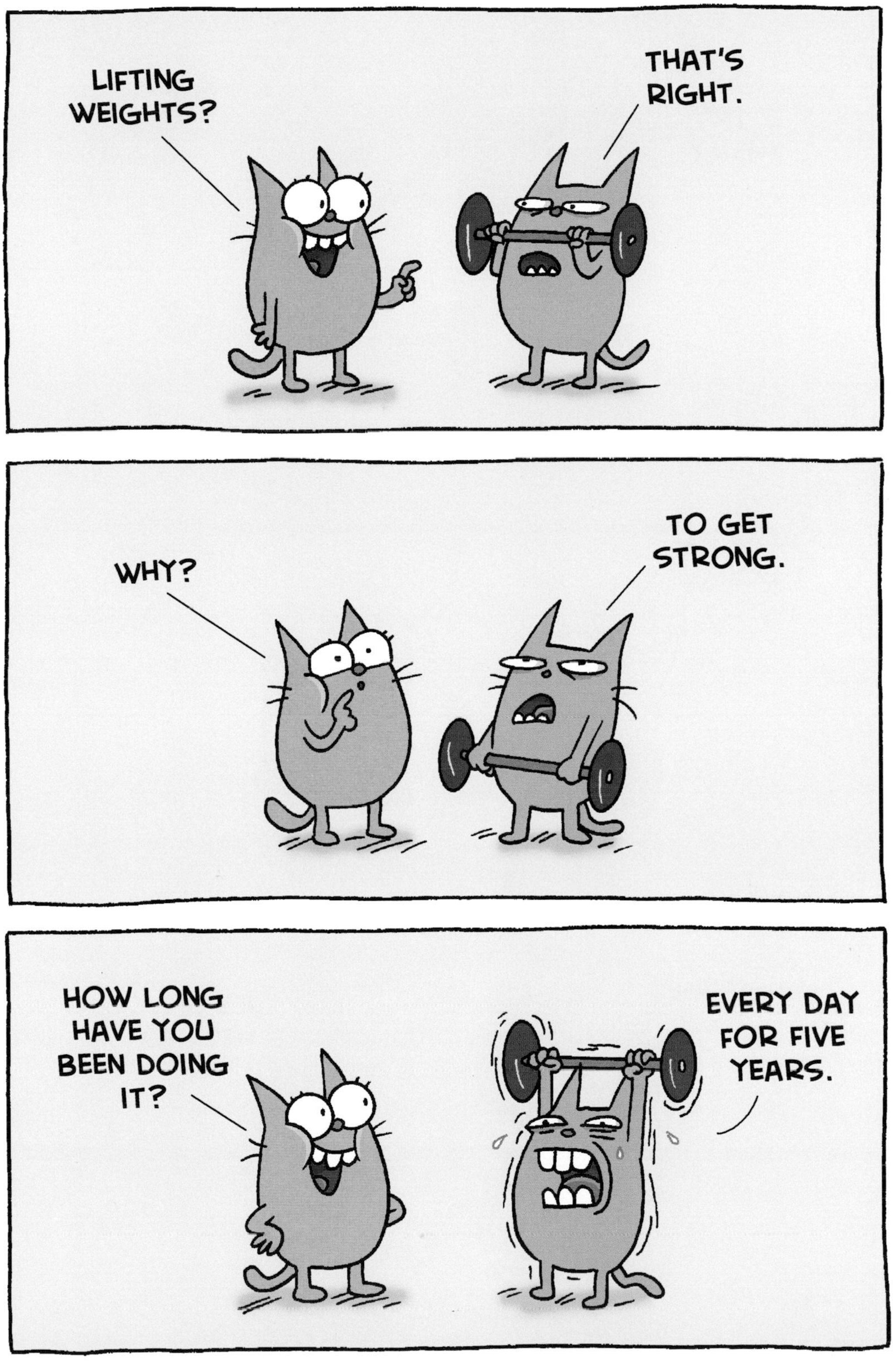
LIFTING WEIGHTS?
THAT'S RIGHT.
WHY?
TO GET STRONG.
HOW LONG HAVE YOU BEEN DOING IT?
EVERY DAY FOR FIVE YEARS.

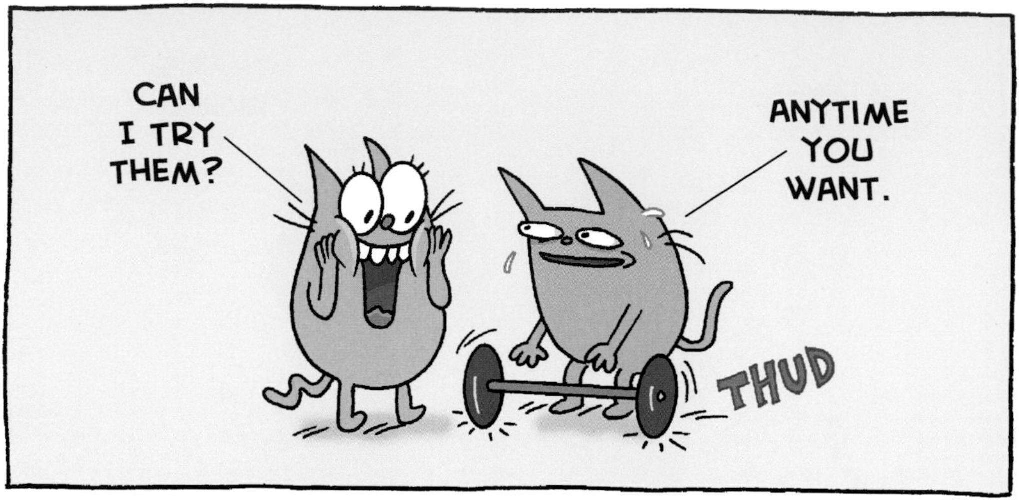
CAN I TRY THEM?
ANYTIME YOU WANT.
THUD

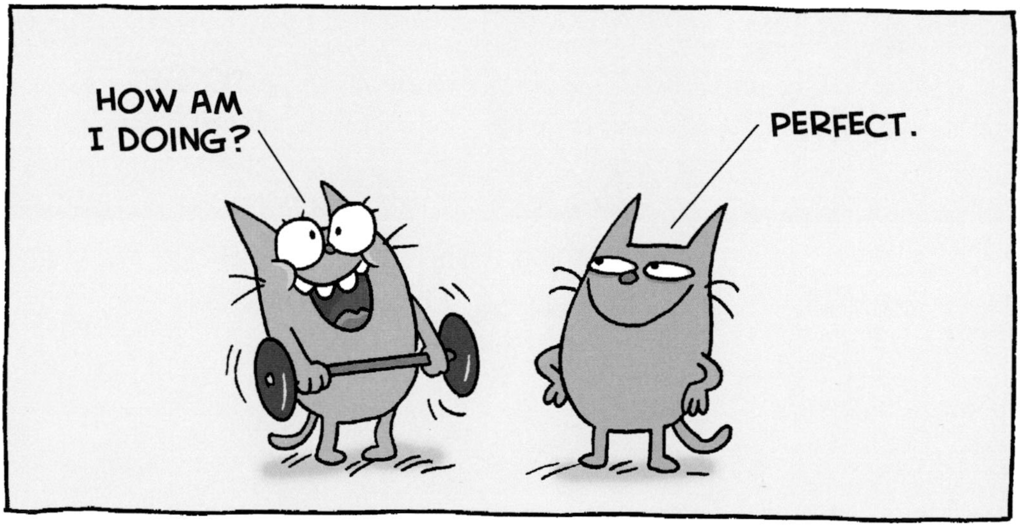
HOW AM I DOING?
PERFECT.

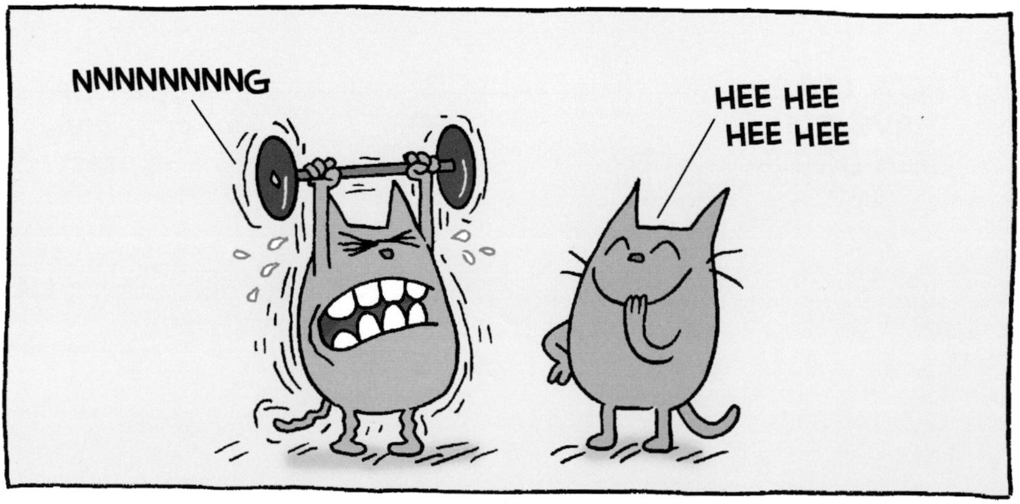
NNNNNNNNG
HEE HEE HEE HEE

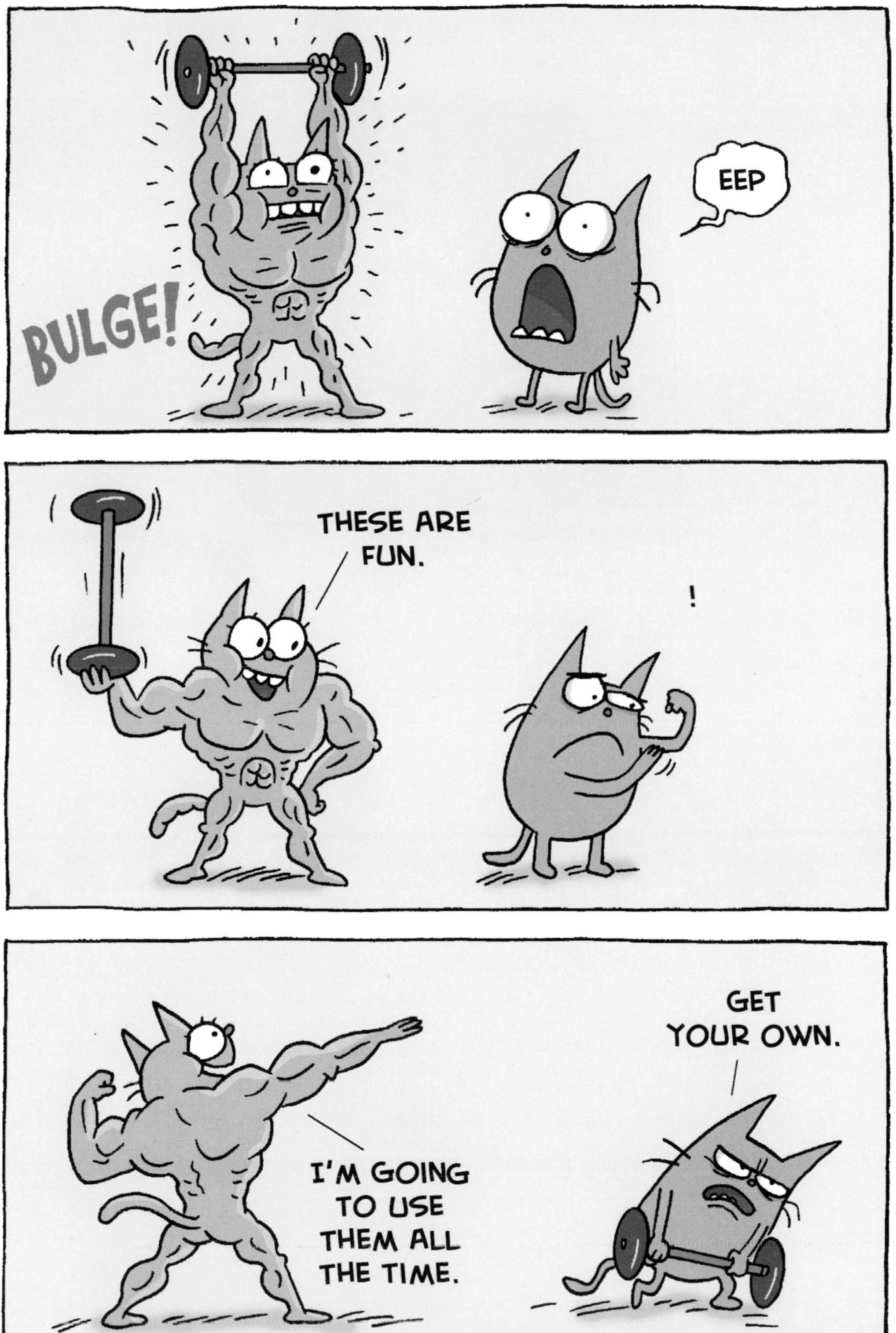
BULGE!
EEP
THESE ARE FUN.
!
I'M GOING TO USE THEM ALL THE TIME.
GET YOUR OWN.

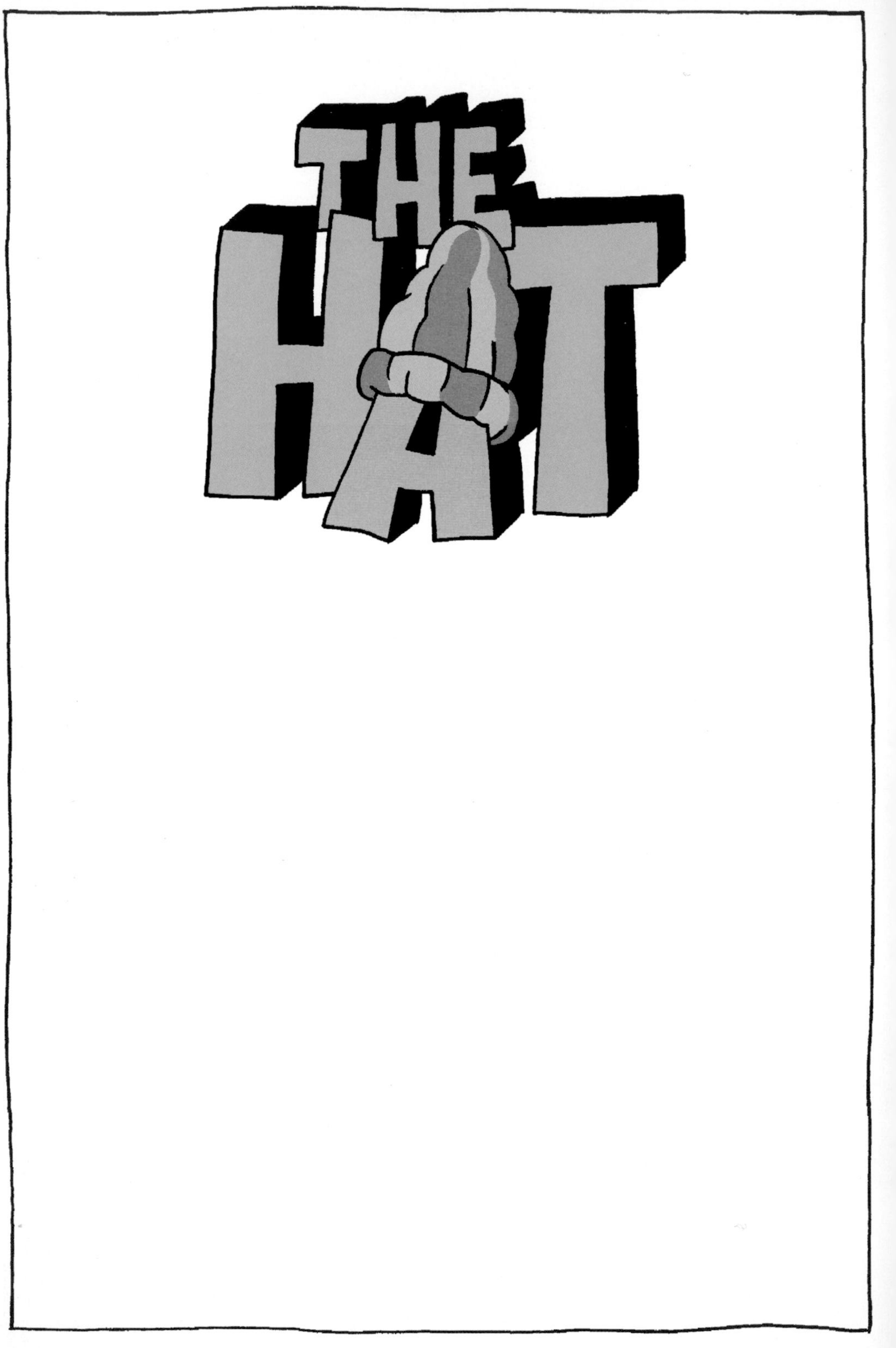
THE HAT

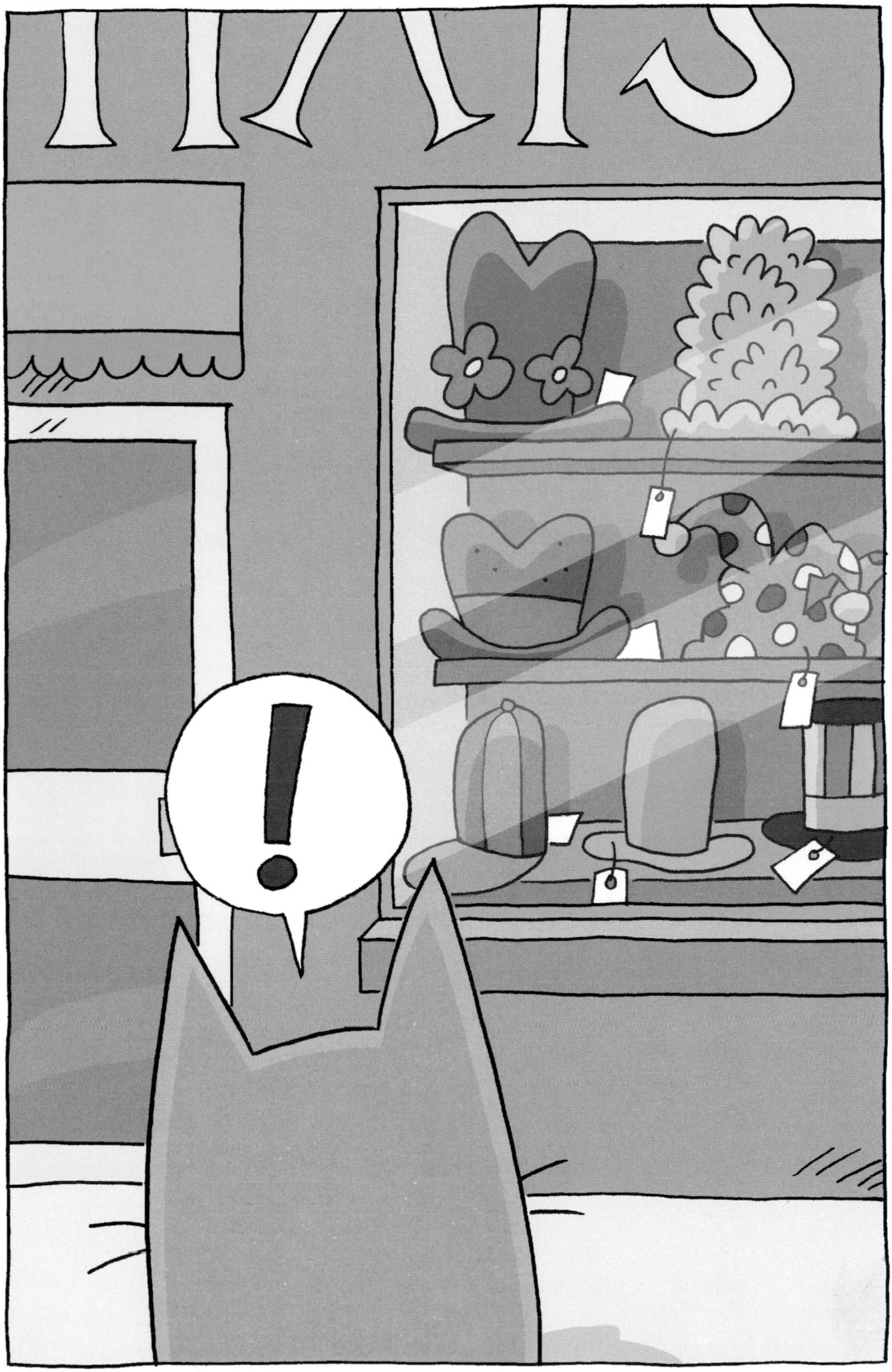
HATS
!

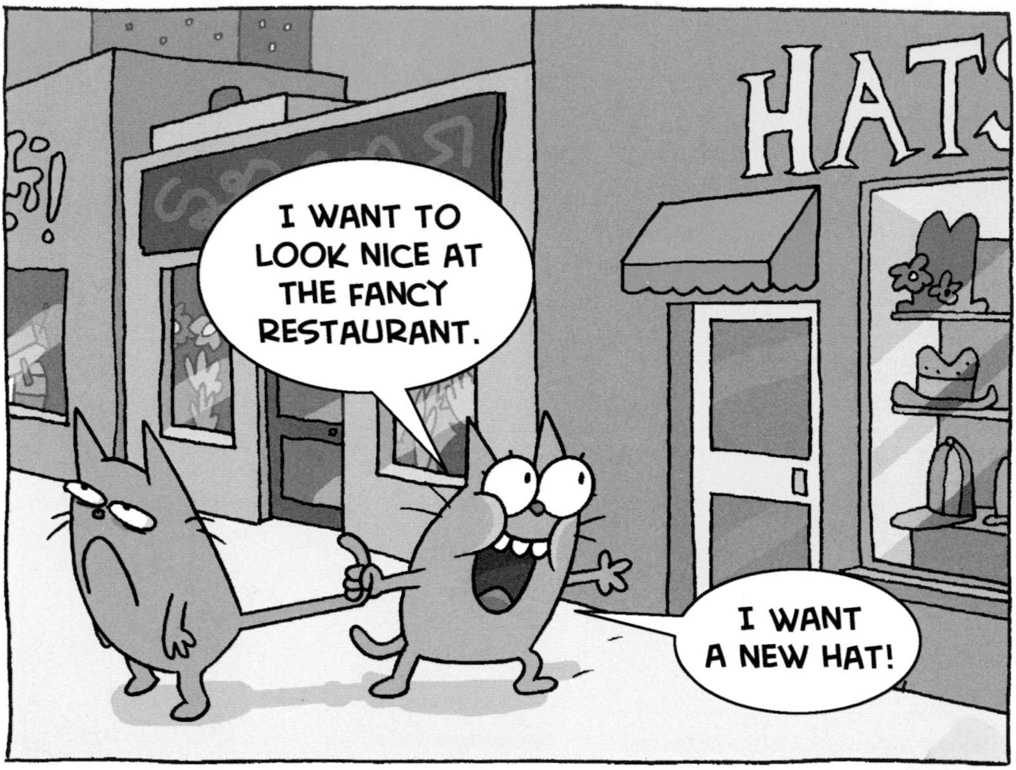
HATS
I WANT TO LOOK NICE AT THE FANCY RESTAURANT.
I WANT A NEW HAT!

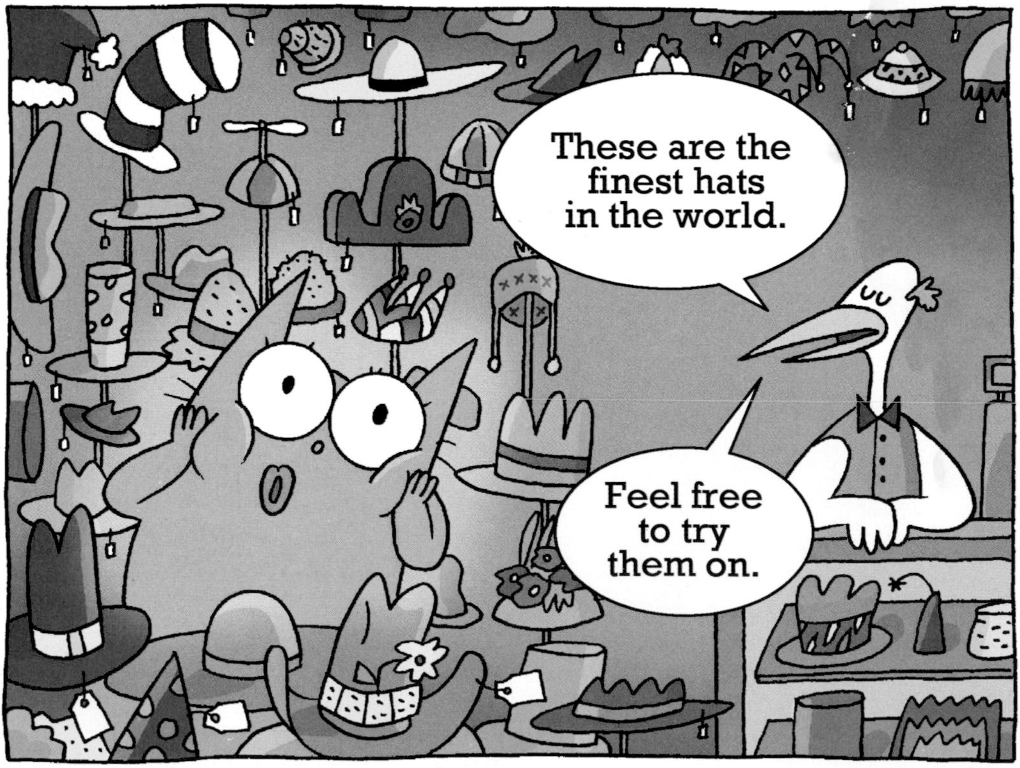
These are the finest hats in the world.
Feel free to try them on.

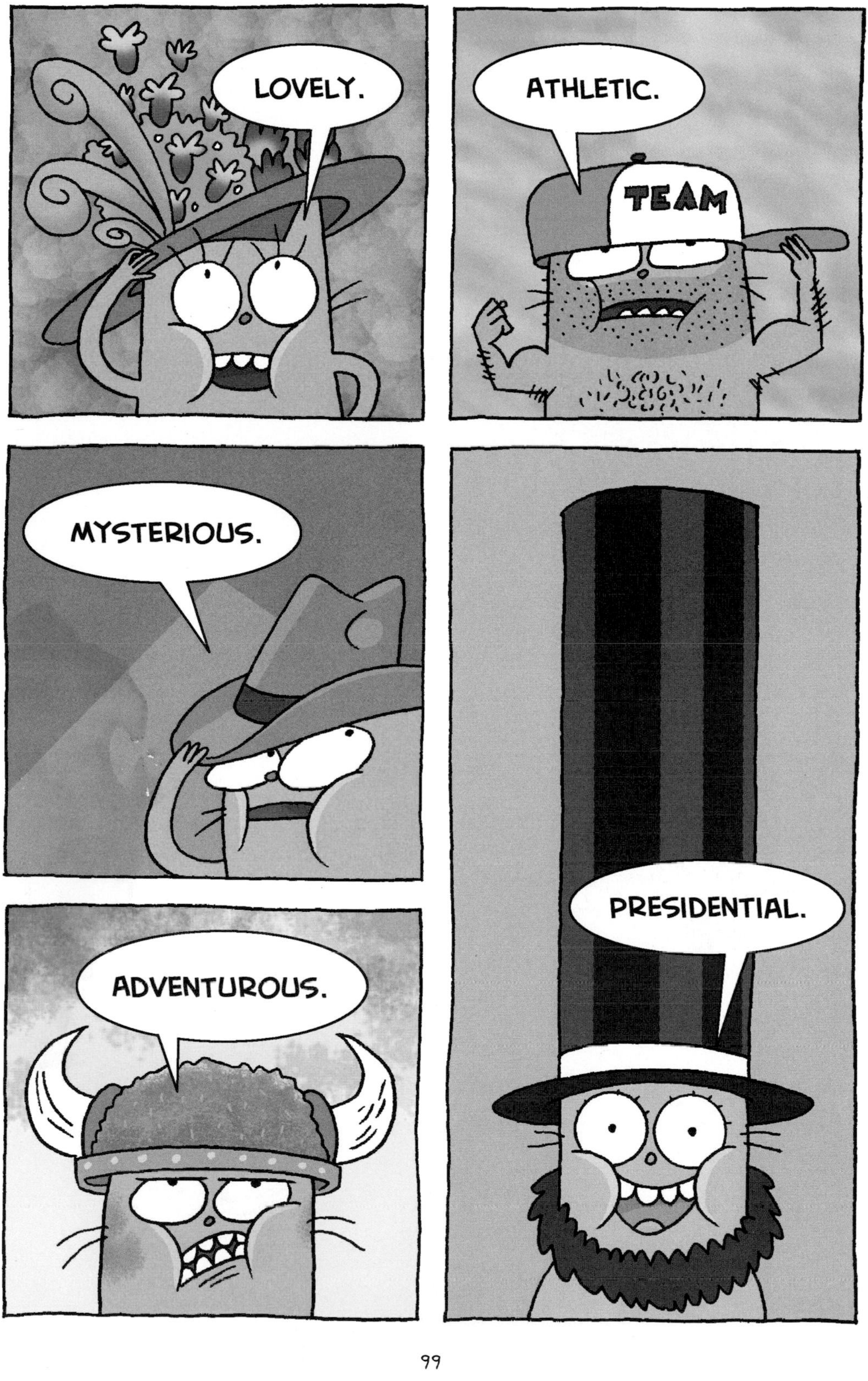
LOVELY.
ATHLETIC.
TEAM
MYSTERIOUS.
ADVENTUROUS.
PRESIDENTIAL.

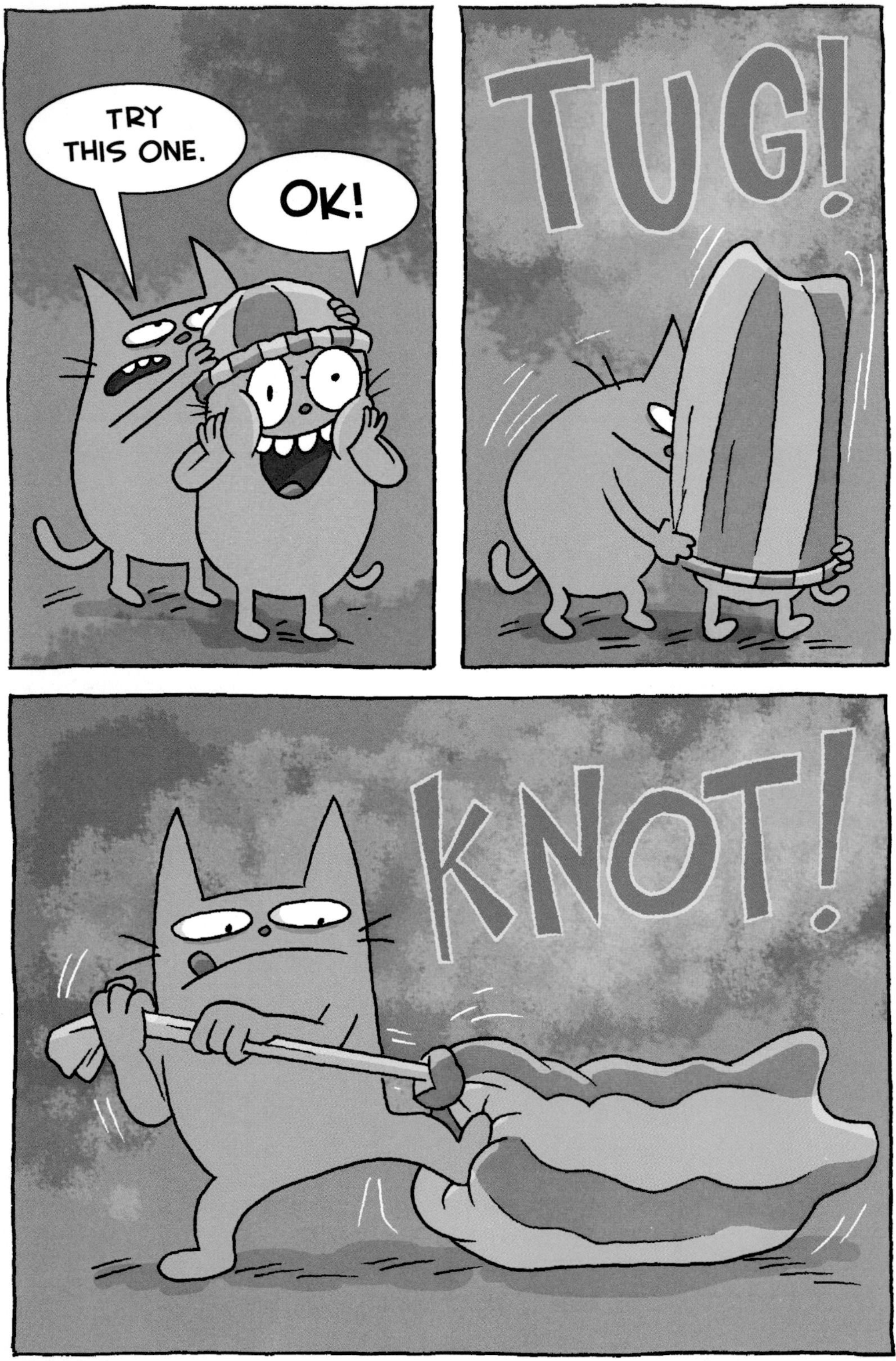
TRY THIS ONE.
OK!
TUG!
KNOT!

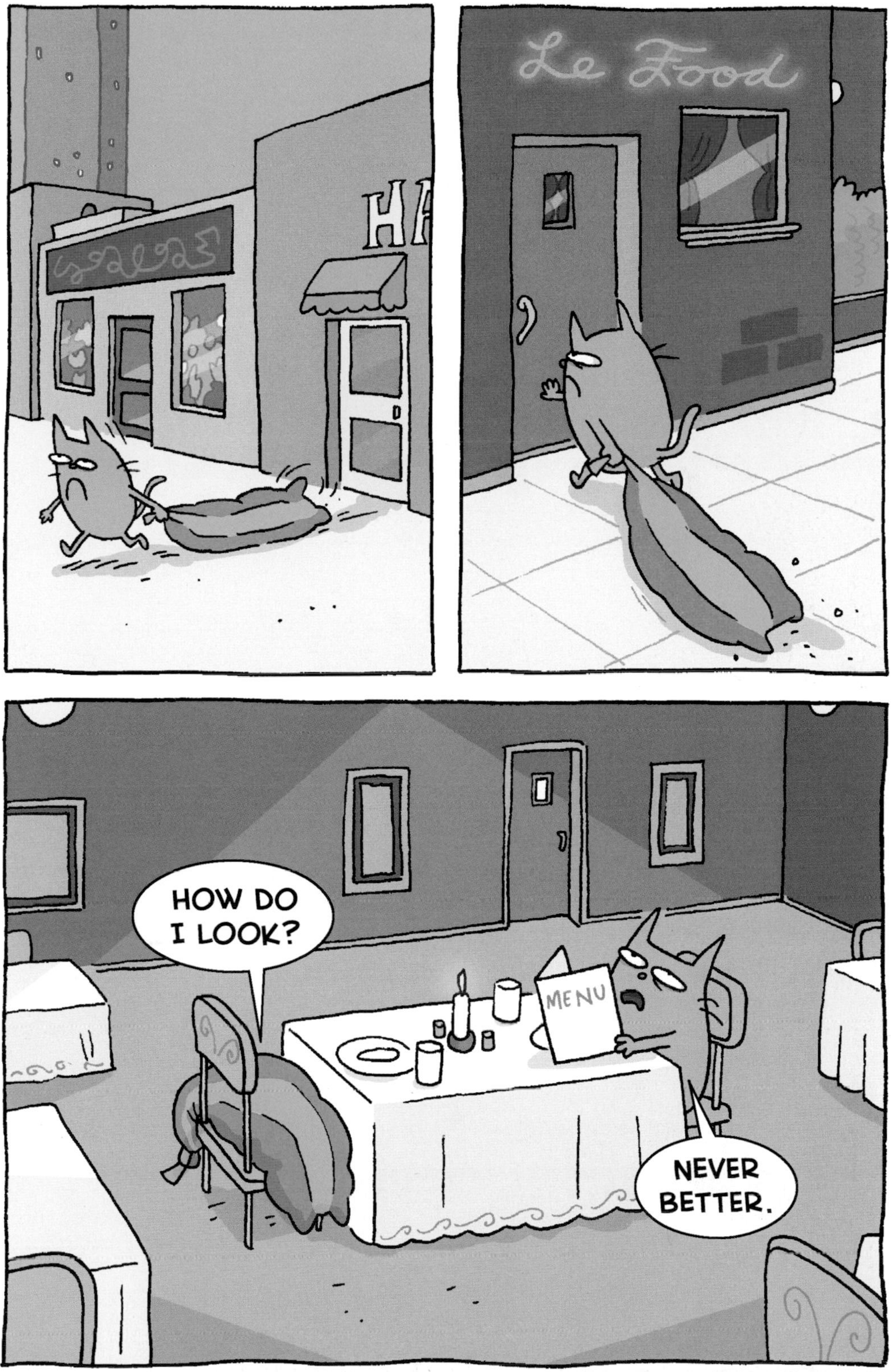
Le Food
HOW DO I LOOK?
MENU
NEVER BETTER.

SHOWER

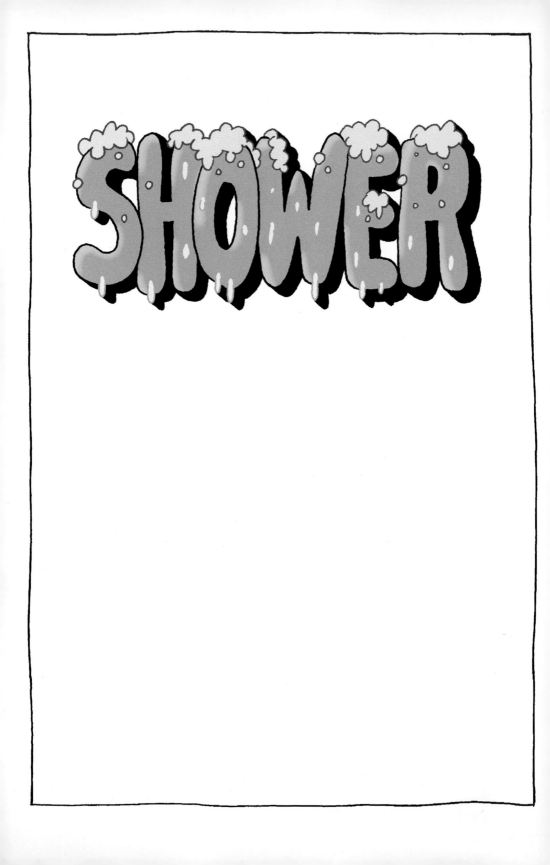

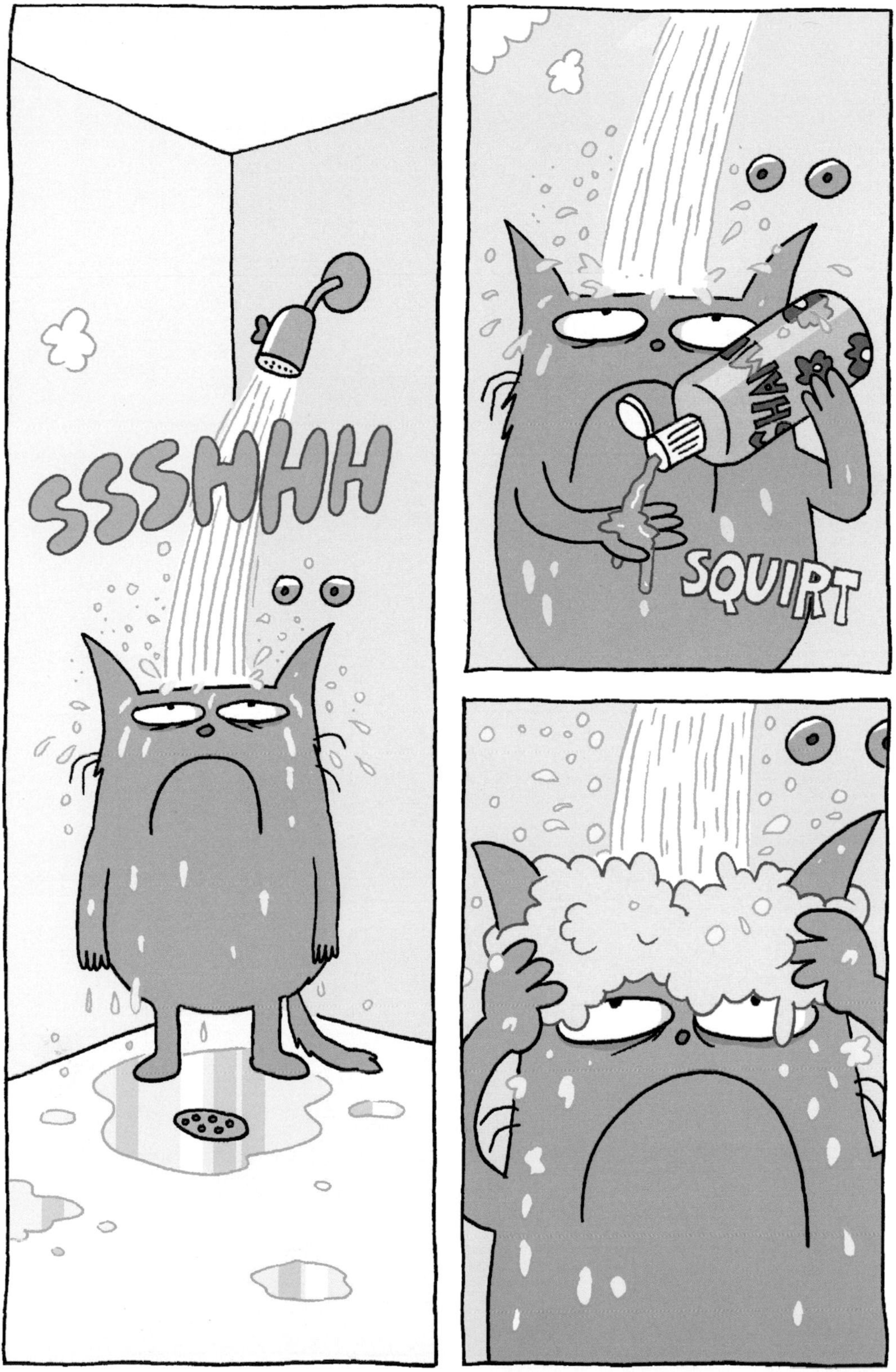
SSSHHH
SQUIRT

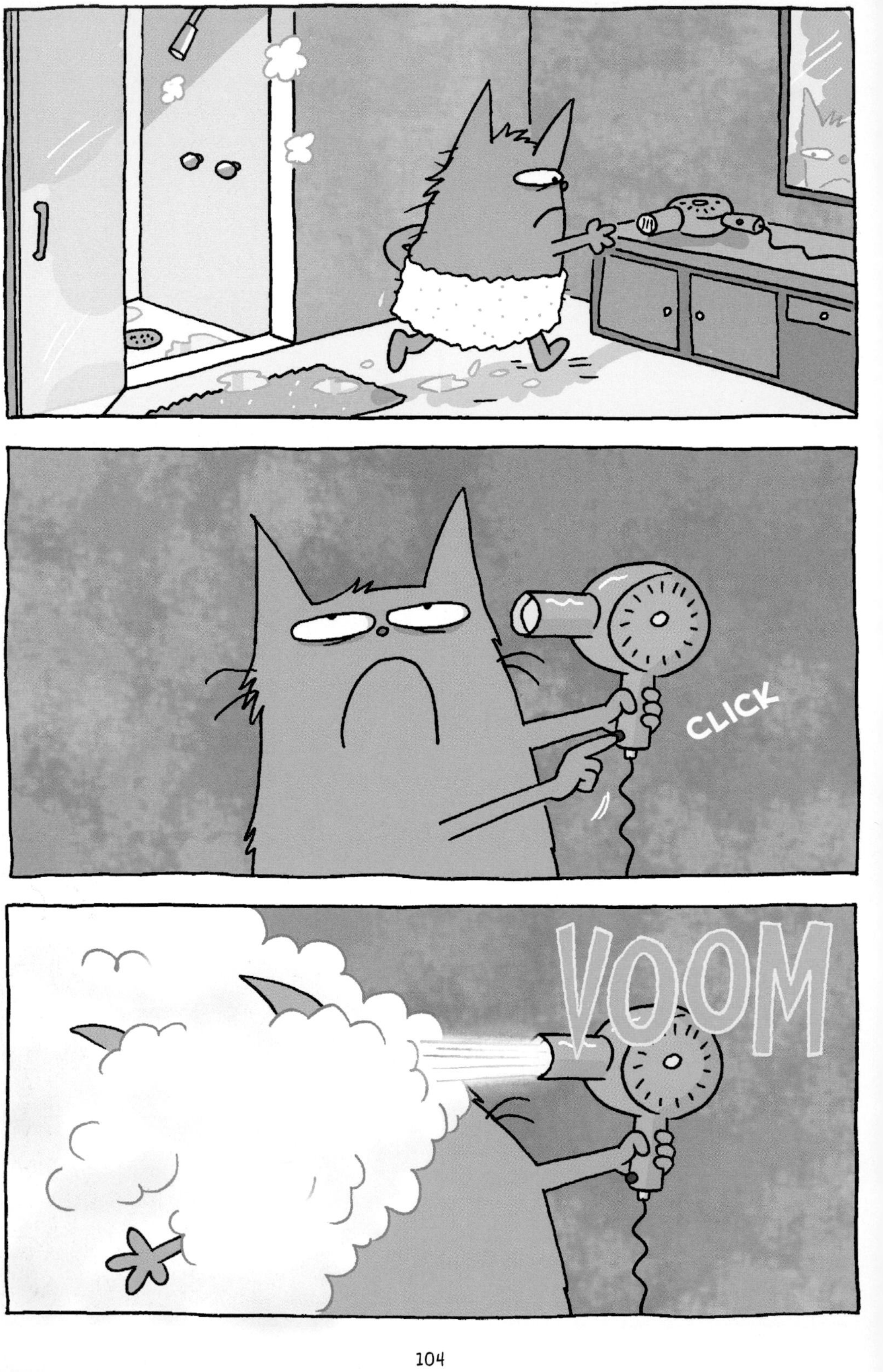
CLICK
VOOM

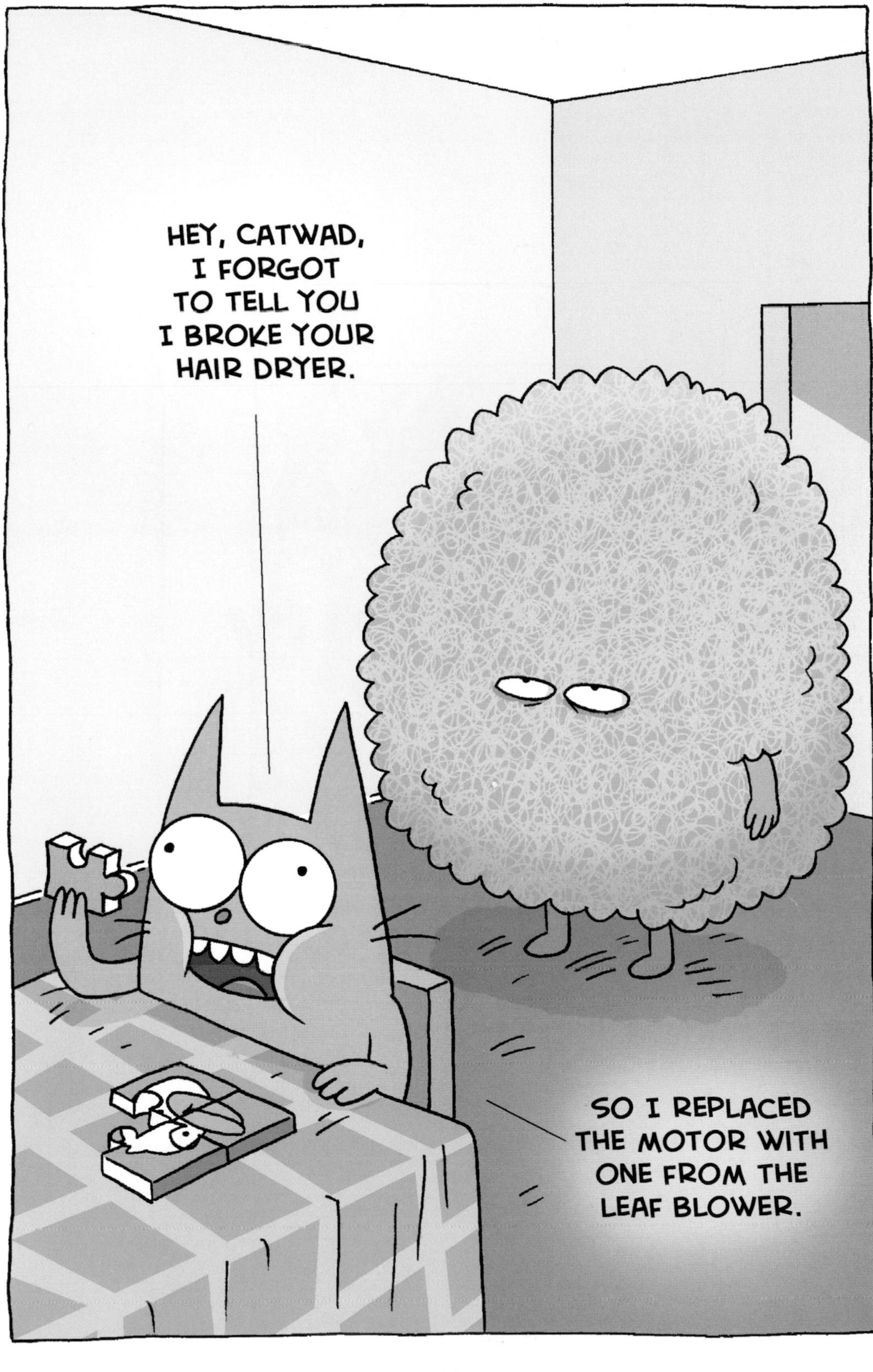
HEY, CATWAD, I FORGOT TO TELL YOU I BROKE YOUR HAIR DRYER.
SO I REPLACED THE MOTOR WITH ONE FROM THE LEAF BLOWER.

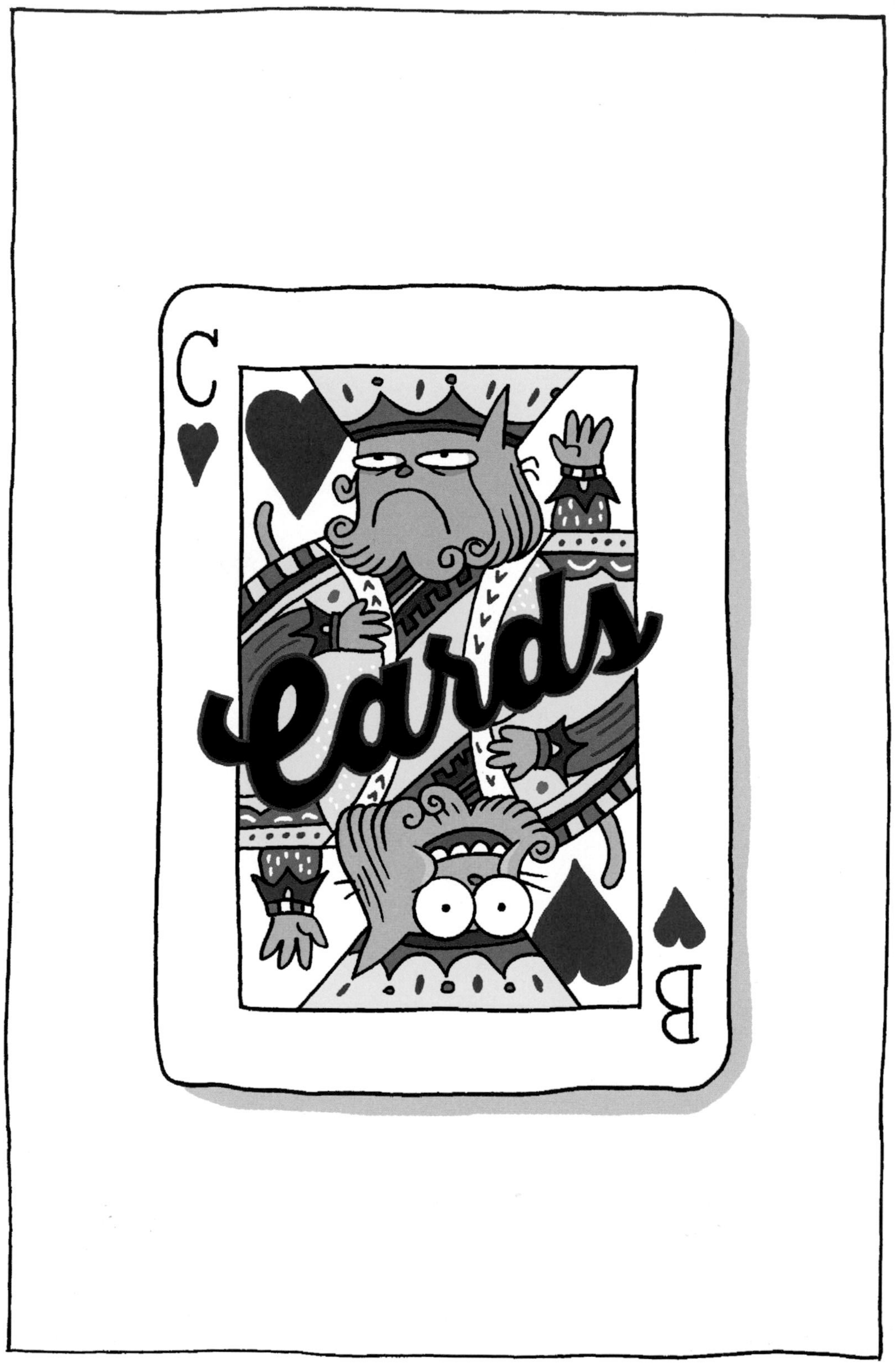
C
Cards
B

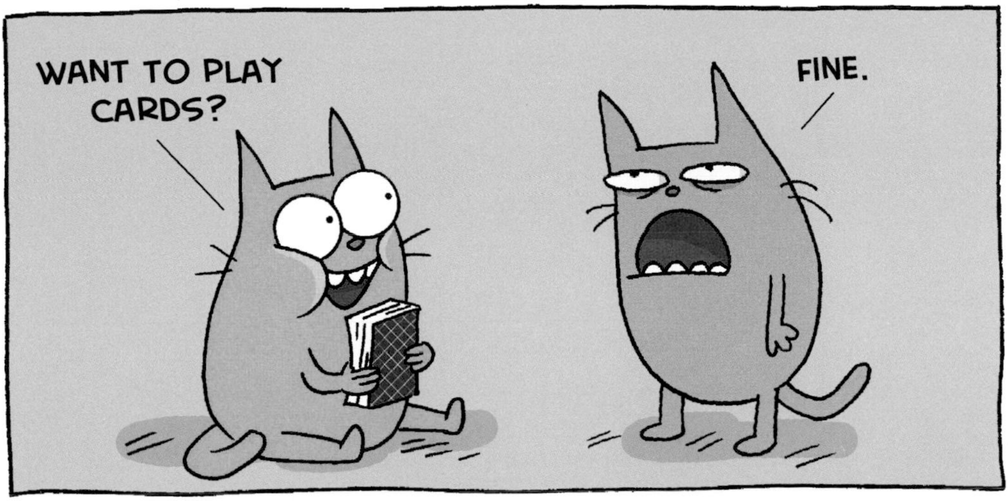
WANT TO PLAY CARDS?
FINE.

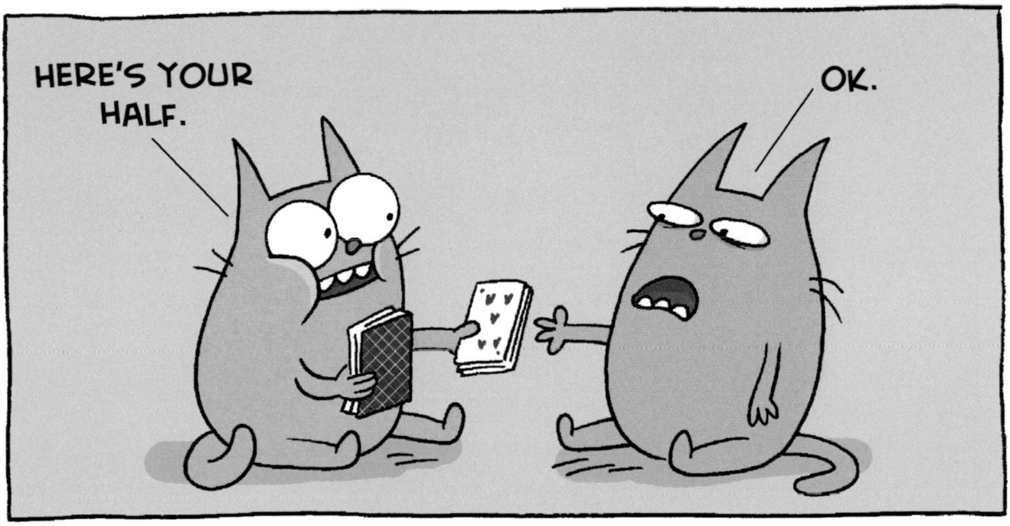
HERE'S YOUR HALF.
OK.

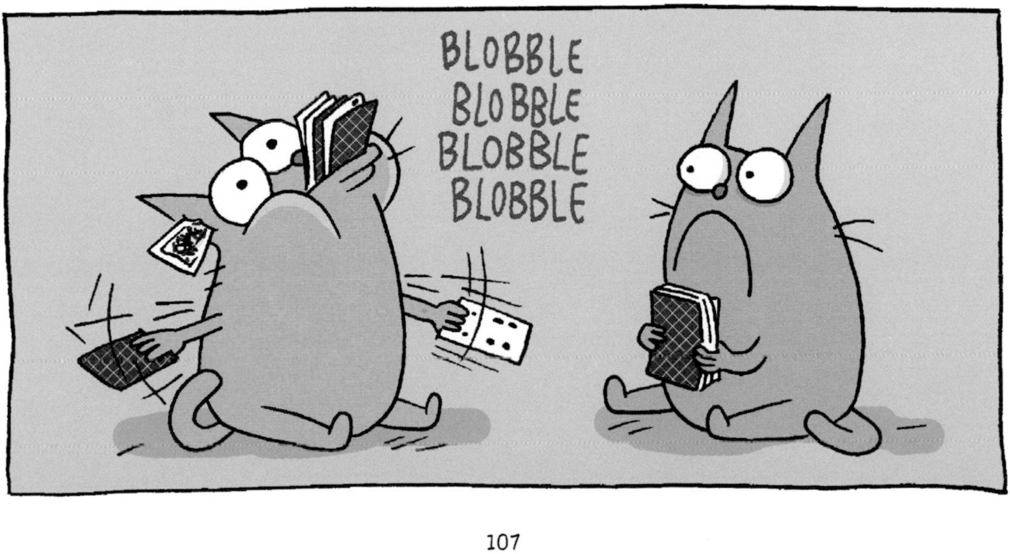
BLOBBLE
BLOBBLE
BLOBBLE
BLOBBLE

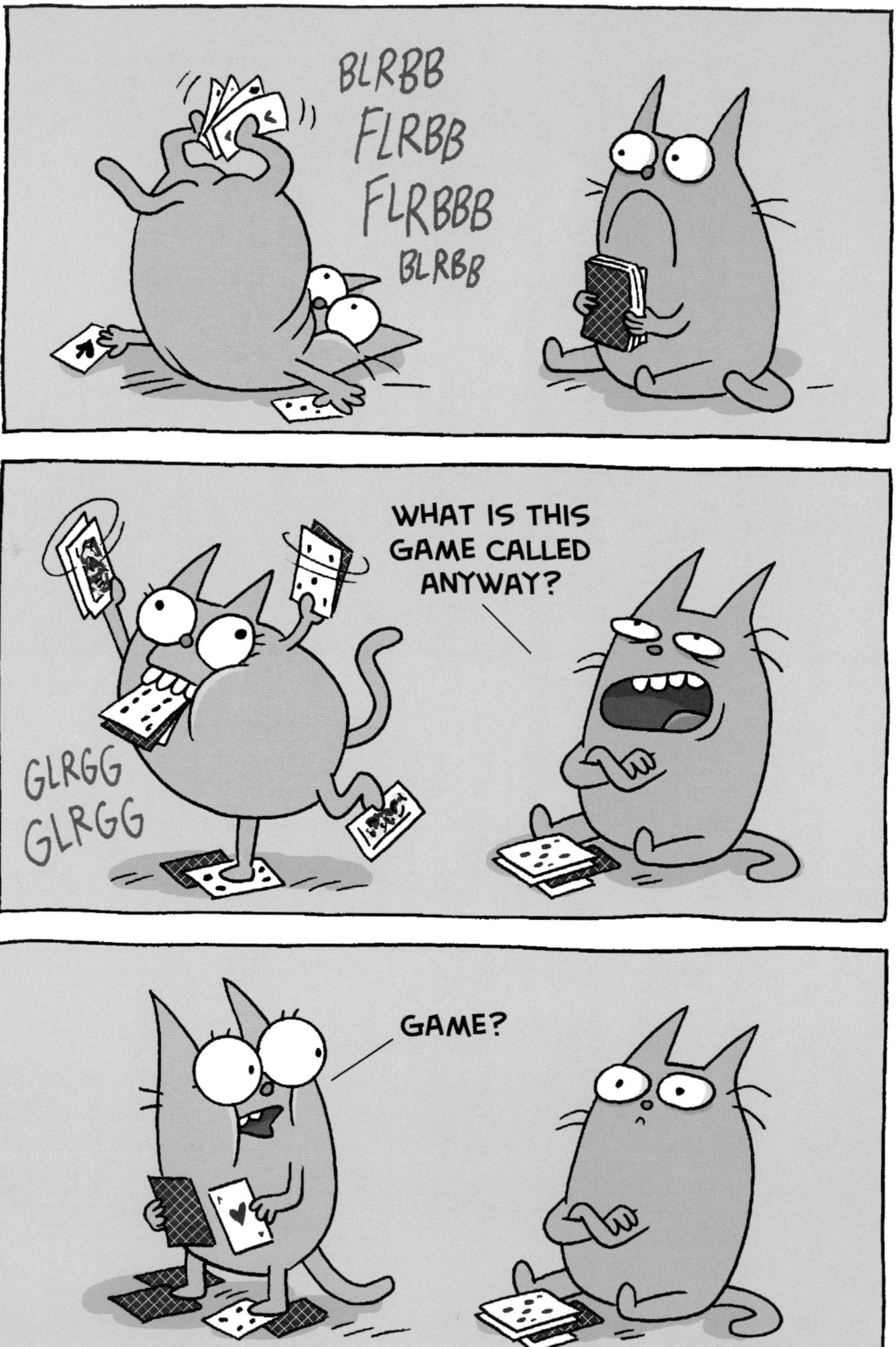
BLRBB
FLRBB
FLRBBB
BLRBB
WHAT IS THIS GAME CALLED ANYWAY?
GLRGG
GLRGG
GAME?

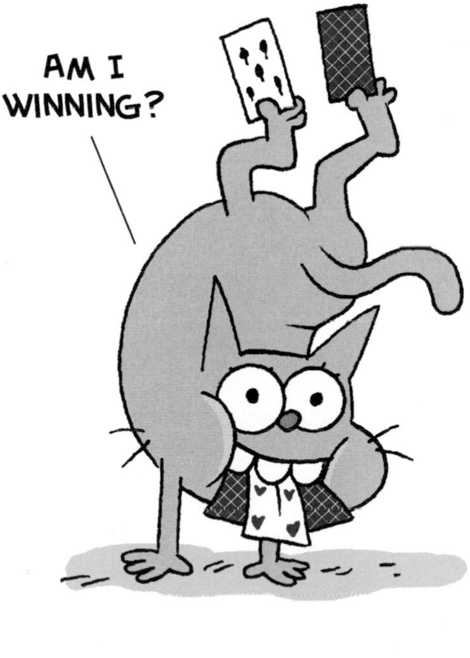
AM I
WINNING?

PLANT

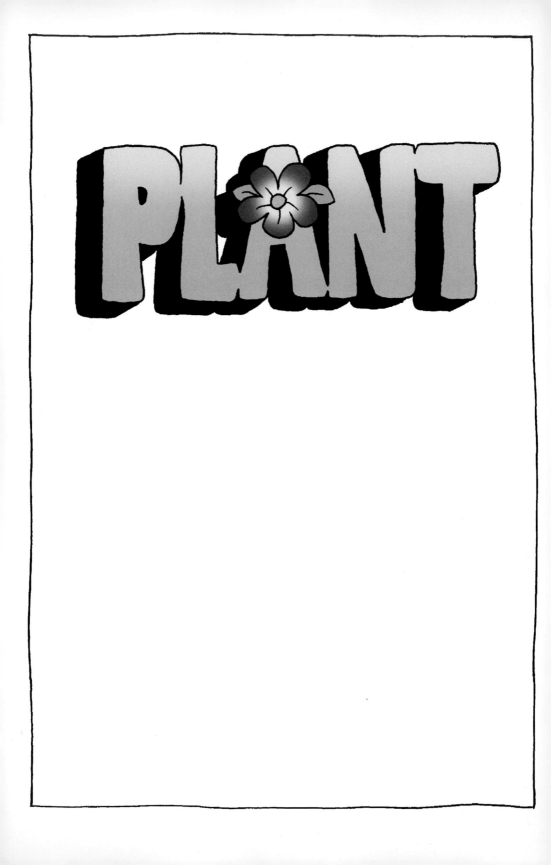

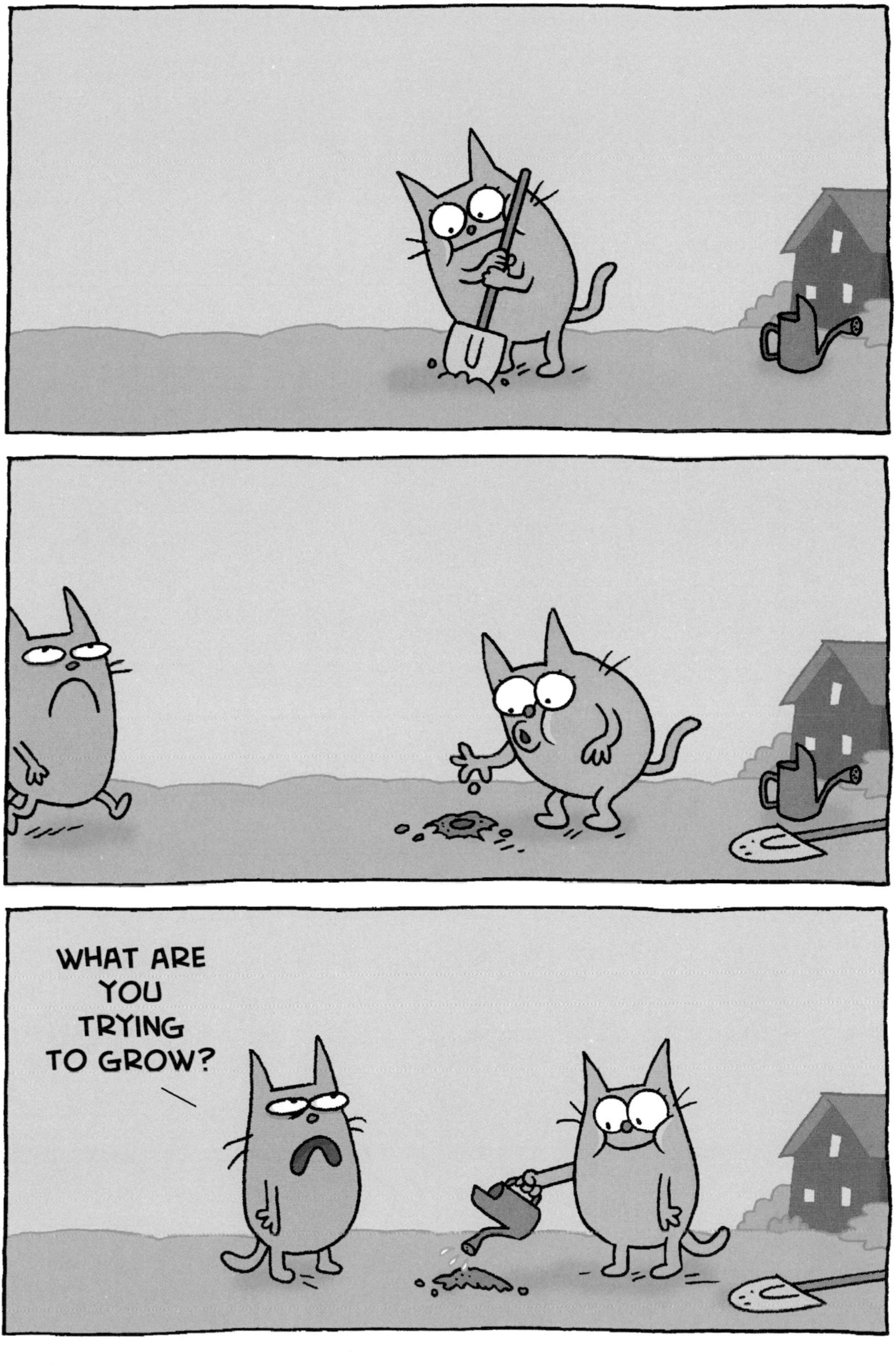
WHAT ARE YOU TRYING TO GROW?

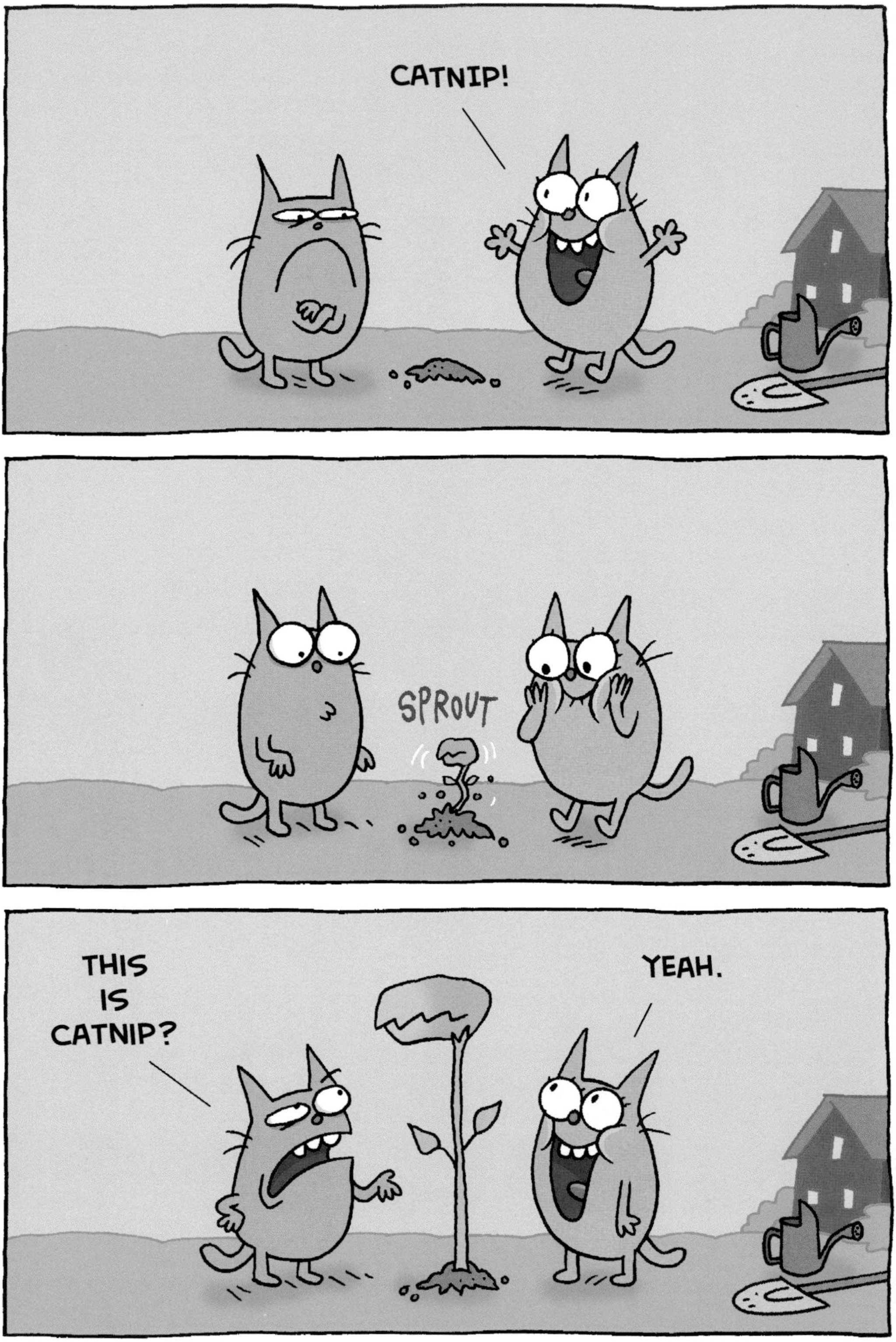
CATNIP!
SPROUT
THIS IS CATNIP?
YEAH.

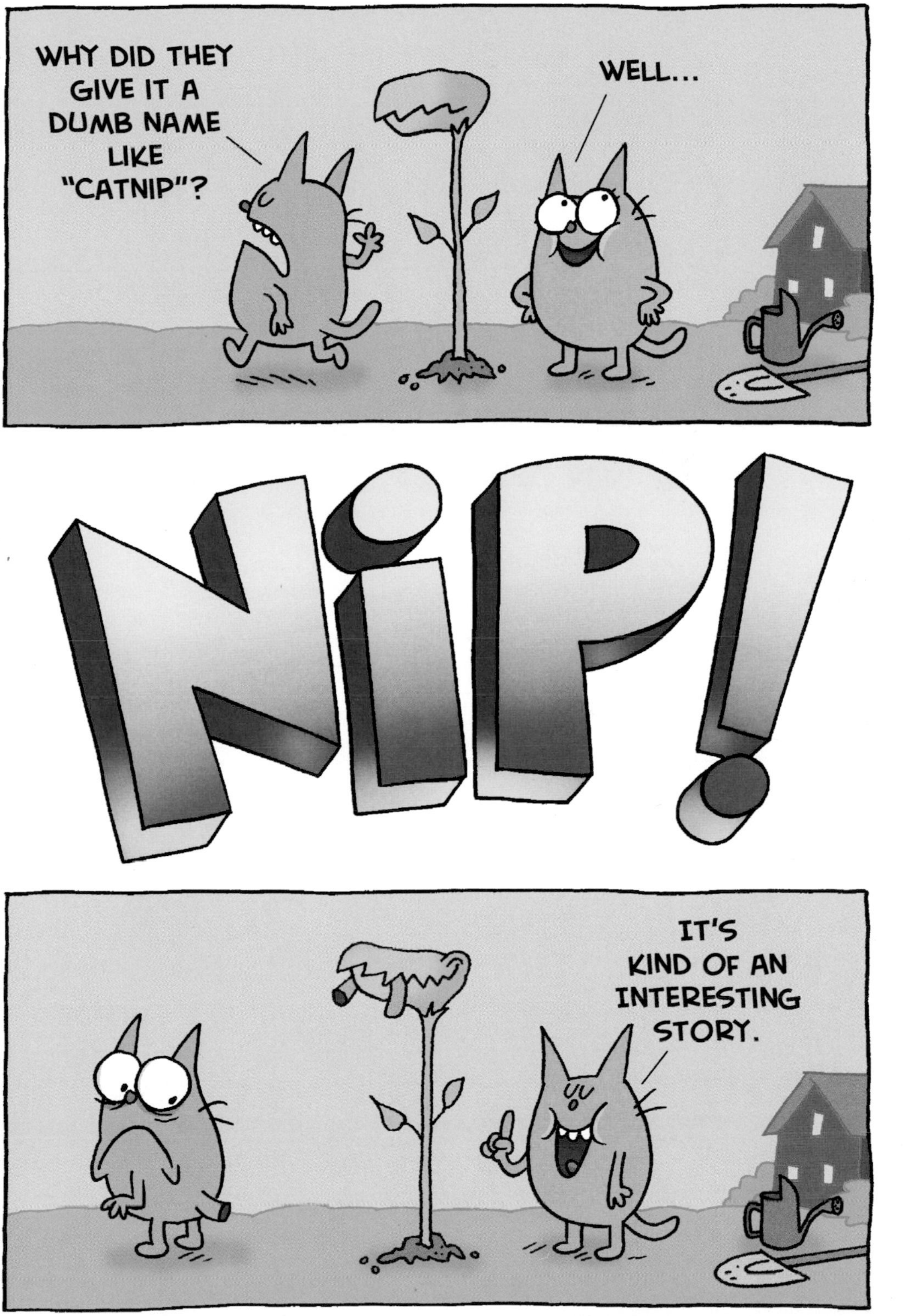
WHY DID THEY GIVE IT A DUMB NAME LIKE "CATNIP"?
WELL...
NiP!
IT'S KIND OF AN INTERESTING STORY.

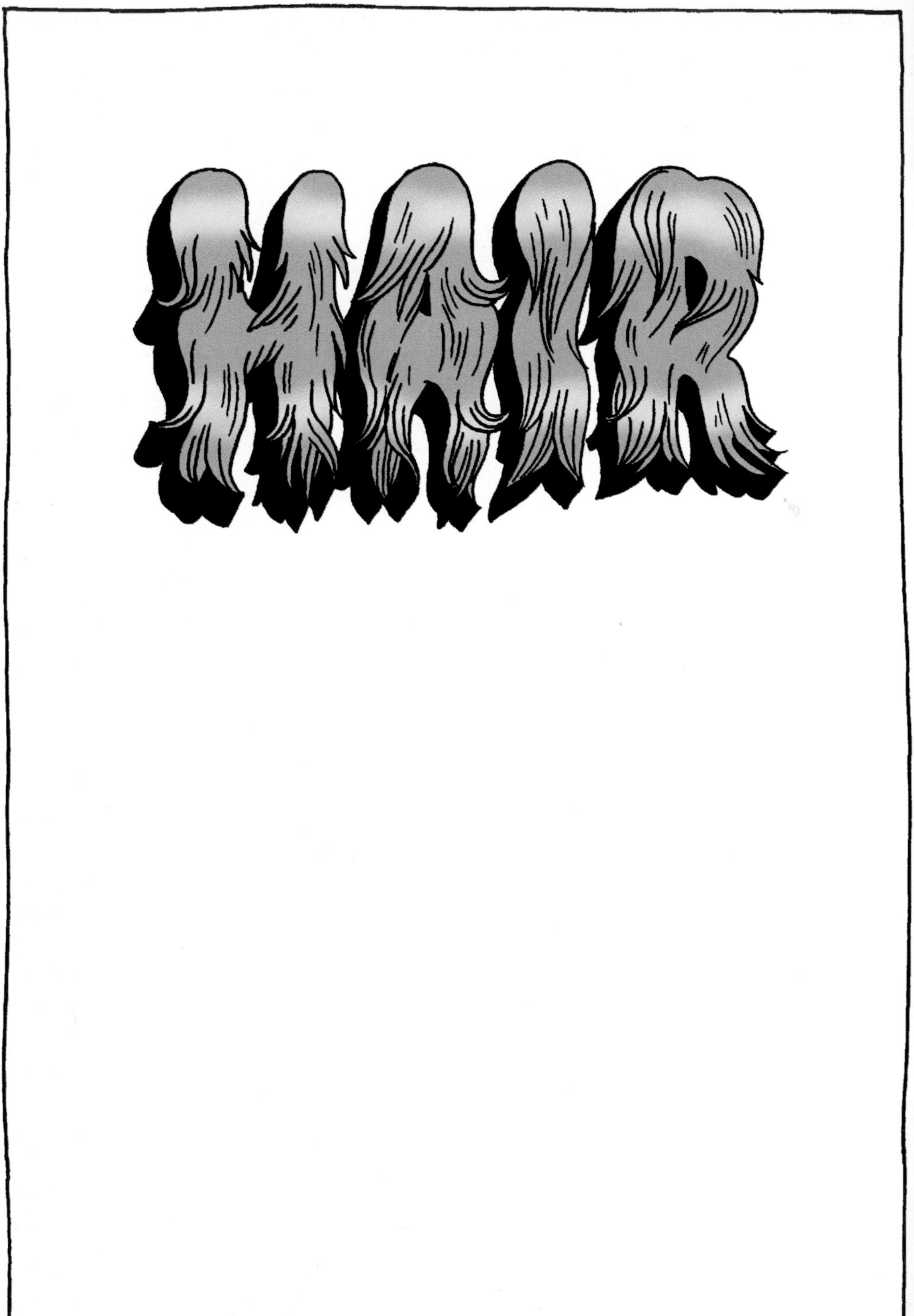
HAIR

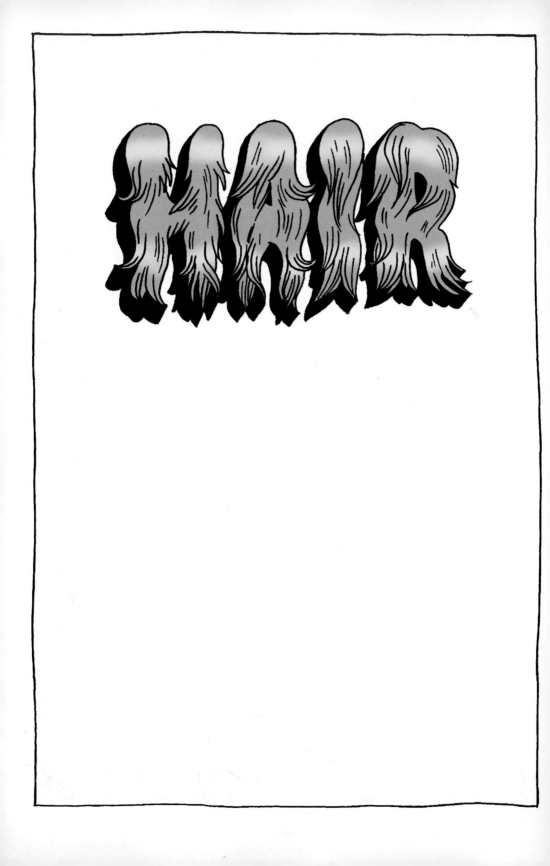

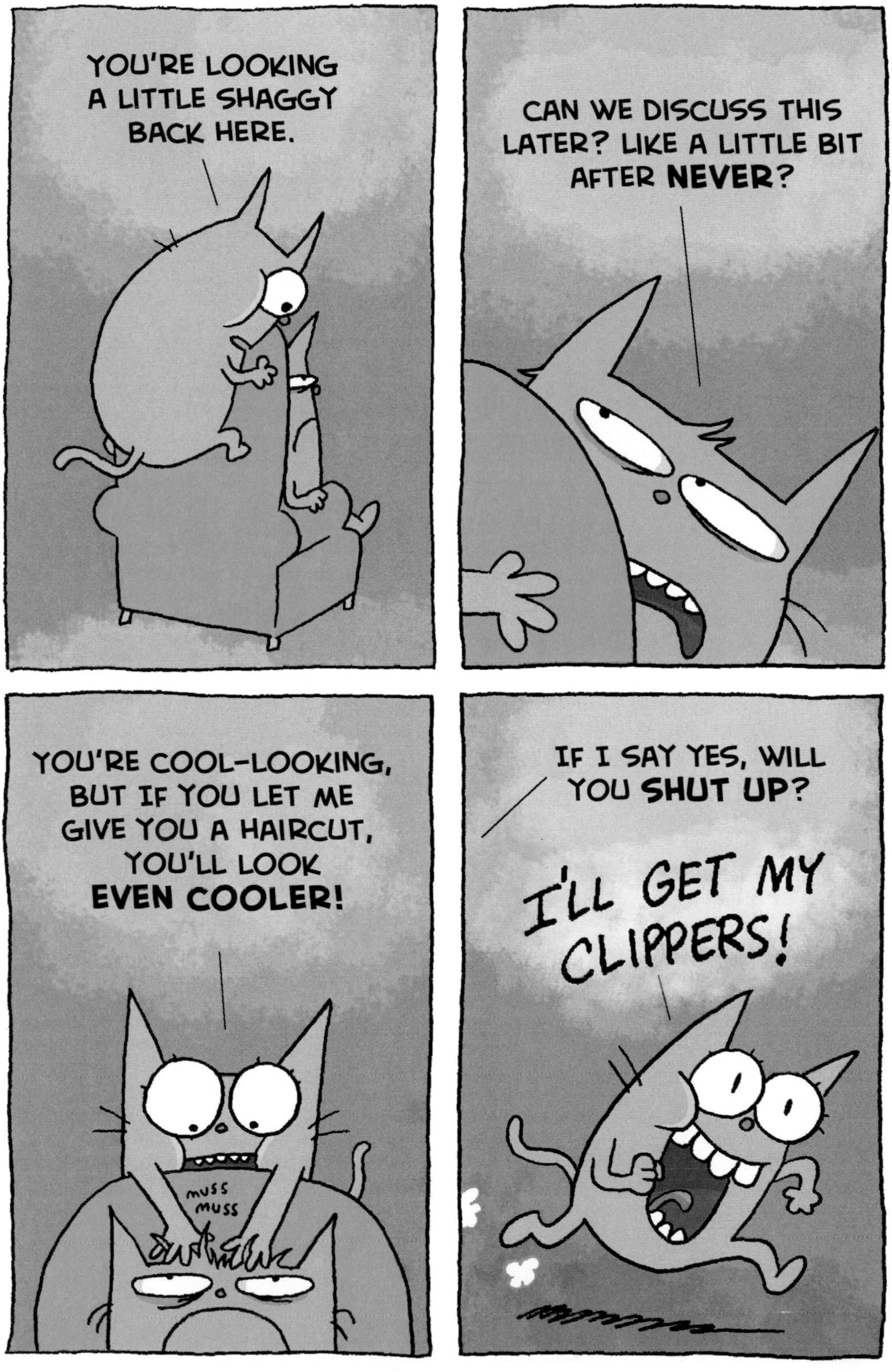
YOU'RE LOOKING A LITTLE SHAGGY BACK HERE.
CAN WE DISCUSS THIS LATER? LIKE A LITTLE BIT AFTER **NEVER**?
YOU'RE COOL-LOOKING, BUT IF YOU LET ME GIVE YOU A HAIRCUT, YOU'LL LOOK **EVEN COOLER!**
MUSS MUSS
IF I SAY YES, WILL YOU **SHUT UP**?
I'LL GET MY CLIPPERS!

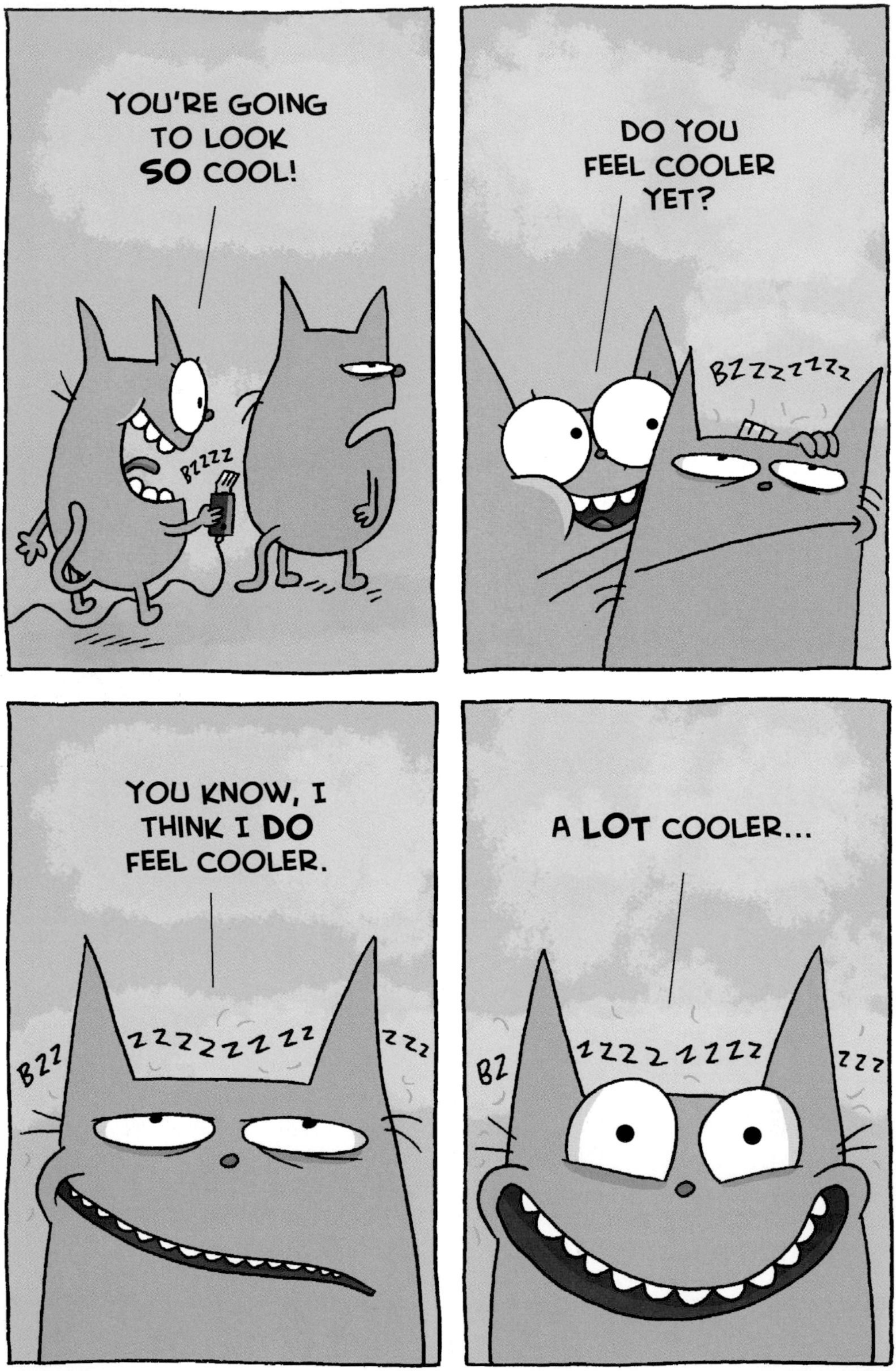
YOU'RE GOING TO LOOK **SO** COOL!
BZZZZ
DO YOU FEEL COOLER YET?
BZZZZZZZZ
YOU KNOW, I THINK I **DO** FEEL COOLER.
BZZ ZZZZZZZZZ ZZZ
A **LOT** COOLER...
BZ ZZZZZZZZ ZZZ

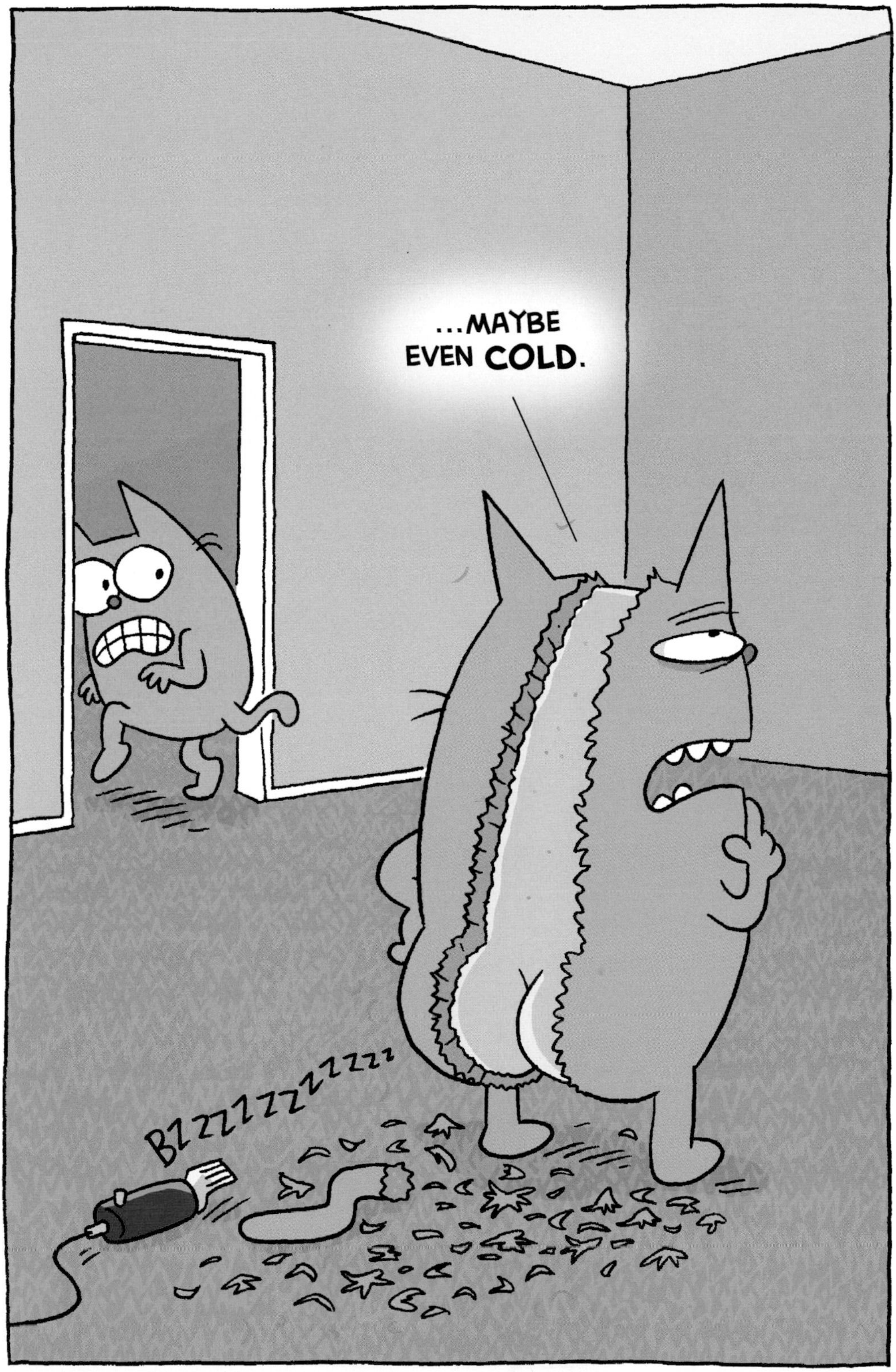
...MAYBE EVEN COLD.
BZZZZZZZZZZZZZ

PAINT

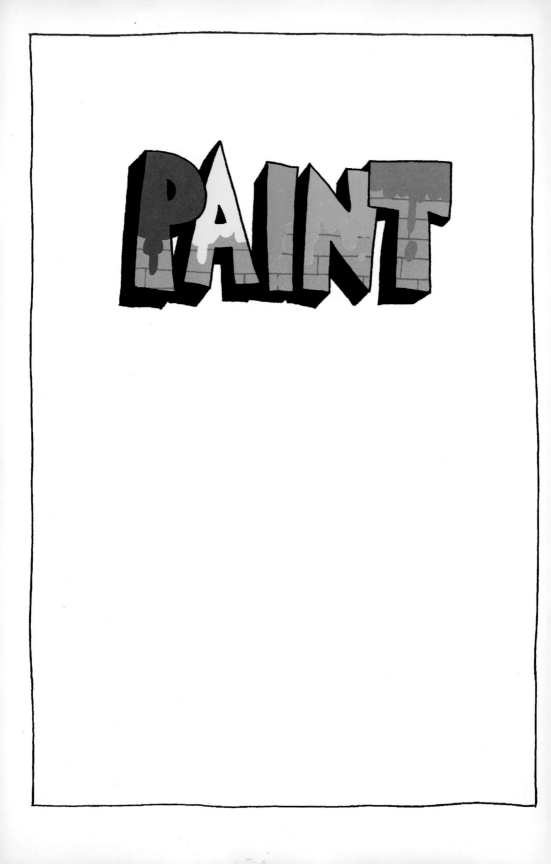

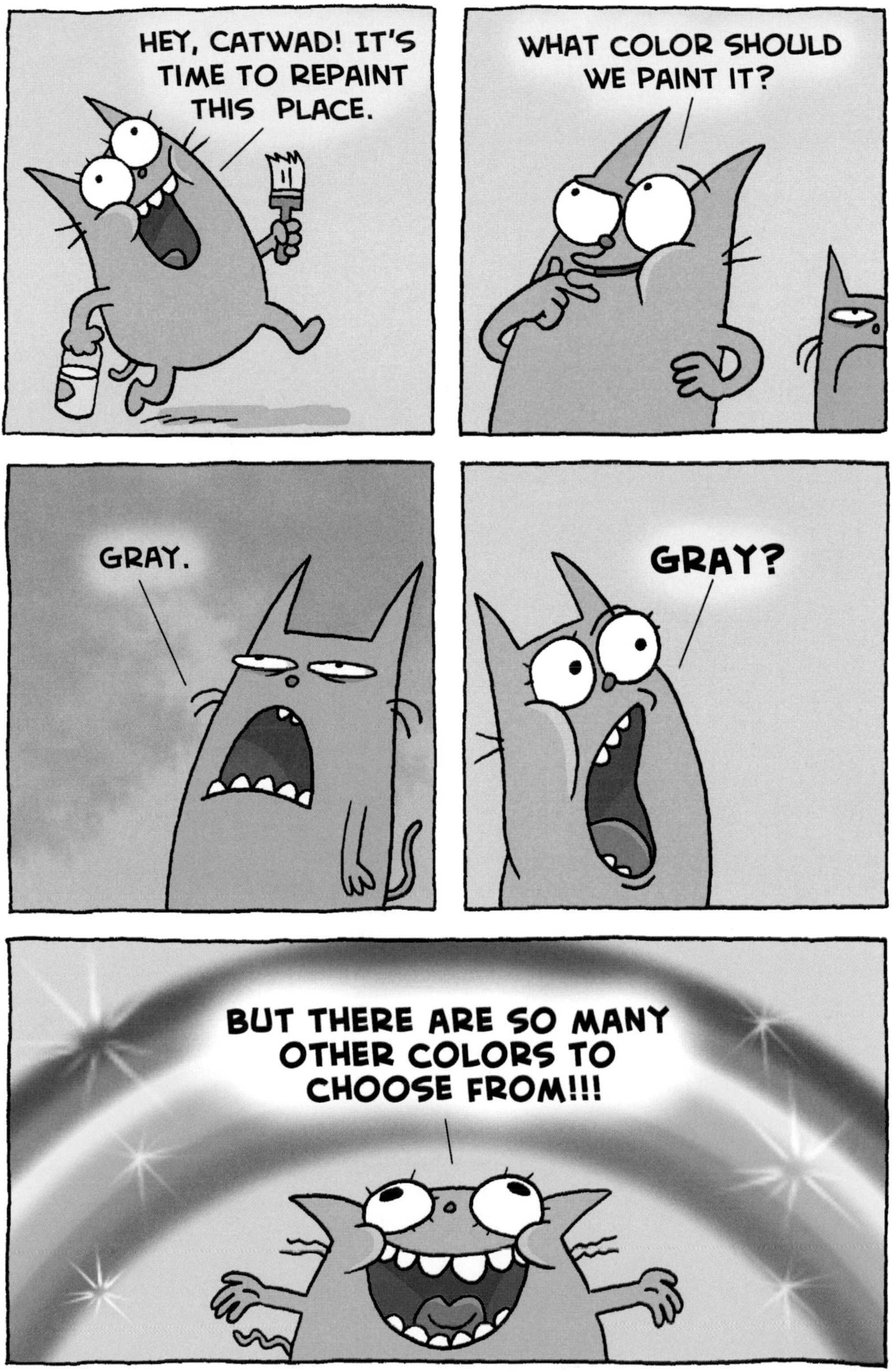
HEY, CATWAD! IT'S TIME TO REPAINT THIS PLACE.
WHAT COLOR SHOULD WE PAINT IT?
GRAY.
GRAY?
BUT THERE ARE SO MANY OTHER COLORS TO CHOOSE FROM!!!

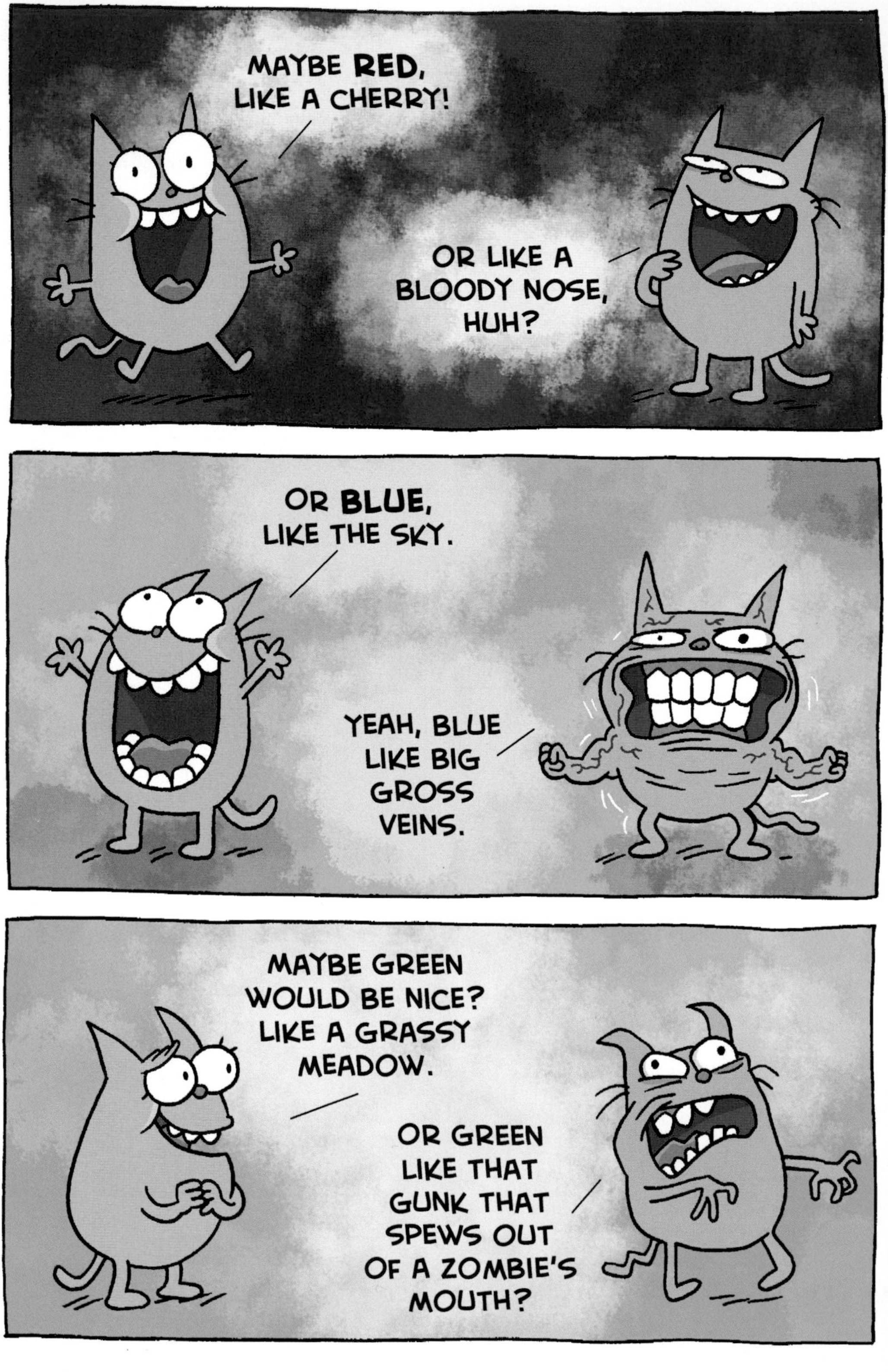
MAYBE **RED**, LIKE A CHERRY!
OR LIKE A BLOODY NOSE, HUH?
OR **BLUE**, LIKE THE SKY.
YEAH, BLUE LIKE BIG GROSS VEINS.
MAYBE GREEN WOULD BE NICE? LIKE A GRASSY MEADOW.
OR GREEN LIKE THAT GUNK THAT SPEWS OUT OF A ZOMBIE'S MOUTH?

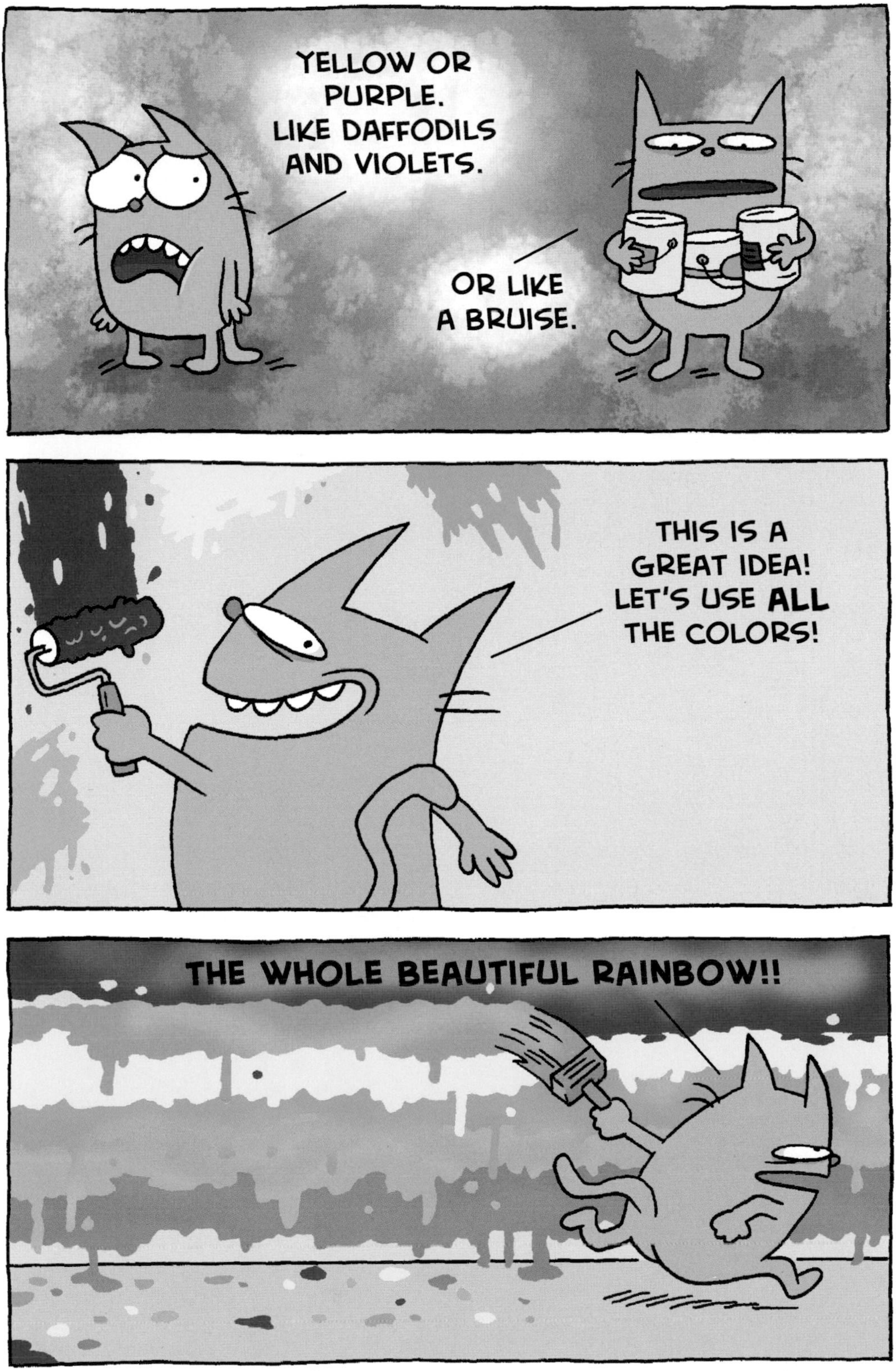
YELLOW OR PURPLE. LIKE DAFFODILS AND VIOLETS.
OR LIKE A BRUISE.
THIS IS A GREAT IDEA! LET'S USE **ALL** THE COLORS!
THE WHOLE BEAUTIFUL RAINBOW!!

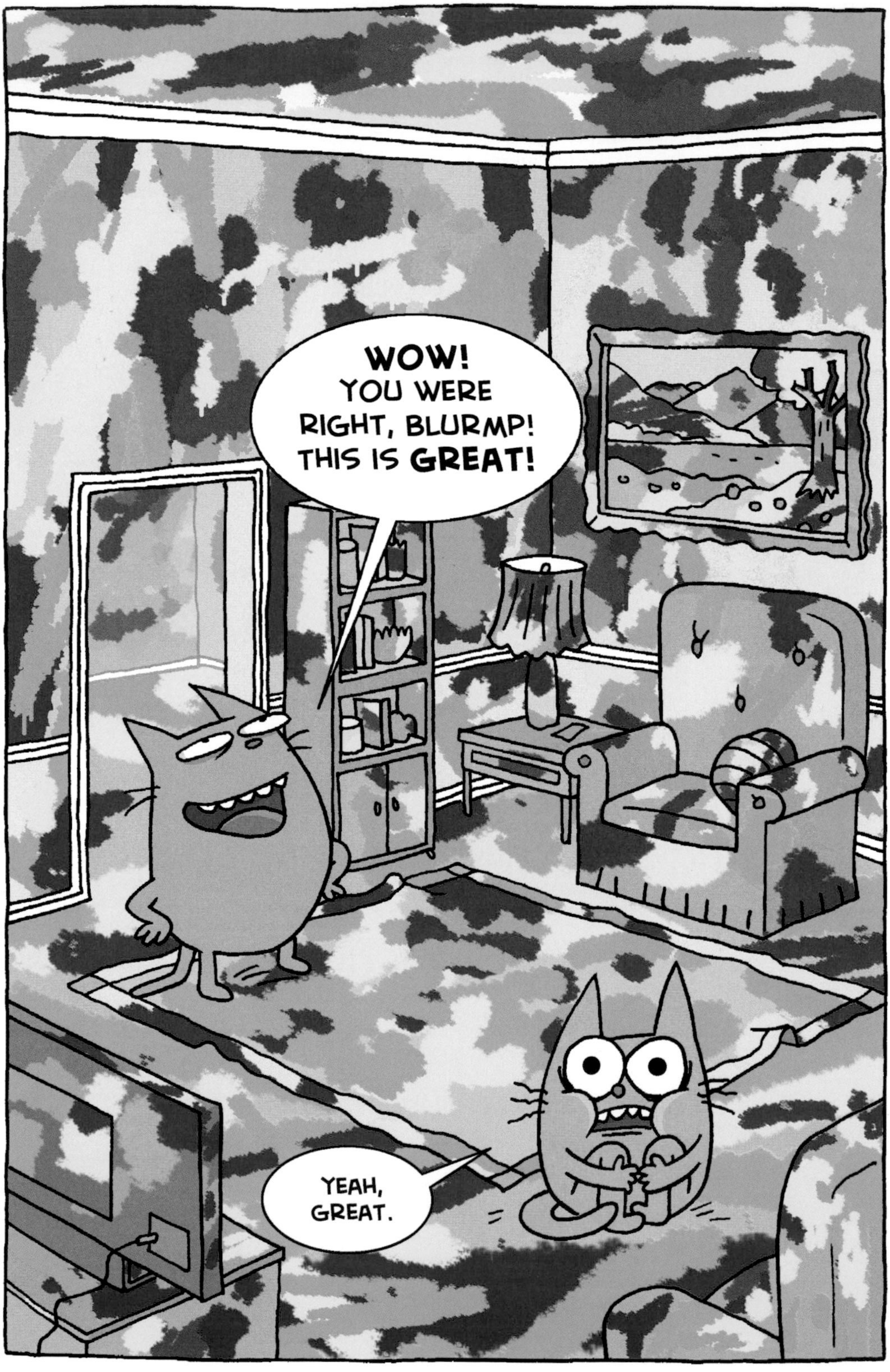
WOW! YOU WERE RIGHT, BLURMP! THIS IS GREAT!
YEAH, GREAT.

BONUS ACTIVITY! HOW MANY DIFFERENCES CAN YOU SPOT BETWEEN THE TWO PICTURES?

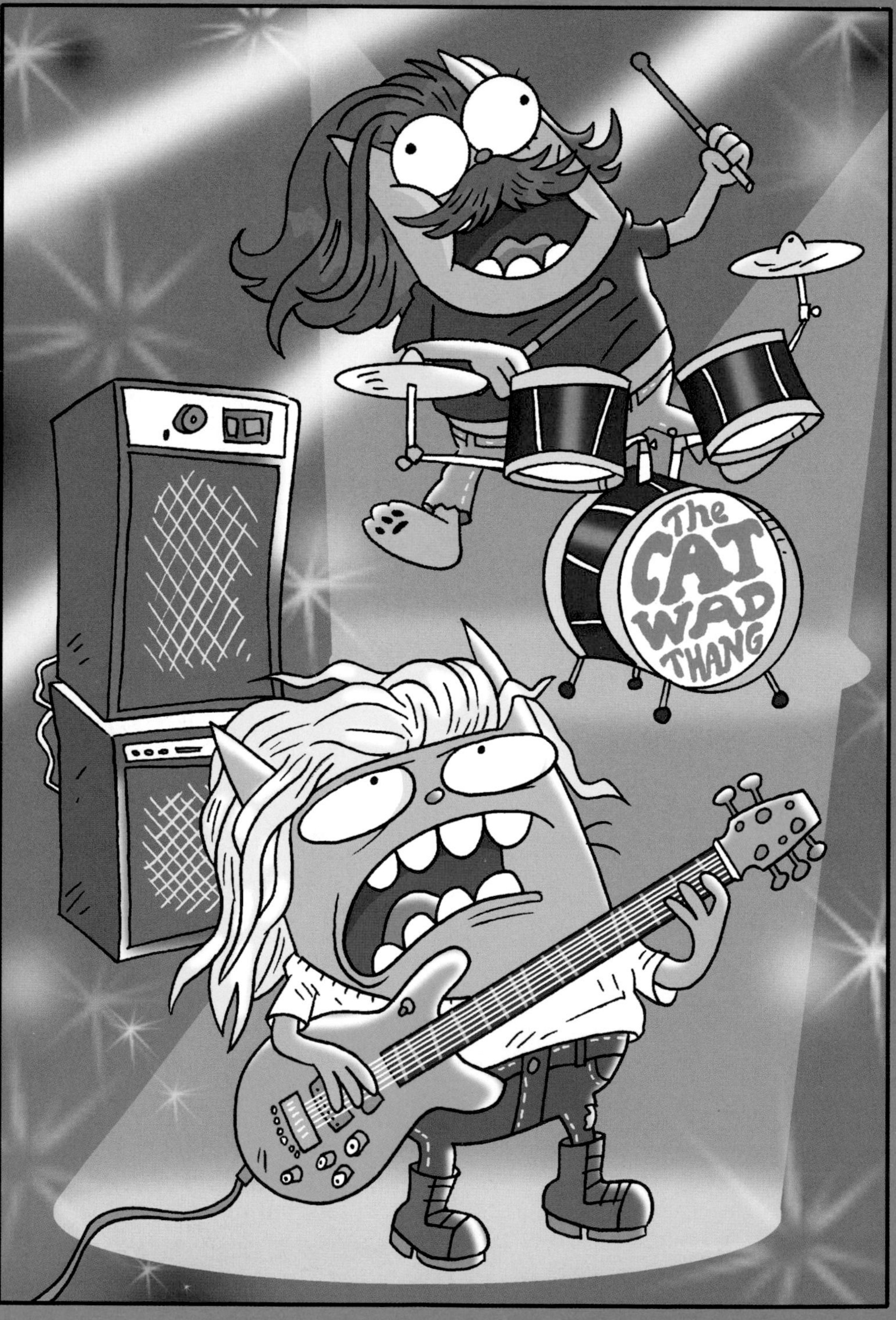

The CAT WAD THANG

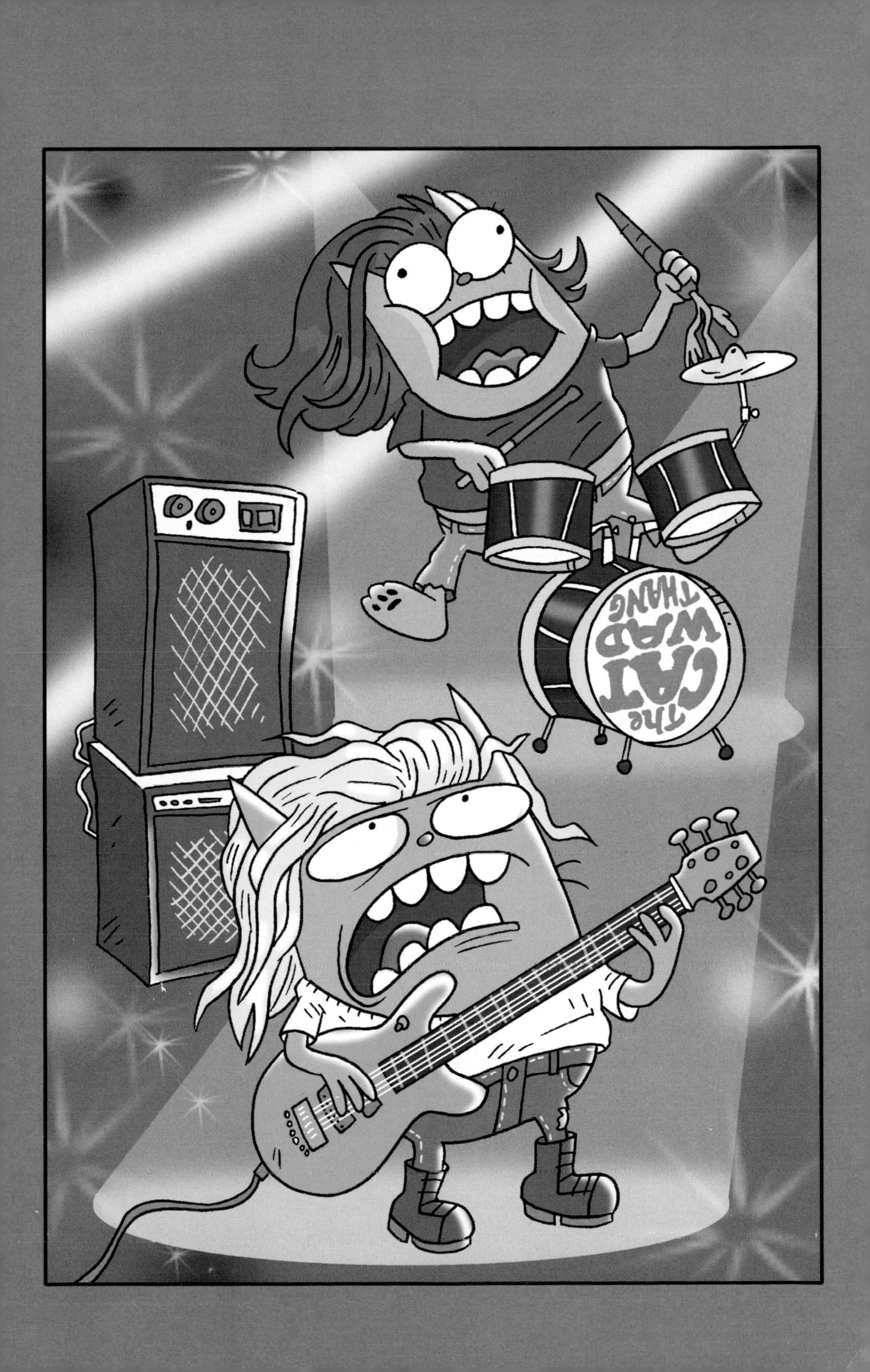
The CAT WAD THANG

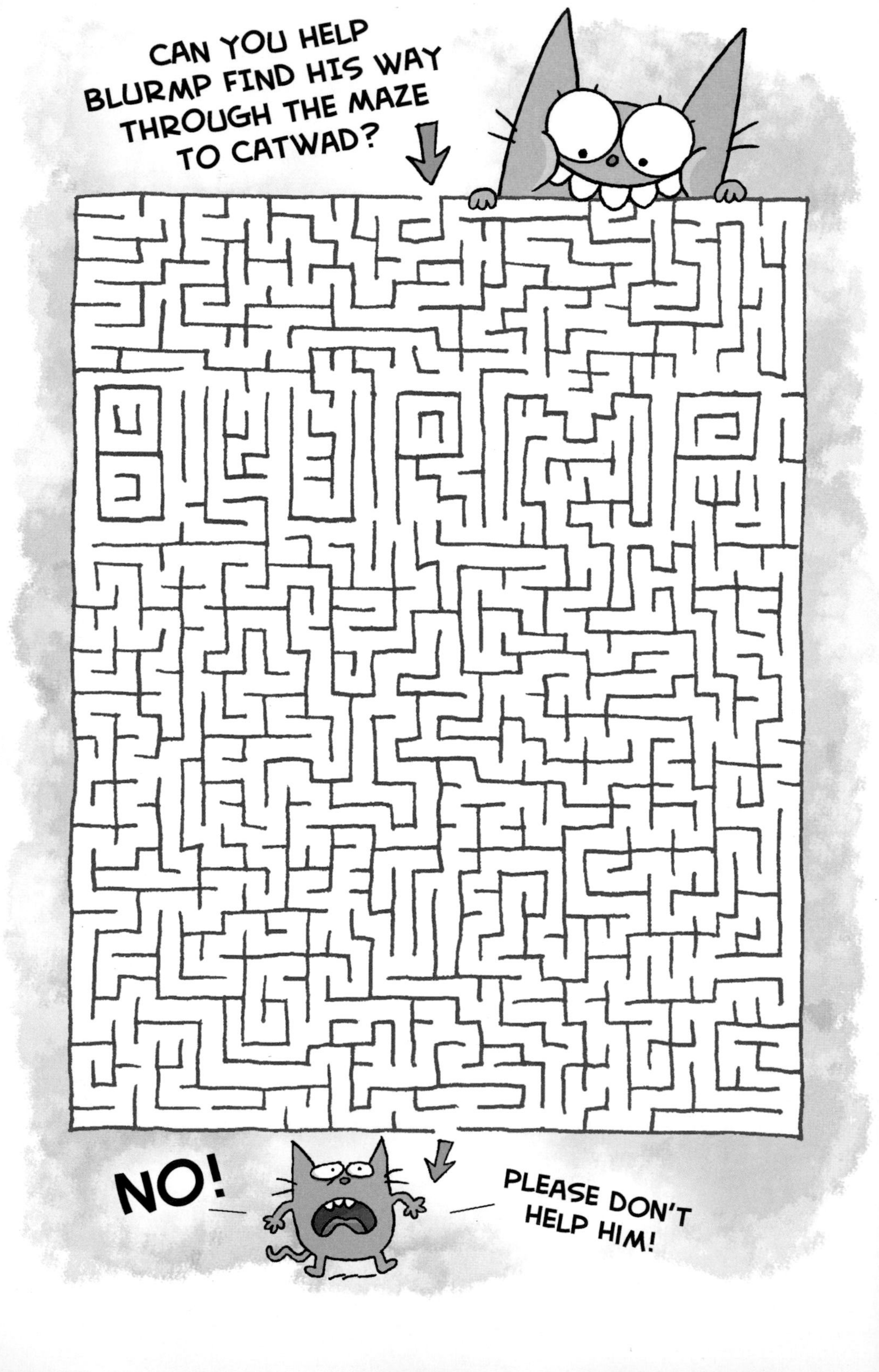
CAN YOU HELP
BLURMP FIND HIS WAY
THROUGH THE MAZE
TO CATWAD?
NO!
PLEASE DON'T
HELP HIM!

DON'T MISS THE FIRST BOOK!

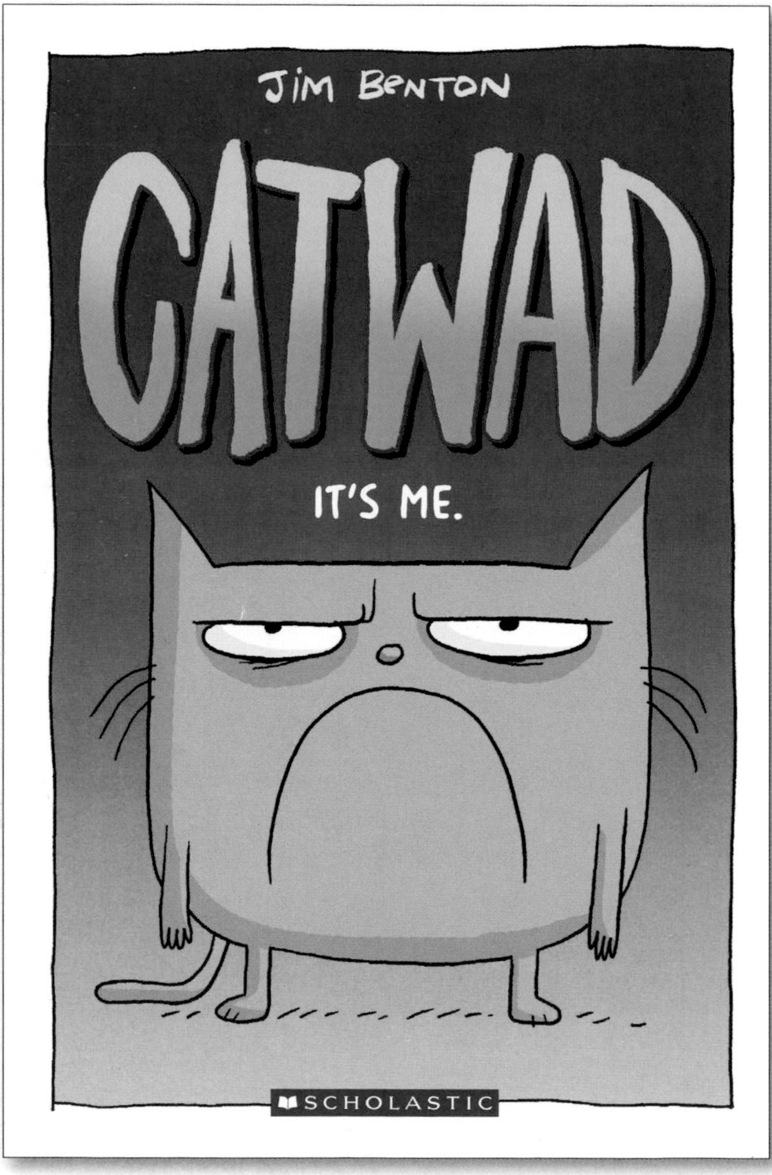
JIM BENTON
CATWAD
IT'S ME.
SCHOLASTIC